I0823994

A TWISTED TALE

Anthology

EDITED BY ELIZABETH LIM

WITH NEW *WHAT-IF* TWISTS BY:

Livia Blackburne • Liz Braswell • Jen Calonita

M. K. England • Elizabeth Lim • Micol Ostow

Kristina Pérez • Farrah Rochon

Disney • HYPERION

LOS ANGELES • NEW YORK

Printed in the United States of America
First Hardcover Edition, October 2023
3 5 7 9 10 8 6 4
FAC-004510-24210
Library of Congress Control Number onfi le.
ISBN 978-1-368-08041-5

Visit disneybooks.com

Logo Applies to Text Stock Only

To Britt Rubiano

For believing in the magic and making dreams come true.

—E. L.

Contents

Foreword

In early 2021, I was on the phone with my editor at Disney Hyperion, Brittany Rubiano (the true mastermind behind the entire A Twisted Tale series, who has overseen and edited the publication of almost every book), going over the finer points of my Blue Fairy Twisted Tale, when I had an idea.

"What do you think about an anthology of Twisted Tale shorts?" I asked out of the blue. "There's so many more possible twists we could explore, and some might work better in a short-story format."

Britt's always been wonderfully open to her authors' brainstorming and pitching ideas, and she said she'd share it with her team. About a month later, I received an email from Britt saying that Disney wanted to go ahead with the anthology idea and asking whether I'd like to edit it.

Now here I am.

This is my first time editing an anthology, and what a

joy it's been. I grew up on Disney, watched *Cinderella* and *Snow White* on my treasured VHS tapes so often that their color faded, and fantasized about writing the next generation of songs to spread magic and laughter across the world. In my wildest dreams, never did I think I'd get to write stories about my favorite characters and, more important, meet and collaborate with a host of authors who share the same love for Disney that I grew up with.

In this anthology, you'll find stories by veteran Twisted Tale authors Liz Braswell, Jen Calonita, and Farrah Rochon, all three of whom have become writerly sisters to me. I'm also delighted to welcome Livia Blackburne, Megan K. England, Micol Ostow, and Kristina Pérez to the Twisted Tale family.

When I conceived the idea of this anthology, one of my goals was to welcome stories from films that have not yet enjoyed their own Twisted Tale novels. I'm especially excited to spotlight original twists on *Bambi*, *Brave*, *The Lion King*, *Robin Hood*, *The Sword in the Stone*, and *Treasure Planet*.

Something I also hoped to achieve was to further explore the possibilities in new twists for the series. As I write this, there are thirteen published Twisted Tale novels, and each takes a Disney film and reimagines one pivotal aspect to create a new story with the characters we know and love. This was an opportunity to explore fresh what-if scenarios for those beloved films.

In this anthology, you'll find new twists—some bending only a few scenes in the film or exploring a potential prologue, like how Madam Mim met Merlin before the events of *The Sword in the Stone.* There are stories that follow characters off the screen into a new adventure, like a tale about the triplets from *Brave* as teenagers, and stories that twist the entire film in a new direction—for instance, what if Mufasa gave up his throne (*The Lion King*), or what if Aurora knew the truth about her curse (*Sleeping Beauty*)?

Twists aside, there are tales of adventure and courage, of romance and growing up, and of love and family—a little something for everyone, with a generous dash of Disney magic.

I present to you *A Twisted Tale Anthology*.

—Elizabeth Lim

Cast Out

What if Snow White learned magic?

by Livia Blackburne

Cast Out

What if Snow White learned magic?

by Livia Blackburne

The castle's grand feast hall had a magnificent flagstone floor, made of sleek gray stones from distant mines. The floor was regal and stately, fit for a king.

Snow White loathed that floor.

To be more accurate, she loathed the spaces between the flagstones—cracks that were too narrow to sweep out easily but wide enough for crumbs to lodge inside. Cleaning the floor meant crawling through the hall to remove bits of debris by hand. Even if she bunched up her skirts for cushioning, her knees always ended up black and blue.

"I'm almost done," she told Dottie. "I don't think the section over there is very dirty."

Her conversation partner clicked her beak skeptically. The sparrow was a good listener and enjoyed staying with Snow White as she cleaned. Dottie *especially* enjoyed eating the occasional cake crumb that Snow White dislodged, and sometimes she'd bring Snow White a sponge if she needed it.

Snow White was battling a fossilized piece of venison when Dottie's siblings, Blue and Featherlight, flew in, chirping madly. At their panic, a chill ran over Snow White. It seemed that most of her existence could be split between two states: the hours when her stepmother was present, and when she was not.

Imperious footsteps echoed down the hall, and Snow White stood as they neared. She wasn't sure why she wanted to be on her feet when her stepmother entered. It wasn't as if the Queen didn't know what Snow White was up to, since she was the one who'd forced her to work as a scullery maid in the first place. But something in Snow White wanted to send a message that she was more than her current circumstances. Snow White had been a beloved daughter once, and a princess. She still was a princess.

The Queen swept into the room, beautiful as always with her statue-like features and tall, regal frame. The black satin of her hooded gown clung to her arms and head like a second skin.

"Have you finished cleaning the dining room?" She didn't even look at Snow White when she spoke, as if the princess were not worth even that tiny acknowledgment.

"I'm almost done." Snow White kept her gaze down and her tone respectful. Humiliation was nothing new, and she could endure any amount of it if she focused on the presence of the animals around her.

The Queen strode through the hall, scanning the floor. "There are crumbs between the flagstones."

I haven't had time to clean that part yet. But Snow White bit her tongue.

"Shoddy work," said the Queen. "I don't know why I feed and clothe you when you don't even earn your keep."

Snow White thought back to that morning, when she'd visited Dottie at the birdbath and watched the sparrow splash water with her wings. She remembered the joy she had felt then. How they'd laughed. She took that joy and held it close.

The Queen slowed in her speech, as if suspecting that Snow White was not completely listening. "You'll have no midday meal," she said. "If you remedy your work by tonight, I might think about giving you supper."

Snow White curtsied. "Yes, Your Majesty."

Snow White spent another two hours cleaning the feast hall, ignoring the gnawing in her stomach as mealtime came and went. When she finished, she slipped out without waiting for her stepmother to inspect her work. The Queen would always find fault with something. Better to leave and trust she had cleaned well enough to avoid punishment.

Snow White still didn't understand why the Queen disliked her so, only that the icy glares and edged comments while her father had been alive turned into full-fledged malice after he'd died. For a long time, Snow White had tried to puzzle it out, wondering if she'd done something to offend the Queen. She'd done her best to be an obedient and dutiful stepdaughter, but nothing made a difference.

She checked the position of the sun through the window. If she went to the kitchen now, the cooks might sneak her some bread, but she hated putting the servants at risk. Better if she found something to take her mind off her hunger.

"How about an adventure?" she asked the birds. They tweeted their approval.

Snow White grabbed a dustrag so she'd have an excuse for wandering. If the Queen had her way, Snow White's world would be narrowed to her room in the cellar, the kitchens, and any halls the Queen had her clean. But whenever she had the chance, Snow White liked to explore the older sections of the castle. There Snow White found artifacts of a happier time: handkerchiefs, baubles, letters left behind by visitors long gone, portraits of the royal family that the Queen hadn't yet removed. It was a risk, but these wanderings were one of the few things Snow White felt still belonged to her.

Hardly anyone ever bothered her once she was in the old castle, but Snow White had to pass her stepmother's rooms in order to get there. As a precaution, she asked two of the castle mice to run ahead and play lookout. She stayed alert as she followed.

"Snow White, come in."

She froze. It was a strange voice that had spoken—hollow

sounding, male, and otherworldly in a way Snow White couldn't explain. The voice came from a side corridor that led to her stepmother's bedchambers. Snow White did sometimes hear odd sounds when she mopped the hallway floors—rustling, ringing sounds, the occasional shriek.

But Snow White had never heard anyone call out her name before.

"Snow White. Lovely maid. Come in."

Snow White gripped her dustrag and backed up against the wall. The mice circled back, rising inquisitively to their haunches. Snow White waved them away. Whatever this was, she did not want the animals near it.

"Who are you?" she spoke into the empty air, softly enough that no one should have been able to hear. Still, she suspected she would get a reply.

"I'm an observer. A reflector. An agent of truth."

"Why do you keep calling me?"

"Truth is hard to come by in the castle, yet I sense it in you. Come in, and we will talk further."

Was someone playing a trick on her? Snow White wondered what kind of being would lure her into the Queen's rooms. "I can't go in. It's locked."

"You are mistaken. This door bears the same weakness as the ones you've discovered in the tower bedrooms."

Those words sent a chill down Snow White's spine. Had this mysterious speaker seen her exploring the castle? Once, in the old wing, Snow White had leaned against a locked door while pushing down on the handle. To her surprise, it had given way. She hadn't thought much of it at the time, since those chambers were always empty.

"The Queen would punish me if I went into her rooms."

"You can risk punishment now or face far greater evils later. Dark days are coming for you, Princess."

Snow White wondered what those greater evils could possibly be. She was already a scullery maid without a father or a real mother. The Queen punished her whenever it suited her mood.

And yet, Snow White couldn't help feeling intrigued by the mysterious voice. She supposed she had little to lose.

Taking a deep breath, Snow White slipped down the side corridor to the Queen's bedchambers. A quarter turn on the doorknob until it caught, and then a push. The door creaked open, revealing a cavernous room with high ceilings. For a moment, Snow White stood at the doorway, taking it all in. On one side were a giant four-poster bed, dressers, and cabinets. On the other was an alcove with stairs leading to an enormous wall mirror.

There was no one inside.

"Where are you?" she asked.

"A wall holds me, but it does not limit me."

A flash of movement caught her eye. Snow White glanced at the wall mirror and jumped back in horror at the face floating there. It looked like a mask one might wear to a ball, and it was illuminated with green light. As Snow White's pulse slowed, she crept closer.

"Are you an enchanted mirror?" she asked in awe.

"I am truth and honesty, the kernel of everything that is."

She wondered if it must always speak in riddles. "I don't understand."

"You are a princess of royal blood. The true heir to your father's throne. Your heart is pure and honest, but misfortune and danger stalk and seek you."

"Misfortune and danger? My father is already dead. I'm a scullery maid. What other misfortunes await me?"

"There are those who mean you harm. You must protect yourself."

"Who means me harm?"

"Your stepmother is a great sorceress. You, too, can harness magic to do your bidding."

Was the mirror refusing to tell her who wished her harm, or had it provided the answer? Then the other part of its message hit her. "Harness *magic*? How?"

But the mirror did not answer, falling silent for the remainder of her visit.

"I can't stop thinking about the mirror," said Snow White as she scrubbed at a stubborn berry stain on the kitchen floor. Dottie fluffed her wings in sympathy.

Snow White had long ceased to feel self-conscious about talking to animals. They'd always taken to her, even in the years before her father died. And afterward, when everything changed, it was the animals who'd saved her from despair in the face of the Queen's cruelty. Their love had convinced Snow White that she was indeed worth loving, and their joy had convinced her there was happiness yet to be found in the world. It was with the strength they lent her that Snow White had chosen joy over bitterness, and their constant companionship kept her on that path. Still, Snow White yearned for the freedom, the familial love, the sense of *home* of her early years. And now it seemed even this new, dimmer version of her life was in danger.

The berry stain was finally fading. Snow White put down her brush and shook her sore arm.

"What was it the mirror said it was—an instrument of truth? I do feel the honesty of its words," she said to Dottie, who'd been joined by Blue and Featherlight. The three sparrows stared back solemnly.

But even if the mirror was telling the truth, how could she heed its advice? It had said she must find a way to learn magic, and she had no idea how to do that.

She turned to the sparrows. "I think I need to go into the Queen's room again. Can you stand watch for me?"

It was midmorning, and the Queen was holding audience until noon. So Snow White had the sparrows stand sentry over the high courtyard window outside the throne room. Then she gathered her courage and entered the Queen's bedchamber again.

The mirror spoke as soon as she went in, frightening Snow White half out of her wits.

"You are wise to heed my advice, Princess."

Snow White put her hand to her chest to calm her racing heart. "You scared me."

"I am not the one you should fear."

"Then whom?"

"You know the answer."

There it was again, that shiver across her skin, the instinct she wished she could deny. Strange that Snow White would still resist believing that the Queen would cause her grievous harm, even after years of her cruelty. Perhaps it was a residual wish to believe she still had family who loved her.

Snow White looked around, unsure what she was looking for. Was magic the kind of thing that could be written down? Or perhaps, if the Magic Mirror was here, there would be other enchanted objects, too.

The mirror's empty eyes followed her around the room. The bedchamber wasn't as clean as the rest of the castle, probably because the maids were never allowed inside. There was dust in the corners, and the surfaces were cluttered with bottles and jewelry. Snow White saw a wardrobe filled with luxurious gowns and a chest with jewelry, scarves, and blankets.

A bit of white under a dresser caught her eye—a corner of parchment, maybe? Snow White saw that it was one of several sheets that had fallen underneath the dresser. She pulled them out and dusted off the cobwebs. They looked almost like pages from a cookbook, except the recipes were written in fancy calligraphy and were for things she'd never fathomed before.

Colored Flame Potion
Shrinking Charm
Cleaning Charm

Snow White's heart pounded. "This must be from some sort of spell book."

The mirror made no answer. Its face had disappeared from the surface.

Ah. So she was on her own once more.

Snow White looked again at the parchment. Could she possibly attempt the spells herself? The thought terrified her. Still, if the pages had gathered that much dust, perhaps they wouldn't be missed. And it wasn't as though she had the luxury of being picky. Before she had a chance to second-guess herself, she stuffed the parchments into her bodice and hurried out.

Not all the cellar rooms had windows, but Snow White was thankful that hers did. On nights with a full moon, the moonlight came through in a silver beam. If Snow White placed the pages of spells underneath, she could make out the words without lighting a lamp.

She'd looked through the spells with fascination. The colored flame potion read like a kitchen recipe—like one of the pies the castle cooks taught Snow White to make after her chores were finished and when her stepmother was otherwise occupied. Except the ingredients this recipe asked for—moonbeam from a crescent moon, ashes of a broken heart—were things that Snow White had never seen in any kitchen. The cleaning charm looked practical, but the incantations were written in a script she couldn't pronounce. She finally settled on the shrinking charm. It seemed to be a poem with a series of hand gestures. Snow White placed a small stone on the floor in front of her to use as the object of her spell.

Snow White squinted at the diagrams. The illustrated gestures were complicated, often requiring both hands to form elaborate shapes. She painstakingly copied the gestures, one after another, until she could remember them all. Was it as simple as saying the words at the same time?

There was a flutter of feathers next to her. Dottie hopped onto her lap and nestled in her skirts.

"You're supposed to be asleep," said Snow White.

The sparrow chirped, looking between her and the spell.

"You want to see me try this? I'm worried something will go wrong."

Dottie looked up at her with clear eyes. The animals had always been more sure of her than Snow White herself.

Well, there was no point in delaying. Haltingly, she spoke the incantation as she worked through the gestures.

Nothing happened.

Snow White deflated. "I suppose it wouldn't be that easy, would it?"

She looked over the diagrams again. Had she gotten a step wrong? Maybe her little finger was supposed to be straighter. But changing that didn't seem to help. Neither did stretching the vowels or holding her hands higher up. Snow White tried variation after variation until her hands started to cramp.

"What was that?" Snow White asked. "I felt something."

Dottie chirped.

"I felt something warm in my fingers. It's gone now, though."

What had she done differently? She'd spoken more forcefully, perhaps. Snow White tried again, modifying her voice, raising and then lowering her tone. There it was—the warmth when she spoke from the bellows of her stomach.

A thrill went through her. If she had a way to sense the magic, then she could work her way closer to the spell. Snow White dove in with renewed determination, adding a pitch adjustment here, a curled finger there. The power in her hands grew with each change. She felt it building through her arms, rushing through her fingers as she finished the incantation. The warmth surged to the tips of her fingers and exploded in a flash of light. White-hot pain burned her fingertips.

The stone remained unchanged.

Snow White blew on her fingers. She couldn't see in the

darkness, but she suspected her skin was red and blistered. "I was almost there, Dottie, but the power got stuck. I need to release it somehow."

Leaning over the parchment, she spoke the incantation again. This time, as she neared the end of the spell, she pointed her finger at the stone. The warmth moved through her finger and out of it. A spark of light arced through the room.

The stone disappeared. Dottie took flight, twittering in alarm.

Snow White scarcely dared to breathe as she moved closer to investigate. Was it completely gone? And then she saw it: a pebble with the same red hue as the stone, but a fraction of its size.

"I can't believe it, Dottie."

Dottie hopped around the pebble and pecked at it. Snow White wanted to run outside and shout her victory to the stars. Instead, she picked up the parchment again. "It says here, to undo the spell, you just do everything backward."

Well, that had some logic to it, though it was easier said than done. Putting everything in reverse felt like a completely different spell, and Snow White ended up with several more singed fingertips. But the learning went faster this time, and soon she spoke the words that restored the stone to its original size.

"Maybe I really can do this," she whispered. "Maybe I can save myself."

———

"I shrank so many things last night!" Snow White finally gave in to the urge to twirl around her stepmother's room. Who'd ever have thought she would gush to a mirror?

Her eyes were dry and her fingers smarted. She'd hardly slept the night before. Instead, she'd stayed up, charming object after object. She'd shrunk a spoon to fit in her palm and turned her extra skirt into one sized for a doll. Not everything had worked, though. A cut rose from the vase by her bed stayed the same size, as did a leaf and the apple she'd saved from dinner. Perhaps the spell worked only on nonliving things.

"You do well, Princess." The Magic Mirror's voice was level as always, its empty eyes devoid of emotion. "But shrinking charms will not protect you from the Queen's magic."

Snow White wished that the mirror would at least let her celebrate her victories. "These spells are the only ones I've found."

"There are other sources of magic here. You must find them."

"If it's so important, why can't you tell me where? Aren't you supposed to see everything?"

"The Queen's dark magic blocks my sight."

Not for the first time, Snow White wondered if she should trust the mirror. But everything it had told her about her stepmother fit with what she'd already suspected, or even known, in the way that her bones sometimes knew things that her mind didn't.

"Why does the Queen want to hurt me?" she asked.

"Your beauty."

"My beauty?" Snow spoke to both the mirror and her own reflection in it. It was true that many called her beautiful. "But my stepmother is beautiful, too."

"Your beauty surpasses hers."

Snow White looked down at her hands, callused and red from scrubbing, and at the rags that hung from her too-thin frame. "Is that really all there is to it? She's jealous?"

The mirror did not reply. Snow White glared at it, wishing it didn't have to be so cryptic. Then something caught her eye. The mirror's surface looked different. Her reflection had darkened, as if the mirror had turned into something like dark glass, and there was a hint of a shadow behind it.

Snow White stepped closer. Was there something behind the glass?

"May I . . . ?"

The mirror didn't respond. Gathering courage, Snow White put her eyes up to the mirror, cupping her hands to block the light. Through the glass, she could see the stone of the wall behind it. She also saw something brighter, like the metal handle of a lever.

"What is that behind you?"

Snow White ran around to the side of the mirror and slid her fingers along where it pressed against the wall. Try as she might, she could not pry the mirror away from the stone.

"There's a lever behind you," she said. "It's important isn't it?"

Snow White pried at the mirror again, wondering at how far she'd come since the days when she'd been frightened even to talk to it. Still, the mirror stuck tightly to the wall. Then Snow White felt that flicker of instinct, the same intuition that had led her to cast the shrinking charm.

She stepped again in front of the mirror. Its surface still had that darker, less reflective quality. It reminded her of the surface of a lake. Rippling, almost. Liquid.

She reached through it.

It felt like plunging her hand into cool water but lighter and airier, with a thrill of magic within. Eddies caressed her skin. Her fingertips bumped against the smooth rock wall, then the cold metal of a lever. She pulled.

A grating sound filled the room. The sparrows fluttered up in alarm and flew circles around the Queen's bookshelf. Except it wasn't a bookshelf anymore. It had opened away from the wall like a door, and beyond it was a corridor, dusted with cobwebs and lit by torches that gave no smoke. Snow White's heart pounded as she stepped through.

The air smelled like it did right before a thunderstorm. Stairs wound down in wide circles until the passageway leveled out into an underground chamber. The clicks of tiny claws on stone swelled around her, then faded away. Snow White stifled a scream at the sight of a skeleton hanging from a hook. Was that her stepmother's handiwork, too? It finally dawned on her how much danger she was in. What was a trivial shrinking spell compared to this palpable evil? Snow White took a steadying breath. She'd come that far. And she had a feeling that the magic she sought was ahead.

Across the chamber was a door that opened into a workshop. Shelves lined the room, loaded with tome after tome, strange artifacts, and jars filled with things she didn't want to identify.

She took a book by the spine, then snatched her hand away when pain lanced through her fingers. Gingerly, she tried the leather-bound volume next to it. This one didn't attack her, and she hefted it onto the dusty table. There were all kinds of spells here, some to bring sickness and death, some to cause nightmares. Snow White paused at a life-giving spell and a shield spell. These seemed helpful, but she worried her stepmother would notice the book missing if Snow White took it.

Snow White fingered the pages, thinking of the ones hidden under her pillow. Would the tome fight back if she harmed it? She didn't have time to worry one way or another. Quickly, she took a knife from the table and cut out the pages for those two spells. Then, stuffing the pages in her bodice, she ran back up the stairs, racing through the secret passageway.

"Kill her," came her stepmother's voice.

Snow White's heart nearly jumped out of her chest.

"But, Your Majesty!" It was a man speaking now. After a moment, enough of Snow White's wits returned to realize that both voices were coming through the wall. She leaned up against the stone to hear better.

Her stepmother's voice was low and commanding as ever. "You know the consequences if you fail."

"Yes, Your Majesty."

The voices died down, and Snow White backed away, shaken. It was one thing to suspect that her stepmother had her enemies executed, but it was another altogether to hear these commandments spoken. She quickened her steps toward the passageway's exit.

Her stepmother's bedchambers were blessedly empty when Snow White came out. She closed up the bookshelf, then fled back to her room. Footsteps sounded on the stairs soon after she shut her door, followed by an imperious knocking.

Snow White struggled to catch her breath as the Queen swooped into her room, her visage like the mythical beauties of legend. Could this otherworldly woman truly be jealous of her? Snow White moved out of the way, hoping she didn't look nearly as shaken as she felt. It seemed impossible that the Queen wouldn't be able to see the truth of what Snow White had just done.

"Have you finished all your cleaning for today?" the Queen asked.

Snow White curtsied. "Not all of it. I was just getting back to it."

The Queen waved her hand airily. "Leave that for now. I wish to have more flowers for the ballroom."

Her stepmother never let unfinished chores go without punishment. Something was deeply wrong.

"Shall—shall I pick some flowers from the gardens?" asked Snow White.

"No, I want wildflowers. Go gather them in the forest. My huntsman will accompany you for your safety."

That was when Snow White saw the man waiting outside—bearded, with muscled shoulders and wearing woodsman's clothes.

He bowed. "Your Highness."

His was the voice she'd overheard in the passageway. Now that she saw his face, she realized she had seen him about the castle. She believed she'd once made his family some hand pies when he'd told the cooks his young son had grown ill. At once, Snow White knew without a doubt that this man was to kill her in the meadow.

Cold erupted over her skin. She needed to think, to stay calm.

"Thank you, Stepmother." She kept her eyes down and her expression serene. "The wildflowers should be beautiful at this time of year. May I have a few moments to freshen up and gather my things?" She looked to the Huntsman. "I can meet you at the stables if you'd like."

The Huntsman bowed. "Yes, Your Highness. I shall await you there." Did she imagine the tension at the corners of his eyes?

Snow White curtsied again as they left, her skirt fisted so tightly in her hands that it was a wonder it didn't disintegrate. The moment their footsteps faded, she grabbed her bags and sprang into action. She needed to flee the castle, though she didn't know where to go. As Snow White frantically thought through her options, she shrank her extra clothes and threw them into a basket.

As Snow White glanced out the cellar window, she saw the Queen crossing the courtyard toward the stables. A harebrained idea occurred to her. If the Queen was down here, then her bedchambers were empty.

Snow White sprinted up the stairs.

"She's going to have her huntsman take me into the woods and kill me," Snow White said to the mirror as soon as she charged through the door. Dust danced in sunbeams around her. Her stepmother's furniture felt sinister in its stillness. Snow White's skin itched with the fear that something would spring to life and capture her.

A swirl of green fog obscured the mirror's face. "You must run."

"Can you come with me? Maybe I could shrink you to fit into my basket." No sooner had the question left Snow White's lips than she thought of a hundred reasons why it couldn't possibly work. Would the Queen have a protection charm on such an important artifact? Would it remain attached to the wall even if Snow White did manage to shrink it?

"You may attempt to bring me," said the mirror.

That was as much encouragement as she needed. She spoke the shrinking spell. There was a flash, and the mirror dropped to the floor with a clatter that sent panic lacing through Snow White's chest. She scarcely breathed as she went closer. It had shrunk to the size of a hand mirror, and she saw with relief that no cracks marred the glass. Snow White carefully placed it into her basket and ran back down the stairs. She needed to go out the garden door. From there, she could slip out the back gate.

It was hard to move both quickly and quietly down the back stairs, especially while carrying such precious cargo, but Snow White did her best. At the ground floor, the stairs split into two—one flight heading to her room in the cellar and the other leading to the garden. Snow White took the latter route and threw her weight into the heavy garden door.

"Snow White?"

Her stepmother's voice echoed through the halls. Snow White froze, unsure whether to answer or run for her life. Perhaps this was the panic that deer felt the moment before a hunter's arrow found them.

The Queen stepped into view. "What is taking you so long?"

Every muscle in her body screamed out to run, and yet, the Queen's gaze rooted her to the spot.

Snow White took a shaky breath. "I'm sorry, Stepmother. I'm on my way."

"Come, then. My huntsman is waiting."

The Huntsman didn't look like a murderer. He was older, perhaps old enough to be her father. Strong arms. No malice in his eyes, and he addressed her with respect every time he spoke. But there was a long knife in his belt, and an axe hung from his saddle. He watched her closely as they rode.

Snow White rode sidesaddle, her panic rising as they went deeper into the trees. She'd lost her chance to flee the castle alone. Could she possibly outrun the Huntsman in the woods? He rode a war stallion, and she had but a pony.

The Huntsman stopped. "Will this meadow do for flowers, Your Highness?"

"Yes, thank you."

He didn't seem inclined to follow her, and Snow White wasted no time getting to the far side of the meadow. The ground was covered with flowers in every hue—fuzzy cornflowers in pink and blue, shy forget-me-nots with delicate lilac petals. Under any other circumstance, Snow White would have loved to spend an afternoon there. She felt the Huntsman's eyes on her back as she started gathering.

A small purple flower caught her eye. She couldn't name it, but the bell-like blossoms looked familiar. Then she realized where she had seen them before. The flower looked exactly like the blooms depicted in the shield spell she'd taken from her stepmother's spell book. She picked several handfuls.

Snow White looked over her shoulder to see the Huntsman tending to his horse. He was no longer looking at her. Carefully, she brought out the mirror and laid it down in the tall grass.

"Mirror, I couldn't get away," she whispered.

The glass reflected the clouds and the trees above. No face appeared.

"Mirror?" She picked it up and looked into it. Her reflection stared back, nothing more. A coldness emanated from the frame, the same chill she'd felt in her stepmother's spell room. Had the Queen found the mirror missing and cast a spell on it?

Snow White's hands began to shake. She was out there alone with a man who planned to murder her, and her one ally had gone dark.

"Come back. Please come back." Her voice broke. She shook the mirror and wiped its surface with her apron, but all she saw was her own distraught face.

Then she saw the blade of a hunting knife rising behind her. The Huntsman's eyes appeared, cold with determination.

Snow White screamed, throwing up her arms.

A spell. She needed a spell. But her tongue froze in her

mouth. She squeezed her eyes shut and waited for the blade to fall.

But no metal pierced her skin. Something thudded on the ground in front of her. Snow White opened her eyes to see the hunting knife embedded in the dirt. The Huntsman stood over her, his face ashen.

"I can't do it. Forgive me. Run away, Princess. Never come back."

The next hours passed in a blur. Snow White ran through the trees, fleeing from shadow to shadow as the forest transformed into ghosts from her nightmares. Finally, she calmed enough to realize that her fears were making things seem more frightening than they actually were. It was then that the forest animals approached her and led her to a cottage in the woods.

What followed was one of the strangest yet most wondrous evenings she'd ever experienced. The house belonged to seven kind little men. Not only did they welcome her into their house for dinner, but they agreed to let her stay with them. They even volunteered to sleep downstairs so that she could have the upstairs bedroom to herself.

She was grateful to have found the kind men. The next morning, she awoke feeling fresher and braver. She came downstairs and cooked a big breakfast, then stood by the door to see her new hosts off as they left for work.

"Have a good day, Grumpy," she said. "I'll have a gooseberry pie ready for you this evening."

Grumpy attempted a scowl, but Snow White could see the smile trying to sneak out. She was starting to realize he was not nearly as bad-tempered as he pretended to be.

Doc doffed his hat, solicitous as usual. "Now, Princess, be careful," he said. "The Queen is a tricky one."

"I know," said Snow White. "Don't you worry. I'll be just fine." In the clear light of morning, she could almost believe it.

After her new friends left, the forest animals gathered around her. Dottie and several blue jay friends perched on the windowsill, two deer peeked in through the doorway, a family of rabbits sat around the fireplace, and two squirrels sprawled atop the dining table.

Snow White inhaled. She wished she could revel in this cozy home, but she still had that uneasy feeling that she was not quite free from the Queen's wrath. "Well, there's no reason to tarry," she said, clapping her hands. "Let's get the washing and cooking done, and then I have some spells to practice."

She delegated the dishes to the rabbits and the sweeping to the squirrels, then instructed the birds to forage for berries. The only task she didn't trust the animals to do properly was the baking, so she rolled out dough and assembled the gooseberry pie herself. When everything was clean and the pie sat ready to bake, she collapsed into a chair, giving herself a few moments to sip a cup of tea.

"Shall I try some spells?" she asked after a while.

The fawns shied away, but the rabbits jumped and

twitched their ears. Snow White took out her bag and laid its contents on the table: wildflowers that she'd picked at the meadow, the spells she'd cut from the Queen's book, and the Magic Mirror, still ominously dark. Snow White's gut clenched at the sight of the mirror. Perhaps if she became better at magic, she'd be able to fix it.

She spread the parchments in front of her.

"What do you suppose a life-giving spell does?" Healing magic would certainly come in useful. The spell itself looked similar in form to the shrinking charm, with an incantation and accompanying hand gestures.

It took Snow less time to learn this spell than it'd taken to learn the shrinking charm. She was starting to get a feel for magic done right, the warmth and the gathering of power that told her she was on the right path. On her fourth try, she felt the familiar surge working toward her fingertips, and she pointed at a cut wildflower.

A spark of light leapt from her finger to the flower, spreading from the leaf where it landed to the very edges of the flower's petals. Then a new green shoot grew out of the stem. One of the deer nibbled at it.

"Oh, you don't want to eat that," said Snow White, but the creature just wagged her tail.

"Well, the spell seems to work," Snow White went on, placing another cut flower at the center of the table. "Let me try it again."

Snow White repeated the incantation. The power gathered in her hands.

The deer belched.

Snow White jumped. The spell shot out at an angle and hit the Magic Mirror. For a moment the glass glowed brilliantly, and then it went dark.

Snow White grabbed the mirror and looked over its surface in panic. Had she broken it? No cracks or noticeable damage. And the surface was . . .

Snow White stared. Images flickered across the glass and disappeared again. There was Snow White as a little girl, playing with her father. Snow White older and mourning her father's passing. Then more recent images of her fleeing the hunter. Was the mirror regaining its magic? But as she watched, the pictures faded away.

A prickle of possibility ran through her. Maybe the life-giving spell could bring the mirror back to life. Snow White drew a deep breath and placed it back on the table. As carefully as she could, she spoke the spell again and directed it straight at the mirror. Once again, the mirror glowed. Once again, images of the past flitted across it, but they were short-lived.

Snow White cast the life-giving spell on the mirror five more times. Each time, the images appeared briefly before disappearing. Was the mirror getting better with each successive casting? As much as she wished it to be true, it didn't seem so.

Snow White sat back in her chair. Repeating a failed spell over and over again didn't seem wise. Maybe it would be better to move on to the shield incantation.

This spell required a mirror, and of course, Snow White

had one in front of her, albeit a rather extraordinary one. It felt wrong to use what had once been such a powerful artifact as a magical prop, but she didn't have any other options.

Snow White read carefully through the steps. It was complicated, requiring not just incantations but weaving a garland of flowers around the edge of the mirror. Snow White grabbed two of the blue wildflowers, knotted their stems together, and started to braid. The work reminded her a bit of crocheting without the hooks. After a while, she fell into a rhythm. Her fingers started to smell like perfume.

She was brought out of her concentration by the sun striking her eyes through the front window. She turned her chair and kept weaving. Just a few more knots to go.

Finally, Snow White put down her handwork and admired it. It was a bit messy, but it looked pretty close to the picture. The birds flew in to look.

"Do you like it?"

The birds tweeted their approval. Snow White held up the braid again, but then she looked closer. Wait, that wasn't right. Somehow she'd woven a pattern that was the mirror image of the one on the parchment.

"Oh . . ."

The dismay must have come clearly through her voice, because the family of rabbits nuzzled her ankles. Snow White rubbed at her temples. Her eyes were tired from such close work, and her fingers ached. Her seven hosts would probably be coming home soon.

"Perhaps it'd be better to start again tomorrow."

The sparrows and blue jays helped her clear the table of fallen petals, and Snow White carefully stowed the mirror and parchments in the cupboard.

"All alone, my pet? The little men are not here?"

Snow White jumped. An old woman peeked in over the open top half of the cottage door. As Snow White's heartbeat slowed, she saw that the woman was frail, wrinkled, and stooped. On her arm, she carried a basket of apples. Snow White felt a surge of compassion for her. It must be a hard life, to be so old and to still have to wander the land selling wares.

"They aren't here," she answered. "Do you know them?"

The peddler woman sniffed the air. "Making pies?"

The woman certainly was odd. Snow White wondered if she was hard of hearing. "Yes, gooseberry pies."

"It's apple pies that make the menfolk's mouths water. Pies made from apples like these. Would you like to try one?"

The crone held up a perfectly smooth red apple. Snow White could smell its fragrance from across the room.

"Oh, they do look delicious."

"Go on," said the peddler woman. "Have a bite."

There was a flutter of wings. The birds flocked around the peddler woman's head, pecking at her and pulling at her cloak. The woman cried out.

"Stop it! Stop it!" Snow White shouted over the confusion. "Go away. Shame on you. Frightening an old lady."

The peddler woman covered her face with her arms as Snow White escorted her inside and sat her down at the table. She didn't know what had gotten into the birds. Snow White had never seen them givc anyone a stern look, much less attack.

"Sit down, madam," she said. "I'm so sorry. I'll bring you some tea for your nerves. And would you like some cake?"

"That would be lovely, dearie."

Something about the old woman's smile made Snow White uneasy. Or was it simply the animals' strange behavior getting to her?

There were two slices of leftover cake. Snow White walked to the cupboard where she'd stored them next to the flower-wreathed magic mirror. Sneaking a glance at the old woman, Snow White angled her body so the woman wouldn't see. Speaking under her breath, she cast a life-giving spell at the mirror and then angled the reflective surface over her shoulder.

The image came instantly: Snow White biting into an apple, then falling lifeless to the ground. The old woman cackling and turning into her stepmother.

Snow White swallowed a cry and hurried to put the mirror down before she dropped it. The images the mirror had shown her before had been of the past, but this one seemed to be a warning. How had the Queen found her so soon? Snow White quelled the overwhelming urge to flee. As weak as the peddler woman looked, Snow White wasn't sure she'd be able to outrun her. It took everything she had to force a smile onto her face. Then she picked up the cake and brought it to the table.

"It's not as good as it is fresh out of the oven, but I hope you like it," she said shakily.

The old woman smiled again. Now that Snow White knew what to look for, she could see her stepmother's smirk, that bit of ice, beneath the unfamiliar face.

"It's delicious, dearie. Let me repay you with this apple." She once again held out that luscious fruit. Even though Snow White had seen the truth of what it was, her mouth watered.

"Thank you," she said. "I'm not hungry now, but I will keep it for later."

"You must have a bite now." The old woman leaned in conspiratorially. "I'll share a secret with you. This is a magic wishing apple. One bite, and all your dreams will come true. There must be something your little heart desires."

Snow White looked around for the animals. A few sparrows peered in from the window, and three chipmunks crowded near the door, but the rest were gone.

"Perhaps there's someone you love?" asked the Queen. "Come now. A lovely maid like you simply must have a bite."

It was hard to think with the peddler woman pushing

the apple so insistently. She was going to get suspicious if Snow White kept refusing. Maybe there was some way of convincing her that her ploy was working.

Gingerly, Snow White took the apple. "Maybe just a bite," she said. She put it to her mouth, turning away so the Queen couldn't see that it didn't touch her lips. Even so, the apple's fragrance filled her nose, tempting her to have just one taste. Snow White mimed eating it, then made herself go limp, just as she'd seen in the mirror. She slid off the chair and let the apple roll out of her hand.

Had that been convincing enough? Snow White kept her breathing as shallow as possible as footsteps came near, paused next to her, and then headed away. The door opened and closed. She counted to one hundred before finally opening her eyes. Sunlight streamed in through the windows. Everything was quiet. The apple lay undisturbed, several paces away. Slowly she pushed herself up and walked to the door. Where were the animals?

"You're cleverer than I thought," said the old woman from behind her.

Snow White turned. There was the crone, next to the stairway.

The old woman stood straighter now. The stoop was gone from her back. Step by resolute step, her stepmother closed the distance between them. "I used to think you were useless and stupid, but you've escaped death twice now. Perhaps I've underestimated you."

Snow White should have known right away that something wasn't right. It had been too quiet. Her animals had not come to her.

The Queen continued her slow advance. "Maybe my mistake was not wanting to get my hands dirty. Perhaps the basest methods are still the most effective."

She reached a wrinkled hand into the folds of her cloak and drew out a long knife. Then, with a speed that did not belong to any elderly woman, she ran at Snow White.

A cacophony of birdcalls. A blue-and-brown cloud streamed through the windows, straight at the old woman's face. The Queen screeched and slashed her knife at the sparrows and blue jays. The birds scattered, and Snow White's heart seized when she saw that one sparrow had fallen to the ground.

"No!" The sight of that limp body spurred her to action. She cast the life-giving spell at the fallen bird, but her aim was off. The spell hit the gooseberry pie, which immediately sprouted legs and walked off the table.

The Queen stared at the pie. "Where did you learn that?"

Three rabbits rushed through the door and crowded around the Queen's feet as a fawn tugged at her cloak. Snow White cast another life-giving spell at the fallen sparrow and went soft with relief when the bird shook itself and hopped onto its feet.

There was another storm of wings. The rest of the birds

surrounded Snow White and pulled her toward the door. As they fled, Snow White heard the Queen chanting the life-giving spell. Was she healing herself? But the Queen hadn't been hurt, had she?

It didn't feel right. Snow White dropped behind a water trough just as a bolt of light sailed overhead and struck a tree, which immediately shriveled.

That had been no life-giving spell. The words had been the same, but the Queen had spoken them in reverse.

A killing spell.

"There's no use hiding," the Queen said. "I'll admit I'm impressed you picked up some magic, but I know a fledgling caster when I see one. Come out, and no more of your animal friends get hurt."

The Queen's voice dropped as she started chanting a new spell. Snow White peeked around the water trough to see her stepping outside. Overhead Snow White saw the birds gather to fly at the Queen again.

"No!" she shouted. "Save yourselves!"

She should have worked harder at her magic. It seemed so foolish that she had thought she could protect herself with walking pies when the Queen had missiles that killed on contact. Could she flip the life-giving spell herself? She racked her brain, trying to visualize the hand gestures in backward order, but a burst of magic exploded on the grass next to her and her mind went blank. It was no use. She might have been able to flip the spell given a quiet hour to practice, but figuring it out right then was impossible.

Though she *did* have practice with the backward shrinking charm. Snow White pointed at a pebble between herself and the Queen, turning it into a boulder as her step-mother neared. As Snow White darted farther away, the Queen spoke and the boulder exploded into hundreds of jagged pieces. Snow White covered her head with her arms as sharp rocks pummeled her skin.

So much for that idea. What she really needed was a shield, but she'd gone and braided those flowers backward.

Backward.

A germ of an idea formed in her mind. She had no idea if it would work, but she was out of options. Snow White heard chattering behind her and turned to see one of the squirrels.

"Can you distract the Queen so I can run inside?" Snow White asked.

The squirrel sprinted toward the Queen, circling her and then biting her leg before scampering off. As the Queen screamed and gave chase, Snow White made for the cottage door, ducking inside and throwing open the cabinet. There was the Magic Mirror again, still nestled in its backward-braided nest. It was useless as a shield, but perhaps . . .

Footsteps sounded behind her. The Queen stepped through the door, knife in hand.

"So it was you who took my mirror."

Snow White turned to face her stepmother. "Why do you hate me so much?"

"It was your beauty that first irked me. But now I see you're a threat in other ways."

The Queen advanced toward her. Snow White backed against the far wall, clutching the mirror in one hand and the spell page in the other. She began to chant, starting with the last word and working shakily forward.

As the Queen raised her knife, Snow White ducked and held up the mirror. The birds screamed. Snow White finished the incantation. There was a blinding flash.

And then silence.

Snow White blinked the afterimage of light from her eyes. Everything was so quiet that she wondered if she'd lost her hearing. Cautiously, she looked around. A sparrow limped across the floor with one wing dragging. A squirrel crawled up to nuzzle it.

The Queen was nowhere in sight.

The mirror lay on the floor a few paces away; its surface looked cloudy. Snow White peered into it, only to spring back at the sight of the Queen's face—her real face, not that of the crone who'd been hunting her. She was surrounded by thick mist, and she was banging on the glass. As Snow White stared in horror, the Queen's eyes fixed on her, and her features contorted into a snarl. Snow White shrank away and wondered how she could ever have thought this woman beautiful.

"A shield spell is meant to keep things out," she whispered. "Spoken backward, it becomes something to lock things in."

Carefully Snow White took the Magic Mirror, wrapped it in cloth, and then slipped it into her bag. Leagues away, her castle stood empty, and her country awaited a ruler.

"Come," she said to the birds around her. "Let's get dinner ready. And then it will be time to go home."

A First Mission

What if Mulan became the Emperor's advisor?

by Elizabeth Lim

A First Mission

What if Mulan became the Emperor's advisor?

by Elizabeth Lim

Mulan drew a deep breath and swept aside the tassels dangling over her face as she hurried down the palace's cavernous halls. It was her first day as an advisor to the Emperor—an Imperial Councilor of China, as her official title had it—and somehow, the blue silk cap on her head seemed to weigh far heavier than her soldier's helmet ever had. And the helmet had been made out of iron!

"That's just because you're nervous," she told herself.

She had a right to be nervous. At least when she'd been a soldier in the army, she'd had a clear idea of what was expected of her: fight to defend China. But the war was over, and thanks to her, Shan-Yu had been defeated. It was unheard of for a woman to be a military hero, and the last thing Mulan had anticipated was for the Emperor himself to publicly honor her in front of the entire capital, then ask her to become one of his advisors—the most coveted and respected position in the Imperial City, offered only to the top scholars in all of China!

The invitation had startled her, and at first she'd refused. "With all due respect," she'd said, "Your Majesty, I'd like to go home to my family."

"Go home, then," the Emperor had agreed. "But should you change your mind, my offer will stand. When and if you are ready, return to the palace, and there will be a post waiting for you."

Mulan had thanked him graciously, but she'd had no intention of staying in the Imperial City. After all, she missed her family terribly and couldn't imagine being apart from them again.

And so she'd returned home—a hero, but more important to Mulan, a daughter most loved. Three months of eating home-cooked food and sleeping in her own bed; spending time with her parents, Fa Li and Fa Zhou, and recounting stories about training to be a soldier; helping her grandmother with the daily chores; walking down the village streets and being greeted as a person of her own worth, rather than as a girl in need of a husband. What Mulan relished most was how the young girls in her hometown came up to her, whispering, "I want to throw tea on the Matchmaker one day, too."

How Mulan had laughed.

"What will you do now that you're home?" the girls asked her.

Mulan stopped laughing. "I . . . I don't know."

And then she had started to reconsider the Emperor's request. For days she'd wavered, sitting in the garden and simply pondering. She grew restless. Before joining the army, she'd never even left her village. How could she expect to come home and not be changed? Every day she itched to go somewhere, to explore the lands beyond her hometown. To do her part for China.

"I want to go," Mulan had admitted to her grandmother. "But all this time, I fought so I could come home—to my family. It feels like a betrayal to leave you again."

"It's an invitation," Grandmother Fa had reminded her. "Not a life sentence. You aren't leaving us. You can always come back. Besides, if I were you, I'd miss that handsome captain."

Mulan had smiled. She did miss her friends from the army. And of course she missed Shang. He had come to meet her family, charming her parents and grandmother over dinner. But his visit had been far too short.

Deep down she knew she'd already made up her mind. She needed to go back to the Imperial City. Not only to continue serving her country but also for the young women in her town, the young women in China. She'd been given the extraordinary chance to set an example for them and for the generations that came after: she could show all of China that a woman was capable of anything—not only of becoming someone's wife.

For the last time, Mulan fidgeted with her hat. All that would start with her making a good impression on her very first meeting. But . . .

Cri-Kee chirped encouragingly. *Why the nerves?* the cricket seemed to say. *You've got this. Come on, now. Pick up those feet, hup hup!*

"I'm not nervous," Mulan murmured under her breath to both Cri-Kee and herself. "I'm lost."

It was true. The Emperor's palace was an endless maze of red-painted halls and courtyards and gardens, and though she'd spent all of the previous night studying the map she'd been given, she must have made a wrong turn somewhere. The Grand Council Room was nowhere to be found.

There were only five minutes until the meeting started. Mulan couldn't be late on her first day! Hurriedly she approached the nearest guard, who was already eyeing her skeptically; he'd clearly never seen a woman dressed in the advisors' robes before.

"Which way is the Grand Council Room?" Mulan asked him politely.

Before the guard could respond, a familiar figure strutted out of the nearby hallway, and Mulan's stomach sank the moment she recognized him.

Cri-Kee made an *uh-oh* squeak and dove behind Mulan's collar, out of sight.

"Chief Minister Chi Fu," Mulan greeted, summoning a respectable tone she hoped hid how much she disliked the man.

Their dislike was mutual. From the very moment the Emperor had appointed Mulan into his trusted circle, Chi Fu had made his disapproval of her—a *woman*—known. But much as the man rankled her, Mulan knew better than to overlook his years of service as the Emperor's most trusted advisor. Chi Fu certainly looked the part of an important official. There was not a wrinkle in his deep blue robes, his sash was evenly tied and knotted, and even his hat behaved—unlike Mulan's.

"Come, come, we don't want to be late on our first day, do we?" he said, tilting his head. He tugged on a long whisker, clearly reveling in Mulan's helplessness. "Were you just asking the guard for directions?"

"Yes." Mulan swallowed her pride. "I needed help finding my way."

She waited for Chi Fu to make some snide remark about how women couldn't do anything, let alone navigate the intricate passageways of the palace, but he merely looked her over. "I'm going there myself." Chi Fu waved his fan forward. "You may join me."

"Thank you." Mulan had to hide her surprise. Maybe she had misjudged Chi Fu.

The older advisor walked too briskly for them to chat, and when they arrived at the meeting, minutes later, Mulan immediately straightened.

The chamber was possibly the grandest she'd ever entered. The ceilings were impossibly high, held up by slender red pillars with gilded dragons snaking along the sides. On every wall hung tenets from every emperor in the dynasty in the most elegant calligraphy, and statues of China's greatest sages stood in long lines, a reminder of the room's commitment to loyalty, justice, harmony, and peace. She was in such awe she almost didn't notice the Emperor himself, seated at the head of the chamber, waiting for her.

"Welcome, Fa Mulan," he greeted, motioning for her to come forward.

Mulan obeyed, but once she reached the Emperor's side, she immediately knelt and bowed deeply.

"Your Majesty, it is my honor to serve you."

The old man smiled kindly at her. It was a blasphemous thought, which Mulan would forever keep to herself, but the Emperor reminded her a little of her grandfather. He'd passed away when she was a child, but he had been kind and wise, and had a way of encouraging her to know her worth. That was the feeling the Emperor inspired in her, as if he could see through her nervousness and worry.

"Fa Mulan is my newest advisor," said the Emperor as he faced the men present. "She is a hero of China, and as all of you are aware, I owe her my life." A long and deliberate pause. "I am very glad that she has elected to join us in the palace. Please make her welcome here."

"Sir, Your Majesty," all the officials said in unison.

For the next hour, the council discussed the aftermath of war: rebuilding villages that had been ravaged, shipping rice and grains across the country, and building new roads to expedite the process. Mulan could barely recognize most of the locations discussed, let alone keep up with the subject at hand.

By the time the meeting was nearly finished, Mulan felt completely overwhelmed by so much information.

All the other council members formed a line around the Emperor. It turned out they were complaining to him—about her!

"Your Majesty," they said in low voices—voices that still carried across the cavernous audience chamber—"every councilman—and *woman*—must prove himself worthy of giving you counsel. This has been tradition for centuries."

"Yes, yes."

"Wait, Mulan," called Chi Fu. He smiled at her slyly. "This concerns you."

"Indeed it does." The Emperor crossed his arms. "Mulan saved all of China from being conquered by Shan-Yu. She saved my life. She does not need to prove herself."

On every other occasion, Chi Fu immediately deferred to the Emperor's wishes, but this time, the corner of his lips lifted ever so briefly. The chief advisor made a show of sighing. "I understand, Your Majesty. You are so wise and gracious." A pause. "However, it would seem like favoritism, wouldn't it? After all, Mulan has no experience in this role. She has no training." Chi Fu unrolled a scroll. "According to her records, her studies of the classics are dismal, and she was a poor student."

Mulan's face flamed. That was true, she couldn't deny it. "My being uninterested in the classics has nothing to do with my being a woman," she said, not caring if it sounded brash. "It's hard to be interested in what men have to say when all you think we should do is bear sons."

The advisors gasped collectively.

But the Emperor smiled. "Then tell us, Fa Mulan. What should a woman do?"

Mulan lifted her chin. "A woman is equal to a man," she said firmly. "She should have the chance to be educated as a man, and she should be able to speak her mind and be heard and listened to."

One of the advisors snorted. "Next you'll be saying that women should be able to own land and take the civil exams!"

The men laughed.

"Well, why not?" Mulan challenged. "Or are you afraid that we'll surpass you all?"

Their laughter died.

The Emperor steepled his fingers. "I hope you are all taking notes on what Mulan has said. China needs both men and women to make its future bright; why do we reward men with freedoms that women do not share? It is a fair point, Fa Mulan, and not one any have been brave enough to bring to my attention. I thank you."

Chi Fu looked like he had choked on a fish bone. "Even still, that does not change the fact that she has no experience, Your Majesty. It's one thing to learn to become a soldier; it is quite different to become a minister—for her every decision to directly affect the citizens of China."

The other ministers murmured their agreement, each one avoiding her gaze. Mulan had a feeling Chi Fu had spoken to all of them in advance of the meeting.

"I'd be happy to prove myself," she spoke up.

"There is no need," said the Emperor. "Each of my ministers will guide you until you adapt to your new position."

The Emperor's word was law, but as Mulan surveyed the room, she could feel that Chi Fu's words had appealed to the other advisors. She'd never earn their respect if she always relied on the Emperor for support. "I would benefit greatly from your many years of experience," Mulan said humbly to the room full of men. "But if there is a way I might prove myself, I would gladly take it."

"There is a disaster in the northeast province of Hongjing," said Chi Fu, a little too quickly. "This may be the perfect opportunity for our newest advisor."

Hongjing? Mulan's ears perked up. The area was famous for being an important center of the silk trade. "What happened there?"

"Heavy rains have started to flood the province," the Emperor said, "and our traders are concerned about the silkworm farms. Hongjing is at the heart of our significant silk trade. Their silkworms are the finest in the country, and they must be saved. The rain is predicted to continue, and the floods will worsen. We must act soon."

"You have a warrior's training, Mulan," said Chi Fu

snidely. "This mission should be easy for you, like waging battle against worms."

Mulan ignored the remark. "I can do it."

"I will come, too," said Chi Fu. "It would be good to have a senior official overseeing Fa Mulan." He gave Mulan a smile she didn't like.

"The floods will be dangerous, Chi Fu," warned one of the ministers. "Are you sure you are up for the task?"

Chi Fu harrumphed. "Of course I am. I spent months on the front line of the war!"

"Very well. You shall leave immediately," said the Emperor. "Take one carriage and leave quietly. General Li Shang shall escort you."

Whatever misgivings Mulan had about Chi Fu vanished when she heard Shang's name. A flutter rose to her stomach, and she beamed as she bowed to the Emperor. "Thank you, Your Majesty. I won't let you down."

"Whose idea was it to invite *him*?" Shang whispered as Mulan secured her horse, Khan, to their carriage.

"Quiet," Mulan whispered back. "He might hear you."

"I hope he does."

Mulan had to smother a laugh. Since being promoted to general, Shang spent much of his time with the ministers of war, devising ways to defend China from future attacks. But before that, he had come to visit Mulan in her hometown—had even stayed with her family for a week before duty had summoned him back to the capital.

"You sure soldier boy isn't the reason you're going back to the capital?" Grandmother Fa had teased when Mulan announced her decision to become the Emperor's advisor.

Mulan smiled shyly. "I'm the first woman ever offered a position in the Imperial cabinet. I can't turn it down. Besides, I want to help China. Right now, this is the best way."

Grandma Fa smiled at her slyly. "Maybe so, but it won't hurt to invite him to dinner every now and then, don't you think? Who'd turn down dinner with the Emperor?"

Mulan had to admit her grandma was partially right. She *was* glad to see Shang again. Very glad. It was like old times, except she wasn't the soldier Ping following under his command. This time, her rank was equal to his. She rather liked the change.

Mulan opened the wooden window that allowed her to peer into the booth where Chi Fu sat. "Thank you for joining us, Chi Fu. If the weather's fair, we should make it to Hongjing in two days."

Then she closed the window and turned to Shang.

"Shouldn't you be sitting inside, given you're in charge of this mission?" he asked.

"And be stuck with Chi Fu for two days?" Mulan shook her head vehemently. "I'd rather sit in the rain with you. And my lucky cricket."

Mulan glanced at Cri-Kee, who had found a straw hat to help him keep dry.

"Lucky indeed," Mulan murmured with a chuckle. To

Shang, she said, "Thanks for getting the map on such short notice."

"That's a perk to being a general," said Shang with a grin. "An endless supply of maps, ropes, and—"

"Watery congee?" Mulan supplied jokingly.

"All right, the military's food is not . . . great. But I'm counting on you to bring me leftovers from one of your dinners with the Emperor. Though not even an Imperial meal can hold a candle to your grandmother's cooking."

Mulan grinned. "You still miss the dinner you had at my home?"

"The man can eat!" Grandmother Fa had praised Shang when he visited their family for dinner. It was custom for the hosts to offer their guest an ample helping of every dish, and Shang had managed to polish off every plate and even have seconds and thirds—the best compliment there was to Mulan's grandmother's cooking.

Shang's eyes softened. "I miss *you*, Mulan. I'm glad you're here."

Before Mulan could reply, Chi Fu popped out of his booth, peeking at the driving seat. "Are we going any time soon?" he yelled, tapping both of them with the rolled-up map. "The entire river will be flooded by the time we arrive." With a flourish, Chi Fu took out a scroll and made a show of recording their late start.

"Loitering at the gates," he muttered, "ignoring Imperial priorities in favor of useless small talk."

Mulan made a face. Of course Chi Fu was going to be

recording their every move. A bad report was not something she wanted, especially for her first official assignment. "Come on, the catfish is watching."

And so they focused ahead, driving briskly past the Imperial City south toward Hongjing. Before long the sky changed, and the clouds ahead didn't look promising. Mulan glanced back at Chi Fu, who lay snoring in the back of the carriage. "I guess he's saving his energy."

Shang took out an imaginary brush and pretended to record: "The Emperor's oldest, most valued advisor spent the journey sleeping in the carriage, basking in the northeast sun as he absorbed the details of the Imperial edict and map during his slumber."

"Shang." Mulan slapped the general playfully on the shoulder, but she couldn't help laughing. "Let him sleep. Maybe that'll put him in a better mood when he wakes up."

Chi Fu was not looking forward to this mission at all, but what choice did he have? He had to protect the council's best interests, and it was not in anyone's interest to have a *woman* join their ranks. A *woman* whose opinion the Emperor seemed to respect, sometimes even above Chi Fu's. That couldn't happen.

He sat in the back of the carriage with their supplies: a week's worth of food, notes, and blankets. How could he humiliate Mulan in the Emperor's eyes?

He let out a sigh and opened one of his writing books to record some ideas. It was growing dark, and the light in his lantern was growing dim. He couldn't read in such lighting! Of course he couldn't; the lantern was *so* dirty. He took out the candle. There. Much better.

But as the rain grew heavier, it became difficult to read amid the sound of water sploshing under the wheels. The carriage trundled over an uneven plot in the road, and Chi Fu rocked forward in his seat, accidentally dropping his candle.

The flame touched the stack of papers stuck inside Mulan's otherwise *empty* notebook.

Let them burn, Chi Fu thought. Until something else caught his eye—the map!

The edges were singed, and the rest was quickly burning up. Cursing under his breath, Chi Fu hastily tried to stomp out the fire with his foot. But the flames spread quickly, and Chi Fu let out a terrified squeal.

"Help!" he shouted. "Help!"

Smoke coiled out of the window, and Mulan and Shang stopped the carriage in alarm. Shang pulled Chi Fu out into the road so hard that his back landed on the soaked ground.

Fortunately, it was raining heavily. It wasn't long before Mulan and Shang put out the fire. But the damage was done. The map was ruined.

And Shang was eyeing Chi Fu as if he'd done it on purpose. Shang wouldn't dare say so out loud, of course, but Chi Fu recognized the look.

"How dare you glare at me that way, Captain—"

"General," Shang corrected him.

"It was an accident," Chi Fu alleged. "Why would I stoop so low as to burn our only map?"

Shang gave him a hard look; it was clear the general didn't believe him, but he let him go. Chi Fu grumbled to himself and bemoaned his scorched sleeves and the smell that now permeated the carriage cabin.

As he snuffed a spark on one of his whiskers, he felt a hint of guilt at having sabotaged their mission. Sure, he had wanted to find a way to unseat Mulan, but the fire had been an accident. It wasn't like he wanted to be stuck on the road for who knew how long with this company.

He looked around the countryside. Still, perhaps it was for the best. If Mulan couldn't complete a task as simple as retrieving China's precious silkworms from a flood, then she'd be deemed too incompetent for her role at the Emperor's side and ousted from the council. Perfect.

"Well, Fa Mulan," Chi Fu said, "which way do we go now? Left or right?"

"Left," Mulan said, after a moment's pause. "Or is it right?" She gritted her teeth, clearly uncertain. Then she closed her eyes as if visualizing the map and drew a deep breath. "It's left. We'll make through the hills to stay above the water. There's another path to the city. We follow this road."

"If you're sure, then lead the way." Chi Fu gestured,

pretending to defer to his fellow council member. Then, when she and General Li turned back to driving the carriage, he leaned back against his seat and hid a smile.

Maybe this would be easier than he'd thought.

It rained the next day, and the next. And there was no sign of Hongjing. Mulan was starting to lose hope, when, on the third afternoon, the rain finally began to recede.

"Oh, no," Mulan murmured as the horses whinnied. The rain had finally stopped, but the worst was far from over. Down the hill was a small village, with trees that were far too short. A river coursed beside the village, overflowing with rainwater. Mulan's gut rose to her throat as she pushed Khan forward for a better look.

"The village is completely flooded," she breathed. "Shang, we have to do something!"

He was already reaching into the back of the wagon for the rope and supplies they had brought.

There were children floating on planks of wood, and families that had built makeshift boats out of their roofs. Mulan held her breath. They had to get everyone they could safely to the top of the hill. She jumped off the wagon.

"What are you doing?" Chi Fu blustered. "We haven't reached our destination."

"We have to help the families here."

"Absolutely not! Our mission is to retrieve the silkworms. There will be forces sent to help the families later."

"By then it'll be too late."

"Silk is China's treasure," said Chi Fu, obstructing her way. "The silkworms are what we came for."

"China's people are its treasure," Mulan said. "If you're so worried about the silkworms, you can go and retrieve them first." She offered Chi Fu their spare horse. "But Shang and I are going to stay here."

With a sniff, Chi Fu took the reins for the horse. "Someone has to follow orders and look after China's best interests. No surprise that it is me."

The words made Mulan flinch, but she let go of the reins and watched as Chi Fu mounted the horse.

"And make no mistake, this is going on your record, Fa Mulan."

Mulan scoffed. Her record was the last thing on her mind. "I'll deal with the consequences later."

She watched as the advisor trotted down the road, holding an umbrella unsteadily against his side as he ferociously wrote in his record book, an action she knew was meant to spite her. When he was out of sight, she let out a sigh and turned back to Shang.

"You did the right thing," he said, touching her shoulder. "The silkworms will have a dozen guards watching over them. These people need our help."

"I know," said Mulan. "Thanks, Shang. I'm glad you're here."

The blush that crept up his cheeks almost made Mulan

laugh. She grabbed his hand, then towed him toward the village.

For the rest of the day, she and Shang helped search for the missing, reunited children with their families, and lent their hands to salvaging what they could from the town. Whatever supplies she and Shang had—food, water, blankets, and wood—she gave to those who needed them more. They led everyone in the village to the top of a hill, safe from the flood below, and built a fire the children gathered by for warmth. As evening fell, spirits rose, and the children clapped whenever Mulan and Shang hauled up a sack of rice or flour that had been saved from the flood. Not long after, Mulan smelled buns rising in bamboo steamers, and before she knew it, a little girl with two braids tugged at her sleeve.

"Are you hungry, Fa Mulan?"

In her hand she had a steamed bun. "There's cabbage inside. Mama says vegetables will make you strong. I want to be strong like you."

Mulan knelt beside the girl, her heart swelling. "Did you have one already?"

She nodded.

"Thank you," said Mulan.

"I wonder if you'll give a bite to General Li." The girl grinned before running off with her cousins, who'd found a wooden ball.

It was the first break Mulan had taken since Chi Fu left, and as she and Shang shared the bun, she noticed the children giggling at the sight of them.

She smiled back.

"What's on your mind?" asked Shang.

"How nice this is," Mulan replied. "Feeling like I'm doing something for China, going on missions and getting to eat next to my favorite general."

Shang inched closer to her. "It'll be the first of many."

Once they had finished their snack, Mulan and Shang helped the villagers set up tents to spend the night.

In the morning, Chi Fu was back. He held his head high and carried a wide box on his lap, with two more boxes strapped behind him on the horse's rear.

"Behold, China's treasure has been saved!" he cried as his horse ascended the hill. "No thanks to Fa Mulan."

No one applauded his arrival; the villagers merely ignored Chi Fu.

With a harrumph, he made for one of the tents, making a show of scribbling notes. "Day four, and Mulan did nothing to help retrieve the Imperial silkworms," he muttered, loud enough for her and Shang to hear.

Shang curled his fists at his sides. "What a useless, pompous—"

Mulan shook her head. "There's no point getting upset."

"Of course there is. I won't stand for him trying to get you fired over this."

"If he does, then I'll go home," Mulan said calmly. "I didn't want to be an advisor in the first place."

"You didn't want to be a soldier, either," Shang reminded her. "But you turned out pretty good at it."

"Only pretty good?"

Shang smiled, and Mulan did, too. "You'll make a great advisor. You know how I know? Because you have the courage to do what you know is right rather than what others have told you to."

The words warmed Mulan. But before she could come up with a reply, she spied Chi Fu emerging from the tent. He was wearing silk slippers and chasing after a child who had taken his hat to play with.

"Why, you ill-mannered young rascal!" Chi Fu cried. "Give that back. Give that—"

"Chi Fu, watch out!" Mulan shouted as Chi Fu ran down the hill and slipped into a puddle of mud. He fell, ungracefully plopping into the muddy tracks. But as he tried to get back up, he couldn't find a foothold. He let out a scream as he started to skid, down and down the hill—into the river.

Mulan gasped. "We've got to help," she said to Shang before grabbing Cri-Kee and leaping onto Khan. Shang mounted his horse, and together Mulan and the general went speeding down the hill after Chi Fu. But there was no way they could keep up.

Luckily, she and Shang had some experience in daring rescues. She threw a glance at her fellow soldier, and he nodded, already knowing the plan. He quickly began tying an arrow to one of the ropes they had brought. The water was fierce, and the window for saving Chi Fu was narrow.

"You ready to be a hero, Shang?" said Mulan.

"Always ready," said Shang, lifting his bow and firing over Chi Fu's head.

"Catch the rope, Chi Fu!" Mulan shouted as the arrow hit a tree and the trailing rope landed in the river.

The advisor swam toward the rope, but the currents were against him. It was hopeless.

"Hang on," said Mulan, kicking off her shoes. She dove into the river after Chi Fu, swam with all the strength she could muster, and grabbed the end of the rope. The waves were strong, but her training in the army had prepared her well. She wouldn't give up.

"Got you," Mulan said, hooking an arm over the Emperor's advisor. She tied the rope around Chi Fu's waist, then made a loud whistle. At the sound, Shang freed the arrow from the tree, and his horse changed directions, dragging Mulan and Chi Fu away from the flood and back up to safety.

Chi Fu's teeth chattered, and he didn't say a word as Shang wrapped a blanket around his shoulders and set him before the fire. One of the village children offered him half her steamed bun, which Chi Fu silently accepted.

"You'd think he'd at least thank you," said one of the villagers, frowning as Mulan and Shang left Chi Fu to prepare for the trip back.

"It's all right," Mulan said, drying herself with a blanket. "What matters is he's safe."

"Do you really have to go?" asked a little boy.

At least five children surrounded Mulan, and she mussed the boy's hair. "I'm afraid so, but I'll come back one day to check on you and your families."

"Why do you have to go?" another child asked her.

"We have to see the silkworms back to the palace, where the Imperial weavers will take care of them." Mulan smiled at them, and Cri-Kee hopped onto the boy's shoulder. "Don't worry, I'll ask the Emperor to send more food and supplies your way so you can rebuild once the floods have cleared. And first chance I get, I'll ride back to check on you all."

"With General Li Shang?"

"Yes," Mulan promised. Then, trying to hide her reluctance to leave, she turned to the carriage.

Chi Fu had already stepped back inside. He didn't say a word to Mulan or Shang, even when they began their journey back to the Imperial City.

When Mulan glanced back at him, Chi Fu was asleep, still hugging the crates of silkworms.

"I have to hand it to him," she murmured to Shang. "He does take his job seriously."

She glanced at the record book tucked tightly under his arm and wondered just what he had written about her. She sighed. Her first and last mission was done. To her, it had been a success, but she knew Chi Fu wouldn't say so in his notes.

"At least I'll have plenty of stories to tell back home," said Mulan cheerfully. "You'll visit me, won't you?"

"It won't come to that," said Shang. "But I'll visit you no matter where you are."

Her heart skipped, and she scooped Cri-Kee into her pocket. "Then I have nothing to worry about."

Three nights later, they arrived in the palace. Chi Fu strode out of the carriage, again without another word to Mulan or Shang. "These are of the utmost importance," he told the guards who awaited. "See to it that they are delivered to the Imperial weavers for inspection."

"Yes, Your Excellency."

Chi Fu grunted and spun on his heel for his quarters. In spite of all the trouble he had caused for Mulan during their mission, she was grateful he had come with them. Without him, they wouldn't have been able to salvage the silkworms.

Mulan bowed. "Thank you for your help, Chi Fu."

He raised his chin. "I have a report to make to His Majesty; I don't have time to converse. Be sure to report to the council hall tomorrow morning. And be on time." He raised his chin, ignoring Shang completely.

Mulan tried not to wince. The severity of his tone made it seem a sure thing that she was going to be dismissed in the morning. Well, she wouldn't leave without a fight. She'd explain to the Emperor what had happened. Surely he would understand.

Cheer up, Mulan, she thought. *Is it so wonderful to work for the Emperor? You have to get up early all the time, wear that awful-fitting hat, and listen to men talk all day long.*

She swallowed hard. *You could be back home feeding the chickens and praying with Grandma right now. And seeing how Mushu's doing up in the temple. He keeps saying he's got the best view in the house—*

She shook off the thoughts. "I can't give up," she said to Shang. "It's not just about showing the council members that I can do this. It's for me, too. I know I'm right for this job. I can explain to the Emperor." She inhaled a ragged breath. "I'll do the best I can—before I give up."

"His Majesty will listen to you," Shang assured her. "He likes you. Just watch, this whole thing will blow over, and you'll be honored with dinner with the Emperor."

Shang always knew how to cheer her up. She smiled at him. "I hope you have more than armor in that wardrobe of yours, General. If I ever get an invitation, and I'm allowed to bring a guest, it's going to be you."

Shang's eyes widened. "Me?"

"Of course. You made such an impression on my grandmother, I know you'll make one on the Emperor, too."

Shang blushed. "I miss your family."

"They're expecting you to visit again," Mulan said, feeling brazen. "Especially my grandmother."

"Oh, I won't let her down," replied Shang.

The young general reached for her hand, holding it tenderly as he walked her back to the Emperor's palace.

The mood was solemn the next morning in the council hall. Mulan had been one of the first to arrive, and not one of the councilors greeted her when they took their places.

"Let us begin with a report of the Hongjing mission," said the Emperor. "Chi Fu, if you wouldn't mind."

Chi Fu rose. He wore his typical self-important smirk, and Mulan wished she could hide under the table, but she straightened in her chair. If she was about to be lectured, then dismissed, she would endure the words with dignity.

"Fa Mulan has surprised me," Chi Fu read aloud from his records. "One would think that the hero of China, a soldier molded by General Li himself, would know how to follow orders. But she never even made it to the city. Instead, she spent two days in some unnamed village, building fires and steaming bread with children."

The advisors murmured their disapproval, but Chi Fu wasn't finished. "I went to complete the mission myself. When I arrived in Hongjing, the silkworms were safely waiting for me. Every single one was accounted for, and the Imperial weavers in Hongjing had done an admirable job protecting them from the storm.

"When I returned to the village to show Mulan and General Li the silkworms I had rescued, I had expected them to recognize the error of their ways. But instead, they had built a camp for the refugee villagers on a hill and completely ignored the Imperial mission to rescue the national treasure. I was so distressed to see this that I intended to leave the camp at once and return China's treasure to His Majesty."

He cleared his throat. "But then I fell—into the flood. . . . I was certain that I was about to find myself in Heaven."

His voice softened. "Mulan risked her life to save me, and it is thanks to her and General Li Shang that the silkworms are also safe."

Mulan looked up, surprised by the sudden shift in Chi Fu's tone.

"I hereby record that Fa Mulan has proven herself a valuable asset to this council, and should be instated as a full member."

Mulan blinked, hardly able to believe it. But the words had come straight out of Chi Fu's mouth, and he had meant them. He was even smiling at her. She didn't think she had ever seen him smile. Not without something up his sleeve, anyway.

"Congratulations, Mulan," Chi Fu said. "Maybe a woman should serve on the council after all."

She bowed her head. Then she turned to the Emperor. "Your Majesty, that's actually related to something I'd like to discuss during the next meeting."

"You can discuss it with me at dinner," announced the Emperor. "It's time we held a banquet in your honor, after all you've done for China." He tilted his head, humor shining in his kind eyes. "I hear there's someone you may wish to bring as a guest."

Mulan's smile widened, and she bowed deeply. She knew exactly whom she'd invite.

Et Voilà

What if Remy had met Colette first?

by Liz Braswell

Et Voilà

What if Remy had met Colette first?

by Liz Braswell

Another Thursday shift was over. The lingering-est customer had left, the last pot had been scrubbed and dried, the final tally of supplies had been carefully conducted. Gusteau's was *closed.* Colette, the chefs, and the entire staff always gathered in the kitchen and shared a midnight snack and social wind-down from a hard day.

(Skinner was the only one at Gusteau's who often skipped this ritual. He was either too busy in his office, going over proposals from those who wanted to cash in on Auguste Gusteau's legacy, or already gone in that ridiculously large, leather-upholstered car he was so proud of.)

Colette wished she could miss that night's gathering, too. She used to love the communal, weary toast of "santé," muttered with glasses in hand, the feeling that they were all participating in the same unending battle. But she was tired—*really* tired. Flat-out exhausted from a physically and mentally demanding job that went into the wee hours of the morning every night.

And then there was being the only woman in the kitchen. It was twenty-first century Paris, and things did not seem to be moving as quickly in the world of cuisine as they did in the political or even corporate worlds.

Lalo, the head of the kitchen under Skinner, *had* immediately accepted her as an equal when she first joined the staff. But the dessert chef and the garde-manger, Pompidou and Larousse, let their prejudices (slowly) dissipate only once she had proved herself in the kitchen. Mustafa (the maître d') still made sure none of the patrons knew when it was a woman who had created something amazing. He claimed it was because of *their* prejudices, of course, not his, which might have been true—but then again, it was a chicken-and-egg situation.

And Skinner . . . well, in the end, despite his general nastiness, he was a practical man, more concerned with money than haute cuisine. When Colette had offered to work for less than an equally skilled male *rôtisseur* chef, he had gleefully hired her and gleefully promised to put her out on the street if she failed to keep up with her male coworkers.

Colette had outlasted eight garbage boys, three *poissonniers*, and one *saucier*. And she was still standing, defending Auguste Gusteau's legacy, showing her commitment with a toast at the end of every night.

But . . . was this it for the rest of her life? A continual

grind, a constant need to prove herself? When did she "win"? When could she rest? When she became chef de cuisine? Was that even what she wanted anymore?

Because she was ruthlessly honest with herself, Colette knew that she was not as creative a chef as her idol. She could make literally anything she was told to, all from memory and certainly as well as the very best chefs. She could even improvise based on what produce was freshest, what fish were available, what special cuts the butchers had set aside for her. But when it came to true culinary creativity—like Gusteau's, like Rene Renzeli's, like Kitty Korman's—she didn't have that final burst of inspiration that meant genius.

Colette was fine with that. She had little interest in chocolate salmon skin, wasabi foam, or smoked-at-your-table and fermented sort-of drinks. A five-star meal served with enthusiasm and perfection was her idea of a good night. They *used* to serve that up at Gusteau's . . . but now they were just going through the motions. Repeating and re-repeating the same recipes and menu, hoping to win back the stars that were lost—one because Auguste Gusteau faltered, another because he died.

And . . . all right . . . her life was feeling a little empty in other ways those days. She loved the kitchen camaraderie at some other establishment late at night, but men in the culinary world were, unfortunately, *porcs*. They either treated her condescendingly, dismissively, or as competition to be destroyed—but more because she threatened their manhood than their careers.

In short: they made terrible boyfriends.

Colette stepped out into the brisk Paris air—that smelled vaguely of dumped soup vegetables—and sighed. She looked up, hoping to find a wishing star, but it was pointless: the sky was a black void, with no answers or ideas.

She shook her head, adjusted her leather jacket, and took off for home on her motorcycle, just one more shadow in the gloomy city night.

The lights of Paris had never looked more magical.

Not to the moonstruck tourists, not to the honeymooning lovers, not even to the artists and musicians and creators who still made pilgrimages to the City of Light. The sky overhead was rich and velvety in its sumptuous blackness, a perfect backdrop for the urban landscape. But there was something particularly effulgent that night about the streetlamps, the festoons, the fairy bulbs lighting up the sides of the Eiffel Tower.

For a rat who had spent the past several days moping in the sewers below, seeing the city laid out before him from a rooftop vantage was almost enough to overwhelm his little rodent heart. Especially after the last few days; they were the worst Remy ever could have imagined. His entire world had fallen apart—and it was all his fault.

He had become too cocky, too sure of himself, too eager

to share—no, too eager to *show off* his knowledge of the human world, of television and books, and most of all, of food. There was no reason to bring his brother inside the old lady's kitchen where Remy had been secretly hanging out, learning to cook.

Emile was different from Remy—he was a *real* rat. And he acted the way a real rat does when cornered: panicked and wild. So when the old lady discovered the literal rats' nest and pulled out her old gun and began shooting, Emile took off, running around frantically.

And then the house collapsed, and the rat colony's home with it. All because of Remy.

Django, their father and leader of the colony, did *not* panic or go wild. He kept a cool head and led everyone to safety.

Well, almost everyone—Remy couldn't even make his getaway like a normal rat. He just *had* to run back for the cookbook, which apparently he prized beyond his own safety and the love of his family.

Whom he had never caught up with or found.

Cold, wet, alone, and hungry in the sewers, he had stewed in misery for countless days and nights, unsure exactly how much time had passed in that eternally moist and twilit realm, sleeping now and then curled up with that book.

But when the ghost of Auguste Gusteau began talking to him from the pages of the book he had saved, Remy knew it was time to leave, to ascend into the world above. He was losing it underground.

He emerged into the open air, and it was a revelation. He had no idea he had been sulking all that time under the city of *Paris*!

"Not bad, eh?" Auguste asked, floating next to the little rat.

"It's amazing! And look, your restaurant!" Remy gushed, pointing at the lit sign. "Seems like it's missing a couple of stars, though."

"Ah, yes, well . . ." The ghost looked thoughtful. "Someone needs to work on that . . . maybe you!"

"Yeah, right," Remy said. "I don't think anyone would let a rat like me work in a fancy human place like that."

"Well, let's take a look around anyway, shall we?" the ghost said, spinning. "What have you got to lose?"

"Not much else," Remy said. He scampered down the roof, chasing the little ghost into the streets of Paris, his tail waving gracefully behind him.

The magical night faded slowly, first going grey and then Bay of Biscay blue. A normal city rat would spend daylight hours sleeping or hiding or slinking in the deepest shadows, far from humans, cats, and dogs. But Remy wasn't a city rat, much less a normal one, and this was his first time in Paris. He wasn't going to waste the day *sleeping*.

Without any particular direction in mind, he wandered the streets, letting his nose guide him. So it was no surprise that his first stop was the Marché Président Wilson, the large outdoor market. Remy hadn't intended on gawking like a tourist, but his first view of the open-air food stands that endlessly stretched down the street stopped him in his tracks.

And, oh, all the *smells*! There were things he couldn't name—things that didn't tickle whichever ancestral memory knew what might be edible and what might be necessary to run away from. *Bird*, but not the little hens the old lady in the house cooked, or the sparrows and siskins of the gardens. *Fish*, but from the sea, and so fresh they smelled of salt and the tangy water they had been swimming in just that morning, and—

That was when a market cat whipped out a fast, ancient paw and nearly swiped his eyes out.

Instinct took over. Remy scampered on all four feet—*yuck*, he would have to wash his forepaws later—into the gutter, up the curb, and finally along a spindly trellis sporting roses. The cat was faster than he expected; she leapt and nearly pinned his tail. But even before his mind could properly process that, he was already balanced on the edge of a brightly striped café awning, swaying high above people sipping their café au lait.

The cat hissed her disgust from below, knowing full well the potential kicks she would receive from the ungrateful café patrons if she went too close. Half of her left ear was missing: she was smart, a survivor.

Remy gave her a saucy little wave.

Although he would have preferred to be down in the market and right alongside the humans who were squeezing fruit, arguing prices, and clicking fashionable heels while picking up a baguette for later, staying up high seemed the safer bet. He leapt from awning to awning along the buildings, then to the cloth roofs of the market booths, where he could peer over the edge.

So many different kinds of fruit and vegetables! Eggplant of all sizes, in every shade of purple, white, and black! Dozens of onion-scented things that weren't the traditional farmhouse variety: leeks, scallions, long green onions, calçots, chives. . . . Ten different kinds of peaches! Remy felt drunk on the sweet, sugary smells that wafted up from the fruit as the sunlight hit it.

He almost fell to the ground when he came to the *fromageries*.

The combination of fine cheeses being sold from those booths was too much for his refined nose, which was already a thousand times more sensitive than a normal rat nose. It was like he was eating by breathing, like he was swimming through an ocean of *fromage*.

Oooh! There were discreet garbage cans for the vendors, set away from the public; despite the early hour, they were already half full of rinds, parings, bits of wax, and bad ends.

Remy's feet began, as if of their own accord, to lead him to them.

"Ah-ah-ah! No, Remy. Remember: Cooks *make.* Thieves *take.*" Auguste wagged a translucent finger at the rat.

"Do you *know* the soup I could create with the rinds alone?" Remy asked sadly.

"Yes, because I have the 'clean out your fridge and crisper drawer' recipe for broth in my book," Auguste said with a smile. "No doubt you could put together something truly *magnifique* from the waste . . . but let it be from your own kitchen, eh, Remy? For people who love to cook, food *comes* to you."

"My own kitchen," Remy said with sigh. "You don't even know what you're talking about. You're an imaginary ghost."

"That is why I know exactly what I am talking about," the chef said cryptically, fixing his toque. "Come, let's take your mind off this cheese. Let us take a peek *inside* my restaurant, to see what the chefs there are up to these days."

"Now you're talking!" Remy said cheerfully. It was hard to stay sad for long in Paris.

Paris, Colette thought, *is killing me.* Fridays were always a challenge, but this one was just grueling. The hard-partying customers had no imagination, ordering the same greatest hits. She felt like an animated GIF of someone making *steak frites*: cut, sear, don't bother to check how the person wants it because it is always medium rare, salt, done, repeat, repeat, repeat.

Outside, she took a deep breath . . . but had to cut it

short before she retched. The piles of refuse in cans and sacks next to them was getting out of control. They had to hire another garbage boy soon. There were only so many times Larousse would pick the shortest straw for the job before realizing he was being tricked.

A rat poked its nose tentatively out from between the bins. Colette's face pulled back in an automatic rictus of disgust. She lifted her foot away, both to avoid any potential contact and to prepare herself for stomping the horrid thing out of existence. That's all the restaurant needed: to lose another star because of rats in the kitchen.

But the rat—smaller than most of the ugly vermin that haunted the alleys of Paris—showed no interest in her or her feet. It scampered over to the outside faucet they used to hose down the garbage area and scrubbed its paws assiduously under the drips. Was that normal? Colette frowned, thinking. Some mammals did that sort of thing, right? When it was done, it padded back and forth between the piles of spilled offal, tentatively sniffing the air.

"There is a whole pile of rotten eggs right there," Colette said archly, pointing. "Bon appétit, furry horror."

The rat looked up at her . . . disappointedly?

Yes, there was definite disappointment on the rodent's face.

Feeling vaguely insulted but curious, Colette watched as it went back to wandering around thoughtfully and sniffing, more like a human than a rat.

Suddenly it paused, tail almost straightening in surprise and delight. Using its front paws *like a human would*, it pulled out a rind of brie. And instead of wolfing it down or packing it into its cheeks for later (Did rats even do that? Colette wasn't sure), it held the rind in a paw and considered it thoughtfully.

Seeming to be struck with inspiration, the creature began eagerly searching around until it pulled out the end of a *pain couronne*, a broken-off ball of bread that made a pretty crown if done right (and they always were at Gusteau's). Very carefully, almost as if not to get its paws dirty, the rat smeared what little cheese was left on the rind onto the bread, then carefully broke up the rest into little bits and sprinkled it on top like Parmesan.

It paused, seeming to admire its handiwork, then frowned as if something wasn't quite right.

"Colette, you are going mad," Colette admonished herself. "You have worked too many late nights, and you are seeing things."

The rat nosed around until it found the greens off the ends of some carrots, which made the chef shudder involuntarily. *Bitter.* She never understood why rabbits loved it—or hipsters. The rodent used the sharp pull tab from a soda can to delicately slice off the greenest, softest tips of the fronds and placed them on the bread and cheese.

Finally satisfied, the rat took a deep sigh and—

Did *not* devour the impossible sandwich. It looked up

into the air next to it in surprise, like a spooked animal. It chittered disconsolately, very obviously arguing with, warning off, or being threatened by something only it could see.

"Rabies?" Colette wondered aloud. But it wasn't foaming at the mouth or snarling. It sounded almost like it was pleading.

Finally, the rat looked *sadly* back at its little treat and pushed it away, back into the garbage pile.

Huh. Maybe it's trained, Colette thought. *Maybe it's a pet rat. Maybe the owner taught it not to eat street food in case it's poisoned.* "Here, you strange little thing."

She reached into the pocket of her jacket and pulled out what was going to be her midnight snack: a simple slab of *pâté de campagne* with some thinly sliced cornichons, wrapped in wax paper, and a tiny jar of the mustard they sold in giant plastic GUSTEAU bottles at the *supermercados.* She broke off a corner of the pâté and, without even thinking, expertly balanced it on a slice of cornichon, adding another slice on top at a rakish angle. What was the point of eating, if not to eat well? Even if you were a rat . . .

She held it out. The rat's eyes widened in surprise.

It approached, slowly and cautiously, at the last moment rising up on its hind legs to take the offering with its paws. "Yuck!" Colette yanked her hand back, suddenly aware of how close the fetid animal was to her own chef fingertips.

The rat, surprised, also jumped backward—but

grabbed the pâté first. It tumbled over, the morsel clutched to its belly. It immediately righted itself, gave her a salute, and ran into the darkness.

"*Oui*," Colette decided. "I am going mad."

"See? What did I tell you? For people who love to cook, food *comes* to you," Auguste said, twirling in the air happily. They were alone at the other end of the alley, enjoying the last morsels of the unexpected treat.

"You know, it really did," Remy said, wiping his mouth. The pâté was delicious. "I hope she comes back tomorrow night."

Colette let herself sleep later than usual on Saturday morning, worried about what she had seen—thought she had seen—the night before. Maybe she was getting sick; maybe she really was working too hard. Normally she rose far earlier than she had to, to visit the market: she never trusted herbs picked out by anyone besides herself. Even Skinner had finally come around to admitting that she had the best nose in the kitchen. But one day of letting Horst shop wouldn't be the end of the world. She had a nice hot shower (in the tiny bathroom she had to install herself in the illegal loft) and a double espresso made exactly right in her precious Gaggia coffee machine.

("You should wait to get such an expensive thing for a wedding present," her father had said. "Bah, why wait?"

Colette had responded, and put a good chunk of her savings into something she enjoyed every day.)

After a luxurious sit, sipping her espresso and watching the feral cats prowl around the alley of the club downstairs, she felt like herself again. She threw on her jacket, took the steps down two at a time, hopped onto her motorcycle, and sped off.

Okay, maybe she had *five minutes* to check out the day's selection at the Marché Ornano. Maybe she could even skip the line if she promised Lucas a nice tray of leftovers later. After perusing the vegetables, she found herself picking through the discounted items, too: the day-old bread, the pinched-looking kumquats. What would a rat make with "garbage" like that?

Trying not to think about it too much, Colette put the items in her basket.

But all day she couldn't stop thinking about the weird little rat and its culinary particularity. She barely remembered the ride from the market to the restaurant and actually nicked her thumb with the knife, something she hadn't done in years. When Larousse and Horst presented a potential new garbage boy, she only nodded yes, sure, whatever; they needed one immediately. He was even cute in a country sort of way, soft lips and nice hair . . . and he had some connection with Gusteau; his mother had been friends with the chef or something. She would have to ask about this later.

"Hey, Colette, wake up," Lalo teased. "What's with you? You're never like this."

Colette growled and continued chopping.

At the end of the night, instead of hanging out with everyone else, she immediately went outside, to the back step.

Oui.

The little rat was waiting for her. With big eyes and a hungry, expectant look.

"Okay, rat." She took out the food she had and slapped it down, one ingredient at a time, like she was pounding a paillard. "Heel of bread. *Fromage Salers.* A bit of hollandaise. A kumquat. Two slices of sweet pepper. Let's see what you can do, eh?"

The little rat rubbed his paws together and got to work. He (she didn't know why she thought of it as a *he* now) ran up to each ingredient, sniffed delicately, ran his paws over it. He *tore off* a large piece of the cheese and rejected it, throwing it into the garbage.

Colette frowned. What was wrong with it? What could he tell?

He delicately stirred the hollandaise with a toothpick, tasted it, frowned. Then he started to peel the kumquat.

"You don't—" Colette began. But before she could finish telling him that you ate the peel and fruit together, that it was the peel that was sweet and not the fruit, he had very carefully hollowed out one end of the kumquat and then, using the blade of a broken plastic knife, cut the rind into a perfect spiral and pulled it apart like a child's bright orange spring toy. This he carefully laid on the inside of the old bread.

He turned to face her. He wiggled his front toes as best he could, and drew his paws apart. Like something exploding. Like . . .

"You want a—fire?" Colette asked.

The rat nodded.

Obeying his request like it was all a dream, she pulled out her lighter, flicked it on, and carefully put it on the ground between them.

With a frown of intense concentration, the rat took the cheese he hadn't rejected and gently stabbed it with a toothpick. Rotating it with a serious look of concentration on his face, he slowly roasted it over the flame until the *fromage* was just the slightest bit gooey and burnt on one end. He immediately dotted it on the bread, in between the curls of kumquat peel. He shredded the pepper into the tiniest strips—tinier than matches, more like fingernail clippings—and scattered them on top. With a dramatic air of finality, he slammed the bread shut and turned to her, paws out. *Voilà!*

Colette frowned distrustfully—not just because a rat had made a sandwich; who knew where his paws had been?—but because the combination of ingredients was disgusting.

But she politely tore the sandwich in half, presenting him with one the same size as hers, and bit in.

"What," she said as the tastes hit her mouth.

The tastes didn't so much *blend* as overlap, one flavor after another—salty, sweet, briny—combining into a magnificent pièce de résistance: sparkling citrus fireworks right before she swallowed. It was like nothing Auguste Gusteau had ever made—at least, not outside of his own kitchen late at night. It was something else. A very delicious something else.

"Not bad," she said grudgingly.

The rat clasped his little paws together, almost sweetly.

The next morning Colette headed straight for the market, skipping the espresso and shower. No more day-old bread or bruised produce this time—she wanted to see what the rat could *really* do. She bought onions, cheese, bread, eggs, herbs. She paused at the meat and decided to pass. A cooking rat was one thing; a rat who could safely cook meat so all the pathogens were killed was maybe pushing it. Especially with chicken.

(She slapped herself on the forehead. A rat was *cooking dinner*, and she was worried about the possibilities of salmonella or *E. coli.* She should have been concerned with the bubonic plague.)

(Or, you know, the fact that a rat was making her dinner.)

When she got to the restaurant, she put the nonperishables in her locker and the rest in a bag in the fridge on which she wrote: *Colette's. Touch and I will kill you. I will.*

She washed her hands—thinking of paws—and wrapped them around a lovely steaming bowl of cappuccino

Pompidou had made. Feeling a presence, she looked up and found the new garbage boy—Linguini? Something ridiculous like that—gazing at her.

"Uh, hi," he said, clearing his throat noisily in a way that made Colette—and everyone who worked hard for a clean, hygienic kitchen—wince. "I just wanted to say . . . you're really amazing? I've been watching you . . . *not* in a creepy way!" he added quickly, putting his hands up. "I mean, like, you're hypnotizing. Um, also not meant in a creepy way. You just chop so fast. And it's like you know what you're doing twenty steps down the line. . . ."

"Actually, I am thinking *forty* steps ahead," she responded smugly. "I have to, to be a woman and get this far in the job."

Linguini looked confused. "But it shouldn't matter that you're a woman. What's the title of Gusteau's book again? *Everyone Can*—"

"*Anyone Can Cook*, yes." She stuck a finger in his face; while the steaming coffee in her other hand sloshed precariously, it did not spill. "But not anybody can make a living at it. It's a man's world, or hadn't you noticed?" She whirled that same finger around, indicating the other chefs and employees.

"Oh. That's terrible."

That was all he said. And he said it so genuinely! Like he really meant it, and it wasn't patronizing, and he wasn't just mouthing a platitude.

Colette narrowed her eyes at him suspiciously.

"I'll bet anywhere else you'd be running the show," he added, clearly meaning that, too—even if he was beginning to sweat a little under her glare.

"Thank you," she said, still suspicious. But she flashed him a razor-sharp smile before turning around to get to work.

If she wasn't as distracted as she had been the day before, she also didn't feel the usual excitement of the evening rush. Now it was just a routine to get through before she could go back to this new, absurd thing in her life.

When the night was over, she quickly pounded an espresso with the crew—someone was also ironically pouring around some sort of horrible American pink energy drink; she wouldn't touch it—and then grabbed her food out of the cold room and slammed out the back door, practically knocking over Skinner, whom she didn't even see.

But he saw her.

"Okay, rat," she called out, throwing open the back door and kneeling on the stoop. "Come out. You have work to do."

The little rat came pattering forward (on his hind legs; that was weird, but, eh, it kept his front paws clean) and looked at her expectantly. She reached in the bag and set out the groceries.

"And the crowning touch!"

With a final flourish she pulled out a little camp stove and a fuel canister. She used to *love* camping when she was younger, just riding into the mountains and living out of a tent for a day or five. But she didn't have much time for that sort of thing anymore. . . . With quick, deft movements that spoke of years julienning carrots and dicing potatoes, she put the little burner top on, opened the valve, and lit it with her lighter. A bright little ring of blue flame appeared, and the rat practically danced with joy.

He needed to stand on an old anchovy can to reach the pot, but that was their only real difficulty as they cooked together. While sometimes he made choices with the ingredients she would not have, they both thought like chefs. So he would puzzle over what was next and then point, and she would nod and then chop.

"I should be running my own place," she muttered with a snort. "And I am here, sous-chef-ing for a rat. What's next? Garbage girl for a cockroach?"

But she didn't say it with any malice. This was the first new and interesting thing that had happened to her in years. And the rat could cook. He might not be able to handle a big knife, but he had some big ideas about flavor and texture that were genius. This onion soup, for example, was next level.

"*Mon dieu*—whatever is that heavenly smell?"

A middle-aged man in a tiny fedora was walking by, glued to his phone, but suddenly stopped and sniffed the air. He looked around, confused; the restaurant was obviously closed. Then he spotted the two chefs.

Colette started to panic; there was no way she could hide the camp stove, the little pot of soup, the *rat* toasting some baguette slices just at the edge of the flame (after he had rubbed them with garlic). What if this man reported her to Skinner? Or the police? Or, even worse, the health inspector?

"We are . . . having a little picnic," she said with a Gallic shrug.

"Ugh! Is that some sort of trained *rat* stirring the soup?" the man cried. "Disgusting!"

The little rat winced as if he had been physically hurt. Colette's temper immediately engaged.

"You know what's disgusting? That stupid little hat you're wearing. What are you, ten years old? This isn't Brooklyn, you ancient hipster."

"I'll have you know—"

"GET OUT OF HERE!" Colette ordered, practically spitting.

The man looked at her, and the rat, and decided to leave—muttering under his breath as he went.

The little rat was still slumped, staring dejectedly into the soup.

"Forget about him. He was a jerk," Colette said, wondering how to put a hand around his shoulders and then deciding maybe not to.

The rat nodded, quickly, like a child trying not to cry.

"Here, I want seconds. That idiot didn't know what he was missing."

The rat straightened up, threw his shoulders back, and set about serving another bowl, complete with garnishes.

After their mostly silent little feast, Colette assiduously cleaned up the steps, sweeping away the crumbs that were too small for even Remy to consider, and put away her stove. She made little whickery-whick noises as she adjusted the leather straps on her bag and put on her helmet.

Remy watched her do all this with folded paws, feeling a little lost and lonely. He gave her a wave goodbye and tried not to look upset.

Colette seemed to notice his mood.

"You sleep here, right?" she asked, trying to be polite. "Here, in the alley, with the . . . garbage cans?"

Remy just nodded, knowing his squeaks would never be understood. He shrugged.

She looked around.

"With . . . all of your little ratty friends?"

He shook his head sadly. He hoped she understood: No friends. No family.

"You're not . . . *from* here, are you? Not from Paris?"

He shook his head more energetically. Maybe she *could* understand a little!

"Are you from some kind of lab? Where they . . . make

smart rats? And, uh, train them to cook, or something . . . ?"

He gave her a look, but it was obvious even as she spoke that she realized how ridiculous she sounded.

"But you *are* an amazing little chef," she insisted, getting down on one knee to get closer to his eye level. He appreciated that. "You must have had some sort of training, right? Maybe you were the pet of—er, I mean, you *lived* with someone who could really cook, and they taught you?"

Remy spread his paws helplessly. How could he explain it to her? He had learned from his nose, and the television at the old woman's house, and the book, and his own trial and error. There was no way to make her understand that. So he just shook his head helplessly.

There was an awkward silence.

The human looked around, perhaps searching for something to say. But the only obvious thing was the dark, cold night. This tiny part of Paris was quiet and lonely at these hours . . . and honestly, it smelled pretty bad. Even to a rat who used to eat garbage with his family.

"Okay, well, why don't you come with me?" she finally said. "It's probably safer for a strange little rat like you, anyway."

She put out her hand.

Remy immediately ran up her arm, joyful and grateful. She carefully put him into her pocket, where he could be safe and warm and still look out. Together they rode off into the most beautiful night of all, lights and stars and speed all around them.

"You see, Remy? Everything is working out."

Auguste and Remy sat on some steps at the Parc du Champ-de-Mars, watching the sun rise. The Eiffel Tower stood at one end like a parent minding her tiny children. There was a little bit of sandwich left over that Colette had thoughtfully folded into a newspaper for Remy, and he nibbled it and should have felt content.

But he sighed.

The dead chef looked concerned. "Remy, what is wrong? You are cooking! You're in Paris! You've made friends! A *human* friend! You never imagined that was possible. . . . And she loves what you cook! So what is the problem?"

It was true. Everything he had ever wanted—and some things he hadn't even dreamed of—was happening. But . . .

"Oh, absolutely. In a million years, I never thought I'd be cooking for a human who trusts me. A human *chef*, no less! But I will never be accepted into the world of haute cuisine. Not really.

"And I miss my family, Auguste. Even my dad. It's all my fault we lost our home. We had the best situation ever. And now the entire colony is gone. Who knows what happened to Dad and Emile? I don't even know if they're okay. I was showing off because I wanted to prove how wrong he was . . . and . . . I just . . . really *miss* them."

"Oh, Remy," Auguste said sympathetically, putting a ghostly hand on his back. "You will find your family again someday. I know it."

Linguini paced around Skinner's office nervously. His lightly curly hair visibly jiggled in time with his restlessness. He picked up things, put them down, occasionally dropped something. He pulled the curtains aside and looked out the window. Colette was pulling up on her motorcycle. Linguini felt his heart skip a beat. But—was that a *rat* in her front pocket?

Like it was the most natural thing in the world, she and the rat touched fingers (paws), and then it jumped down and scuttled into the shadows. She got off her bike, and it was like, oh, they were just saying goodbye for the day to go to their separate jobs. She to cook, he to . . . do whatever it was rats did.

Linguini sighed. Could Colette get *any* cooler?

He let the curtain fall back and resumed his pacing. He had been called in there for a verbal thrashing. Most likely someone had found out about his fooling around with the bouillabaisse. Anybody could cook, right? So why couldn't *he*? All right, he wasn't cooking exactly. He was . . . playing around. He just couldn't help meddling, picking, poking at stuff. Like he was doing now in the office: looking at things, fiddling with things, arranging things, picking up and playing with things. . . .

His mother always laughed about his touchy, nervous, clumsy habits—which were particularly jarring considering how good he was on his feet, like on his roller skates. *"Mon petit Tyrannosaure,"* she called him. "My little *T. rex*! So sure and powerful with the back legs, and bumbling with the little front ones." Even while he was remembering this, his fingers were wandering, flipping through the stuff on Skinner's desk, exploring his private doodads, rearranging them, opening his drawer. . . .

Brochures, receipts, the letter his mother sent with him to give to Skinner . . . Huh. There was some new, official-looking paperwork clipped to it. It looked legal, like something from a lawyer.

As he read through the documents, Linguini's eyes grew bigger and bigger, and his hands stopped what they were doing, staying perfectly still.

Colette felt bad for the little rat, who still seemed down. People were so mean and unhelpful! Poor thing. It seemed like all he wanted out of life was to cook.

And why not? Who got to decide who was allowed in the kitchen and who was not?

On her break she went out and bought a nice piece of fish and a small pan to add to her growing collection of utensils and private groceries she had apparently begun stockpiling at the restaurant. She made it through the day without incident, good or bad, and at eleven p.m. went out the back door, dragging an old wine crate with her. The little rat, looking confused but intrigued, watched her push it up awkwardly on its end.

"Mise en place," Colette said, grunting a little. "Everything in its place before you even start to cook, right? But perhaps you know that already as a tiny chef."

The rat nodded enthusiastically. He scampered over—as always, on his hind legs—and sniffed each ingredient she pulled out, thoughtful and obviously already calculating what to do with it.

"I think we are ready to level it up—how about some filet of sole tonight?" She held up the beautiful, clean-smelling pale fish. The rat grinned. She carefully placed it back down on its paper and took out some vegetables, some herbs, a jar of breadcrumbs.

The rat frowned at the last thing and put his paw on it, shaking his head.

"We're not dredging it and frying it?" Colette asked, amused.

The rat nodded, then shook his head, then nodded, then shrugged helplessly. He pointed at the vegetables and her knife.

"Okay, boss," she said with a shrug. "We'll do it your way. But slowly, eh? I can't always tell what you want."

She began chopping: turnip, leek, onion, carrot. The rat stopped her once, holding two claws apart: *Make the pieces smaller.*

"Minced? Yes, Chef! But I think if we're going beyond a mirepoix with whatever you're planning, maybe we could add the parsley stems, too?"

Not something she would normally do. Not something to be found in any of Gusteau's recipes. But the less waste, the less they had to hide. Plus it was crunchy and added a deeper note to the mix. The rat seemed to agree it was a good idea and gave her a sharp nod.

And so they cooked together: He heated butter in the new pan, turning it this way and that over the flame. She chopped and mixed and did all the things that required a large knife or human fingers. They were able to communicate with minimal sounds, pointing, holding something up to be smelled or felt, tapping when confused or frustrated—which was rare.

It was after midnight when they finally finished, but Colette wasn't tired at all. She felt revived, excited about the simple act of cooking like she hadn't been in a long time. What they were doing was new and whimsical; he was a partner whose ideas were truly up to her knife skills.

The resulting piece of fish was a thing of art, coated in tiny, colorful bits of vegetables like breadcrumbs, the skin perfectly crispy. And the smell . . .

"Bon appétit," Colette said, toasting him with a piece on the end of her fork. The rat toasted her back.

"*Mon dieu*, it really is a rat cooking!"

Colette and the rat both turned their heads away from

the latest, most exclusive restaurant; and, of course, neighborhood locals who, no matter their income, were fiercely Parisian at heart—who loved a good meal far more than any destination diner.

The nights passed, and the numbers trickling in started to grow.

This was the most fun Colette had in a long time, preparing limited quantities of new things for a truly appreciative crowd. And she was learning a lot from her little co-chef: it was okay to go off recipe, to try unexpected combinations of tastes that weren't in Gusteau's book. The rat treated her like an equal—all right, there was a lot to unpack there, him being a rat and all—but their creations together were truly that: shared creations.

It was the best of times . . . but of course, it couldn't last forever.

The first hint of future trouble was when Larousse sidled up to her at the main sink one morning. He looked this way and that to see if anyone was listening.

"Colette, I've heard about your little side project, the Midnight Kitchen. If *I* know about it, if everyone knows about it, *Skinner* will hear about it, too. I don't think he would be happy you have a second job, or that one of his star chefs is serving food that's not Gusteau's. . . ."

Colette tried not to let herself preen at hearing "star chef." It was true, of course, but you couldn't let that sort of thing go to your head.

"*What?* I haven't heard about this," Linguini squeaked, suddenly between them. "Uh. Colette? What's the Midnight Kitchen?"

He tried to sound casual, but his cheeks were a little flushed. He was *jealous*! Colette found herself almost smiling for the second time in the conversation. For her, it was a record.

"It's a secret. But you can come tomorrow night, as my special guest," she said. "But you *stay silent* about it."

"Oh, I promise, absolutely. Mum's, uh, mum's the word!" he said, making a strange gesture that might have been an inability to decide between zipping his lips and just putting a finger to them to mean *hush*.

"Colette," Larousse said warningly.

"I'll do something about it," she promised.

She just wasn't sure what.

And while she wondered, word continued to spread.

And obviously not just about the food—because Paris is full of great food—but also because there was a *rat* involved with the cooking. Unique, novel, unheard of . . . and, to those of a certain set, utterly disgusting.

"Can you *believe* it? A rat. *Cooking*. For humans!"

"I've heard he's *completely assimilated*," another rat said, hissing in disbelief. "He's even standing on two feet like one of them."

"Garbage and raw food aren't good enough for him

anymore, I guess. I hear he thinks he's some kind of fancy chef, even."

"Wait, what's this?"

Django whipped his head around from where he was overseeing food distribution in the sewers. It was hard dividing an uneven apple core equally between two interested (rat) parties.

"You say something about a rat hanging out with humans and doing weird stuff with food?"

"Yes, it's all *over* . . ." one of the gossiping rats began excitedly.

"EMILE!" Django shouted, not bothering to listen to the rest.

A few food piles away, Emile was grinning from ear to ear, albeit with a piece of meat gristle hanging out of his mouth. "I heard, Dad. It's Remy! It's *got* to be!"

"He made it here," Django said in wonder. "He's alive! We gotta go find him!"

Larousse was right, Colette decided. Things were definitely getting a little too dicey operating out of the alley behind Gusteau's. She thought she was being clever by having Linguini leave the restaurant out the front, walk around the block, and then meet her in the back alongside the other Midnight Kitchen patrons. But when she opened the back door, she almost dropped her produce bag.

A hungry crowd awaited her, filling the alley.

There must have been twenty or thirty people milling around, arguing over who had gotten there first and pretending to know what was on the menu from some secret social media post. It was only luck that no one still in the restaurant had heard them yet.

(Linguini was standing politely in the back; he gave her an enthusiastic wave. He was wearing a *jacket.*)

Her rat was also there, a little removed from the crowd atop a garbage can. He was obviously trying to gauge the safety of a situation that was rapidly growing out of control. Colette tried to catch his eye—maybe they should both just sneak home?

And then something happened that was straight out of a horror movie.

And then something happened that was straight out of the most wonderful, impossible dream.

At first Remy thought his perfect nose was finally failing him when he caught the scent.

But no—

Coming around the corner and up the alley like a miracle were *rats*. Wall-to-wall rats. Dozens of them. And leading them was . . .

"Dad!" Remy cried.

"Son!" Django cried back.

"Remy!" Emile shouted in delight. "It really *is* you!"

Any worry that his dad or his family would never speak

to him again immediately disappeared, like a cloud of steam released from an unlidded stockpot.

Remy leapt down into the rat crowd and threw his arms around his father.

"We thought you were dead!" Emile said, joining them in a group hug.

"You sure make strange choices," Django said, looking at Colette, her bags, and the crowd, "but you're *alive*!"

Of course what all the humans saw was a disgusting pack of rats, chittering and squeaking and poised to attack.

Everyone panicked and began screaming.

(All right, that wasn't strictly true; at least four people pulled out their phones and immediately began filming and posting.)

Colette had one bad moment before rationality won out: it was obvious that her rat friend simply had other rat friends and family. It wasn't a plague; it was a reunion.

And . . . were they actually hugging? Like tiny people?

If only it had ended there, maybe she could have gotten everything back under control.

"Aha!"

Like the grossest, biggest rat of all, Skinner threw open the back door where he had been hiding and pointed a finger at Colette.

"J'accuse!" he shouted.

"Oh, my god," a bystander said, turning her phone

from the rats to film the two chefs. "Is this really happening? Chef-off at Gusteau's *and* a plague of rats? Let's go!"

"You have been stealing food from the kitchen! I have been watching you! And you are . . . cooking with rats!" Skinner screamed. "*YOU ARE FIRED!* And maybe sued."

"I have *not* been stealing food!" Colette shouted back. "I have been buying my own, you lying snake!"

"What's that about snakes? I do *not* like snakes," Django said, whipping his head around to look at Colette. "What's your human friend going on about up there?"

"Uh-oh," Remy said, surveying the shrieking, phone-cluttered chaos. "I think the jig is up. I'd better go help her. Dad, you gotta leave—they're going to get animal control, or dogs or something, if you stay around."

"Uh-uh. No way. Not again," Django said firmly.

"I'm in the eighteenth arrondissement," Remy said, turning to leave. "Rue Hermel! Look me up!"

"What are you saying? What is this human talk?"

"JUST GO!" Remy begged.

"Not this time," Django said, and nodded at Emile.

They each grabbed one of Remy's arms and scampered off, dragging him away from Colette, being a real chef, and everything he had ever dreamed of.

Colette had to summon every ounce of pride to walk straight-backed into the kitchen of Gusteau's the next day to gather her things. All the other chefs just stared at her silently.

Could she blame them? They probably thought she was mad. *They* had never talked to a cooking rat before.

Or—perhaps more important—taken on a second, secret cooking gig.

The only one who said anything was Lalo, and all he did was pat her shoulder and say, "I'm sorry."

Skinner kept watch over her every move as if he was afraid she would steal the pepper.

When she had gathered all her things and put them into a cabbage crate, she turned to take one last look around the kitchen that had been everything she had ever dreamed of.

Well, maybe it wasn't everything she had dreamed of anymore. But it had been her home for the past ten years, and these now-silent chefs had been the closest thing to family.

And after the meme with the rats died down, no one would remember her or care what had happened to her. Unless you were an Auguste Gusteau, chefs came and went anonymously in the dark and busy world of restaurants.

"Yeah, I'm out of here, too," Linguini said suddenly.

But not spontaneously; it felt like something he had prepared. So did his dramatic tossing of the scullery rag over his shoulder and into a clean pot.

Which still made everyone—including Colette—wince.

"Linguini, I appreciate the support," she said, "but you don't need to quit."

"I'm not," Linguini said mysteriously.

"Good riddance," Skinner growled at the two of them.

"You have no idea," Linguini said.

"What does that even mean?" Skinner shrieked as the two of them went out the back door.

Remy was waiting for them outside—and so were Django and Emile. Remy had asked (demanded, screamed, pleaded) to come back to check on Colette; they wouldn't let him out of their sight again.

"So this is the little chef who caused all the big problems," Linguini said, bending over to look at Remy closely. Which was surprising—Remy didn't think that humans could actually tell them apart. "Nice to meet you, Little Chef."

Remy grinned and waved.

"What am I going to do?" Colette moaned, collapsing on the steps. "This place was my life."

"Not anymore," Linguini said, trying to sound suave.

Then he saw the murderous look on Colette's face.

"I mean, I'm sorry, that came out the wrong way—I was trying to be—I just mean maybe it's time for something new. With my help."

"Linguini," she said with a wry smile, "I like you, but I'm not sure how you can *help* me."

"You *like* me?" he squeaked. "I mean, wait, we can talk about that later. But what would you say about help from the owner of one of the most famous restaurants in Paris—and all of its subsidiary businesses?"

"What are you talking about?"

Linguini pulled out a sheaf of papers. "It turns out Gusteau was more than . . . um . . . one of my mom's *friends*. He's actually my dad. Skinner tried to hide that from me. With no will specifically naming business partners as beneficiaries . . . well, it's all mine now. The fancy lawyers say so."

"This is real?" she said slowly, looking over the papers.

"One hundred percent. And as the new owner, I think some changes are due around here. Like, instead of Gusteau-themed oven mitts, why don't we invest in talented young chefs? My dad wasn't entirely right. Not *everyone* can cook. I can't. But those who can should have the opportunity. And *you* can cook, Colette—and you, Little Chef. You need your own place to shine instead of hiding in the shadows."

"You can't be serious. Are you serious?" Colette asked. "Because if you are playing with me on the worst day of my life, so help me, Linguini . . ."

"I'm not! Promise! There's more than enough profit to start a small bistro. And maybe another one, with a rotating residency of new chefs."

Colette was silent for a moment. Then she looked up and grinned.

"What are they talking about, those two?" Django demanded.

"I think Linguini there is offering to start a restaurant

for me and Colette!" Remy cried with joy, dancing up and down on his toes.

"Really? In a building? Where you get food with that weird human money stuff?" Emile narrowed his eyes suspiciously at the two humans and sniffed the air. "Because I gotta tell you, it seems like they're *really* talking about how much they like each other."

"Yeah, look at the way he's leaning toward her," Django observed with a father's wise eyes.

"Huh. You think?" Remy asked in wonder. "Well, that's great! For all of us."

He could practically see it, a place for *everyone*: the outliers, the dreamers, the lovers of good food. A place where the strangest pairings made the most sense.

Behind them all, a ghostly Auguste Gusteau smiled, the lights from the Eiffel Tower shining through him.

The Envelope

What if Anastasia had a change of heart?

by Jen Calonita

The Envelope

What if Anastasia had a change of heart?

by Jen Calonita

Had the house always been this still?

Anastasia contemplated this as she sat in the dimly lit parlor and tried to learn how to knit. It wasn't going well, but then again, neither had starting a fire (hers died out within an hour). Too bad there was no one around to ask for a tutorial.

In the weeks following "the incident," Anastasia became the only one who bothered to get out of bed. Drizella and Mother spent their days under thick quilts in bed with the curtains drawn, their only company being an occasional visit from an on-the-mend Lucifer (who was still hobbling around after his fall).

The three Tremaine women didn't converse with one another; they barely uttered a sound. The ticking of the clock was the only indication that time still trudged on without them. With Cinderella gone, there was no one to shout at to make the fire, fix their breakfast, wash the dishes, do the mending. The bells they'd once rung for service sat collecting dust. Even the home's pesky rodent problem had been solved. The moment Cinderella left, they did, too.

The Tremaine women were living like ghosts, and she was the only specter up and about, attempting to keep things running. *Attempting* was the operative word.

"Mother?" Anastasia asked that morning. "Shall we have a music lesson today?"

"Why would we? There's no one to impress." The whites of Mother's eyes were the only thing visible in the dark room. "No one will ask for your hand now."

"You don't know that." Anastasia attempted being optimistic, which felt like trying on a new hat—a little uncomfortable, but something she wanted to get used to. What other choice did they have? "In time, people will forget what happened with Cinderella, and—"

"Don't say her name!" Mother shouted so fiercely the windows rattled.

Anastasia backed out of the room, shaking. She didn't have better luck with her sister.

"Get dressed? Why?" Drizella moaned, the top of her dark hair sticking out of a tangle of pillows that had a faint odor. "No one will ever set foot in this house again."

Her sister was right, of course, and it was easy to be bitter. In the days following the incident, their mother had tried to tell the world their side of the story, but it was clear from the whispers she heard through friends and in the village that people had already formed an opinion. They loved a good transformation story, and Cinderella had risen from the ashes to win the heart of the Prince after enduring years of abuse from a cruel stepmother and stepsisters who treated her like hired help (so they said). All anyone could talk about was Lady Tremaine locking Cinderella up to keep her beauty hidden from the duke and his footmen. But the glass slipper had inexplicably turned out to be Cinderella's, and when she escaped, what had happened at the Tremaine house was revealed by the Grand Duke. The Tremaines were shunned because of it.

Being angry—at herself, at Cinderella, at her mother and sister—worked at first, but Anastasia quickly realized it wouldn't fix things. Invitations to events in society had ceased. The house was cold because Anastasia couldn't keep the fire going, the air was stale thanks to windows that hadn't been opened, and dust piled up on windowsills like a first snow. (How had Cinderella kept up with all these chores?) Drizella's and Mother's doors stayed firmly closed, and Anastasia was left alone, trying to pick up the pieces of their lives to no avail. Visitors were nonexistent.

Which was why the knock at the door that came that afternoon sounded so foreign.

Who would bother calling on the Tremaines?

Anastasia certainly didn't expect to find a handsome gentleman at their door.

"Hello, miss." The young man's face broke into a smile at the sight of her.

It was one of the Prince's footmen, judging by his livery, which included a blue velvet jacket with the royal family's emblem over a gold vest. He was so tall that his white stockings seemed to go on for miles, and he had shortly cropped brown hair and dark eyes that were two different colors—one gray, one green. How unusual! But it was the sight of an actual smile that stopped Anastasia in her tracks.

"Your Grace." Anastasia grabbed the folds of her eggplant-colored gown and dipped into a curtsy without even thinking. If there was one thing Mother had instilled in her girls, it was proper etiquette. She was just thankful that, unlike her mother and sister, she still bothered with her appearance. "How can I help you, Mr. . . . ?"

The footman blinked in surprise, showing off his long eyelashes. "Oh. It's Benoit, Miss. Please call me Benoit."

A first name, no less! "Nice to make your acquaintance, Benoit," Anastasia said, her own voice sounding foreign on her lips. She spoke so rarely now, she could hear the rasp, as if she were waking from a long slumber. "I am Anastasia."

"Tremaine, I presume?" he said.

Anastasia felt her stomach tighten. "Yes."

He pulled his right arm from behind his back and offered her a crisp white envelope.

"This is for you."

Anastasia blinked in surprise. The envelope had the

name *Tremaine* handwritten on it in familiar script. What was this? An angry letter from a mob come to burn their home down for what they'd done? She'd had that nightmare more than once the past few weeks. Anastasia peered out beyond Benoit to the tree line, looking for axes and torches in broad daylight. She saw none. Still, she did not reach for the envelope.

Benoit stared at her, confused. "This is for your family, from the future princess."

Anastasia faltered. This was even worse than she had suspected. Could Cinderella be laying claim to their house? Technically, it was hers. Were they being tossed out on the cobblestone streets?

Benoit waved the invitation like a fan. "I promise the envelope won't bite. Or maybe it will! A biting envelope—now that would be an exciting development in this saga, don't you think?" He smiled wider.

This saga. He knew what her family had done. Her heart hardened once more. "Do you think I'm a fool?" she demanded.

Benoit blinked. "Miss?"

"Why are you being so nice to me? You clearly know what is being said about my family, and yet you stand here acting like a jester, talking about biting envelopes instead of spitting in my face like some have done before." She closed her eyes at the memory of the last time she was in the village. Mother had been begging for bread, and much as Anastasia tried, the loaves she'd attempted to bake kept burning. Counting the few coins she could find in the house, Anastasia made her way to the bakery, reveling in the freedom she felt at being outside again. But the moment she stepped up to the counter to order, she knew it had been a mistake. Monsieur Gagnon spit at her when she asked for a loaf. Then the others in line did the same. Remembering her shame, Anastasia moved to shut the door in Benoit's face.

Benoit boldly put his hand on the door to stop her. "I'm sorry. I don't mean to make you feel foolish."

"Then why exchange pleasantries when you clearly know who I am and what I have done?" Anastasia heard her voice waver.

"I was trying to be kind." Benoit cast his eyes downward. "I've been where you are before."

Anastasia paused. "How so?"

He stared at her again, his one green eye so striking Anastasia couldn't look away.

"My father . . . he got into some trouble a few years ago and muddied our family name. We couldn't show our faces in the village. It was a very lonely time. The clock seemed to move so slowly."

"Yes. As if the second hand has stopped completely," Anastasia whispered, holding on to the door for support. Her hand was so close to his now, all she would have had to do was reach out to touch it. She didn't.

Benoit swallowed hard. "So you can see why I volunteered to come today." He shifted slightly. "Others refused, but I know what it's like to be made an outcast. I wanted you to know it doesn't have to be forever."

At this Anastasia tsked, the bitterness taking hold again. "So you can see my future, Benoit?"

"No, but I speak from experience." His voice was rushed. "When I came of age, I was certain there was no way I could ever find employment—let alone in the royal household. My father said I was a fool to try applying, but the Prince saw me differently." He smiled softly. "He believes in second chances, and so I try to do the same. We are more than our mistakes." He held out the letter again. "It's clear the future princess agrees. This is an invitation to the royal wedding. She asked that I see to it her family receive one."

"Her family? Meaning *us*?" Anastasia couldn't believe what she was hearing.

Benoit smiled coyly. "Unless there is another Tremaine family in the village I don't know about. If so, then I must get going and find them." He pulled a gold pocket watch out and looked at the time. "I have several invitations to make for the Prince and princess before sundown."

Anastasia wasn't sure how to respond. "But . . . we . . . I . . . she . . ." It wasn't just her voice shaking now. It was her whole body. She'd spent the past few weeks angry with Cinderella, and here the girl was again one-upping her with . . . with . . . forgiveness! It was unfathomable.

After all that had happened, how could Cinderella still consider them family?

It suddenly occurred to Anastasia, shamefully, that Cinderella was good in a way she would never be. But . . . if Cinderella wanted them at her wedding, then perhaps Benoit was right—she could be more than her mistakes. He'd found his second chance. Was it possible she could have one, too? The thought filled her with hope. With trembling hands, she reached out for the invitation.

Someone snatched it away first.

Anastasia whirled around in surprise. Her mother was standing on their doorstep in her nightdress, her hair untamed, dark circles visible on her pale face. Under normal circumstances, Anastasia would have told her mother to hurry back inside. Appearing unkempt was not the Tremaine way. But her mother's eyes were wild, and these were not normal circumstances.

"What are you doing?" Mother rasped.

Anastasia attempted to calm her. "Mother, it's all right." She looked from Benoit to Mother, her face flaming with embarrassment. "Cinderella has sent us an invitation to her wedding."

Mother waved the envelope in Benoit's face. "Is that so? The girl wants to rub our noses in her triumph? Well, I won't allow it!" She ripped the envelope in half and then in half again.

"Mother, no!" Anastasia dropped to her knees to catch

the falling pieces of paper, but several had already caught on the wind and began flying away.

"Leave our home at once!" Mother shouted at Benoit. "You tell the girl we are not her family!"

"Mother!" Anastasia gasped.

"We want nothing to do with her!" Mother continued. "You hear me? Nothing!"

Benoit stumbled backward in surprise, practically tripping off the steps as Mother yanked Anastasia inside and slammed the door. She was up the staircase before Anastasia could even catch her breath.

Anastasia threw open the door again, desperate to apologize. To tell him Mother didn't speak for her. To beg him not to tell Cinderella such things. To thank him for being so kind and understanding. But by the time she made it to the steps, all that was left of Benoit was the dirt kicked up by his horse as he galloped away.

Anastasia stood there for a moment, hot tears falling on her cheeks. Any fleeting bits of hope drifted away like the pieces of the invitation. *Run away,* a voice in her head suggested. But where would she go? Who would dare help a wicked stepsister, as she'd heard herself called? It was hopeless. Anastasia took a step backward and felt her slipper connect with something on the ground.

She looked down. Benoit's pocket watch stared back at her. He must have dropped it in his haste to avoid Mother. Anastasia picked it up, then turned the timepiece over in her hands. She stared at the inscription on the back: **FOR BENOIT, ALWAYS BE TRUE, PAPA.**

Be true, Anastasia thought. That was something she had never been. Her thumb rubbed the etched lettering over a single word—*Papa.*

She hadn't thought of her own father in a long time.

I'll love you always, Strawberry. That was what he called her—his strawberry. They'd grown the fruit on their old estate, and she ate them night and day till her lips were stained pink, which had always been her favorite color. He had died when she and Drizella were young girls, but she could still picture herself sitting on his lap in front of the fire when he returned from a trip. He was the one who had taught her to read, always keeping a small *berlingot* hidden in his jacket pocket; the hard candy was a reward for getting through a tricky passage. The sweets had been their secret. Mother wouldn't have tolerated her girls eating anything between meals, but Father had been the one up for merry-making, for acting out a story, for seeing the bright spots in the world.

Those bright spots were gone now, and he was gone, too. Forget the stillness. Their home had become a tomb in which they all would rot.

Father, she thought desperately. *Help us.*

She wasn't such a fool to believe he would answer. There was no such thing as fairy godmothers—or godfathers, for that matter. She was on her own.

Mother had never liked to speak of Father. To her, his death was a failure, something he had done to them. (The same went for her stepfather, who had embraced her and Drizella as his own. When he died, he was scorned, too—as was his child). All she had to remember Father by were a few fading memories. If only she had something tangible of his, as Benoit had his father's pocket watch. Maybe such an item would give her hope. *We are more than our mistakes,* she repeated to herself.

If a possession of Father's existed, there was only one place she'd find it. A place she never dared step: the tower, where they'd stored old things from their past life. That was Cinderella's dreary quarters. Then again, she was no longer there.

Quietly Anastasia ascended the stairs, tiptoeing past Mother's and Drizella's rooms and taking the narrow steps that led to the dilapidated attic. Cinderella's perfectly made bed sat empty in the corner. The rest of the furnishings were sparse—an old dressing partition and a small table she remembered discarding that Cinderella apparently used for her water basin. Anastasia's face burned once more as she thought of her stepsister toiling away in this dismal space.

Walking across the room, Anastasia spotted a door that led to the storage area. Inside she found an equally tidy space—Cinderella had clearly left her mark on everything. Behind the racks of unworn dresses and coats, Anastasia found several boxes and trunks. As soon as she saw the one marked *FT* for Francis Tremaine, she knew she'd found what she was looking for. A very rusty lock prevented her from throwing the top of the case open and diving in. Anastasia looked around for something to break the decaying metal with. Spotting a pair of black heels (*shoes*, how ironic), Anastasia picked one up and began chipping away. Finally, the lock popped off.

Anastasia sat down and sorted through his things, wondering why Mother had never shown this trunk to her. The contents were exactly as she expected: old coats, a hat, what looked like a baby's quilt, and a stack of books. She held one of the fraying leather-bound books up in wonder. She remembered this! Father had read her fairy tales all the time. After he died, the books had disappeared. Mother wanted her girls to focus on more "attractive" hobbies—music and etiquette—not on something as useless as *reading*. Anastasia went to put the book back in the trunk when something fell out from between the pages.

An envelope—this one very old. She picked it up and stiffened when she saw her father's handwriting. The note was addressed to her and Drizella.

How had Mother missed this?

Hands shaking, she tore it open and began to read. *My dearest girls . . .*

In neat, tight cursive that mirrored her own (he had taught her that, too, of course), Anastasia read, her eyes tripping over words in excitement to see what he had written.

I long for you and your sister to do things I never had time to do before I became ill. When I was a child in Lille, I pretended to do so many things—watch a sunrise from the bow of a ship, explore a cliff on horseback, swim in the shadow of a great waterfall. You and your sister can do these things! That is my great wish for you. To live and to find great love like I found with your mother. Above all else, I hope you remember what I have taught you—that showing kindness to others, even when it isn't returned, is the greatest gift you can give this world. Have faith, girls, and I know you will do great things. I will be looking down on your adventures from above and smiling with happiness. All my love, Father.

Anastasia leaned against one of the trunks and let the letter flutter from her hands. It stared back at her from the floor, taunting her, making her question her every decision and action over the past few years. It also made her wonder how well she remembered Father.

For a man dying, his letter was so full of life, something she clearly was not. She was a disappointment. She hadn't done any of the things he wanted her to do. She'd certainly never found great love. Mother wasn't concerned with such trivial things—she just wanted her girls to marry someone who would elevate their status.

Was that how her parents' story had played out? Father hadn't been wealthy, clearly, and yet he and Mother had what he called a "great love."

Who was this man her mother had fallen in love with? She couldn't fathom how Father's cheery disposition matched up with Mother's grim one, but then again, maybe

Mother hadn't always been that way. It made her wonder: Had Mother changed when she lost not just one husband, but two?

Anastasia sat in that attic, remembering, till shadows danced on the walls. The years blurred together, the lessons from Mother mixing with the contrasting words from Father. If Father had still been alive, what advice would he give her now? *It's not too late to do better, to live differently. Be kind,* she thought. *Like Cinderella.*

Her stepsister.

A girl she had treated shamefully.

Anastasia closed her eyes and thought of her father's words: *I hope you remember what I have taught you—that showing kindness to others, even when it isn't returned, is the greatest gift you can give this world.*

That was what Cinderella had done for the Tremaines, and her kindness was certainly never returned. Anastasia thought back to the night of the ball, when she'd torn strips of fabric and beads from Cinderella's finished gown—one she'd sewn herself in whatever little time she had. She had been terribly cruel to the girl, who had no family to speak of but her stepmother and stepsisters. *Oh, Cinderella,* Anastasia thought, tears falling. *I'm sorry.*

But what good was her regret now? Cinderella had risen above them, and Anastasia was the one left to tend the cinders.

Gingerly, as if it were the finest china, Anastasia picked up the letter again and looked at her father's handwriting. It made her wonder who Francis Tremaine really was, aside from an excellent reader, writer, candy hoarder, and maker of dreams.

Why don't you find out? a small voice inside her asked.

Anastasia wasn't used to voices. Especially ones that were cheery and filled with aspirations. But she knew she could not stand the chilly silence for much longer, so maybe that was why she chose to listen. Grasping the letter and rushing out of the attic with it, she yelled for Mother and Drizella to get up and join her in the sitting room, shouting so loud she could have woken the dead. Mother wasn't amused, and neither was Drizella, who looked more drawn than ever. Maybe a good adventure was just what they needed.

"Child, what is wrong with you?" Mother huffed.

"I found a letter from Father!" Anastasia exclaimed, and she saw her mother's eyes flicker. "It was addressed to Drizella and me."

"Francis?" Mother whispered. A look of sorrow mixed with longing crossed her face for a moment. These were emotions her mother didn't usually express. Then, just as quickly, her face went hollow once more. "Drizella and *me*," Mother corrected. "And I don't recall your father writing you a letter. He was too busy abandoning us, leaving me to fend for myself with two small girls."

"Abandoned? Mother, he died," Anastasia said gently.

Her mother looked flustered, and her speech, for once, wasn't polished. "He swore he'd never leave me. Never leave us," she said quietly. "Instead, I found myself alone in a cruel world, and nothing has been the same since. . . ." Her tone sharpened. "Where did you find that letter?"

Anastasia tried to imagine what it would have been like to be a mother with two young daughters and a fear of how they would make their way without any income, any real power. And then Mother had met Cinderella's father, and he'd died, too; her worst fears realized a second time. Was it any wonder she had hardened? "I found it in his trunk. Father writes about us traveling, seeing the world together."

Surprisingly, Mother and Drizella said nothing. They were listening to her for the first time in weeks! Anastasia kept going.

"I thought that might be the very thing we need to do right now after . . . the incident. Get away from this house and everyone who knows us." Anastasia inhaled fast and went in for the kill. "I know exactly how we could start our trip, too—by visiting Father's old hometown."

"Lille?" Mother's laugh rang hollow, and Anastasia noticed the sadness in her eyes as she spoke. "It's a hovel. Your father and I never told people where we were from. I hardly think he'd want us to pay it a visit."

"Never even heard of it," Drizella said with a yawn and turned back to her room. "And I don't care to see it now. Who wants to go to Lille when our beds are so inviting?"

"Drizella!" Anastasia said impatiently. "We are wasting away in here. Don't you want an adventure?"

"You are not adventuring anywhere," Mother said. "We are not leaving this house until this all blows over. We certainly aren't going to embarrass ourselves by attending *her* wedding."

"Her name is Cinderella," Anastasia said, her voice shaking as emotions got the better of her. "She didn't need to invite us, but she did so out of the kindness of her heart. Perhaps we should be there for her."

"I don't know what's gotten into you, Anastasia, but we cannot show our faces at that castle." Mother's voice grew quiet. "I don't care if we were given an invitation. If people saw us there . . . what would they think of us?"

Her mother was embarrassed. Anastasia didn't blame her. But this was their chance to make things right. "Cinderella wants us there, and I'm sure Father would think we should make the effort. We'll go together, and all will be fine," Anastasia said hopefully. "Maybe this will be our chance to begin again."

Her mother shook her head. "Don't be a fool! Burn that letter—it's filling your head with nonsense! I don't want to hear another word about it."

"I'm not burning Father's last words!" Anastasia hugged the letter to her chest.

"Do not open the front door again," Mother continued. "And do not bother me with such trivial things. . . . What I need right now is tea. Fetch me some."

Lucifer meowed at her feet, his black tail swishing as he

eyed Anastasia devilishly. With a bandage on his back left leg, he couldn't move fast these days. (Mother usually yelled to Anastasia to carry the cat up and down the stairs.) But the accident hadn't changed his personality. It was as if that cat could understand Mother and liked her best when she was being cruel.

"Anastasia? Do you hear me?" Mother repeated.

"But, Mother," Anastasia started, feeling her resolve begin to wane.

Mother turned back to her room. "Your father had his head in the clouds. 'Adventuring' . . . as if any respectable person would waste time on such follies. What this family needs is money. Going to Lille will take the last of what we have!" She slammed the door behind her.

Anastasia looked over at Drizella, who was still standing in her darkened doorway. "We could still go, the two of us," she said hopefully. "We should learn more about where Father's from, don't you think?"

"Women don't travel alone." Drizella sniffed. "We would need a proper companion. And who would be seen with us?"

Anastasia hadn't thought of that. Traveling with Mother was one thing, but journeying to a strange town as two unmarried women would not be the easiest of feats—especially without spending much. Still, she was willing to try. Something told her learning Father's story was the key to finding herself. Not letting her mistakes be all there was to her story. If Father had been good and kind, maybe, just maybe, there was a chance she could be, too. "We will hire someone to take us. We can sell some of our things—our dresses. We have so many!"

"Sell my things? What has gotten into you?" Drizella scoffed.

Anastasia felt the hope that had been slowly rising inside her begin to deflate again. Mother's mind couldn't be changed. Drizella seemed a lost cause as well. Could she hire someone to take just her? Was that proper? Who would even agree to such a thing?

"Stop daydreaming and get Mother's tea," Drizella said. "I'll take some, too."

So that was it, then—she was to be their new Cinderella. The thought made her want to die inside. *Father, please,* Anastasia begged. *Send me a sign. Should I go to your village? How?*

Drizella slammed her door, catching Lucifer's tail in the process.

The cat screeched, banging into the small table in the hallway and making it sway. Anastasia caught it before it could topple and take the water pitcher down with it. In her haste, she felt something slip from her pocket and hit the floor. She looked down.

Benoit's pocket watch.

Anastasia picked it up, and a plan began to form. It was reckless, but it just might work.

Packing up some of her dresses had been easy. Mother hadn't left her bedchambers again. She had begun to call for Anastasia, however, asking for tea or a light meal to have in bed. Once Drizella caught on, she started asking the same, and soon Anastasia found herself running from room to room, delivering food or fresh linens. It was hard work, but Cinderella had always done it without complaint, so Anastasia tried to do the same. That very morning, she had delivered trays with enough crackers, bread, and fruit to last them the day—or at least long enough for her to get away without anyone being the wiser.

And then she was off, walking the long distance to the village with a dozen dresses that she sold to Countess Garnier. The older woman, with four daughters of her own, loved a good bargain and a juicy piece of gossip—Anastasia Tremaine forced to sell her clothes! But Anastasia didn't care. Now she had enough money to make it to Lille. All that was left to do was find her escort.

Am I mad? she wondered as she trudged through the village, going shop to shop looking for Benoit. *Asking a man I've spoken to for mere moments to accompany me on a trip?* She laughed out loud, and people stared. *Possibly. Surely. Yes. But what of it? I finally feel as though I am* doing *something worthwhile.* After several hours, she finally spotted him delivering another wedding invitation.

"Benoit!" she called out. "Wait!"

"Miss Tremaine? Is that you?" Benoit looked up in surprise—*but not embarrassment,* she thought—at the sight of her. He was even more handsome than she remembered, and she could feel her heart pressing against her chest the moment he neared.

"Yes, it's me. Please call me Anastasia." She lowered her hood, revealing her red hair (which she had always thought was her best feature), and dropped into a curtsy. "I've been looking for you. I have something of yours." She reached into her cape pocket and pulled out the velvet handkerchief she'd wrapped his pocket watch in.

His unusual eyes brightened. "You found it!" He took the watch from her, holding it up to the afternoon's waning sun to admire. "I didn't know where I dropped it. I searched everywhere, retracing my steps to all but your manor." He raised his right eyebrow. "I was afraid of your mother's wrath if I knocked on your door again."

Anastasia felt her cheeks flush as she thought back to Mother's behavior. "She wasn't having a good day," she admitted. "I'm sorry about what she did with the wedding invitation."

Benoit cleared his throat. "Please don't give it another thought. The good news is you found my timepiece and returned it to me." He stared at it again. "My father had it commissioned before he died."

"I'm sorry for your loss," Anastasia said softly. "I lost my father when I was young, too."

"Then you understand," he said. "Even after all the trouble he got our family into, he was family. This is all I have left of him. My mother presented it to me when I got my position with the royal family. It's my prized possession. I have it back because of you."

Anastasia's heart pulled. "I'm glad I could bring it, but it's not an entirely selfless act, I'm afraid. I have something to ask of you, too."

"Oh?" His right eyebrow rose higher. "Would you like a new invitation?"

"No." Anastasia flushed. "I will not be attending the wedding."

Benoit's face fell. "The princess will be sorry to hear that."

Anastasia wasn't so sure. And now that her mother and sister had refused, she knew she could not go alone. Maybe she didn't deserve to be there, after all. Besides, the sight of her stepsister on her wedding day might make Cinderella sad. It would be better this way. She had work of her own to do. "Yes, well, there is something else I was hoping you could do for me." Anastasia felt her palms begin to sweat beneath her white gloves. "I was hoping you could accompany me on a trip to Lille. Incidentally, I have been thinking of my own father, and that is where he was from. I've realized I barely knew him, and I'd like to know him better." She faltered. "I don't have much to offer you." She pulled some shillings from her pocket that Countess Garnier had given her. "But I sold enough to get us a carriage to use for travel. I can't go alone, and I . . . don't know who else to ask."

Benoit's hand closed over her own clasping the shillings, and Anastasia inhaled sharply. "Keep your money. It would be my honor to accompany you. Lille isn't far—half a day's trip at most. I have off Thursday and Friday, if you're available then."

Available then? She was available every day! And Thursday was the next day! "Yes, that would be lovely. Thank you! I can meet you back here at first morning light." She wouldn't add that she'd use some of her earnings to rent a room in town for the night so that she wouldn't have to return home. If she did, she feared Mother wouldn't let her out again. She was officially on her own for the first time, and it was both exhilarating and terrifying.

Benoit bowed slightly as if she were someone to be revered. "Till then, Anastasia."

True to his word, Benoit was waiting at the stables at dawn. At first, Anastasia worried they'd have nothing to talk about, but their conversation never ceased—him telling her about castle life, which was fascinating; her reveling in each new sight as it went by, wondering about its unique history, which he admitted he had never thought of before in all his journeys through the kingdom. It was the longest conversation she'd ever had, and it made the time pass quickly. By late morning, they arrived in Lille.

"It's beautiful," Anastasia observed as Benoit helped her down from the carriage. Already she could see how different it was from their own village. Or maybe it was just that this one was nestled into the rocky countryside, sitting alongside a river where small boats drifted by. Cobblestones lined the tiny, packed streets where homes and shops intermingled in straight lines.

"So where do you want to start?" Benoit asked.

Good question, Anastasia realized. Where would they find someone who might have known Francis Tremaine? His family was as long deceased as he was. His name didn't belong to a storied family or one that owned a shop. She tried to think back to anything Mother might have told her about him. It wasn't much. All she had were her memories, and her memories were about stories and laughter and . . . "Sweets! Perhaps a bakery or a sweet shop? My father always carried candy in his pocket."

Benoit looked around at the shops in the square. "Aha! If your papa loved sweets, why don't we try the *chocolaterie*? At the very least, they'll have some delicious delicacies we can take with us on this quest."

Anastasia smiled. "That sounds like a wonderful suggestion."

Even though the day was only just beginning, it felt different. Maybe it was being in the village where no one knew her or her history, or maybe it was walking the same streets her father had once walked, but she felt unencumbered in a way she never had before.

A bell rang on the door as they entered. The sweet smell of chocolate greeted them along with glass counters full of candy, cookies, and chocolate.

"Hello!" a woman called out as she dusted a cake with powdered sugar. "How can I help you?"

"Hello," said Benoit. "First off, we'd love two of those, three of those, and maybe a bag of those to take with us." He looked at Anastasia and winked. "Need to bring something home for the other men."

Anastasia smiled. "We were also hoping you could help us find someone who might have known the Tremaine family. My father was Francis. He died almost a decade ago." It still hurt to say those words after all this time.

The woman searched her memory for a second, scratching her head and almost dislodging the white cap her hair was tucked into. "Tremaine . . . Tremaine . . . Francis . . . No, I'm sorry, child. I don't recall ever meeting someone with that name before."

Anastasia tried to hide her disappointment. "Thank you anyway," she said, taking the bag of treats from her. What if this trip—the deception of leaving without telling her mother or sister, the decision to travel with a man she barely knew—had been for nothing?

"But my shop is only a few years old," the woman added. "I might not be the best person to ask."

"Thank you," Benoit said, then tucked into his first cookie. "We'll keep searching." He handed Anastasia a sugar cookie. "Have a bite of this. It will help."

Anastasia did as she was told, feeling the warm sugary concoction hit her tongue. She had to admit, the sweetness helped.

"Better?" Benoit read her thoughts. She nodded. "Good, because that was just our first stop. We can't give up now. Perhaps we could find town records, or find out where he lived?"

Benoit continued to offer suggestions as Anastasia scanned the signs above shops. Something told her someone here knew her father. Maybe it was the tingling she felt at the back of her neck, or the way the wind seemed to whisper his name whenever it whipped past her, but she knew his memory was here somewhere. The question was, where? The market was a possibility, but when her eyes landed on a picture of a book, she knew she'd found the next place to stop. "The library!" she said, rushing ahead.

"To the library!" Benoit said, charging after her, the two of them laughing.

The room was small—just a few shelves with books, and only one person inside browsing while a librarian worked, but the smell of leather drew her in. She recalled a memory of herself reaching for a book that was just out of reach. *Here you go, Strawberry,* she heard her father say as he took the book down for her. *Enjoy your adventure.*

Adventure.

"Can I help you?" asked the librarian, high on a ladder, shelving a book with a purple spine.

"Yes, I was hoping you might be able to help me find someone who knew my father, Francis Tremaine. He died ten years ago, but his family resided here their whole lives."

The librarian thought for a moment, then shook his head. "Sorry. I've only been open a few years, and that name does not sound familiar."

Anastasia's hope began to wane again. So many new establishments in this storied village! "Thank you, sir."

Benoit smiled at her sadly. "Don't worry. We will keep searching."

"I'm sorry to interrupt, but did you say Tremaine?"

Anastasia turned around. An older woman stood before them, holding a cane in one hand and leaning on a bookshelf with the other. "Francis Tremaine?" She didn't give Anastasia time to answer. "Yes, you must have. I knew him as a boy, and you look just like him."

Anastasia looked at Benoit in wonder, then back at the woman. "You knew my father?" The woman nodded, and Anastasia felt her heart lurch. She moved in closer, hoping to hear more. "Please forgive me. I'm his younger daughter, Anastasia. What is your name?"

"Mathilde Boche." She let go of the bookshelf to clasp Anastasia's hand. "My son was friends with your father when they were children."

Anastasia felt something inside her stir. "Do you have some time to talk? I'd love to know more about him," she said.

The old woman smiled. "Time? All I have is time. I live alone, and getting around is hard these days. It would be my pleasure to have your company."

Benoit led them outside to a sunny bench in the square, then stepped back to give Anastasia and Mathilde their privacy. It was there Mathilde told her story after story of a young Francis and Mathilde's son Paul, running through the countryside pretending they were pirates or sea monsters or sometimes even animals.

"Your father loved creatures big and small," Mathilde said. "One time he tried to bring an injured raccoon home, and his mother forbade it." She gave Anastasia a look. "Your father didn't take no easily—he set up a place for that raccoon in the shed and took care of him till he was nursed back to health. That's how Francis was—someone who treated everyone fairly, whether it was a wild animal or the town beggar. He had the kindest heart."

The woman's words reminded Anastasia of someone, momentarily distracting her. She realized with a start that it could have been a description of Cinderella.

The older woman went on. "And he was so in love with your mother. Those two were never apart. Anytime I saw them together, they were singing."

"Singing?" Anastasia gaped. Mother? She tried to picture her parents together, young, in love, and happy. "I've never heard my mother sing before." In music lessons, her mother was always strict about arrangements and technique, but she never sang a note.

"She was quite good," Mathilde insisted. "You should ask her to sing for you. She might like that. I am sorry to hear your father is no longer with us."

Anastasia clasped the woman's hands, feeling a rush of emotions for her. "Thank you. This afternoon was truly a gift, and this small town . . ." She looked around. "I feel like I've entered a storybook."

Mathilde laughed. "Your father always said the same thing. Lille is small and humble, but it is magical." She looked at Anastasia curiously. "So you are enjoying your visit?"

"Why, yes!" Anastasia gushed. "Here, I feel like I could be anyone I want." She looked down for a moment. "Maybe even someone my father would be proud of." She felt Mathilde give her hand a squeeze.

"Then why don't you stay longer?" Mathilde's eyes twinkled. "When you found me in the library, I was about to leave a post seeking someone to assist me around the house. Light labor, company, for a warm bed. I am getting on in years and could use the help. My home isn't large, but it is cozy."

"You would want to hire me?" Anastasia gaped. "Are you certain? You barely know me."

"I like what I see," Mathilde replied. "You've got some of your father's fire in you. I suspect you'll make a fine worker and an even better friend. What do you say?"

Anastasia felt her heart start to beat out of her chest. A million thoughts formed at the same time. She pushed away the ones telling her all the reasons she couldn't stay: Her mother telling her she was above this sort of labor (even if that had not been the case at home lately, as she waited on her mother and sister). Her sister telling her she was ridiculous and that she should wait for something better to come along. Her own doubts telling her how hard it would be to truly leave home.

But a louder sentiment rang through. This was it. Her fresh start. A chance to carve out a different path. She'd be a fool not to take it. "I say yes!" Anastasia said, laughing as she threw her arms around Mathilde. It only occurred to her afterward that it was the first time in a long time she'd shown affection to someone. It made her feel like anything was possible.

Benoit was waiting near the carriage when Anastasia left Mathilde. As soon as he saw her, his face broke into a smile. "How did your afternoon go?"

"I got a job!" Anastasia burst out.

"A job?" Benoit's face fell. "Here?"

She filled him in on Mathilde's offer, along with the stories she'd learned about her father. Benoit listened patiently, not interrupting till the end.

"So does this mean you won't be returning with me?" Benoit asked.

Anastasia shook her head. "I think my place is here . . . for now." His smile wavered slightly. "I keep thinking about something you said to me that day you came to our door—we are more than our mistakes. I want that to be true, Benoit." Her lower lip trembled. "I want to be someone my father—and my stepsister, Cinderella—can be proud of. I think if I'm here, learning more about my father from Mathilde, I might find a bit of his kindness in me, too." She shrugged. "I don't know if that makes sense."

"It makes all the sense in the world." Benoit placed a hand over her hers, and she felt a warmth spread from her toes to her head. "A woman who sells her own gowns to raise funds for a trip to her father's birthplace seems like a woman who could do anything."

Anastasia laughed. "It was quite impulsive!"

This had been an adventure . . . and who said it had to end now? If she could find a way to walk in her father's footsteps, surely she could learn to be someone who strove to make the best of the time they were given. Her mother and sister would be angry she had left, but maybe someday she could return and help pull them out of their own darkness. She could be someone who learned from her mistakes . . . and accepted others' forgiveness as well.

That gave her yet another new idea. "Benoit? About the invitation."

Benoit looked at her again, his right eyebrow twitching. "Yes?"

She bit her lip before speaking. "Would you tell the Prince and princess it would be my honor to attend the wedding?"

"Yes!" Benoit exclaimed. "I would be happy to pass along that message."

Anastasia smiled, wondering if she could be so bold as to ask Benoit a question very much on her mind. "And you? Will you be at the wedding as well?"

"Yes, I believe I will be," he said softly.

"That's wonderful news." Anastasia's grin widened as she pictured herself dancing in Benoit's arms at her stepsister's wedding. That was a future she hoped she could make happen. She *would* make happen. *I'm coming, Cinderella,* she thought. *And I'm ready to show you who I can be if you'll let me.* Anastasia held out her hand. "I guess it's time for me to bid you adieu, for now," she said.

Benoit looked down at her hand before lifting it to his lips and kissing it. "Till we meet again, Anastasia."

Anastasia's breath stopped for a second, and her heart started to beat wildly. "Farewell, Benoit." Then she turned and began to walk through the village—her new village—back to where Mathilde was waiting. The sun warmed her face as she walked fast, then faster, to a future full of uncertainty and challenges, but also so much promise.

Anastasia Tremaine's adventure was just beginning.

A New Dawn

What if Mufasa gave up his throne?

by Farrah Rochon

A New Dawn

What if Mufasa gave up his throne?

by Farrah Rochon

The morning sun crept up on the horizon like a panther on the hunt, stealthily advancing across the Pride Lands and the jagged rock formations that lined its borders. Pride Rock boldly lorded over the vast terrain. As the highest point of the savannah, it was the only place for the king of this African land to preside.

Simba prowled along the edge of the towering rock, his attention focused on the area still smoldering from a recent brush fire. He stopped and sniffed the air.

Nothing but ash.

Just because he didn't smell anything out of the ordinary didn't mean trouble wasn't lurking. Simba had sensed it for days. First there was the mysterious illness that took out a family of aardvarks the week before, and then the previous night Simba got word that a colony of flamingos had been attacked.

Something told him that both were intentional. And only the beginning . . .

There had been talk of a group of lions who had been cast out of their prides and banded together to form their own. They called themselves the Wasaki—the Evil Ones. Any pride that proudly claimed such a label had only one thing in mind: destruction.

The marauding group had hit several prides in the past few months. From what Simba had gathered, the Wasaki swooped in and violently overtook their targets. They pillaged all the resources and desecrated the land before moving on.

It was his job to ensure Pride Rock would not become the Wasaki's next victim.

"Kuume," Simba called. The lioness ran to his side. "Make your way to the southern border where the collection of baobab trees shields the land. Stand guard there until I send someone to relieve you. Don't take your eyes off that large boulder just beyond the trees. If we are being targeted, that will be the attackers' approach." He was sure of it.

The lioness gracefully bowed her head before taking off at a brisk clip down the side of Pride Rock.

Simba turned to the three remaining lionesses who had gathered with him on the edge of the outcropping. He issued orders and breathed a sigh of relief as each, even Tandi and Olee, heeded his command without question. It had been two years since he'd technically taken over as the leader of the pride, but he still found himself wanting to defer to the elder lionesses. They were his parents' contemporaries, and it felt strange to order them around. But it was the role he held.

Well, at least he was *supposed* to hold that role. Some of the residents of Pride Rock still saw him as a wet-behind-the-ears cub. One resident in particular.

"You seem busy today."

Speak of the . . .

Simba turned and stood up straight.

"Hello, Father," he said to Mufasa. Simba tried not to wince as he observed his father gingerly making his way toward him. His steps were measured. Careful. Even with the brace Rafiki had fashioned for him, Mufasa moved extremely slowly. His pain was evident, his face often contorting with discomfort.

It had been nothing short of a miracle that his father had survived the fall after Simba's uncle Scar had pitched him into a mass of stampeding wildebeests. He'd lived, but the incident had left his body badly broken. There were some days when Mufasa could not make it out of the alcove where he and Simba's mother, Sarabi, spent much of their time.

"You sent Kuume to the southern edge of the Pride Lands," Mufasa said. "Why?"

"Because I need her to stand guard there."

His father laughed dismissively. "For what, Simba?"

"For protection," Simba answered. "Nala heard whispers

while out on a hunt. She believes an attack is imminent, and I believe her."

"Nala tells fanciful stories. She always has. Don't you remember when you two were cubs? You would both make up wild tales."

"We are no longer cubs, Father. Nala has grown into one of our most efficient huntresses. Who do you think brought in those gazelles that fed the pride this week? I won't question her."

"I know you are hesitant to question Nala, my son. She has been a good friend to you and a decent huntress, but neither of you have enough experience in running a pride to know if an attack is imminent. You cannot base such decisions on whispers one hears around the watering hole."

Simba swallowed down his frustration. Arguing would do him no good. This disagreement had been going on for the past two years, ever since his mother had convinced his father to abdicate the throne. Soon after the incident with Scar, it had become obvious to everyone on Pride Rock that Mufasa's injuries would not allow him to continue performing his duties as leader of the pride.

But his father had a hard time letting go. And for two years, Simba had to deal with Mufasa second-guessing every decision he made.

"This isn't only about what Nala reported," Simba said. "We haven't had to deal with another pride trying to overtake our lands for the better part of a year. You know better than anyone that we are well overdue for an attack."

It was one thing to be declared king, but it was another thing entirely to maintain that status. There were lions all over this land waiting for their opportunity to take over Pride Rock. They had to remain vigilant at all times, but Simba's instincts told him they must be even more so lately. An attack was on the horizon; he could feel it.

"Trust me on this, Father," Simba told him. "You taught me to rely on my instincts, and they tell me that Pride Rock is in danger."

"I have taught you well, Son, but there is still much you have to learn."

Simba bit his tongue to stop himself from lashing out. He'd done all he could to prove to his father that he was more than capable of taking complete reign over this pride, but no matter what he did, it was never enough. Mufasa continued to treat him like a young cub still learning how to pounce on unsuspecting zebras. Simba didn't know what it would take to make him see that their pride was in good hands.

Just then, Simba felt the short hairs below his mane stand on end. An uncomfortable sensation swept over him seconds before a familiar voice drawled, "Well, well. If it isn't my two favorite people."

Simba whipped around and growled.

Scar.

"What are *you* doing here?" Simba hissed.

"Now, Simba, is that any way to greet your beloved uncle?"

"You're no uncle of mine," he snapped.

"Simba," Mufasa said in a warning tone, "we've been over this."

"Yes, we have," Scar muttered. "And if I must say, it has become rather tiring. I've apologized to my dear brother for our little . . . misunderstanding. And *he's* forgiven me. Don't you think it's time you did, as well?"

Scar sauntered toward Mufasa, his tail brushing back and forth along the ground. He whipped a cloud of dirt onto Mufasa's paws as he came alongside him. "Oh, oh, pardon me, Brother," Scar said.

Simba's eyes narrowed.

It had been months since Scar last visited Pride Rock. He'd spent the past two years dropping in for a few weeks at a time, then leaving without so much as a goodbye. Simba remained wary of his dubious comings and goings.

When it came to his uncle, he was suspicious about everything he did, everything he said.

Why couldn't his father see that Scar was never to be trusted?

Mufasa's decision to forgive Scar after the incident that had almost killed him was another ongoing issue between Simba and his father. Mufasa believed Scar's excuse that he'd been trying to help him as he dangled off the side of that cliff but had lost his grip.

A lie.

Simba had been there. He'd witnessed the hatred and

jealousy in Scar's eyes as he stood above the gorge. He still saw that hatred on those occasions when Scar allowed his mask to slip. That his father had taken Scar at his word continued to confound Simba.

Then again, his father had always had a blind spot when it came to seeing the evil in his brother.

Simba didn't. He saw his uncle for what he was. Which was why he never let his guard down around Scar.

"Come, Brother," Scar said. "Why don't we go down to the watering hole."

"No!"

Both his father and Scar turned in astonishment at Simba's exclamation.

"It's just the watering hole," Scar drawled. "What do you think I am going to do? Try to drown my own brother?"

"That's exactly what I think you would do," Simba bit out between clenched teeth.

"There's always dozens of animals around. Don't worry, Simba. If I ever thought of harming Mufasa—which I wouldn't," Scar said with a saccharine smile, "the last place I would consider doing so is at the watering hole. Too many witnesses."

Simba's paws flared with the innate urge to pounce. He managed to curb it, but only slightly.

"I've told you a million times, Simba, things are good between me and Scar," his father said. "You have no need to worry."

The two turned and started in the direction of the watering hole. As he watched his father and uncle walk away, Simba could not shake the troubling feeling that something was amiss.

If it were up to Simba, Scar would never set foot on Pride Rock again.

And the thing was, the decision *should* be up to him. As the leader of the Pride Lands, Simba was supposed to decide who resided there and who didn't. He was supposed to be in charge of what the pride did to protect their land, and when they decided to hunt and where. But that's not the way things had worked over the past two years. And Simba wasn't sure how much longer he could take it. He couldn't be half in, half out of such major responsibilities.

He knew this would all come to a head sooner or later, and it seemed as if he was on the precipice of having to make a decision he was loath to make.

Either Mufasa would be the leader or Simba. But there could be only one.

The thought of breaking off from the pride was something that had floated across Simba's mind numerous times the past year. But it felt like a betrayal even thinking about it. He knew in his heart that his father could not lead the pride anymore, and if Simba were to abdicate and leave, the pride would be more vulnerable to attack than they'd ever been before.

But his father was making it impossible for Simba to stay. The way he continued to undermine Simba's decisions *also* made the pride more vulnerable. It confused the others, forcing them to choose whose word they should listen to.

If Mufasa insisted on interfering with Simba's leadership, it would not end well for anyone.

"Simba? Simba?"

He turned at the sound of the familiar voice. Moments later, Nala appeared from around one of the boulders. Simba's heart gave a little stutter step, but he quickly shut down any inkling of affection. He did not want anyone to think his feelings for her had anything to do with how he was running the pride.

He turned and affected his sternest face. "Yes, Nala?"

She stepped back and let out a soft laugh. "Why so glum, Mr. Serious?"

"I have a lot of work to do," Simba said.

She rolled her eyes. "Yes, yes, I know. You're the leader of the pride." She sent a cloud of dust sailing up around his feet. "I don't care that you're king. Stop being so full of yourself."

Simba allowed himself a small laugh. He couldn't maintain this stoic countenance around her. "Fine. What is it that you want?"

"Actually, this *is* pretty serious," she said. "Duma just came back from a hunt. She said that the berm on the southwestern side of the Pride Land was breached overnight."

Simba froze, a rush of unease slithering down his spine. "Is she sure?"

Nala nodded. "I went out to see it for myself before

coming to you, just to be sure. It was trampled, and not by elephants or antelope. There are *lion* tracks. And it wouldn't be anyone from our tribe, because you specifically told everyone to avoid that area."

"Are you certain my father didn't come behind me and tell them that they could?" Simba asked with a derisive snort.

Nala walked up to him and placed her right paw on his back. "I know things are . . . uncomfortable between you and Mufasa. Just give him time."

"It's been two years," Simba pointed out. "How much time am I supposed to give him?"

"However long it takes," Nala said. She gave him a knock on the back of the head. "Now enough with the pity party. Do you want to check out what's happening at the berm or what?"

Rubbing his head where she'd clocked him, Simba turned to her and said, "Show me."

Simba and Nala raced across the parched ground, kicking up dirt and dust in their wake. The entire area was going through a peculiarly dry season, which was another reason Pride Rock was such an attractive spot for other prides. The river that ran through their land still overflowed, while so many in neighboring areas had dried up due to the massive drought that had seized much of this part of the continent.

Protecting their home was the most important thing Simba could do as their leader. If another pride were to come in and force them off Pride Rock, he wasn't sure how many of the older lions and lionesses would survive either the fight or the journey to find another home.

The pressure of it all consumed him day and night, but it was his duty to think of such things and make sure all members were cared for.

When he and Nala came upon the berm, Simba knew within moments of seeing it that Duma had been right.

"There are at least two different sets of paw prints," Simba said as he sniffed the earth. "Judging from the size, I'd say one belongs to a full-grown lion and the other to either an older cub or a lioness." His eyes traveled in the direction of the prints. "I think they have their eyes on the watering hole on the western edge of Pride Rock."

"Simba! Over here," Nala called. He ran to her side. "Look at this." She pointed to yet another set of tracks. She and Simba followed them to some short brush. There, they found the skeleton of a small rabbit, which had obviously been someone's dinner.

Simba nudged the bones with his paw. "There isn't much decay, so the kill was recent." He sniffed the air. "Possibly last night."

"You think they've been doing reconnaissance?" Nala asked.

"I have no doubt," he said. He turned to her. "Do you remember which pride was around when you heard those other lionesses talking? Was it the Wasaki?"

She shook her head. "I wish I knew, but they were

speaking in such low tones, I only caught a few words here and there."

Her answer gave Simba pause. He was basing several important decisions on the details Nala had given him. Could he be sure it was all correct information? Could putting all his focus on Nala's reports cause him to miss something else? Was he possibly putting the pride in danger by relying only on secondhand accounts and his own gut instinct?

And was he setting himself up to be seen as an incapable leader by his father?

If his hunch was wrong and the information Nala had provided was faulty, it could lead to a catastrophic outcome for them all. He wouldn't have to worry about deciding to leave the pride. He would be forced out.

Or worse.

Later, as most members of the pride lay underneath the blazing African sun, enjoying much-needed rest, Simba continued to pace back and forth along the cliff that looked out over the Pride Lands. The situation at the berm, combined with his run-in with Scar, made him too edgy to settle down. Even if he tried to sleep, he knew it would evade him. Better that he keep watch while the lionesses who would eventually stand guard rested.

He heard the whisper of soft steps seconds before Nala appeared.

"You're going to wear a trench into the earth," she said. Her words held more unease than humor, which told Simba much about how scared she was for him. He hated to worry her but could also admit that it felt good to know she was concerned about his well-being.

"I have a bad feeling about all of this," Simba told her.

"I share your bad feeling," she said as she came up alongside him. They walked in step, their bodies in tune as they had always been.

Simba stopped pacing and turned to her. He hesitated for a moment, unsure if he should voice the thoughts that had plagued him so much lately.

"If I were to leave the pride, would you come with me?"

Nala's head reared back. "Leave the pride? Why would you even think of doing such a thing, Simba?"

"Because I don't know my place here anymore," he said.

"Your place is as our leader."

"Is it?" Simba asked. "I'm not so sure of that."

"Of course it is," Nala insisted.

"It's not easy to step into the role of such an effective ruler."

"Simba." Her voice was strident. "Your father was a brilliant ruler, but his time has passed. I know he has been stubborn and he thinks you aren't mature enough to be at the helm of the pride, but it doesn't matter what Mufasa thinks. *You* are the sole and rightful heir to the throne. *You* are our leader."

"That's just the thing, Nala. It *does* matter what my father thinks, because many of the lions still look up to him. They respect his word. And if the pride doesn't know if they should defer to me or to my father, then 'leader' is a meaningless title." He shrugged. "It's also singular. There can only be one. If my father isn't willing to step down completely, then maybe I should just walk away."

"What about what's best for the pride?" Nala asked. "I don't care what Mufasa or anyone else says, you're the one who is best to lead this pride into the future."

Her unwavering belief in him was like a balm for Simba's battered ego. If every member of this pride eventually gave up on him, at least he would always have Nala's support. And just maybe a bit of her love, as well.

"Thank you for saying that," Simba said softly. "It means a lot."

"I know what you're capable of." She covered his paw with her own and caressed his neck with her head, gently rubbing back and forth in a soothing motion.

Simba's eyes narrowed as he stared at a figure walking his way. "Kuume? What are you doing here? Why aren't you at your post?"

The lioness looked at him in confusion. "Zazu flew by not too long ago and told me I no longer had to stand guard," she answered.

Zazu. His father's majordomo. The red-billed hornbill was supposed to work for Simba, but he never consulted with him on anything concerning the pride. Zazu remained loyal to Mufasa and refused to recognize anyone else as leader.

This had to end. His father's interference would eventually jeopardize them all.

With a determination he'd failed to muster until this point, Simba marched into the cave where his mother and father were resting.

"Father," Simba said, "may I speak to you? Outside?"

"Simba, is everything okay?" Sarabi asked.

"No, it isn't," he answered.

Mufasa stood and, with his brace tied to his right front leg, walked out of the cave.

"Yes, Simba?" he said once they'd cleared the cave entrance.

"Why did you send Zazu to Kuume? I gave her a specific order, and you gave her permission to defy it."

"Watch your tone," Mufasa said, his tail swishing from side to side in a clear sign of growing aggression.

"My tone should be the least of your concerns," Simba snarled.

"Simba! Stop this at once!" He turned at his mother's horrified voice.

"It must be said, Mother," Simba told her. He returned his attention to Mufasa. "You go behind my back, undermining my direct orders. Undermining *me*! Everything you are doing is putting this pride in danger, and I refuse to live this way even one more day. You need to decide right here, right now, Father. Will I be allowed to lead this pride, or do I *leave* this pride?"

Mufasa bared his teeth.

"You would leave your pride?" he asked. His growl was filled with anger and disappointment.

"You give me no choice," Simba answered, his heart thudding dully. "I cannot do what is being asked of me if you continue to get in my way."

"I'm trying to *help* you, Simba! You haven't yet developed the instincts you need to lead the pride into the future. Just look at what you did today. You foolishly sent lionesses to patrol the borders based on some story from Nala. You didn't think to—"

The blow came from out of nowhere.

Mufasa crumpled to the ground, his brace skidding across the dry soil as two full-grown lions pounced on him.

"Father!" Simba charged at the lions. "Attack!" he yelled over his shoulder. "Attack! Attack!"

He slammed into the two lions, knocking them off Mufasa's back and following them in a tumbling roll that took them close to the edge of the cliff. Simba scurried away from the edge, hustling to find his footing.

He howled as sharp teeth plunged into his right flank. The debilitating pain shot through his entire body, causing his knees to buckle and rendering him useless. Simba tried to pull away, but the other lion just bit down harder.

He swiped his unfurled paw across the face of one lion, then immediately sank his teeth into the other's neck. The second lion violently twisted his head, shaking Simba loose and sending him crashing into the hard ground.

Bursts of white-hot light flashed behind his closed eyes as a sharp pain thundered in his head.

"Simba!"

He heard Nala's voice seconds before the lion with a grip on his side was forced off of him, taking a chunk of Simba's flesh.

He looked up and recoiled at the horrifying chaos that had been unleashed. Kuume and Duma were locked in a fierce battle with two invaders. Another set of lionesses had Empurra and her mate, Akiki, up against one of the boulders shielding the cave where the elder members of the pride dwelled. Simba called on a strength deep within and pushed himself off the ground. He hurried to their aid. He could not allow the attackers to reach the others.

They managed to bar the lions from entering the cave, but the battle was nowhere near over.

An additional half dozen lionesses, all baring their razor-sharp teeth, rushed at them from all sides. How many were there? How long had they been waiting in the wings, poised to attack?

And why hadn't he seen them coming?

He'd known the Wasaki were getting closer. The previous few prides they'd targeted were in this area. He should have been better prepared.

Being caught unawares had put the pride at a disadvantage. However, knowing Pride Rock like the back of their paws made up for it. Kuume used a short bush as a shield, rounding it and attacking two intruders from behind. Simba climbed up a large outcropping, about five feet in the air, and dove onto the lioness attacking Akiki. He swung his paw behind him and connected with the jaw of another lion.

Out of nowhere, Simba felt a strong blow to the middle of his back. He slid several feet before landing against the wall, pebbles crumbling around him.

He looked up and blinked twice before his vision cleared.

The sight before him both robbed him of breath and made him see red.

Scar.

"I knew it!" Simba growled. "You're with the Wasaki, aren't you?"

"I *am* the Wasaki," Scar snarled.

"I knew you weren't to be trusted, you traitor!"

"And I knew you weren't fit to be a leader," Scar said. "Get him!"

A trio of lionesses besieged Simba, sinking their sharp teeth and claws into his flesh, ripping his mane out by the roots. The pain was so great he nearly passed out.

But at the sound of Nala's cry, Simba was instantly alert.

He looked up to find her rushing toward him. A new lion twice her size advanced on her from her left side.

"Nala, look out!"

The lion caught her before she even saw it. Something broke in Simba at the sight of Nala being attacked with such disregard.

A roar unlike any he'd ever released traveled from the depths of his being. He hefted himself up from the ground and charged at the lion, ripping him away from Nala and pummeling him to the ground. They tumbled along the dry earth, their limbs tangling up together. Duma joined in, and together she and Simba subdued this latest attacker.

"Where is he?" Simba growled.

He searched the area until his eyes landed on Scar. He looked a few yards ahead of where his uncle trekked, and spotted Mufasa still prone on the ground.

"Father," Simba whispered.

He took off for Scar, galloping toward him and pouncing. He landed on Scar's back just seconds before the traitor reached his father.

Scar unleashed a blood-curdling roar as Simba clamped down on his neck with his teeth. He flung his uncle against the side of a boulder and pounced again, unrelenting in his fight.

"I knew better than to trust you," Simba said.

He stomped on Scar's head with both paws, relishing in his uncle's broken, feeble cry.

"Simba, please!" he heard his mother yell from somewhere to the right of him. "You'll kill him!"

"He deserves it," Simba said.

"Don't, Son," Mufasa said.

"He brought these intruders to Pride Rock," Simba said, stomping on Scar's face. "He betrayed us yet again. He betrayed *you*, Father. You forgave him once, but he doesn't deserve to be forgiven again."

Simba pressed his paw against Scar's windpipe, grinding back and forth, ignoring his uncle's pleas for mercy. The fevered need to squelch the life out of Scar was so strong it scared Simba. He didn't realize he was capable of such hate and violence. But the desire to protect those he loved drove him to eliminate this threat to their well-being, by any means necessary.

"Simba," Nala said over his shoulder. "This is not who you are. Don't allow him to turn you into a monster." Her soft voice drew him out of the bloodlust daze he'd been in, but not enough to take his attention away from Scar. He knew how his uncle operated. He wouldn't give Scar the chance to get the upper hand.

"Yes . . . yes," Scar choked out in a hoarse breath. "Show your uncle some mercy."

"You deserve no mercy," Simba spit out. But as he pressed his paw against his uncle's throat, repulsion rushed through him. He'd been taught to kill only for sustenance and defense. His sense of honor would not allow him to take a defenseless life—even Scar's. "Lucky for you," Simba continued. "I've inherited more from my father than I first thought."

With a growl he released his hold on Scar's neck.

The older lion coughed up blood and spittle.

Simba walked around him in a tight circle, his tail swishing back and forth, pitching dirt at Scar's crumbled body with each sway.

"You will leave Pride Rock. And you will never, ever return," Simba said. Simba kept his eyes trained on Scar as he called out to the other lions and lionesses. "Nala, Akiki, Duma, Kuume. Help me escort my uncle and his friends out of the Pride Lands."

"Have some mercy," Scar begged. "Like it or not, we are cut from the same cloth."

In less than a second, Simba was in front of him. He leaned forward until his nose was mere inches from Scar's, then released a terrifying roar. Scar's ragged mane billowed from the force of it.

"I will never be like you. Get. Moving," Simba warned.

Together, Simba and the others marched Scar, along with the lions and lionesses who'd survived the battle, from Pride Rock. They slowly made their way down the side of the large rock formation, past the watering hole, and to the very edge of the Pride Lands.

"You are forever expelled from this pride and this land," Simba told his uncle. "I don't want to hear of the Wasaki terrorizing any other prides ever again. If I catch even a whiff of you or your friends, I will not be as charitable as I have been today. Leave, and never return."

This time, Simba didn't trust Scar enough to turn his back on him until he and the banished crew were but dots on the horizon.

After some time had passed, he felt a gentle nudge against his neck.

"Come, Simba," Nala said softly. "It's time to return. Pride Rock needs its leader."

By the time they made it back to Pride Rock, the sun had begun to set over the Pride Lands. Simba gestured for the others to go ahead of him before he climbed up the rock formation. The moment he reached the top, he noticed a figure standing in the shadow of one of the boulders. One paw supported with a brace.

Simba wasn't sure he could talk to his father just yet. His emotions were still too scattered after the ordeal their pride had just endured. He tried to skirt around the boulder, hoping the pretense of not seeing his father would work, but Mufasa called out to him.

"Simba, I need to speak to you," came his deep voice.

Simba shut his eyes and took a deep breath. After a moment, he turned and headed for his father. He stopped when there was still about five feet separating them.

"I owe you an apology," Mufasa started.

Simba's eyes widened. "Wha—"

"I'm sorry for not trusting in you," his father said. "You were right. I never gave you a chance to be a true leader of the pride." He puffed out his chest. "The truth is, I wasn't ready to give up the throne. I was forced to, and I have resented it for two years. It pains me to say this, but I have resented you, Son."

Simba winced, but he understood. He'd been a cub when his father first suffered his injury, but now that he was grown, he was able to fully grasp the difficulties his father must have faced. He'd been a strong, virile, competent leader, and in a heartbeat, his own brother had robbed him of his duly earned position.

"You prepared me to take over as leader one day, but none of us expected that day would come so soon. If I could go back in time and change it, I would, Father."

"But we can't," Mufasa said. "It is time I accept that." He sighed. "I must also accept that you were right two years ago. Scar intentionally threw me to the wildebeests that day."

"Father—"

"If I had listened to you, and banished Scar from this land a long time ago, the pride wouldn't have had to endure today's battle. Instead, I put all of us in danger because I didn't want to concede that you were right."

"It's done, Father. It's over. We defended Pride Rock, and it will stand for years to come. I will make sure of it."

Mufasa nodded. "I know you will. You showed us all today what a fierce protector you are, and that you are more than capable of leading this pride into the future."

With an unsteady shift of his paw, he released his brace. It took Simba a moment to recognize what his father was doing.

"No," Simba said as Mufasa slowly bent his head in a humble bow.

"Yes," his father replied. "I pledge allegiance to you as the leader of our pride."

The entire pride gathered around them in a semicircle.

Emotion welled in Simba's throat.

"Maybe I have been wrong in some ways, too," he said. "I've been so fixated on proving that I'm up to the task that I've disregarded the wisdom that is right in front of me. You were right when you pointed out that neither Nala nor I have the kind of experience you have." He looked to his mother, who stood with Tandi and Olee. "That all of you have. It is time I acknowledge that I still have lots to learn."

Simba walked over to his father. He placed his paw on his father's shoulder. "I would be honored if you would be at the helm of an advisory council comprising the elders in our pride. You all still have much wisdom to pass on, and as heir to the throne, it is my duty to learn as much as I can for the sake of our pride."

Mufasa nodded. "And that, my son, is the sign of a fine leader."

His father gestured to the outcropping that protruded from the front of Pride Rock. "Go and take your rightful place," Mufasa said.

Simba stood up proudly, his chest thrust forward and his head held high. Slowly, he walked toward the ledge. One by one, each member of their pride bowed in deference.

As he reached the edge of the outcropping, Simba surveyed the vast Pride Lands, marveling at the kingdom laid out before him. He was exactly where he was meant to be.

He was home.

He stood with and for his pride—all of them, even (or maybe especially) the lions who would disagree with him.

And he would help usher them all into a new dawn.

Rattle the Stars

What if Jim Hawkins joined the pirates?

by M. K. England

Rattle the Stars

What if Jim Hawkins joined the pirates?

by M. K. England

Jim Hawkins could deal with people who talked in their sleep. Everyone had their quirks, and on a ship crammed full of crew flying through space toward a planet that would make them all rich . . . well, there were plenty of quirks to go around. He could put up with a lot for the chance to lay his hands on the pirate captain Nathaniel Flint's legendary treasure trove.

He could *not* put up with sleep-talking in the Flatula language. Turned out, Jim had a limit, and that limit was a tentacle farting repeatedly and directly into his face as he slept.

Jim tumbled from his bottom-bunk hammock and landed in a heap, groaning the unhappy protest of the barely conscious. No point in trying to go back to sleep with all that racket, so he rolled over, his lean frame drowning in his oversized tan tunic, and pushed up to a sitting position. He ignored his black jacket, which had been a poor substitute for a blanket anyway, and grabbed for his boots, pulling one on in a half-asleep daze. He reached for his other boot . . . only for it to hop away, far out of his reach.

He sighed and ran a hand over his face, his sleep-tousled brown hair flopping into his half-lidded eyes. Too early. Not awake enough for games. Especially not games that involved a suddenly alive and hopping boot. He'd seen a lot of weird things so far on his voyage aboard the RLS *Legacy*, the solar galleon sailing them ever closer to fabled Treasure Planet, and many of those weird things had involved one particular creature.

"Morph?" Jim croaked, his throat dry from sleep. It had to be Morph, the ship cook's fist-sized pet blob of space goo, hiding inside the boot and making it hop away from him. The floating pink ball of irritation was too playful for his own good, funny to the point of becoming obnoxious. Like now. Of course, most things ranked significantly higher on the annoyance scale on scant few hours of sleep.

Jim had been up late that night, wallowing in grief and hating himself over the events of the afternoon. His brain kept replaying the horrifying scene over and over again: the nearby star going supernova, turning the space around them red-orange with fire and burning debris. All hands tying themselves to the mast to keep from being thrown from the ship during evasive maneuvers. The chaotic scramble to adjust the sails as Captain Amelia expertly guided the vessel through the calamity. The black hole that collapsed into existence in the former heart of the star.

And Mr. Arrow, Captain Amelia's stoic and loyal first officer, spiraling off into the void, his untethered safety line trailing in his wake.

Jim hadn't actually seen that part with his own eyes, but he could picture it all too well. If he'd only secured the ropes better, Mr. Arrow would still be alive. It had been his responsibility, assigned to him by Captain Amelia herself. *Make sure all lifelines are secured good and tight,* she'd said. And he'd done it, he'd swear on *anything* that he'd done it. But not well enough, apparently. Thanks to Jim, the boulder of a man was now a tiny crush of atoms at the center of a black hole.

Silver, the ship's cyborg cook, had found Jim up on the deck contemplating his worthlessness just a few hours earlier, before he'd managed any sleep. They'd started out as adversaries when the captain assigned Silver to show Jim the ropes during their voyage. It was babysitting duty, and they'd both known it. But before long, they'd developed a rapport. Silver taught him about ship work, and Jim learned and worked hard. They'd grown to almost like each other. And then had come the supernova, when they'd clung to the mast together, Silver's bulk shielding Jim from the raging fires as Captain Amelia sailed them to safety.

They'd lived. They learned that Mr. Arrow had not. They learned that it was Jim's fault. And Jim had crumbled.

When Silver had found him on deck earlier in the night . . . a flicker of embarrassment lit inside Jim's chest at the memory. But there was warmth there, too. Jim had been feeling lower than he ever had in his life, and Silver had said all the right things, even held him while he cried into the man's soft chest. It had been . . . soothing. Maybe even kind of like how it would be to have a father, Jim imagined. Not that he knew what that was like. His own father had ditched him and his mother so long ago he was barely a fuzzy memory. He was probably dead, for all Jim knew.

He wrenched his thoughts away from that old scar, from the new and fresh wound of Mr. Arrow's death, and focused on the immediate problem at hand: his escaping boot, and the mischievous little creature inhabiting it. Far easier to deal with.

"Morph, knock it off. It's too early for this," Jim droned, dragging himself across the room to where the Morph-boot had hidden behind a chest. He leaned over, ready to make a grab for it—only to receive a kick in the rear and a raspberry in the face as the boot shape-shifted into Morph, then darted away with the real boot grasped in his tiny pink limbs.

Jim gave chase, his gait uneven as he stumbled up the stairs leading out of the hold with only one boot on. His belt struggled to keep his wide-legged and far too large trousers from slipping, but it held on valiantly as he chased Morph from bow to stern. *Nothing wakes you up like a wild goose chase across an interstellar sailing ship. Or a wild . . . pink space goo chase?* Whatever. He was awake, but not quite awake enough for eloquent thoughts.

Jim recovered the boot not long into the chase, but only because Morph had abandoned it in favor of spitting water directly into Jim's face. Big mistake, though—a little cold water had been all Jim needed to finally wake up and pursue Morph in earnest. He cornered Morph in a small belowdecks storeroom, both of his boots securely on his feet where they belonged. With tiptoeing steps, he crept through the quiet, windowless room over to a barrel and peeked inside . . . then dove in headfirst.

"Ha, busted!" he said, capturing Morph in one hand and laughing as he fell all the way inside the barrel, miraculously not squishing all the juicy purple fruit stored inside. The little creature attempted to flee again and again, his tiny voice chittering with delight all the while.

Then a harsh, scraggly voice lowered to conspiratorial tones reached Jim's ears, along with footsteps on the stairs leading belowdecks. Jim froze, the laughter dying in his throat, and he gently covered Morph with his other hand to silence the little creature. As the voice neared, Jim strained his ears to listen.

"Look, what we're saying is we're sick of all this waiting," the voice's owner said. It was Birdbrain Mary, one of the crew members. Jim leaned closer to where light streamed through a two-inch-wide notch cut in the barrel, squinting to force his eyes to focus.

"There's only three of them left," another crew member said in his raspy reptilian voice. "We are wanting to move."

Then Silver's cyborg arm came into view, his voice low and menacing as he shook a balled-up fist.

"We don't move till we got the treasure in hand," he said.

Jim blinked in confusion. What were they talking about? Moving where?

Another voice provided terrifying elaboration.

"I say we kill 'em all now," said Scroop in a low, menacing growl.

Jim's blood ran cold. He hated that voice. Scroop scared the pants off him, if he was honest. And what did he mean, *kill 'em all*? Who was he planning to kill? And *Silver* was in on killing someone, just hours after he'd been comforting Jim over Mr. Arrow's untimely death? Jim blinked and looked again, just to confirm that he was really seeing whom he thought he was. But sure enough, it was Silver, with his cybernetic arm and leg, his long black coat wrapped around his large bearlike body, and a black tricorn hat on his head.

"I say what's to say!" Silver snapped, grabbing Scroop by his long, narrow face and shaking. "Disobey my orders again like that stunt you pulled with Mr. Arrow and, so help me, you'll be joining him!"

He lifted the spidery man off his six spindly legs and threw him straight into Jim's barrel hiding place. The whole barrel rocked, and Morph nearly escaped his grasp, but Jim managed to catch him tight between both palms, barely keeping his own panicked breathing under control. His stomach did a complicated flip as he processed the words he'd just heard.

Scroop killed Mr. Arrow.

Mr. Arrow's death hadn't been Jim's fault after all.

A crash of relief was immediately subsumed by a burning wave of anger. Jim hadn't failed to secure the ropes and caused Mr. Arrow's death. He'd been beating himself up for no reason. His tears and pain and self-hatred had been for nothing. Scroop had *murdered* the man.

And he'd deliberately blamed it on Jim.

Scroop landed out of Jim's line of sight, but the sound of six needle-thin legs *tick-tick*ed on the deck as Scroop got to his feet somewhere very near the barrel. Jim held his breath, holding as still as possible—and then his eyes went wide as one of Scroop's vicious crab-like claws dipped into the very barrel he was hiding in, right in front of his face.

"Strong talk," Scroop said as he felt around for a plum. "But I know otherwise."

"You got something to say, Scroop?" Silver asked as Jim frantically scooped up one of the soft purple fruits and held it up for Scroop to pinch between the points of his claw.

"It's that boy," Scroop rasped, his arm retracting from the barrel with the plum in his grasp. "Methinks you have a soft spot for him."

He pierced the plum with the knife-sharp tip of his claw, letting the dark juice bleed out as the other crew members rumbled their assent.

Jim's gaze stayed fixed on Silver, watching through the gap in the barrel for the cyborg's every reaction . . . and there was *something*. Blink and you'd have missed it, but his expression slipped for just a moment, a vulnerable point exposed. Fear, maybe? For himself, or for Jim?

Then Silver's eyes darkened, and every emotion Jim imagined he'd seen there flickered and died out.

"Now, mark me, the lot of ya," Silver said. "I care about one thing, and one thing only: Flint's trove. You think I'd risk it all for the sake of some . . . nose-wiping little whelp?"

Nose-wiping little whelp.

Was that what Silver really thought? A bolt of pain hit Jim square between his ribs, knocking the breath out of him, so intense he wondered for a moment if he'd been found and shot. He'd thought . . . earlier that night, he'd been sure Silver had *meant* the kind things he'd said. That Silver had maybe even started to care for him, just a little bit. Had he really read things so wrong?

"What was it, now?" Scroop continued, sneering. *"Oh, you got the makings of greatness in ya."*

Silver's face as they'd talked that night had been so earnest, his voice warm and parental and sure. If he had been acting, it was a really good act.

If he was acting right then, though, it was equally good.

What was the truth, and what was bluster? Could he be trusted or not?

"Shut your yap!" Silver said, sharp as the knife tipping his cyborg arm. "I cozied up to that kid to keep him off our scent. But I ain't gone soft."

His eyes, hard as pure steel, dared a single crew member to challenge him.

Then, a call from the lookout in the crow's nest: "Land ho!"

They had arrived.

Treasure Planet. Home to Flint's trove. Jim's map had led them true, but the finish line for their voyage was still ahead. A planet was a big place, after all, but the little golden orb that held the map would take them right where they needed to go. And only Jim knew how to open it.

That orb was currently locked in Captain Amelia's office for safekeeping and guarded by a contingent of two: Captain Amelia herself (cunning, fierce, an excellent shot) and the dog-faced astronomer Dr. Doppler (kind, doddering, of no use in a fight). Against sixteen pirates?

They'd be massacred. The mutiny would be all too easy.

And time was up.

The crew cheered, reptilian grins stretching and fleshy arms pumping the air in victory as they all flooded the decks above to get a glimpse of the double-ringed planet.

Everyone but Jim, who huddled in the barrel, struggling to process, Morph cupped in his hands.

You got the makings of greatness in ya, Silver had told him.

A lie. Or was it?

He let Morph slip from between his fingers, squeezing his eyes shut against the pain and humiliation. The little creature darted off to follow Silver to the main deck above, leaving Jim alone in the barrel.

Of course it had been a lie. Of course a man—a pirate, Jim realized—like Silver wouldn't be taking a useless boy like Jim under his wing.

He slipped out of the barrel, stumbling and dazed, rubbing a hand over his face to bring himself back to reality.

Kill, they'd said.

They were planning a mutiny, planning to kill everyone standing in their way. He had to warn Captain Amelia.

Jim made a break for it, rushing for the stairs, but was brought up short.

By a shadow. By the distinctive gait of Silver's cybernetic peg leg.

Oh, *no.*

Jim glanced around, frantically surveying the room for another exit, even briefly considering a leap back into the barrel of plums. The room was tiny, though, with no windows or other doors. He had about two seconds to make a decision. Trust Silver, or no?

With nowhere else to go, he stuck to his original exit plan, hoping to play it off like he'd only been belowdecks for a few seconds. Silver covered his surprise quickly, looking to either side for witnesses before continuing down the stairs, forcing Jim back belowdecks.

"Jimbo," Silver said with forced casualness, blocking the exit with his big ursine body. "Playing games, are we?"

"Yeah," Jim said, feeling a table bump against the small of his back. Trapped. He had to stall. "Yeah, we're playing games."

"Oh, I see. Well, I was never much good at games. Always hated to lose."

A barely audible click—the distinctive sound of a tool sliding into place on Silver's cyborg arm. And that decided it.

No matter what Silver's true feelings were, it was clear: he was willing to put them aside for greed. For Flint's trove. And he was apparently willing to put Jim aside by force, if needed.

That made Jim's decision much easier. He needed to do the same.

So, Silver hated to play games and lose?

Too bad.

"Hmm," Jim said, feeling behind himself for the curved scissors he knew were on the table. His fingers found the slender handle and wrapped around it, holding tight. "Me too!"

Then he lunged forward, left hand already held out to block Silver's pistol arm, and pressed his own blade to Silver's throat. The man's eyes went wide.

"Jimbo . . . what—" he began, but Jim pushed the scissors harder against Silver's neck.

"Now here's the way this is gonna go," Jim said, forcing his voice into a steady surety he absolutely did not feel. "I heard everything. I know all about your little mutiny plan."

One last gut check was in order. Was he really going to do this? Bullets of nervous sweat beaded on his forehead, but he doubled down, using all his willpower to keep the blade from shaking.

"I know what you're here to do," he said again, and slowly lowered the curved blade away from Silver's throat. "And I'm gonna help you."

Silver held his hands up and took a slow step back—then frowned as Jim's words registered.

"Now, Jimbo, you—wait, what?"

Jim slid one finger over the curved blade of the scissors thoughtfully, in what he hoped was a vaguely threatening manner. He'd never threatened anyone before, and it was probably painfully obvious. Hopefully his pitch would be good enough that it wouldn't matter.

"You heard me," he said, pointing at Silver with the scissors. "I know how to open the map. You need me. You need this ship to get down to the planet and haul off the treasure."

Jim took a step forward, closing the gap again, the blade always between them. "But you don't need Captain Amelia or Dr. Doppler."

Silver blinked. "Right. So . . ."

Jim took a breath to steady himself. This was the critical part. The make or break. He had to sell it with pure, blustery confidence.

"So you're going to let them go," he said, infusing as much assurance as he could into the words. "And I'm going to stay. We put them in a lifeboat and drop them off, then we head down to the planet and get rich."

Silver's mouth hung open in astonishment, the silence broken only by the sounds of the crew running about on the main deck above, chattering with excitement as they prepared the ship for the descent to the planet. After a moment, he shook his head, his voice gentling.

"Jimbo, this isn't you. You're not like me. You don't want to be like me. Last night, when we was talkin', I thought—"

Hurt flared in Jim's chest, and he lashed out in retaliation, letting every bit of his pain twist his face into ugliness.

"I'm sorry, did you think I had a soft spot for you?" he said, throwing Silver's words back into his face. "I care about one thing and one thing only: Flint's trove."

Direct hit. Silver's face fell, exposing that flicker of vulnerability Jim thought maybe he'd imagined earlier. Maybe everything Silver said on deck under the stars hadn't been a complete lie. Or maybe that was just what Jim wanted to believe.

Too late now, in any case.

Jim was committed. This path was for the best, either

way. The whole point of the journey had been to use the riches he'd find on Treasure Planet to rebuild his mother's inn. With her entire livelihood a burned-down wreck, she needed this from him. He had to get her that money, no matter what it cost him personally. And he'd still get to see the legendary Treasure Planet, too, like he'd always dreamed of as a boy.

Beyond that . . . who knew?

"Are you sure about this, Jimbo? The life of a pirate ain't what it's like in the storybooks. The crew is a rough sort, and they ain't like to take easy to ya. Our work is bloody, and you're certain ta get your hands a mite stained, being with us."

"Who said I wanted to stick around? Maybe I want to take my cut of the treasure and split," Jim said, though in all honesty he hadn't even considered it. Did he want to be a pirate? It wasn't exactly a life that his mom would be proud of. But there would be plenty of adventure, excitement, riches, and . . . a family, of sorts. A crew. Something to be part of. When he'd first met Captain Amelia, he'd thought that maybe he could find that with the Royal Navy. A ship and crew of his own, and the wide-open galaxy before him. The Interstellar Academy would never take someone like him, though. Was the life of a pirate really all that different?

"I s'pose that'd be your right," Silver said, shaking Jim out of his consideration. "We'll give you an equal cut—"

A startled laugh sputtered out of Jim.

"Equal cut? Like I'm just one of your regular crew? I'm the only one who can open the map. You're only on this ship because of me. The ship only made it to Treasure Planet because of *me*. I want twenty-five percent. And I have one more demand."

The corners of Silver's mouth tightened. "Careful, now. You're driving an awfully hard bargain here, Jimbo."

"It's not negotiable," Jim said, gesturing sharply with the blade. "Scroop has to pay for killing Mr. Arrow. I won't see the treasure shared with someone like him. I won't *reward* him for dumping an innocent man into a black hole . . . then blaming it on *me*."

Silver hesitated, considering.

"Are you sure, Jimbo? You know what you're asking for? There'll be no easy way out with Scroop. If he's off the job, then we can't let him live. If we were to dump him on some random planet, he'd spend the rest of his life hunting us—"

"It's him or me. That's the deal," Jim said flatly. "Besides, he was stirring up a mutiny against *you*, too, trying to convince everyone you'd *gone soft* over the *nose-wiping little whelp*. You really think you can trust someone like that at your back?"

Silver winced at that one, nodding to acknowledge the jab.

"You make a fair point there, Jimbo. Perhaps you're fit for this life after all," Silver said. "Scroop's been stirrin' up trouble fer as long as he's been part of the crew. Manipulative, that one is, and always looking for the chance to cut in on my leadership. Takes a sight too much enjoyment in being cruel, too, if I'm honest. Bit disturbing."

He rubbed his chin thoughtfully, then cut his eyes back to Jim and softened.

"You know, Jimbo, I . . ." His voice trailed off as he looked down and away. "I didn't mean what I said to the crew. I wouldn't have let them kill ye, but I couldn't let them be thinkin' that I wasn't up to the task of leadin' the crew no more. If Scroop took over, that'd be the end of ye, boy."

Silver rubbed a hand over his eyes, hiding his expression.

"I couldn't have that," he finally said.

"And you couldn't have them tossing you overboard before you ever got your hands on Flint's trove," Jim said with a frank stare.

Silver shrugged in acknowledgment. "Yeah, okay, that too. Benefits us both, me boy."

Above deck, the excited chattering rose in pitch and clamor, and Jim and Silver locked eyes. Time was nearly up.

"We have an agreement, then?" Jim asked.

Silver nodded and held out his non-cybernetic hand for a shake. "We have an accord. It'll be as you say. We'd better move now, though, 'fore that useless, feculent traitor Scroop gets the rest of 'em all riled against me."

Before he could think better of it, Jim strode forward and took Silver's hand, projecting all the confidence he could muster. He could always improvise later if he wanted out. Once the treasure was in hand and he had the money he needed to help his mom, he could decide for sure.

For now, Jim Hawkins was a pirate, and it was time to launch a mutiny.

"Follow my lead," Silver said, and he spun around on his peg leg and marched up onto the deck. Without a blink, he raised his cybernetic arm with the pistol attachment loaded up and fired the second he crested the stairs and had a clear shot.

Scroop fell to the deck, unmoving. Every single crew member froze, too, utterly silent as Silver stared them all down.

It was all Jim could do not to recoil in horror.

He'd asked for this. He'd signed Scroop's death warrant. And it was fair—a life for a life, a murder for a murderer. Wasn't it? Now that there was a dead man in front of him, Jim's sense of justice wavered. As did his stomach. Morph, apparently sensing his distress, flew down from his perch atop the sails and nuzzled into his neck. It took every ounce of Jim's self-control to keep his reaction in check as Silver stepped forward to address the crew.

"All right, you lot, change of plans," he called out, wrenching everyone's attention away from the smoke curling up from Scroop's chest. "We're moving now, and Jimbo here is joining us. Anyone got a problem with that?"

He glared around at each member of the crew, meeting every eye. No one spoke a word. He nodded.

"Good, because if you did, you'd be endin' up like Scroop there. Let that be a lesson to ye all. Someone get that scum overboard. The rest of you lot, take arms and follow!"

Everyone leapt into action, and Jim turned to Silver, unsure.

"What should I do?" he asked.

Silver held up a finger to Jim and called over one of his crew, a single-eyed alien named Blinko.

"Where are the captain and the good Dr. Doppler?" he asked.

Blinko snapped a salute. "They're in the captain's office, sir. Shall we take them out?"

Silver held up a hand. "Not yet. We have other plans. Prepare to break down the door on my command. The captain and doctor are *not* to be harmed, though. Spread the orders."

Blinko saluted again and scurried off to spread the word as Silver turned back to Jim.

"We need that map," Silver said. "We're going to send you in there alone first so you can get it."

He paused, studying Jim for a long moment.

"Last chance, Jimbo," Silver said, his voice grave. "Are you sure this is the choice you want to make? There's more'n one path outta this for you."

Jim forced himself to make eye contact and really, *really* look. Did he mean it?

From the corner of his eye, he could see the last of the

smoke from Scroop's chest dissipating, wispy curls disappearing against the blackness of space.

No. There was no turning back.

Jim took a deep breath, then nodded to Silver.

"I'm ready. Let's do this."

Jim burst through the reinforced door to Captain Amelia's office and locked it behind him, putting on an only partially feigned show of panic. No need to fake the pounding of his heart or the nervous sweat on his brow. Morph flew laps around his head as Jim pretended to gasp for air, gathering himself for the most important performance of his lifetime.

"Mutiny!" he panted, letting his expression go wide-eyed and frantic. "Pirates! The rest of the crew, they're—"

Jim broke off, breathing hard. Captain Amelia's feline face hardened into battle readiness, sharp as the precise lines of her uniform. No more words were needed. She made for the weapons locker in three quick strides, every move exuding grace, power, and purpose.

"Pirates on my ship? I'll see they all hang," she said, her pointed ears moving to stand at aggravated attention. She armed herself (and the doctor, to moderate success), then tossed the smooth golden sphere that was the map to Jim.

"Mr. Hawkins, defend this with your life."

Jim scrambled to catch it, then stared down at the map sphere in his hands.

Well, that had been easy.

The guilt twisted inside his chest as his eyes traced the intricate lines of the orb's surface. Captain Amelia trusted him so implicitly that she'd given it to him without a second thought. And he was about to betray that trust.

A startling *THUD* at the door sent all three of them whirling to face it. Outside, the sounds of shouting and pounding intensified, and a crackling sound preceded the smell of burning wood. They were right outside, cutting their way through.

All according to plan, Jim reminded himself. *Stick to the plan.*

"No time for the, uh, hanging, I think, Captain," Jim said, stumbling over his words. "Are there life rafts or something? Do you have another way out of here?"

"Of course I do. I always have a plan B," the captain said, then threw a glance at Dr. Doppler. "You won't like it, though."

"Oh, my, well, in that case, perhaps we should—" the doctor babbled, his doglike ears flapping with his distress, but Captain Amelia paid him no mind, pointing her gun at the deck and pulling the trigger several times. A sparking hole appeared, just large enough to admit Dr. Doppler's long snout, and the captain holstered the weapon at her side. "Follow me to the longboats!"

Jim let the captain and the doctor go through first, then jumped down with Morph following after, chittering his excitement. They were barely through the hole when the office door burst open to a chorus of cheers and shouts. Captain Amelia led them on a wild race through the ship's inner workings, under pipes and over bits of jagged machinery, the sound of Silver's crew mock chasing them not far behind.

Part of the plan, part of the plan, part of the plan, Jim chanted to himself as the clamor of their pursuers drew closer. He feigned a few stumbles to slow them down, not wanting to get too far ahead of his new piratical allies. All he needed was for the captain and the doctor to reach the longboats ahead of him. One final turn, and they burst into the dock, panting and exhausted. Captain Amelia slammed the door shut behind them and shot the locking mechanism with her laser pistol.

"To the longboats, quickly!" she shouted, pointing to a small boat dangling from a series of cables.

Jim couldn't get there before her, though. He needed her in the boat first if any of this was going to work. He spotted her turning toward the big double lever that would open the docking bay doors below the suspended boat, and he jumped to cut her off.

"I've got this, go!" he said, wrapping his hands around the handle and pointing to the boat. "The doctor has no idea how to get that boat ready."

"Good point," she said with a wry smile, and darted away, leaving Jim to heave at the lever with all his might. The door below the boat slowly began to retract with a series of grinding clanks as Captain Amelia somersaulted into the boat.

Then the pirate crew burst through the door.

Jim whirled to face the group, breathing hard as his muscles sang with adrenaline. Silver strode to the forefront of the group, coming face to face with Jim. After a heavy second, he detached a blade from his cybernetic arm and held it out for Jim to take.

"Go on, Jimbo. Make the cut," Silver said with a solemn expression. "It's got ta be you. Prove to the crew that you're one of us."

The pirates made a big show of firing back at Captain Amelia and Dr. Doppler, but they stuck to the agreement. The captain and the doctor were to survive this encounter. Everything was going to plan.

Jim took the blade from Silver just as Captain Amelia's voice rang out.

"Mr. Hawkins, to me!" she shouted, sighting down the barrel of a rifle. "I've got you covered!"

And there was a moment, a bare handful of seconds, where time seemed to stand still and Jim saw the choices laid out before him. It wasn't too late. He could cut the ropes and jump into the longboat. He could take the map and make the leap, joining the captain and the doctor. He didn't *have* to go through with the plan. He wouldn't get the money from the trove right away, but they could always come back for it.

But could his mother wait that long to rebuild the inn?

It was her only livelihood, her life's work, and the thing that had kept her going after Jim's dad had left. She needed it to *survive.*

And ultimately . . . did he even want to wait?

Jim looked to Silver for one last confirmation. The pirate gave the barest nod.

Jim swung the blade in a wide arc, slicing through the first set of cables that held the longboat aloft.

"I'm sorry. It's for the best," he called out to Captain Amelia and Dr. Doppler, unwilling to meet their eyes. "It's to keep you safe. I'll find you and pay you for the ship once we have the trove."

Captain Amelia caught herself on the railing as the boat lurched under her, suddenly held aloft by only a handful of ropes. Her brows knit in confusion, and she called up to Jim again.

"Mr. Hawkins, what are you—"

He cut through the last of the cables before she could finish.

The last things he saw as the lifeboat fell away were Captain Amelia and Dr. Doppler's astonished upturned faces locked on him.

The pirates gathered behind Jim and cheered as the longboat's sails caught and its engines fired, carrying it—and the last obstacles blocking them from Flint's trove—far into the blackness of space. Jim watched its sails until they were too far away to see, his heart aching.

He'd saved them. They would be okay. A bloodless mutiny.

Well, bloodless except for Scroop. The flash of the shot, the sound of Scroop hitting the deck, the curl of smoke . . . that image would be burned into his brain for a long, long time. Was that the sort of thing Jim would have to do if he continued to walk this path? Was there an option to be a pirate who didn't kill people, who stole only from those who truly deserved it?

But Scroop *did* deserve what he'd gotten. He did.

Jim would keep repeating it to himself until he believed it.

The rest of the crew retreated back to the main deck to prepare for landing, chattering excitedly. All but Silver, who stepped up next to Jim with Morph perched on his shoulder, watching the stars pass beneath them through the open bay doors.

They both let the long silence hang between them, leaving space for the clamor of the crew celebrating their victory. Jim barely heard any of it, his eyes still locked on the spot where Captain Amelia and Dr. Doppler had disappeared, and Silver's words from the night before ringing in his ears.

You gotta take the helm and chart your own course. Stick to it, no matter the squalls. When the time comes you get the chance to really test the cut of your sails and show what you're made of . . . Well, I hope I'm there, catching some of the light coming off ya that day.

And there they were, side by side. Jim had charted a

course he never would have imagined even a day before. The guilt was like a crushing weight in his chest. Seeing Captain Amelia's easy faith in him shattered had changed something fundamental inside Jim. And yet, there was something shining through the cracks, too. Something light, and free, and burning for adventure. The part of him that would soon hold a legendary treasure, present it to his mother, sweep away all her problems, and secure a future of some sort for himself, too. One of his own choosing and making.

"You're something special, Jim," Silver said in a low voice, breaking the silence. "You're going to rattle the stars, you are."

More empty words, or truth this time? Words worth staying for, worth choosing this life for?

Well. Maybe he'd stay, maybe he'd go in the end. Either way, he was free to make his own choice.

"Yeah, I am," he agreed. "I'm gonna be my own man. Watch me."

Silver laid a warm, paternal hand on his shoulder and gave him a pat, then left him to his thoughts, shouting orders at the retreating crew to prepare them for docking at Treasure Planet.

Adventure awaited. Excitement. Riches.

A new life, maybe.

"I'll never be what you want me to be," he murmured, thinking of his mom, his long-gone dad . . . and of Silver, too. "But I'm still here."

Alive, and ready, and making his own destiny.

His hands danced over the surface of the golden map sphere in his hands, unlocking it by instinct until the seams lit with green light and burst forth, projecting the map of the universe against the backdrop of vast empty space.

The whole of infinity laid out before him.

Jim smiled, cupping the universe in his hands.

A Royal Game of Chess

What if history wasn't quite *right about the legend of Robin Hood?*

by Liz Braswell

A Royal Game of Chess

What if history wasn't* quite *right about the legend of Robin Hood?

by Liz Braswell

"You know, there's been a heap of legends and tall tales . . . about Robin Hood. All different, too. Well, we folks of the animal kingdom have our own version. It's the story of what really happened in Sherwood Forest. . . ."

—ALLAN-A-DALE

"Lady Marian!" The maidservant burst into her room breathlessly, feathers literally flying. "They have caught Robin Hood!"

"What?" Maid Marian demanded, looking up from her hymnal. "But that can't be!"

"Aye, I'm afraid it is, lass," Kluck said grimly.

Both were silent for a moment. Then they burst out laughing.

A few days earlier:

A beautiful—if oversized—carriage slowly rolled down the only road through Sherwood Forest. It was pulled by two war elephants, retired from active duty and earning a little extra in their later days by hauling around folks who probably didn't deserve such treatment.

But the carriage: it was a gorgeous thing, with a golden body and purple damask curtains to keep the sun and flies out. Every square inch of the interior was padded thickly with velvet and stuffed with eiderdown. Crowning the whole structure was an actual crown, a replica of King Richard's, cunningly carved from wood and foiled in gold to look like the real thing.

Only . . . it wasn't King Richard riding in this stately manner. It was his younger brother, Prince John, along with his venomous, ever-present confidant, Sir Hiss.

"Sire, you have an absolutely amazing skill for encouraging contributions from the poor," Sir Hiss said (strangely enough, not hissing at all while he spoke).

St. Patrick might have drummed all the legless and scaly beasts out of Ireland, but this large and dun-colored representative of his genus was far too well connected to be so rudely removed from merry olde England.

Prince John smiled in a leonine way that was somewhere between a smirk and a warning yawn. "To coin a phrase, my dear counselor," he drawled, admiring his unvelveted claws, "rob the poor to feed the rich. Am I right? But tell me—what is the next stop, Sir Hiss?"

"Let me see . . . Oh! Yes. The next stop is Nottingham, sire."

"Aha! The richest plum of them all. Notting—*ham*. You see what I did there? It's a *ham*, because it's rich and fatty."

"Yes. Very droll, Your Highness. Your talents are endless. Driver! What's the holdup?" Sir Hiss stuck his very long, scaled neck out the window as the carriage slowed to a ponderous halt. The false king stuck his head out the other window in his impatience to see, much like a small child.

"Oh, Sir Hiss! It's a carnival—fortune-tellers! Oh, let us have our fortunes read!" The crown he wore—not quite the one duplicated on top of the carriage; even Prince John had his limits—tipped precariously on his undersized head with his excitement.

"Sire, this is not advisable. They could be bandits!" Sir Hiss narrowed his eyes suspiciously—which was in and of itself suspicious, since snakes have terrible vision in general. It was only for show. His forked tongue *did* flicker in and out, but it was unlikely he could taste the sort of colorful, drapey garments worn by the women waving at them from the middle of the road, or the sparkling crystals one of them held aloft.

Of course you know what happens next. One mystic praised and prattled to Prince John, snuggling up to him inside the carriage, the creakiness of her voice belied by the slender comeliness of her paws. Their deftness, as well: in short order the prince had lost several rings and even the brooch that held his voluminous sleeve back. And while she endlessly told Prince John what a magnificent future he would have, the other seeress slunk around the back of the carriage and handily retrieved several bags of gold.

Eventually the show was over and the carriage rolled on, a little lighter than before. It would be some time before Sir Hiss managed to convince his boss that they had been had.

The two fortune-tellers watched the prince go, barking fox laughter and slapping their knees at the idiocy of their marks. Finally, the leader flung a cloak around her body, disguising the disguise of her colorful clothes and silver stars.

"Here," she said, handing her coconspirator the rings she had purloined. "Take these to Little John; he can sell them in Mansfield without much suspicion. You've been there too often yourself to sell royal jewels—even criminal pawnbrokers can get suspicious. I'll go into Nottingham and distribute the coins now."

"Just be careful, Marian—I mean, *Robin*," the other fox said, his very masculine voice in stark contrast to the delicate threads he wore. "That old sheriff may be a dummy, but even a dummy gets an idea once in a while."

"I'm always careful, Red," Robin Hood said with a smile.

The two foxes kissed and scurried away to their separate businesses.

Robbing from royalty was always a lark, but in some ways *this* was the best part of the job: seeing the joy on people's faces when they received a little money with which to ease their burdens. The Sheriff of Nottingham had made his rounds right before the royal theft, collecting (extorting) taxes (random amounts; cash) from everyone in the shire. He had even taken the single farthing Mother Rabbit and her family were giving Skippy for his birthday! What sort of criminal did *that*?

"Well!" Robin Hood declared upon hearing the sad tale from the birthday boy himself. She threw off her cloak and fortune-teller costume. All the rabbits, mother included, clapped in joy upon seeing the handsome figure, complete with trademark hat and mask. "Here's a proper present for the young lad of the house."

The hero handed over a miniature bow and several small, neatly fletched arrows.

Skippy leapt about in delight over his new toy. Meanwhile, Robin drew Sis rabbit aside.

"I don't know when your birthday was, but here's an equally important gift to the young lady of the house." The fox handed her a tiny, sharp dagger with a pair of curves taken out of the metal just above the grip. "When I was your age . . . well, I was more into archery, of course. Not something a young lady was supposed to be engaged in. *This* is a throwing blade. Practice, practice, practice! And keep it in your bodice, love."

Sis's large, black rabbit eyes grew larger as she delicately took the dangerous thing, and even larger when Robin Hood winked and put a finger to the side of her muzzle.

"And now, I must be off!" Robin said with a dramatic bow. She swirled her "old beggar" costume cloak on, pulled a large ugly hat over the pretty, feathered green one, and swept out into the rainy, terrible day.

Skippy couldn't wait to try out his bow. Someday he would be just like his hero, but for the moment it was enough that all his friends, his own band of merry men, desperately wanted a turn and were already begging to be first. The game almost ended immediately, however, when the arrow flew satisfyingly, dramatically high—but off target—and through the Maidens' Gate, into the private side yard of the ladies of the castle.

Fortunately, the only person around was Lady Kluck. She was wandering about, muttering to herself and expertly bouncing a shuttlecock off the tip of her badminton racquet.

"Och, ye wee bairns," she said in delight and surprise upon catching sight of the (very inexpertly) sneaking children. "What are ye invading the castle for? Is it time for *rrr*evolution?"

"I lost my arrow," Skippy said both defensively and grumpily. "Robin Hood *himself* gave it to me."

"Oh-ho," Lady Kluck said. "Robin Hood *him*self. Well, then. I think I saw it go under the bush over there, ye wee thug."

While Skippy went to get his arrow (followed by a

more cautious Toby the turtle), Sis hung back, tiniest sister Tagalong hiding behind her.

"Is . . . uh . . . Maid Marian here?" Sis asked, looking hopefully around. "She's so beautiful!"

"Ah, no," Lady Kluck replied, also looking around—a little nervously. "She's, ah . . . in the . . . garderobe? Picking apples? Something that's not happening right *here*—but somewhere at the castle and absolutely normal. *Also*," she added, giving the young bunny a serious look from her left avian eye, "she's not *just* beautiful, you know, with her gowns and dresses and all. She's smart as a whip, and can whip anyone at—uh—badminton."

Sis felt the tip of her tiny dagger, thought of Robin Hood's conspiratorial wink, and wondered at this.

"OOOOOH, I hate that Robin *Hood*!"

Prince John stomped his feet and shook his—by then mostly ringless—fists in the air, throwing a truly epic tantrum in his solar (privately, without even guards around, because Sir Hiss made sure of that). "He has outsmarted us *again*!"

"Not much of an accomplishment there," Sir Hiss muttered. Something had occurred to him after the theft was discovered; he was currently flipping through the royal almanac, confirming his suspicions.

"Sire," he said more loudly, "have you noticed a pattern in Robin Hood's attacks?"

"They always cost me my precious jewels," Prince John moaned, sticking his thumb in his mouth. "Mummy would be so disappointed!"

"Yes, sire. Besides that, sire," Sir Hiss said impatiently. Maybe King Richard was the more stable, slightly more together brother—but maybe inbreeding among royalty had cost them *all* a bit more than they realized. The king had, after all, been incredibly easy to hypnotize and send to the east with the Crusades.

(Sometimes Sir Hiss thought about that and wondered about the asps and cobras and other poor folk who probably wound up having to deal with the nasty, warm-blooded European invaders. Ah well, not his problem.)

"Listen: Robin Hood's attacks on your royal self, and the treasury, and the taxes . . . they all occur when you're out on official visits, away from the castle."

"Well, of *course* they do, you ninny. When I'm in the castle, I'm safe from all the bandits and fortune-tellers. They can only get me out there."

"Yes, sire, but the *taxes* aren't always out there with you—they're with the sheriff, or in the middle of being transported elsewhere. And they still get stolen. All while you're away. And how did those fortune-tellers know to wait for you there on that road, that you were returning?"

"Well, I suppose that makes our next move exceedingly simple, then, you simple snake," Prince John said with a patronizing laugh. "Let us *pretend* to go somewhere and lay a trap for the hoodlum!"

"Sire," Sir Hiss said tiredly, "That might seem like a reasonable plan, but may I remind you that *none* of your, ah, 'reasonable' plans to capture him have worked out?"

"No, you may *not*," Prince John said, lifting the edge of his mouth and allowing just the slightest leonine growl to escape. "We are playing the long game. I'm very good at chess, you know. My royal mind always comes up with the most devious strategies. . . ."

"Why don't we just take extra precautions when you go out, sire?" Sir Hiss pleaded. "More war elephants and rhinosoldiers around the royal carriage, and more guards around the treasury, and—"

"Quiet, you ridiculous reptile!" Prince John reached out with a casual paw and cuffed him across the face.

It *hurt*, and Sir Hiss took a few nauseating moments to recover.

"This will work. Never doubt me. We will *say* we are leaving the castle, under some lovely, clever pretext. . . . Oh, I've got it!"

"My lady!" Lady Kluck burst into the room breathlessly, feathers literally flying. "They have caught Robin Hood!"

"What?" Maid Marian asked, startled. "But that can't be!"

"Aye, I'm afraid it is, lass," the fowl said grimly.

Both ladies were silent for a moment. Then they burst out laughing.

Eventually the old hen wheezed to a halt. "Prince John

claims that they caught a masked bandit on the outskirts of Sheffield, and it could only be Robin Hood. . . . So His Royal Highness is going to *personally* investigate."

"I can't even begin to decide what to think," Maid Marian said, shaking her head. "It's not like I *want* to be found out, mind you—I have so much more work to do. But really! Now completely random men are taking credit for my work—and being punished for it? I suppose I should pity whatever poor soul they think they have. Maybe it's a copycat."

"Copy*fox*," Lady Kluck corrected with a wink. "At any road, the prince and his sycophantic snake will be gone for a few days to investigate. Maybe it's a good time to . . . do some good?"

"Yes, absolutely!" Maid Marian turned her hymnal upside down and expertly flipped its pages until the trick book revealed her secret journal and almanac. "Let's see. The treasury carts are supposed to come in this week from Cornwall. That should be a good load. And as for the Sheriff of Nottingham . . ."

She suddenly frowned.

"What is it, my lady?" Kluck asked with concern.

"I was just thinking . . . *the sheriff*. And his guards, those loud vultures, Trigger and Nutsy . . . None of them can go anywhere without making a ruckus. But you know, I haven't heard a single noise from the stables and mews this morning. Or the barracks."

She rose gracefully, yards and yards of skirt and tippets not at all impeding her strong and lithe body. She leaned out the window, searching. "Surely if Prince John were preparing for a trip, there would be all sorts of shouts and complaints from the men."

"Och, you're right! What a clever thing you are!" Kluck said, lifting her own skirts to flutter up and perch on the sill. "There's neither hide nor hair of preparations going on."

"I'll bet there isn't any masked prisoner at all," Marian said with a smile. "Although I should still look into that. I wonder if he's even a fox."

"Speaking of foxes . . . have you seen much of Red lately?" Lady Kluck asked with a knowing waggle of her eyebrows.

"We had a brief unchaperoned moment at the last heist," Marian said with a dramatic sigh, clutching her "hymnal" to her chest and putting her other hand to her forehead. Then she laughed. "I do long for the day when we can spend all our time together, without hiding our feelings."

"Well, *that* can only happen when our rightful king is restored. Have you had any homing pigeons arrive today?"

"Not yet. We know nothing beyond what the last one said: that there was success in some campaign or other in the Holy Land. . . . What a waste of men and resources! The pigeon did seem to imply, however, that Richard finally understood the dangers back at home and would consider returning soon."

"From your muzzle to God's ears," Kluck said earnestly. "Has he gone again?"

"Not yet; he is taking a day or two with his family before

setting off. Seeing his mother, handing out little gifts to the children and all. Nuts and olives and desert sand taken just steps from where Mount Sinai is supposed to be!"

"Well, isn't that something," Lady Kluck said. "I should like to see the Holy Land myself someday."

"*I* should like to see this masked bandit they found up north," Marian said thoughtfully. "I'll bet he can't shoot as well as I."

Robin Hood did not rob anything for the few days that Prince John was "gone."

But the moment the prince and his small retinue "returned," an armed cart on the road from Cornwall met an unexpected fate.

Marian, resplendent in her peaked hat and mask, stood perfectly still on a tree branch up the road from the cart. No matter how the large branch swayed from the occasional breeze or curious young squirrel, her stance never faltered.

She *lived* for days like that, counting the hours down in her long gowns until she was free to aim her bow and arrow at the bad guys with abandon—and not have to pretend she and Lady Kluck were playing badminton in the lady's court.

The cart was light, basically a surrey pulled by a single elephant. Marian clucked her tongue sympathetically. Any idiot could see that there needed to be a second man—or woman—keeping a sharp eye out for thieves.

The fox raised her bow and took half a breath, aiming her arrow at the elephant's heart.

She tilted it up just a hair and let fly.

Twang. The arrow arced through the air and impaled the elephant's hat; the momentum caused both arrow and hat to tumble into the bushes.

The soldier looked up in dismay. But he did not immediately drop the yoke of the cart, which was impressive. This was an experienced veteran. He looked around suspiciously, and only once he determined there was no one else in sight did he begin to stomp angrily about, trying to find his magically disappearing hat.

Marian then let loose one of her special arrows: one that was dipped in pitch and aflame. It swirled like a comet and landed in a dry thicket of bracken.

She counted to five and then whistled like a grouse and leapt down from the tree. Keeping low to the ground, she scurried around bramble patches and over tuffets to the cart. She was quickly joined by two other shadows that emerged from other parts of the forest. The smaller one ran like she did, his namesake red tail swirling elegantly behind him like a flame.

(Very much less elegant, Little John had disguised his large body with piles of ferns stitched into the back of his coat; it really was uncanny how, when he stood still, you couldn't see him at all.)

All three had just made it to the cart when the bracken

finally caught, sending up smoke and flames with a sudden *whoosh.*

"What now?" the war elephant roared, spinning around. "Fairies? Pixies? I'm being haunted!"

With the guard now distracted, Little John used his massive paws to scoop the bags of money out of the cart and hand them to Red and Robin. As soon as each had as much as he or she could carry, all three hurried back to the safety of the woods, the elephant none the wiser.

"Ha ha! That was a good one!" Red crowed as they threw down their loot. "Not a hair on that giant's head harmed, and we've as good as cleared him out of all his cash!"

"Old Prince John ain't gonna believe it this time," Little John said, and the two bumped their hips together in boyish delight.

"He may, though, at that," Marian said. Her foxy smile had slid away as she sliced open the top of the first bag and saw what lay within.

Sand and gravel and rocks tumbled out onto the ground like spoiled milk.

"Like sand from the Holy Land," she murmured.

Red and Little John stopped their goofing around and gaped at the sight.

Then Red laughed, a good-natured, throaty bark. "Oh, he got you good, there. The prince is way ahead of you. Checkmate!"

"That's no work of Prince John," Little John said with

a growl. A single swipe of his paw was enough to tear open the rest of the bags. Sand and grit spilled from them as well. "That's Sir Hiss right there. He's the only one with half a brain among them."

"I don't believe this," Marian said. She had already planned where the money would go, what good it would do. The orphanage, Friar Tuck's poor box . . . "Those poor hungry children!"

"Oh, Mar—uh, Robin," Red said, putting an arm around her shoulder. "So he got you this time! Let it go. Had to happen someday. We'll just get him where it hurts next time."

"*Twice* as much," Little John promised with a wink.

"All right," she said, taking a deep breath. "*Next* time, then, merry men of mine!"

As if to add insult to injury, no one even questioned where Maid Marian had gone that day. Lady Kluck was prepared to answer in terms neither Prince John nor Sir Hiss could refute: that the maiden was ill abed with *women's difficulties.* But nobody cared.

Perhaps that was because everyone—even the otherwise terrifying rhinosoldiers—was using all their energy to avoid the prince and his latest tantrum.

His shrieks could be heard throughout the castle; his claws had already torn through a priceless Norman wall tapestry. Maybe Sir Hiss shouldn't have said *I told you so* quite so many times—or even once. But eventually the fanged consigliere succumbed to fear and weariness. While trying to untie himself from a particularly painful and annoying sheepshank knot the prince had tied him in, the snake found himself unknowingly echoing Red's own words.

"Yes, we didn't catch him this time, sire. Despite your *very clever* plan." He flexed various parts of his very long rib cage, trying to see where the skin would give the most while tearing the least. "But on the other hand, he didn't manage to steal anything—thanks to, ahem, *my* plan. I would call this a draw. We'll get him on the next turn."

"A *draw*? I don't want a *draw*!" Prince John roared. All right, perhaps it was closer to the howl of an injured cub than the territorial call of a full-grown male lion. "I want to *win*, Hiss! What would Mummy think if I lost to a stupid *fox*?"

Personally, Sir Hiss didn't think Robin Hood was all that stupid. In fact, he seemed to be even cleverer than most foxes, and that was saying something.

"We need something to draw him out into the open . . . something where he will have no chance of escaping," the lion said thoughtfully after a blissful moment's silence.

"Or," Sir Hiss ventured, finally able to pull his tail out of the knot, "we can keep going with the deliveries of fake bags of gold and extra guards and—"

"Rubbish." The prince slammed a meaty paw down on the table where Sir Hiss struggled. Everything shook, including the reptile's heart. A lesser lion he might have

been compared to Richard, but John was still an apex predator who could easily smash almost any animal to a bloody pulp. "We will lure him out into the open with something he cannot resist. . . . He just *loves* showing off, doesn't he? He can't just hold a guard at dagger point; he has to do all of those tricks with his bow and arrows, and . . . That's it!"

His yellow eyes lit up; he slapped his paw on the table again.

"We'll have an archery contest! Yes, he won't be able to resist that! And I have just the prize!"

"Bags of actual gold to hand out to the poor?" Sir Hiss asked warily, unthreading himself through the final loop. He sagged in exhaustion and relief.

Prince John stuck his head into the snake's face and grinned.

"A kiss from our own beautiful fox, Lady Marian! No warm-blooded fellow could resist such a reward!"

"Your niece?" Hiss asked, aghast. "That seems . . . inappropriate. And what if Robin Hood doesn't win? What if it's the sheriff, or some other lowbrow?"

"Robin Hood will win. Don't be daft," the prince said, turning away, already thinking about other things. In his mind, the whole thing was already decided and practically carried out.

"A kiss from *me*?" Marian demanded in outrage. "What am I, a doll or puppy to be handed around?"

Lady Kluck looked at the poster with a critical eye.

"Why, yes, you are. That's the problem with being a Lady and not a Sir, you know. Is it just me, or is this whole to-do a setup to catch Robin Hood?"

"Now you're thinking like a fox. Of *course* it is," Marian said, looking out the window glumly. "And I can tell you for certain that Robin Hood *would* win the contest. And she should. *I* should win the kiss from *me*."

Kluck chuckled and rolled up the parchment that advertised the contest. "Well, I think that might be a tetch difficult to arrange . . . and even if we could somehow pull it off, the jig, as they say, would be up. You have an important job, Missy. There's folks who depend on you. To not *starve*, you know, and to keep the hope of King Richard's return alive."

"I know, I know." Marian sighed and straightened up, patting down her skirts. "I was just being self-indulgent for a moment. Someday, though, I shall be free of this castle, to live my life in the woods with Red and my fellow merry men."

"Even with good Richard's return, I don't know if it's going to work out p*rrr*ecisely like that," Lady Kluck said delicately. "It may be that one of your outlaws winds up as one of his *in*-laws . . . and comes to live in the castle with *us*."

"Well, that would still be something," Marian said with feeling.

The couple's time together alone was almost never just alone time. Either the two foxes were plotting their next heist with the other Merry Men—Friar Tuck, Little John, and the rest—or they were training. No longer a little girl whose whimsical pursuits could occasionally be excused, Marian had to practice in secret, far from the castle. And there was no more skilled archer to compete against than Red! Every day was an adventure with him.

But Marian also longed for the quieter times, like when they managed to spend an hour or so just sitting by the fire, talking quietly and playing chess.

The afternoon of the contest was bright and not too windy, a perfect day for archery. Punch and cyser were served, and the populace was encouraged to drink up and toast the health of Prince John. Some did without meaning their words; some spat immediately thereafter; a few muttered "To good King Richard" into their tankards and under their breath.

A smaller range had been set up for children; the winner of that contest would also get a kiss from Maid Marian (*Yuck,* thought Skippy), as well as a bag of sugared nuts. Allan-a-Dale, the minstrel, wandered around with his lute, singing popular songs—along with one or two borderline revolutionary tunes that drew frowns from the royal guards.

"This is all so exciting," Marian said as convincingly as she could, leaning forward in her seat in the royal box. And to be fair, she *was* looking forward to seeing Red out in the open, in public. He was not as good a shot as she, but certainly the best of the lot there.

"Mmm, it *is* a rather propitious day," Prince John said with a sly look at her. "Tell me, my dear—is there anyone . . . any*thing* you're looking especially forward to seeing?"

"Well, I would be lying if I said I *wasn't* hoping to catch a glimpse of Robin Hood," she said coyly.

"Yes, my dear, of course, we are *all* looking forward . . . to *catching* him."

He snorted and elbowed Sir Hiss. "Did you hear that? That was a good one."

"Yes, Your Highness, very good, Your Highness," Sir Hiss said, only half paying attention. Suddenly his eyes widened. "Look, sire—aren't those some of Robin's Merry Men over there?"

A bear in the ridiculous getup of a peasant with a beak (cassowary, maybe? Emu? Some other giant flightless bird?) was ambling toward them with another very fake-looking bird (stork, or maybe he was supposed to be a plague doctor, with his long nose). This smaller "bird" went to enter the contest; the larger one approached the prince.

"Well, hold my hat and call me mother! Is that the handsome Prince John *himself*?" the creature squawked.

"Sire . . . beware . . ." Sir Hiss hissed.

"Oh, nonsense, you suspicious snake," Prince John said, preening a little. "I am indeed he."

"My word! Isn't this the thrill of a lifetime," the . . . cassowary . . . said as he sat down comfortably next to the flattered lion. Sir Hiss continued to hiss; the prince continued to ignore him.

Horns sounded; the contest began. Trigger and Nutsy had a nephew vulture who made a fair shot: within the red, but no bull's-eye. Several professional huntsmen did moderately well. But it was obvious to all watching that the only real competitors were the Sheriff of Nottingham and the stork bird thing.

(Though the stork's chances in the next heat did not look incredibly hopeful, judging by the width of Captain Crocodile's toothy smile when he made the announcement.)

"And here I was thinking that all the sheriff knew how to do was scare poor old beggars and intimidate the pious," Deacon Mouse huffed to Friar Tuck. Everyone from the church sat together in the front row and shared a bag of fry cakes. "I had no idea he had any actual skill in bow and arrow."

"Well, he's not bad, but he's no Robin Hood," the large badger replied without thinking. "Ehm, not that I would know, bless me. But I've heard stories."

The sheriff nocked and loosed his arrow . . . but it was hard to see what happened next. Later, some people claimed they saw the target *move* and adjust itself to the arrow's position. Whatever the case, the sheriff scored a bull's-eye.

The stork, despite being shoved by the sheriff just as he let go of the string, *also* managed to get a bull's-eye. His arrow whacked the other one clean off the target.

"He did it! He beat the sheriff!" Friar Tuck shouted, leaping up. His robes billowed around him like the petals of a flower. The crowd clapped and cheered; everyone stamped their feet.

"Only Robin Hood could make a shot like that!" Prince John cried.

"I beg your—" Marian started to growl.

"I claim my prize," Red yelled, dispensing with his disguise. He rushed forward and leapt up to kiss Marian.

"Run, you fool!" she said, laughing—but she kissed him back.

"Now! *MEN!* Seize this fox!" yelled the prince.

Captain Crocodile and his men rushed for Red—and Little John, and anyone else who was cheering in defiance of Prince John.

Marian leapt up from her seat and looked around. Everything was in chaos; here was her chance! She could run away with Red, forever! No one was watching. . . .

"Come along, my lady, it's not safe." A hippo guard grabbed her by the arm, and the prince gestured impatiently for them to hurry.

All Marian needed to do was sink her teeth into the guard's wrist. Her canines were long and sharp, and even if they didn't puncture his leathery hide, it would probably be enough of a surprise to make him release her. And then she would be free! A happily ever after in the wilds, fighting for justice until good King Richard came back.

But . . . she was not Robin Hood just because of her skill with a bow and arrow. She was also clever, gifted in strategy, and last but not at all least, on the *inside* of things happening at the castle.

This was what she saw in the two seconds while she debated what to do:

Friar Tuck, being picked up bodily by a rhino. Mother Rabbit's youngest child—Tagalong, was that her name?—crying alone in the dirt. Soldiers running rampant among the good folk of Nottingham.

As Robin Hood, she could rob from the rich and give to the poor. She could occasionally attempt rescues with derring-do. But once she had thrown her lot in with the Merry Men for good, she was Robin Hood for life. And there were some things only Marian could do, like send communiqués to good King Richard and keep track of Prince John's plans and whereabouts.

She let herself be pulled away.

As the guards solicitously helped her through the crowd, they passed the children's archery range. Marian couldn't help it. She grabbed a toy bow left behind in the confusion and let fly a tiny arrow before the guard even noticed.

Only a couple people saw—and refused to believe they saw—a child's brightly feathered arrow go whizzing through the air . . . and then split the winning arrow down to its point, deep in the winning bull's-eye.

Sir Hiss waited anxiously for the prince to decide whether this was a win or a loss, or a draw. On the one hand, they had captured a number of Merry Men—or at least people known to associate with them, like Friar Tuck. And using their traitorous behavior at the contest as an excuse (clapping for the *enemy*, no less!), the royal treasury had tripled taxes upon the rest of Nottingham. The same people who had been cheering for the fox stork thing were now sad and voiceless, having lost their religious leader, their money, and any hope for the future. So that was fun.

On the other hand, the guards hadn't actually captured Robin Hood himself. Little John was locked up along with his friend Red, which was almost as good, but not quite.

"He will come—he *has* to come, to rescue his friends, whom we are going to execute at dawn," the prince growled. "Set up the gallows forthwith!"

"You can't execute Friar Tuck!" Hiss squeaked. "He is protected by the church!"

"I can do whatever I want. I'm the prince."

Hiss started to disagree, then thought better of it. He was just recovering from his boss's previous punishments and didn't want any more bruises.

"If Robin Hood doesn't come . . . well, that's a few more traitors to the crown we'll be without. We can even place their bodies on pikes outside the walls as a warning, like the Britons used to!" Prince John clapped his paws in delight.

Actually, that probably *would* quell any incipient anti-crown desire to insurrection, Sir Hiss thought. Not the actual worst of his daft noble's ideas. Still, things would be much more efficient and far less messy if he could just hypnotize the prince.

"Check and mate to Robin Hood, Your Highness," he muttered, biting his own snaky tongue to keep from saying anything else.

Trigger, Nutsy, and even the sheriff led their own battalions of soldiers that night, preparing for the inevitable rescue attempt. Hippos marched back and forth atop the castle walls; war elephants paraded in the bailey. Rhinosoldiers used their own massive bodies to barricade all possible entrances to and exits from the castle: drawbridge, kitchen door, garderobe pit, side stables. Sometimes a vulture would take to the air, glide around, and light in a nearby tree, keeping keen eyes peeled for trouble. Captain Crocodile strode up and down the hallways with a crossbow, looking resplendent as his red cape flowed out behind him.

"There is *no way* he can get into the castle," Prince John said smugly.

"It seems to be pretty tight," Sir Hiss grudgingly admitted. "Our spies on the ground, the stealthiest minks and otters, haven't seen a thing in the woods. The village is quiet."

"Just you wait," the lion said, rubbing his paws together like a child at Christmas. "This is going to be a doozy."

Deep in the darkest, dankest dungeons, a strangely similar conversation was taking place.

"Robin Hood will rescue us," Little John said confidently. His weight bowed the only bench in the dingy cell, and he had to be careful not to fling his paws out when talking, for fear of literally taking someone's head off. Huddled around him in various stages of despair and sadness were the motley group of peasants, Merry Men, and innocent bystanders the prince's guards had rounded up.

"I don't know," Deacon Mouse said sorrowfully. "I don't know how *anybody* could, with us all the way down here. And all those guards between us and them up there."

"Oh, nonsense," Red said, whirling his hand in the air. "Those guards are *nothing* for Robin Hood. They're dust and twigs—easily dispensable foes."

"He'll do it, don't you worry," Friar Tuck said. "You'll see—it'll be spectacular. Why, I can't wait to see all the cling-clanging and swordplay!"

As a matter of fact, at that very moment Robin Hood was hurrying down the back stairs of the castle to the dungeon, dressed in a scullery maid's rags, with a basket of baked treats instead of a sword.

Despite the careful defense of the castle itself, there were only a few rhinosoldiers positioned by the prison cells; the prince's plan was focused less on guarding the captives and more on capturing his enemy. When it was time to change watches, the bored and grumpy rhinos did it immediately, with all the eagerness of underpaid bullies.

That was when she planned to sneak the key to the

prisoners, while distracting the grunts with ale and sweet buns she had brought with her. How surprised they would all be, undone quietly with a snack, and no swordplay at all. . . .

Although a clever gamer always thought several steps ahead, an even cleverer Robin Hood should have known better than to drift into thought while actively infiltrating enemy territory.

"Girl! What are you doing?"

A surprised voice scratched irritatingly on the ears of an equally surprised Marian. Slithering silently *up* the stairwell was Sir Hiss, flowing like backward water. He stopped; his snaky eyes narrowed in confusion as his tongue flickered in and out, testing the air.

"No, you're no servant girl . . . you're Maid *Marian*!" he said in shock.

Marian gave a silent curse. She had disguised her body and covered her scent, but snakes had senses that were different from everyone else's: taste and smell were all mixed together, and they could somehow detect heat. Like bloodhounds, but stranger. Of all the luck to meet him here!

"I was just going to offer some refreshment to our poor overworked guards," she said, holding up the basket.

But his quick eyes immediately saw the dull flash of bronze she tried to palm away: the key to the jail cells.

"My lady," he drawled, slithering close. "You're not trying to help the prisoners escape, are you?"

"Oh, not at all," she said, trying not to look him directly

in the eye. It was known that he had powers over the mind, though the details about it were sketchy.

"Mmm-hm." The snake nodded, beginning to circle her. "No doubt your poor gullible uncle would believe you. *I* don't. Everyone knows your sympathies don't lie with our beloved Prince John. Everyone knows."

"Sir Hiss, I must protest. I have no idea what you're talking about." Marian rose up on her toes into a fighting stance, ready to drop the basket and grab her dagger—a bigger, less aerodynamically sound one than she had given Sis.

"Maid Marian . . . could it *be*," Sir Hiss drawled, looking like he had suddenly thought of something. "Could it be that—no, could it? That *you* . . . are . . ."

Marian braced herself, ready to fight. The game was over.

". . . secretly *aiding* Robin Hood?"

She almost didn't react at first.

Really? Even the supposedly intelligent Sir Hiss? Could he not put two and two together?

For heaven's sake!

For more than one reason, she pulled back and kicked him solidly where she thought his stomach might be.

Sir Hiss gasped, all the air going out of his lungs and prodigious windpipe.

But he recovered almost instantly, lashing out with horrific speed at her muzzle.

Marian ducked to the side; he struck the wall beside her. She quickly grabbed his thick midriff, clutching him tight. Then threw them both down the stairs, making sure that the snake's head hit each step as she dragged him along.

While he was stunned, she quickly took his tail and lashed it around the railing.

"Not . . . a sheepshank . . ." Sir Hiss begged weakly.

"Long live Robin Hood!" she whispered into where she supposed his ear was.

She hurried down the rest of the steps, panting, her heart racing. That little mistake had cost her several precious moments—the guards were already changing watches, grumbling and gossiping and about to wrap it up.

Red spotted her immediately; his eyes lit up, but he pointed at the guards. They were already getting into position. As quickly and as silently as she could, Marian dropped the key to the ground and kicked it under the door to him.

"I'm going to distract them," she whispered. "While I do that, quietly make your way to the empty jail cells to your left. No one will think to look for you still in prison! Lady Kluck will come along in a bit and lead you all to safety."

"I'll stay with you!" Red whispered back. "And give a couple of the guards the what-ho!"

He made a swishing, swordy movement with his paw.

"You will do no such thing," Marian said with a smile—but a steely nip in her tone. "Escape for everyone only works if we keep it quiet. Not even the three of us together could fight our way past all the guards stationed around the castle. Stick with the plan, soldier."

"Aye aye, captain!" Red said with a bow. "Your word is as good as done."

"Maid Marian! Is that *you*?!" the mousewife whispered hopefully, clambering around Red's tail to get a better view. "Did Robin Hood send you to save us?"

"No, blast it! *I* . . ."

Marian looked helplessly at Red. He shook his head and shrugged, trying not to smile.

"He works in mysterious ways," Friar Tuck said with an apologetic wink to the sky.

"Yes, Robin Hood sent me," she said, giving up. "Now count to ten!"

She approached the guards obviously and loudly, swinging her basket.

"Sustenance for the long night ahead," she said in a sweet purr. "A gift from . . . Sir Hiss."

The rhinos' eyes lit up almost as much as Red's had upon seeing her, and they grabbed the rolls—muttering deep-voiced thank-yous as they did, however. They weren't complete animals. Marian's large fox ears twitched at the nearly silent scurry of the prisoners out of their jail cell and into the next one.

The legend of Robin Hood grew by furlongs that night. As soon as it was discovered that Red, Friar Tuck, and everyone were missing, the castle erupted in chaos. Every spare man and woman was sent to comb the woods and search the shire and scour the roads and beat the bushes . . .

. . . while the prisoners were quietly and calmly led out of the castle through the Maidens' Gate. To Prince John and the outside world, it seemed like black magic.

To the released prisoners, it was, perhaps, a little less exciting than what they had hoped for: a show of swordplay and some bad guys' heads getting knocked in. But at least they were free.

"Nooooooooo!"

Sir Hiss stuck his throbbing head deep into a bucket of cool water as his prince howled mournfully the whole night long.

"Next time Robin Hood shows up, he's going to steal me away, I think." Marian decided, watching the skies outside her window for more homing pigeons from the east. She was safe, for now; Sir Hiss's mind was still addled from the blows she had given him. He didn't quite remember what had happened, though he did look at her mistrustfully now. She just smiled back and batted her long eyelashes.

"Yes, I think I'm done here. Next heist, we'll say Robin Hood rescued me from my life of embroidery and prayers."

Lady Kluck rolled her eyes, knowing she wasn't serious. The prince would recover from his sulk soon and come up with another ridiculous plan to tax the citizens and catch Robin Hood. And there would always be more treasuries to rob, and wrongs to right.

At long last King Richard returned. Marian and Red

were finally able to marry, to everyone's delight—if with a little muttering from royal relatives. Robin Hood was never captured, dead or alive.

But when it was clear that justice had been restored to the land by its rightful king, and all usurious taxes lowered, he *did* disappear for a while.

"Maybe not forever, though," Marian said, carefully folding up her mask and putting it in a chest to hide under the bed. "Kings don't live forever, and I may be of use again someday."

"I do hope so," Red said with a yawn from the goose-down bed they now shared in the castle. "I certainly can't stand all this living in luxury. It's unbearable."

Marian had her paw on the lid of the chest, ready to close it. Next to the mask, nestled in protective cloth, were a dozen sharp-tipped arrows, a bottle of pitch, and other bits and bobbles from Robin Hood's bag of tricks.

She looked up at Red.

He raised his eyebrows questioningly at her.

She grinned and reached for the mask.

The Secret Exchange

What if Eric met Ariel after she rescued him?

by Elizabeth Lim

The Secret Exchange

What if Eric met Ariel after she rescued him?

by Elizabeth Lim

Ariel had never understood why humans feared her father, the great sea king. Why they prayed to him for safe passage across the ocean, or spoke of him in hushed tones, as if he might be listening from the depths of Atlantica.

Then she witnessed the storm.

It came upon the sky without warning, a crack of lightning tearing apart the clouds. At once, powerful winds gathered, and the sea began to howl, waves churning with such strength that Ariel had trouble floating above the surface.

Terror filled the sailors' faces. Only minutes ago they'd been dancing about the ship deck making music as they celebrated their prince's birthday. In an instant the time for revelry was over, and the sailors ran across the deck, firing shouts at one another to "stand fast" and "secure the rigging!"

The storm was relentless. Wind and rain rocked the ship. It careened against the sea's tumultuous waves, and it seemed the sailors' fight couldn't get worse.

A bolt of lightning suddenly struck one of the sails.

Ariel gasped as the flames burst across the sail, traveling swiftly. For so long, she'd been curious about fire. She'd seen pictures of it and imagined a hundred times what it must look and feel like.

But her imagination hadn't come close. The flames were bright and orange, like a beautiful flower. She could feel its heat even from the sea. It traveled swiftly, mercilessly devouring everything it touched. And it grew! Soon it was everywhere, and the only thing the sailors could do was evacuate.

Fighting the current, Ariel swam closer to the ship. Searing sparks flew into the air, and chunks of wood and scraps of cloth fell into the ocean, but Ariel kept going. She had to help. She'd do her best to save any of the humans who might need her, but most of all she was worried about the handsome young prince who had been on the ship: Prince Eric.

She'd been watching him all evening, unable to take her eyes off the way his blue eyes smiled whenever he spoke to anyone in his crew, how his head tilted in concentration when he played his snarfblatt, how his gaze wandered to the sea whenever he thought no one was looking.

The sailors had lowered a rowboat into the water, and

she scanned the faces aboard. She felt like she knew them, had listened to the sweet sound of their names and memorized their faces. There was the old man who'd been with Eric—Grimsby—with several of Eric's friends and even his dog, Max. But where was Eric?

Last she'd seen him, he'd gone back to the ship to rescue Max.

Then a thunderous explosion rocked the ship. Dread rose to Ariel's throat.

Not wasting a moment, she swam toward the wreckage, searching, searching. There! His body was floating against a broken panel of wood. It seemed he was unconscious and barely holding on.

As he slipped into the sea, Ariel dove. She wrapped her arms around his waist and pushed for the surface.

It was dawn when they reached shore, and the storm had finally receded. Ariel gently laid the prince on the sand, and she brushed his dark bangs from his face.

A seagull landed at her side, his familiar face a comfort as Ariel hovered over Prince Eric.

"Is he . . . dead?" she asked Scuttle.

The bird pressed his head to the prince's foot, listening earnestly. "I don't hear a heartbeat."

"No, look, he's breathing!" Ariel exhaled in relief as she watched the rise and fall of Eric's chest. "He's . . . so beautiful."

She'd never been so close to a human before. Her father

despised them and forbade contact between Atlantica and the world above. She wasn't even supposed to go to the surface. But ever since she could remember, she'd been fascinated with the world above the sea. What she wouldn't give to meet and become friends with a human, to get the answers to her burning questions about dancing and running, and to see the items she'd collected in her grotto in actual use.

She turned to Eric, smiling as his cheek warmed to the touch of her hand. He was starting to stir.

"What are you gonna say to him?" Scuttle pressed. "This is your chance."

Ariel was torn. She had a million questions to ask, and she wanted nothing more than to talk to him. But part of her was hesitant. Her father's warnings rang inside her.

Humans are dangerous! King Triton had cautioned his daughters. *They are trouble!*

Eric didn't look like trouble. Beyond the handsomeness of his face—his strikingly pale blue eyes and endearing smile—he looked kind and good-natured. She'd seen the way he'd put his own life in danger to save his dog from the burning ship. How could he be bad?

Ariel touched his cheek again. He was peacefully asleep, and she knew she ought to leave before he saw her. But a part of her wanted him to remember something about her, even if he never saw her face or learned her name.

A song bubbled up to her throat, a melody she sang to herself whenever she yearned to explore more of the world that wasn't hers. Going by the party she'd watched on Eric's ship, it seemed they liked music on land, too. Perhaps it was something a mermaid and a human might have in common.

As she sang, Eric's eyes fluttered. Ariel could see her reflection in his pupils and gently broke off her song. It was time to go.

A dream, she thought, letting go of his cheek. *You'll remember me as a dream.*

"Goodbye, Eric," she murmured, knowing he wouldn't hear. She twisted to leave and darted quickly for the sea.

But behind her, Eric was already half up.

"Wait," he called.

Ariel hid behind a rock.

"Ariel," her best friend, Flounder, said nervously. "Can we go yet?"

"You first," Ariel whispered. "I'll just be a minute."

"Please," called Eric as Flounder dove into the water's depths. "Your voice, it's . . . it's beautiful. Did you save me?"

Ariel froze, unsure if she should follow her friend or wade further into this uncharted territory. Finally, she peeked around the rock. Eric was staring at her, open-mouthed. She gave the barest nod.

"Thank you." Eric touched his heart. He looked just as nervous as she was. "What's . . . what's your name?"

Her father was going to kill her for this. She bit down on her lip, but she couldn't ignore the connection she felt with this human. She liked him.

"I'm Ariel," she said.

"Ariel," he repeated. "That's beautiful, too."

The prince's friends were shouting in the distance. Ariel shrank behind the rock. It was one thing for Eric to see her, but multiple humans?

Eric stepped into the water, his eyes filled with urgency as though he knew they didn't have much time left. "Can I see you again, Ariel?" he asked.

She smiled, then nodded shyly.

Without another word, she leapt into the sea, her heart buzzing with excitement.

Back in Atlantica, Ariel couldn't contain the whirlwind of emotions that coursed through her. She had saved a human! The most beautiful and kind and wonderful human she had ever seen. And she'd spoken to him.

"Eric," she whispered, her stomach fluttering like butterfly fish. "When am I going to see you again?"

She plucked a flower from one of the reef beds and rolled onto her back as she giggled to herself. It'd only been a few days, but every minute she had to wait until she was back on the surface again felt like forever. Was Eric waiting for her already? He'd said he wanted to see her again.

The only thing slowing her down was Sebastian, the court composer—and her father's most trusted advisor. The crab had intercepted her during her return home, and for the hundredth time, was practically begging her not to go back to the surface: "This will be our secret," he said, over and over. "No one is going to know."

"Oh, stop panicking, Sebastian," said Ariel to the crab. "Daddy's not going to find out—so long as you don't say anything."

"*I'm* not saying anything," Flounder said proudly, doing little flips.

"It won't be easy keeping a secret like this for long," Sebastian muttered. "Look at you, with your head in the clouds instead of in the water where it belongs!"

Ever since she had missed performing in Sebastian's concert last week, he'd been treating her as if she were a child.

"Stop being such a worrywart," she said. "Please?"

The crab wasn't convinced, and Ariel let out a sigh. She softened. "Nothing like this has ever happened to me before. We're going to be friends, I just know it."

Flounder stopped midflip to look at her.

"Humans and merpeople don't become friends," Sebastian said.

"Maybe they should," replied Ariel. "We could learn from each other."

As Sebastian harrumphed, Ariel took Flounder by the fin. "Come on, I'll show you."

She swam off to her grotto, not waiting for Sebastian to catch up.

Inside the secret cave was Ariel's collection of human objects. It'd taken years of rummaging through old shipwrecks, of keeping her eyes peeled every time she explored outside Atlantica, but she'd amassed an impressive trove. Ariel swam up to the painting of a woman staring at fire.

She finally understood what it was.

After a beat, she soared to a high shelf in her grotto. "You see this, Sebastian?" Ariel said, picking up an instrument. "It makes music."

Sebastian gave the instrument a critical look. "Doesn't look like much to me."

"See?" Ariel blew.

A brassy noise resounded across the grotto, making Sebastian cover his head. "What was that?"

Ariel peered into the mouthpiece. "I guess I need some practice."

"Give me that," said Sebastian. He blew into the instrument, and the sound he produced was smoother, almost pleasant. "You've got to find the right pressure. Much better."

"You see?" said Ariel. "Not all human things are bad. Why don't you look at it? I bet you could write an entire symphony with it."

Sebastian looked skeptical. "It does have a nice sound, I guess."

"I'm going to learn all about humans," said Ariel to Sebastian. "And I'll show Daddy how beautiful their world can be."

"That's going to take a lot of convincing," said Sebastian.

"Eric will help me," Ariel said. "Scuttle's promised to look out for where he's been waiting, and—"

"You're not really going back up there, are you?" Flounder said, seeming worried.

"I've got to. He wants to see me again. I can't just leave him wondering. . . ." Ariel's voice rose with excitement as she brushed through her hair with the dinglehopper. "I'm going to go up and find him."

"Now?" said Flounder. "But what if there's another storm? What if there're big birds that want to eat fish for dinner, or that bright and burning—"

"Fire?" Ariel supplied.

"Yeah. That was scary."

"Don't worry," said Ariel, chuckling. "The fire can't hurt you if you're in the water."

"Really?"

She nodded. "Will you come?"

"I guess." Flounder gulped. "Okay. What about you, Sebastian?"

The crab hesitated.

"Please, Sebastian?" pleaded Ariel. "We can ask Eric about his snarfblatt. Maybe he'll have an extra one he can give you."

He let out a sigh, and Ariel celebrated inside. She knew music would be the way to his heart. "Doesn't look like I have a choice, does it? All right, but make it quick."

Up they swam, as fast as they could, for the surface.

The sky was still bright, a striking blue not unlike the color of her father's tail. If only she could make him see how incredible the world up there was. The birds soaring through the clouds, the warmth of the sun on her hair, the salty smell of the sea. Ariel loved everything about it.

"Scuttle!" She waved at the seagull. "Any sign of him?"

Scuttle landed on Ariel's arm and padded toward her hand. "You mean the furry one?"

"No, silly. Eric. The one who was playing the snarfblatt."

Scuttle blinked, as if he didn't remember exactly what a snarfblatt was.

Ariel made a motion with her fingers, playing music.

"Oh! The prince!" Scuttle chuckled. "He's been lookin' all over for you."

"Really?"

"He's already taken his boat out three times today! Come on, I'll show you."

Scuttle leapt back into the sky, and Ariel followed him toward the shore. He was right. Not far from the beach where Ariel had left Eric was a rowboat.

Sure enough, it was the prince's. He was playing his snarfblatt, playing a melody that sounded like the one she'd sung to him.

Ariel's stomach fluttered. She caught Sebastian in her hands and scooped him up. "See, what did I tell you? He's playing. Isn't it beautiful?"

Sebastian grunted. "I've heard tuna make better music than that."

Ariel stifled a giggle; she knew the crab was intrigued.

"All right, we've seen him," said Sebastian. "Now it's time to go back."

Unfortunately not intrigued enough to let go of his worries about getting caught.

"Come on, Sebastian, we just got here!"

"And we saw what we came to see," Sebastian said. "Your father's forbidden you from leaving Atlantica. If his guards find you up here—"

"We'll always be afraid of the human world if we never get to know it," Ariel interrupted. "This is my chance to meet a human and talk to one. I'm going."

"Wait!" Sebastian cried as Ariel swam toward Eric's boat. "Ariel!"

Ariel ignored Sebastian and waved to Eric as soon as she was closer.

The prince saw her right away, and he nearly jumped out of his boat with excitement. "It's you!" he cried. "Ariel."

Ariel couldn't stop the grin that came over her face. He'd remembered her name!

"You really are a . . . a—wow." Eric tilted his head in awe. "You know, I didn't used to believe merpeople existed. There have been stories, of course. Myths, legends. But you really are here."

Ariel folded her arms over the side of his boat. It was sweet, how nervous he was to talk to her. She would have loved to let him keep talking so she could listen to his voice.

"Would you like to come onto my boat?" said Eric. "That way we can sit together and talk."

"I'd love that."

Carefully, gently, Eric took her hands and hoisted her onto the rowboat.

"Are you cold?" He offered her his cloak. "You should take my cloak."

She wasn't cold, but she'd never worn anything like a cloak before. It was soft and warm, and she liked how the cloth felt draped over her shoulders.

"What's this?" she said, touching the round metal at the folds.

"That's called a button," said Eric.

"A button," Ariel repeated.

"It fastens the ends together so it doesn't fall off your shoulders." Eric fastened the button. "See?"

"Wow." Ariel looked down at the button. There were so many questions she had about his world. She wanted to know about the ship he'd been sailing, how long he'd been playing the snarfblatt . . . if he knew how to dance.

"What's on your mind?"

"I've never talked to a human before," she admitted.

"I've never talked to a mermaid before," he said, grinning. "Are they all like you?"

"Everyone else is better at following the rules," she replied. "We're not supposed to come up to the surface." She wrinkled her nose.

"Whose rules?"

"My father's," said Ariel. "King Triton."

"Your father's King Triton?" Eric exclaimed. "Wait

until Grimsby hears that. He thinks the stories about the sea king are all tall tales the sailors tell to explain the storms."

Ariel laughed. "Daddy doesn't make all the storms. He's usually too busy in Atlantica. I can't remember the last time he came to the surface." Her voice turned distant. "I wish he would, though. It's beautiful up here."

"It must be beautiful under the sea, too," murmured Eric. But he wasn't looking at the sea as he spoke; he was looking at her.

Ariel blushed. "Tell me what it's like living on land. What do you eat, how do you sleep, and what do you do every day?"

"Well . . ." Eric turned to the basket at his side and lifted it onto his lap. "I brought some food if you want to try. This is an apple, and we call this a salad—"

"A dinglehopper!" she cried when Eric offered her a fork. She took it excitedly and started combing her hair.

Eric gave her an amused look.

"What?

He chuckled. "We use it to help us eat." He speared one of the fruit slices with the fork. "See? You try."

Ariel poked her fork into the slice, then examined the fruit carefully. What an oddly shaped piece of food. The reddish yellow skin along one side gleamed under the sunlight. She bit carefully. She didn't expect the fruit to be so crunchy, nor for it to release a stream of sweet, tart juice.

"I love it!" she exclaimed. "That's . . ."

"An apple," supplied Eric. "It's one of my favorites, too."

Ariel listened raptly and tasted everything that Eric offered her to try. The apples were her favorite, and the bread with butter a close second. Delicious!

After lunch, they talked for hours, barely noticing as the sun began to sink below the horizon. Ariel learned why humans wore shoes and boots on their feet, how many seasons there were in a year, what telescopes did, and how to spit out the olive seeds from the salad Eric had brought. And in turn, she taught Eric how to read a fish's face for emotion, why Atlantica had been kept a secret from humans, and the best tactics for evading sharks.

Come sundown, Sebastian pinched her on the elbow. "You've been here long enough. It's time to go home," he hissed.

Pretending not to hear him, Ariel nudged the crab to one side. Poor Sebastian fell off the boat and back into the water with a small splash.

"Ariel!" he cried.

"What is it?" said Eric. He noticed her looking overboard. "Do you have to go?"

Ariel finally looked at the darkening sky, and her shoulders fell. "My father doesn't know I'm here. He doesn't know about you."

"Because contact between humans and merpeople is forbidden," Eric said, remembering what she'd told him.

"He'll be worried if I stay out any longer," said Ariel.

Reluctantly, she lifted herself off the boat, dipping her tail back into the water. "But I had the best time. I'll remember everything you told me, Eric, and . . ." Her voice trailed. Why was she talking like it was the last time she'd see him?

Because I don't know if I'll see him again, she thought. *And I want to. But I don't know how he feels about me.*

"Would you like to tour my kingdom?" Eric blurted. "I can introduce you to my crew, my friends—Grimsby and Carlotta. They'd love to meet you."

"I'd love to," Ariel blurted back, her heart leaping as Eric grinned at her. She couldn't believe it: an invitation to go on land. She'd get to see all the things she'd only imagined. Puppets and bakeries, horses and trees that grew taller than whales.

Then she shook her tail in the air. "There's just a small problem."

"Oh, right." Eric laughed at himself. "Hmm. How about a ride through the countryside, then? I can ask Carlotta to get you a dress. The skirt can cover up your fins, and we can take a picnic in the fields."

Ariel had no idea what a picnic was, or fields, or even a skirt. But the light that shone in Eric's eyes made her nod eagerly. She'd ask Scuttle later to explain what he meant.

"That sounds wonderful."

"When would you like to come to land?"

Tomorrow, Ariel wanted to say, but Sebastian snapped his pincers at her fin. "Absolutely not. You are not coming back here. You have rehearsals—there's the rescheduled concert. Your father will notice."

Ariel sent the crab a displeased look. "The concert's in three days," she muttered.

Sebastian stared her down. He had a surprisingly piercing stare, for a crab. Ariel had to look away with a sigh.

"I can't tomorrow," she told Eric, making a face. "I forgot I'm singing in a concert. I missed the last one, so I really have to be there, and at all the rehearsals, too."

"How about we meet the day after the concert, then?" Eric suggested. "Do you think you could sneak away for a day?"

Ariel perked up. "I could try."

"That's four days from now," said Eric slowly. "I know you can't stay long because of the rehearsals, but do you think . . . can I at least see you again tomorrow?"

Ariel couldn't hide her smile. "Here?"

"Here's perfect. I'll be waiting."

Both human and mermaid grinned sheepishly at each other, neither wanting to be the first to say goodbye. Nor did either notice the pair of glowing yellow eyes peering at them from beneath Eric's rowboat.

The next day and the next, Ariel and Eric met again. Eric played his snarfblatt—a flute, he called it—and Ariel sang for him. Together, with Sebastian's reluctant participation, they even made new songs together.

"You like him," Ariel teased the crab after their third meeting. "You just won't admit it."

"The boy's got some talent with that flute," admitted Sebastian. "But that's all. He's still a human."

"Music is a language that we share on both land and sea," said Ariel, hiding a smile. Eric had charmed Sebastian, same as he'd won Flounder over by bringing him a set of small floating balls. Flounder couldn't get enough of chasing after them across the surface whenever they met.

At every meeting, Eric brought something from his world to show her, and Ariel brought something from Atlantica. The last time, he'd started to teach her to sail and showed her how to tie knots with simple rope. Then it began to drizzle, so Eric had shown Ariel an umbrella—which bloomed open like a flower to shield them from the rain. It was Ariel's favorite discovery so far, and she couldn't wait to learn what Eric would bring her next.

"Here, I wanted to show you this," said Eric. "You can keep it, but I don't know if it'll get soggy under the water."

"A book," Ariel said, recognizing the object. She hugged it to her chest. "I've always wanted one of these. I found one in a shipwreck, but most of the pages were missing."

She flipped through the book, tracing her fingers across the pictures.

"It's called an encyclopedia," explained Eric. "It has pictures and descriptions of almost everything in our world. I thought you might like it."

Ariel could already imagine herself spending hours poring over it. "We have something like this in Atlantica's library. I'll bring you a copy next time." She pointed at the next object in his bag. "What's that?"

Eric held a small wooden box on his palm. "This is a matchbox," said Eric. "You asked me about fire last time—this is how we make it. Want to see?"

He struck the matchstick against the bottom of the box, and Ariel gasped. There it was, that orange bloom of heat, like she'd seen on the ship.

Up close, it was mesmerizing. The flame flickered with the wind, casting shadows about the boat. The flame traveled down the matchstick, about to graze Eric's hand.

"Be careful!" she cried, remembering the destructive power of the fire during the storm.

Eric blew out the match. Poof, the fire was gone.

"Can I try?" Ariel said eagerly.

Ariel struck the match against the box. Nothing. She tried again, and again. It took her several attempts until at last the flame burst alive on the tip of her matchstick. "I did it!"

Eric clapped. He raised a lantern and motioned for her to light the candle inside.

"It's fuel for the fire," he said. "It'll make the light last longer so that even when it's night, we can see."

Ariel held the lantern, admiring how it illuminated the water. "Flounder, come look at this," she said, lowering the lantern off the side of the boat.

But a large wave rolled toward the boat and splashed against the lantern, dousing the flame inside. It went out with a hiss.

"Oh, no," Ariel cried.

"Don't worry about that," said Eric. "We can light it again." He gave her a sheepish smile. "I guess that's why there's no fire in the sea."

She mustered a smile back at him, but she couldn't help focusing on his two legs and her fish tail. It was one thing to convince Sebastian that humans weren't bad, that they loved music just like fish and crustaceans did, but deep down, she knew that some differences were too impossible to overcome. Water and fire was only one of the many ways their worlds were different and could never touch.

Ariel reached into her bag for one of the fluorescent shells she'd brought to show him and tried to hide how her smile had fallen. She could learn as much about the humans as she wanted, but unless she got legs, or Eric suddenly became a merman—they could never be together.

They'd never be part of each other's world.

Ursula, the sea witch, waited anxiously inside her lair for her two eels, Flotsam and Jetsam, to return. Her home, a cave of whale bones in the darkest part of the ocean, was far from Atlantica. Years ago, she'd lived in the heart of the sea—in the sea king's palace, in fact, as a powerful advisor. Though, to her, the position wasn't nearly as powerful as it could have been, and she'd been banished for trying to steal his trident. Since then, she'd been scheming ways to usurp King Triton's throne, and finally she'd thought of the perfect angle: his precious seventh daughter, Ariel.

At the sight of her eels returning, Ursula's tentacles bloomed to life, and she glided toward them.

"Well?" she said. "How was it?"

Flotsam and Jetsam exchanged looks. "The poor princess is in love. With a prince—a human prince."

Ursula let out a deep laugh. "I knew it! This is too easy."

"They've been meeting in secret," said Flotsam. Jetsam added, "Almost every day."

"Let me guess—Triton has no idea."

The eels nodded.

"Then that needs to change." Ursula rubbed her hands together, laughing to herself. Soon that pitiful fish king would no longer be the ruler of all the seas. Ursula would acquire his trident, and she'd use its power to control the entire ocean!

"I wonder how the great sea king will feel about his pretty little daughter making friends with a human. I think it's time he found out what she's been up to. Why don't you leave a little hint?"

Flotsam and Jetsam smiled. "With pleasure."

The concert was a swimming success. Everyone in Atlantica showed up, and Ariel sang her best. She didn't rush the tempo during her solo, she kept harmony with her sisters, and she remembered all the words. At the end, the applause was so enthusiastic that Sebastian was beaming. Ariel wondered if he had almost forgiven her for missing the concert the first time.

While the concertgoers crowded Sebastian to congratulate him on the spectacular success, Ariel swam into the wings of the concert hall, then back toward the bedroom she shared with her sisters.

She was humming to herself.

"Still singing?" said Attina, swimming up to Ariel's side. Her orange tail glittered with tiny crystals she'd studded on for the concert. "You know, you've been acting strange lately."

"Strange?"

"You're glowing, Ariel," chimed in Arista. "And you smile every time someone talks to you." She paused coyly. "Who's the lucky boy?"

"Come on," Attina said, "we won't tell."

"I . . . I don't know what you're talking about," said Ariel, though she couldn't hide her grin in time.

"You've been like this for days. Smiling to yourself, singing to yourself. Come on, tell us. We're your sisters!"

"We won't tell Daddy," Adella chimed in.

"Tell Daddy what?" Triton interrupted.

All seven royal princesses immediately straightened, their fins going still. One by one they mumbled excuses about having to get some rest or freshen up, and before long, it was only Ariel and King Triton—and Flounder, hiding behind a coral column.

"Tell Daddy what?" Triton repeated.

"Nothing," said Ariel, waving a dismissive hand. "We were just talking about . . . what a great concert that was. And how nice it was of Sebastian to reschedule it."

Triton harrumphed. "Well, you did miss it the first time." His expression turned stern. "Because you were exploring shipwrecks. No more of that human nonsense, hmm, Ariel?"

Thank goodness for Flounder. "No more shipwrecks," he said for her as he swam out from hiding. "Ariel wouldn't miss Sebastian's concert for anything."

Triton nodded. "That's good, Ariel. I'm glad to hear you've been taking your responsibilities seriously. It's time that you—"

Before the king could finish what he was about to say, a seahorse hurried to his side. "Your Majesty," he piped up, "an important delivery for your eyes only."

"Now what could this be?" Triton picked up the scroll and unrolled it in one hand.

"I should probably go, too," Ariel said. "It was a long concert, and—"

"Wait." Triton's grip on his trident tightened. Never a good sign. He crumpled the scroll in his fist, and when he spoke again, his expression was livid. "I ask you again, Ariel—have you been engaging in any more of this human business?"

Ariel didn't answer.

"Have you made contact with a human?"

Her heart stopped. How could he know that? "Daddy, he's—"

That was all Triton needed to hear. "Have you lost your senses?" he roared. "Contact between the human world and our world is strictly forbidden. I've told you this before. You know this! To lie to me—"

"Are you spying on me?"

"I don't need spies," said Triton. "I'm the king; you're a princess. Someone's bound to notice you flouting the laws and going up to the surface."

"Then maybe there shouldn't be laws," Ariel said.

Flounder defended her. "He's not like other humans, sire. He's . . . he's . . ."

Flounder's voice trailed off under the sea king's glare.

"This is between me and my daughter," King Triton told the fish. "You would do well to stay out of it."

Flounder swallowed. "Yes, sire."

"If you would just meet him," pleaded Ariel, "you'd see. Not all humans are barbarians. Not all humans are bad."

"Not another word," Triton said, reproaching his daughter. "You are not to meet this human ever again. You are never to go to the surface again. Is that clear? This is for your safety."

Ariel's lower lip trembled, and she spun away, ignoring the dolphin guards that followed as she swam fast out of the hallway back to her room.

King Triton exhaled. He worried deeply about all his children but about Ariel most of all. And this news that she was in contact with a human—a species that threatened everything they held dear with their compulsive hunting and polluting and wasting! Who knew what they would do with this confirmation that merfolk existed? That was troubling indeed.

Raising his trident, he summoned Sebastian to his side.

The crab was still in a jubilant mood from the concert. "Yes, Your Majesty?" he piped.

"I'm sorry to take you away from the concert hall, Sebastian, but I need your help. Have you been keeping an eye on Ariel, as I asked?"

Sebastian smiled, a little too widely. "Of course I have, sire. Why, what's the matter?"

"She's been off to the surface, to meet a human. Did you know about this?"

Sebastian's legs shook nervously. "Um, I—I tried to stop her! But she wouldn't listen. What could I do? She said she wouldn't sing in the concert if I said anything."

Triton's displeasure deepened the lines in his brow. "All this time, you knew?"

Sebastian swallowed hard. "I'm sorry, Your Majesty. If it's any consolation, the boy truly cares about her. He's not as bad as I—"

"I don't want to hear it, Sebastian," interrupted Triton. "I'm disappointed in you. You know the law."

"I'm sorry, Your Majesty."

Triton frowned. "My daughter is headstrong and

stubborn, I know that. But you put her in danger, Sebastian. You can no longer be trusted to supervise her. You're dismissed from your duty watching over Ariel."

"But, Your Majesty—" Sebastian gulped at Triton's stern glare. "Yes, Your Majesty."

Triton let out a sigh as the crab skittered away. It felt as though he was losing control of what mattered.

Was he being too harsh on Ariel? Had he been too harsh on his entire kingdom? No. Every year, thousands of fish died at the hands of the callous humans. Their kind was dangerous, unpredictable, destructive. There was nothing that would change his mind about that.

The next morning—only a few hours before she was supposed to meet Eric, Ariel was leaning against the wall in her room, numbly counting the leaves on the kelp outside, when her bodyguards allowed Sebastian inside.

She turned her back on the crab. "What are you doing here?" she said flatly. "I heard Daddy said you don't have to watch over me anymore."

"You're sixteen years old, Ariel. You're not a child."

"Tell that to the two dolphins outside watching the door."

"I already did. How else do you think they let me inside?"

Ariel turned away. "Go away, Sebastian. I want to be alone."

"Ariel, please. It's for the best. You're too young to

understand now, but once you see that you and that prince can't be together—"

"Who could have sent that letter?" Ariel interrupted. "I've been thinking about it all last night, and I can't think of anyone. But someone had to be following me."

"It doesn't matter who it was," Sebastian said. "Let's go for a swim around the palace. I hear you haven't left your room since yesterday, and you've been under a lot of pressure—"

"Everywhere I go, the dolphins follow me." Ariel crossed her arms, then she whispered, "Help me out of here, Sebastian, please? Eric's waiting for me. He had this special day planned."

Sebastian nearly dropped his jaw. "You heard what your father said. I watched you the first time, and then? You become friends with a human! Do you know what he'll do to me if it happens again?"

"Please, Sebastian?" Ariel swallowed hard. "I love him. At least let me explain things to him . . . and let me say good-bye? He won't understand why I never came."

Sebastian wouldn't budge.

"Please?" said Ariel.

"What a softshell I'm turning out to be." Sebastian sighed. "All right. I hope I don't regret this."

Sebastian cocked his head at Flounder, who was sleepily lying on a rock. "Come on, you come out with me to distract the guards."

"Thank you, Sebastian," Ariel cried, picking up the crab and kissing him on the head.

Eric paddled around the lagoon, his heart jumping every time anything green wafted across the still waters. But no, it wasn't Ariel.

Where was she? She was over an hour late, which was unlike her. Usually he could count on her being early, like him—waving excitedly as she jumped out of the water. The last time, she'd accidentally jumped straight into his arms. He'd held her for an instant, breathing in the sweetness of her hair, before they shyly parted. But at the end of their time together, they'd held hands.

Had he gotten the date wrong? Or the time?

Or had she changed his mind about him? Maybe she didn't like the books he'd brought, or the chocolate cake. Or maybe she'd found his lesson on tying sailors' knots incredibly dull and boring. Grimsby definitely did.

"Enough," he muttered aloud. "She's a couple minutes late, Eric. That doesn't mean she doesn't like you."

He sighed, aware that he sounded hopeless. But ever since Ariel had rescued him from the shipwreck, ever since he'd opened his eyes and seen her face, heard her voice—she had been all he could think about.

When he went home, he just wanted to talk about Ariel, too. But he had to be careful what he said; Grimsby and Carlotta only knew of Ariel as the mysterious girl he'd been seeing. Eric hadn't told them that she was a mermaid. It didn't seem right to share that without Ariel's permission.

"Maybe I can use this time to practice what I'm going to say," Eric murmured. He was going to confess to Ariel how he felt. He had it all planned. After they went on their picnic, he'd shower her with the flowers he'd picked that morning and play her a song on his flute. Then he'd tell her:

"Ariel, I'm in love with you."

He shut his eyes, letting the words fill the stillness of the air. He'd brought her three dresses to choose from, because he didn't know what her favorite color was or what she might feel comfortable wearing. He'd even packed the picnic basket himself after asking Chef Louis to teach him how to prepare a meal. He'd baked bread for the first time, even made an onion soup that he hoped would be edible. Probably not the best choice, in hindsight, if they kissed.

Eric felt his cheeks heat, wondering if he'd gotten it all wrong. There'd be no kissing if she didn't show up.

"Ariel?" he called, growing worried. He reached for his satchel and rummaged inside for the telescope he'd brought to show her.

There was a splash from afar. Could that be her?

"Looking for someone?" rasped a pair of voices from the water.

Eric leaned over his boat. A pair of eels with mismatched eyes peered at him. But no, the voices couldn't have come from them—

"Looking for your sea princess, perhaps?" the eels said, their mouths opening to reveal their small sharp teeth. "Hmm?"

Eric staggered back.

"There's no need to be alarmed," they went on. "We represent someone who's looking after Ariel."

As Eric recovered, he slowly crept up to the side of the boat again. He didn't like the looks of these creatures. He didn't trust how slippery their expressions were, and how they circled his boat—like he was prey. "Where is she?"

"Follow us," said the eels. "We can help you find her. She needs you."

"Needs me?" Eric repeated, alarmed. "Is Ariel in trouble?"

"This way," the eels said, then dove into the water.

Apprehension churned in Eric's gut. He didn't trust these eels, but if Ariel was in danger, and he didn't go after her, he'd never forgive himself.

The prince kicked off his boots. He didn't have a fishing spear or a harpoon with him, but he'd brought an umbrella. He hooked it under his arm and took the largest breath he could.

Then he dove after Flotsam and Jetsam—straight into Ursula's trap.

Ariel spied Eric's boat and rushed to it. But he wasn't there.

The boat was empty, floating aimlessly across the

lagoon. His oars were still inside. There was a bundle of neatly folded human dresses, a picnic basket with food—still warm—bottles of water and juice, and a satchel full of gadgets Ariel had wanted to learn about.

But no Eric.

"Eric!" she shouted. "Eric!"

Ariel picked up a long metal tube. It had rolled to the side of the boat and wasn't in the satchel along with everything else. It matched Eric's description of the looking device—what was it called? A telescope? Had Eric been looking for her?

As she raised the telescope to her eyes, she saw a pair of boots in the boat.

"Maybe he went looking for you," suggested Flounder. Her best friend dove into the water. "Nope. Don't see him anywhere."

Ariel's gut knotted.

"He couldn't have gone far," reasoned Sebastian.

Mermaid and crab exchanged grim looks. Humans couldn't survive long in the water.

"Eric!" Ariel called out again.

Then, from beneath the surface emerged a flare of white hair and a pair of hooded eyes. "Looking for someone, angelfish?"

"Ariel!" Flounder let out a horrified gasp. His teeth chattered uncontrollably, and he hid behind Ariel's hair. "That's . . . that's . . . the sea witch."

Everyone in Atlantica had heard of the sea witch, how she deceived naïve merfolk and enticed them to her lair with false promises and dark magic. Ariel braced herself as Ursula rose to the surface, her black tentacles writhing with menace.

"What are you doing here?" Ariel demanded. "Get out. Get away from me."

Ursula wore a smug grin that Ariel didn't like. "It's been a long time since I've come up to the surface," she said. "I can't say I see what all the fuss is about. But you, angelfish—you seem to have caught yourself a prince!"

Ariel gripped the side of Eric's boat. "If you know where he is—"

"What will you give me?" said Ursula coyly, opening the shell on her necklace. A light flared from the center of the pendant, showing Ariel a silhouette of the prince, swimming deep within the lagoon.

"She's in there," Flotsam and Jetsam warned him, pointing ahead at something Ariel couldn't see. "She's trapped. You've got to help her."

Eric ventured forward, raising his umbrella to attack the unseen creature. Then the prince's eyes bulged with horror.

The light from Ursula's necklace went out, and she settled it back on her chest, closing it. "You can imagine what happens next."

"You monster!" Ariel cried, lunging at Ursula. "You tricked him!"

"Careful, dear."

Flotsam and Jetsam wrapped their tails around Ariel's arms, immobilizing her.

"Let him go!" she shouted.

"I'm afraid you're too late," said Ursula. "My little pet swallowed him. It won't be long until it devours him whole." The sea witch smiled. "Unless . . . you come with me."

Without giving Ariel a chance to respond, Ursula dove into the sea.

Flotsam and Jetsam loosened her arms. "This way," they said in unison.

Ariel ignored Sebastian's and Flounder's pleas for her not to go. She knew it was a trap, but what could she do? Eric was in trouble—because of her. At the last minute, she reached onto the boat for Eric's satchel.

"Ariel, do not do this," Sebastian demanded. "I'm going to tell your father—"

"Find him," Ariel whispered. "Go, as fast as you can. Hurry."

The crab's eyes widened. Then he swam off as fast as he could while Ariel and Flounder followed Ursula's eels.

It wasn't a long swim, but along the way, Ariel spied Eric's umbrella nestled between two reefs. As she dove to retrieve it, she saw Ursula's "little" pet.

A giant clam, it turned out to be, entrenched deep in the bedrock of the sea. Its maw was as wide as a shark's and snapped tightly shut.

"Eric!" she cried, charging at the monstrous clam, but Ursula pushed her out of the way.

"Not so fast, angelfish," Ursula said. "You want to save your prince? Then how about we make a deal?"

Ariel wasn't listening. She could see Eric's silhouette inside the gigantic shell. He was unconscious, barely breathing. "You . . . you monster! You did this to him—"

"Now, now, there's no need to be rude." Ursula tsked. "You haven't even heard what I'm offering. Your prince—in exchange . . . for you."

"Me," repeated Ariel, drawing a sharp breath. "What do you want from me?"

Ursula's smile widened. "You're the favorite daughter of the sea king—an exceptional addition to my collection." She paused, using her necklace to show them a terrifying grove of lost souls magicked into polyps. "King Triton will come swimming into my clutches."

Ariel clenched the satchel as Flotsam and Jetsam surrounded her. She shook her head at Ursula. "Never."

The sea witch puckered her lips. "Then your prince, I'm afraid, is going to die."

"Not so fast," cried Flounder, bursting out to charge at Ursula. Using the umbrella, Ariel swung at Flotsam and Jetsam and knotted their tails together. Then she rushed toward Eric.

"Hold on, Eric. I'll get you out of there," she cried, trying to pry the giant clam open with the tip of the umbrella. "Come on, please. Open, open!"

When the clam wouldn't give, Ariel opened the umbrella instead. The sudden burst of cloth and wire made the shells part. Inside was Eric, his eyes closed and body limp.

"Quick, you gotta get out of here," Flounder said breathlessly. "Ursula's com—"

"I know. Get somewhere safe, Flounder. You've helped me enough."

As fast as she could, Ariel swam Eric to the surface and hauled him back onto the boat. She started to lift herself, too, so she could help revive him, but black tentacles wrapped around her wrist.

The boat rocked, and Eric's body hit the side. There was the sudden sound of coughing.

Then—"Ariel!" Eric cried. He scrambled forward, still sputtering, grabbing her arms and trying to help her stay aboard.

Ariel gritted her teeth. The lantern was still burning. She reached for it and smashed it over Ursula's tentacles. Immediately, she withdrew, and as Ursula rose from the depths of the sea, Ariel stuffed the picnic basket over the sea witch's head.

"Get the rope!" Eric cried to Ariel.

Ariel snatched it, diving underwater as Eric hurled the boat's anchor at Ursula. The metal weight of the anchor slammed into the sea witch's stomach, and she let out a pained gasp.

Eric dove into the water as Ursula sent his boat spinning. But his attack had bought Ariel the precious seconds she needed to wrap the rope around Ursula's arms and make a tight knot.

"You think a bunch of strings are enough to defeat me?" Ursula strained against her binds, and her tentacles wrestled with the knot Ariel had tied. "I tried to bargain with you two, but it seems we'll have to do things the hard way."

The sea witch seized the prince and princess with her tentacles—and the waters suddenly began to churn.

"Ursula, stop!" someone yelled, voice deep and rumbling.

It was King Triton, with his trident aimed menacingly at Ursula.

"Why, hello, Triton," Ursula said with a huff. "You going to strike at me while I've got your daughter?"

"Let her go." Seething, Triton spoke through gritted teeth.

Eric headbutted Ursula, attempting to attack her with his bare strength, but her grip was strong. They needed more. That was when Ariel realized she was still carrying Eric's satchel. Most of its contents had fallen out, but there was still something inside. Something familiar . . .

The tines were metal and sharp. She grabbed the dinglehopper and, as hard as she could, stabbed it into Ursula's arm.

The sea witch let go of Ariel and Eric with a cry. She reached after the pair again, but Ariel flung the umbrella in Eric's direction. He opened it and wielded it as a shield against Ursula.

"Now, Daddy!" Ariel shouted.

Light blazed from the trident, and before Ursula could escape, it surrounded her, enclosing her in a clam like the one she'd tried to trap Eric inside.

Then, with a swing of Triton's arm, he sent Ursula barreling deep into the sea, someplace where she could never bother them again.

The sea witch was no more.

News of Ursula's defeat traveled swiftly across Atlantica. As King Triton and Ariel escorted Eric back toward shore, dozens of mermaids and mermen that had been under the sea witch's thrall came up to the surface to thank those responsible for saving them.

"The sea witch will no longer threaten Atlantica," King Triton declared to his people. "Thanks to my daughter Ariel, and—"

"Eric," replied Ariel, introducing the prince to her father.

Without smiling, King Triton gave the human prince the barest nod. "And Eric."

When the cheers receded, the sea king used his trident to locate Eric's boat and bring it back to the surface.

"Thank you, Your Majesty," said Eric.

"It's time you go home, young man."

Eric opened his mouth, as if he wanted to say something but then thought better of it. While the prince climbed back aboard, Ariel gathered the remnants of what Eric had brought to show her—the rope, the lantern—and placed them back on the boat.

King Triton watched without a word.

Ariel couldn't bear the silence any longer. "Daddy, I—"

"What was that thing in your hand, Ariel? The thing you used against Ursula," said Triton suddenly, a note of curiosity in his voice, as though he couldn't help asking. "It looked like a small trident."

Ariel tilted her head, surprised by the question. "It's called a fork, Daddy. Humans use it to eat their food." She smiled. "Or comb their hair."

"A fork," mused King Triton. "And what did you use to tie around Ursula's arms?"

"Rope, Your Majesty," Eric supplied.

"A picnic basket," Ariel said, holding up the broken basket she'd thrown onto Ursula's head. "And my favorite: this is an umbrella." She opened it. "Humans use it to cover themselves from the rain."

"Intriguing," Triton murmured. He let out a sigh and lowered his trident as he turned to face Eric. "It was brave of you, young man, to risk your life to save my daughter."

Then he turned to Ariel. "And you, my youngest daughter. You used those items from the human world ingeniously to defeat the sea witch. We would never have known she was keeping all those merfolk captive if you hadn't."

Ariel beamed at her father and at Eric. "So what does

that mean, Daddy?" she asked. "That I can continue to visit the human world? That danger doesn't just come from the surface? That there are things here that might actually help instead of hurt?"

Triton hesitated. "I need to learn more first."

It wasn't a refusal, which made Ariel brighten. "I have an idea."

The hardest part was convincing her father to come up to the surface again. Once that happened, Ariel and Eric had an entire presentation ready for the sea king, which started off with a collection of Ariel's favorite objects from the human world.

"It's called a telescope," she said, demonstrating to her father. "It helps you see things that are far away. Look."

King Triton held the telescope to his eye. His brow rose, and he peered more deeply at the lens. When he lowered the telescope, he admitted, "This might be useful in our kingdom."

Sebastian brought the item to the pile of other human treasures the sea king now permitted in Atlantica.

Eric bowed to the sea king.

"And you, young man, would you like to join us for dinner? I hear from Sebastian that you have questions about the mer-world."

"I'd be honored, sire, but I'm afraid I can't." Eric gestured at his legs.

"Ah, yes." King Triton pointed his trident at Eric, and suddenly the young prince grew a dark blue tail, with fins.

The young prince stared at his new tail in awe. He jumped into the sea after Ariel, but he was still new at being a merman, and maneuvering around in the water was trickier than it looked.

"You'll get the hang of it after a while," said Ariel with a laugh. "I'll teach you."

"Ariel and I have been talking," said King Triton, "and my daughter has convinced me that if you, Prince Eric, were more informed about Atlantica, that could help us both be better leaders in our respective kingdoms.

"Therefore, I've decided there is no harm in you learning what it's like to be a merman, and my daughter what it's like to be a human. An exchange of ideas from one world to the other, if you will. But it will be a trial, first. You may come to my kingdom three days a month, and Ariel to your world for the same amount of time."

"Humans and merpeople could learn to trust each other," Ariel said. "We could warn your sailors against storms, and your people could be more considerate with your . . ."

"Fishing and polluting," King Triton provided.

Eric bowed his head. "Those all sound like wonderful ideas." He sent Ariel a smile. "I can think of no one better than Ariel to find a bridge between our two worlds."

Ariel smiled back at him shyly.

"It'll be a cultural exchange, too." Sebastian raised his claws in delight. "There's nothing that shows off Atlantica better than our music. Shall we have a concert to introduce this young merman to our kingdom?"

"You can play your snarfblatt," said Ariel, still smiling. Then she took Eric's hand, and together they dove—two worlds meeting, just as the sky meets the sea.

Dust to Dust

What if Tinker Bell was working for Captain Hook?

by Micol Ostow

Dust to Dust

What if Tinker Bell was working for Captain Hook?

by Micol Ostow

La Belle Époque Noir (Before)

All children—except one—grow up. Surely you've heard this before. And it is true of fairies, as well. The reason for this is nature, and order, and things that live. But let us not forget that along with nature and order, so too exists magic.

Which brings us to our story—and to a young fairy named Tinker Bell, who above all else wanted desperately to grow up . . . if only her fairy family would allow her.

The days in the Hollow were idyllic; on that point there was no dispute. Tink and her friends spent long afternoons lolling in the lush grass of the glades, the sky a vibrant watercolor of dappled sunlight against mottled clouds. They wove crowns of marigold buds and splashed in dollops of fresh rain. They ate honey cakes, played games, told elaborate, whimsical stories. . . . They traded secrets in hushed tones.

Yes, the days could be idyllic indeed. Magically so. But they were long, too. Amid the gaiety there were also responsibilities, chores to be done. The pixies were each assigned a particular task: embroidery, cooking, laundry. Each contributed to the betterment of the group, a community. And Tink, as her namesake suggests, was the tinker of the lot. Such was her natural proclivity.

Though she was adept at mending the pots and pans of the fairy folk, she had her faults, as well. Specifically, Tink was known for her mercurial temper.

And so it was that one fine spring morning, the wind crisp and the sky a blinding prism of color, Tinker Bell found herself surveying a particularly considerable pile of cookware in need of mending. She sighed, a sound like wind chimes carrying across the air.

A handle to be welded, a spout to be widened . . . It was all so *dreary* when the sky was such a riotous shade of blue and the dragonflies begged to be raced. Causing specific frustration was the knowledge that a swift toss of pixie dust would have the cookware soldered back together in no time. What was the point of toiling with flesh and fingers when magic could complete the task in a fraction of the time?

But no, it was frowned upon. More than frowned upon—expressly forbidden. Something about "the value of honest labor" and "understanding magic as sacred, beyond whimsy." Which made no sense to Tinker Bell, really, for what was flying if not whimsy, when walking served just the same purpose? How arbitrary it all seemed!

She could hear the elders' voices in her head, could see them shaking their heads. *Arbitrary to you, perhaps. Use of magic for such purposes is* dark *magic, a gateway to baser temptations.*

Hmmph. "Dark magic." As though the shade or hue of a magic spell mattered so terribly.

From beyond the swaying sunflower fields, her friends' laughter carried. How had they completed their chores so quickly? She glared at a teakettle, snorted . . . and watched as it jiggled, responding to the force of her disdain.

How easy it would be. The thought was a flicker, a gleam of pixie dust catching the light. Once it landed in her mental periphery, the notion was impossible to shake.

She cast a furtive glance to either side. She was alone. No one would be the wiser if *just this once . . .*

And then she'd have the whole day with her friends to do as she pleased.

The ban against using magic for chores had never seemed so pointless. No one would know if her magic had been tinged with the slightest of shadows.

At her sides her fingers began to wiggle, as though completely independent of the rest of her body. The heady tingle of fairy dust coursed through her.

The pots and pans began to dance.

What could the harm be?

In the end, fairy lore is divided on whether Tink was asked to leave or she flew off in a huff; there are those who insist she had the final say, and even the time and wherewithal to pack a small bag.

The prevailing sentiment, however, was that she was "asked" to leave and that the asking was not so much a question as a strong suggestion, and that to call Tink's reaction and mood as she departed the Hollow a "huff" was to befoul the good name of perfectly reasonable huffs everywhere.

But all *that* is a preamble, insofar as (as with all the best preambles) it preceded what was to become one of the more significant inflection points of Tink's young fairy life. In fact, so deeply focused was Tinker Bell on leaving her beloved home, it scarcely occurred to her what she might be drifting *toward.*

If only more attention had been paid.

By Hook or by Crook (Before)

Tinker Bell had found herself bobbing down an uncharted channel on a velvet-soft lily pad when she came to a stony inlet, the likes of which she'd not seen before.

Strange, she thought. Of course, she knew there was more to the world beyond what she'd seen with her own eyes. And yet it didn't seem that she'd been paddling—drifting, really, and napping once, albeit briefly—long enough to suddenly find herself completely disoriented.

But then it had been a disorienting sort of day. Rebuked by the elders for her experimentations with dark magic! *Be gone,* they'd proclaimed.

With pleasure. Rebuked over something as silly as pots and pans.

She'd show them. If she was gone, as they'd suggested, they'd be none the wiser about her use of magic anyway.

She didn't fly off; that might have caused too much of a stir. She stomped and shouted and pouted. Generally speaking, she enjoyed a dramatic tantrum, storming off to the forest for "air" and sneering at any "friends" who'd failed to defend her when it counted and merely feinted at following her. But she dutifully waited until nightfall to take her more permanent leave.

She set sail in a small makeshift float crafted of reeds and lily pads—easy to steer, difficult to trace or track with magic.

She came upon a tall rock formation. She squinted, not quite believing her eyes—the outline of a human skull? Then, just as unexpectedly, the prow of a ship loomed through the low haze. A tattered flag revealed a leering skull and crossbones waving from the foremast as a shiver tiptoed across the back of Tink's neck.

A figure emerged on the foredeck. The captain, clearly, in a long red dress coat with glittery gold trim. A tall hat with a large feather topped a cascade of fat black curls, and a handlebar mustache snaked over a sly smile that pierced Tink's bubble of nonchalance even across the distance and gloom. This man, this *pirate captain*, radiated cunning, danger.

Tink had been bobbing along on her lily pad for some

time, feeling isolated, lonely, and rather misunderstood. The power and fury of her initial clash with the elders had faded. Perhaps she didn't belong among the fairy folk, after all. Perhaps it was fate that had carried her to this strange, foreboding place. To this sly man with his smug, nasty—yet entirely gleeful—expression.

Even if it were not fate as such—regardless, this was where the current had carried her. She had no plans to go back home anytime soon.

Curious, she felt a twitch at the spot where her wings met between her shoulder blades. Before she knew it, she was aloft, flying toward the ship, toward the dark, menacing . . . and, yes, delightfully eager man—who seemed equally delighted to lay eyes on her.

Hello? she said as she rose to his eye level. Her tone was more of a question than a statement or greeting.

"Well, hello there, yourself," he replied.

Tinker Bell started. She'd never met a mortal who could communicate with a fairy before. Who *was* this creature?

He gave a short bow. "A pleasure to make the acquaintance of so charming a fairy as yourself."

She tinkled, bashful laughter and uncertainty. *How do you do?*

Would another fairy have taken note of the steel-gray tinge of storm clouds rolling in behind the pirate ship, the slight stench of rot on the surrounding winds? Likely. But Tink was at a most impressionable moment. He extended an arm as though to shake, despite the great disparity in their respective sizes, which Tinker Bell immediately decided was a point in his favor.

But as she darted forward, Tink gasped. For where the captain should have had a hand, instead Tinker Bell found herself faced directly with a gleaming piece of metal polished to a deadly shine. The instrument—*no, the weapon*—was larger than the entirety of her body.

She fluttered her wings hummingbird quick and regarded him again. She was all the more intrigued.

The captain chuckled. "What can I say?" he asked. "Some of us are imbued with unique . . . *qualities.* Mine is my hook, as plainly as yours is a formidable grasp of some very powerful magic, yes? And the inclination to put it to use."

Tink flushed as she nodded, pleased that he had somehow divined this of her. What an oddly compelling man! It had been some time since she'd been addressed with such kindness.

He leaned forward conspiratorially. "I should wonder," he began, "does your pixie dust know any limits?"

She shrugged coyly. If it did, she had yet to encounter them. After all, her lack of limits was the reason she was out there in the first place, quite literally adrift. *Not that I've found.*

He cocked a knowing eyebrow at her. "Aye, I see. Is this why you had to leave?"

I don't have *to do anything,* she insisted. Still she glanced away, a gesture of which Hook took notice.

"Your so-called *family*. So quick to cast you out. Aye, but it's a story I know perfectly well, lass."

"Family." All she'd wanted was to bask in the sunflower fields with her friends. Was that so wrong?

"Not at all," the captain said, reading her thoughts as though she'd spoken them. Or perhaps she had. She wasn't quite sure what was happening there, in that strange, unknowable place. "And I'll tell you what's more: *I'd* love to have you for a partner."

A pirate captain, needing her?

He waved his hook, this time as a demonstration, and she flapped her wings, giving a nervous squeak and floating back from him sharply.

"'Twas a scoundrel who cost me my hand," he said, lip curling into an angry snarl. She watched his mustache undulate with his words. "It's been me life's mission to exact revenge. But I do wonder if a bit of pixie dust isn't what the mission needs to carry us to victory."

Tinker Bell's heart raced as restlessly as her wings. A *mission*? That sounded important. She'd never had something so bold or explicit as a mission before. The closest she'd come was her chores—those infernal pots and pans again—decidedly less exciting. All the responsibility of a mission but without, she imagined, the element of adventure.

A mission involving my pixie dust.

"Indeed," the captain agreed. "We need it. To capture the boy."

A boy? Tinker Bell had seen human boys before, but they so rarely believed in fairies that most often they were disinclined to notice one darting directly before their eyes.

"Yes, a *boy*. Though if I'm honest, this one is more like a demon," the captain went on. "Rotten to the core. Don't you wonder why you've never come across this island before, in all your exploring?"

Tinker Bell allowed that she did, in fact, wonder that.

"It's because the fairies . . . *they're terrified of him*. They didn't want you or any of the young'uns to know about the island. He's dangerous, I tell you."

Well, this was growing more interesting by the moment. A secret mission. And a place so dangerous that the pixies avoided it, concealed it from their young?

"Do you think, Miss . . . ?"

Bell. Tinker Bell.

A grin split the pirate's face in two, revealing jagged teeth. "Do you think, Miss Bell, that you might be able to use your pixie dust to help me?"

Tinker Bell sighed with great contentment. *I'm quite sure of it.*

She perched on his hook, the metal cold against her feet, even through her slippers. It felt like the equivalent of shaking hands. There was a sense that passed between them that a mutual accord had been reached.

"Excellent. I think the two of us can help each other. Quite a great deal, in fact." His mustache trembled. "Tell me this: Are you particularly fearful of crocodiles?"

Tinker Bell shrugged. She wasn't *particularly* afraid of anything. And she'd never met an especially aggressive crocodile in the Hollow. It didn't seem he wanted an answer, though.

"Welcome to Never Land, Tinker Bell," the captain went on. "You can call me Captain Hook. I'm so thrilled to make your acquaintance." He cocked an eyebrow at her.

"I just know you're going to help me defeat Peter Pan at last."

Darling (Now)

"Peter's been away so often of late."

Tinker Bell held still, keeping her wings folded close between her shoulder blades so as not to give away any sense of rising consternation at the mermaid's idle comment. Yes, Peter had been to London frequently those days—or more accurately, those *nights*, preferring, it seemed, to wait until darkness fell over the Lost Boys' den and Tink was presumed to be tucked safe in her walnut-shell bedframe.

This was the problem with presumptions. They were so awfully . . . well, *presumptuous*, and the groundwork for many a coup. Hook knew this well (once an Eton boy, after all) and had passed his knowledge along to Tink.

Despite this, she had to acknowledge, in the moment, her creeping discomfort with the process. . . .

She pushed the thought away.

"*You* know where he's been!" A spray of salt water splashed Tink's shoulders.

The mermaid Chelan winnowed her way across the shallows of the main pool of Mermaid Lagoon, where Tink had been trying to enjoy the bright morning sun. It startled the fairy out of her anxious reverie, for which she was at least somewhat grateful, gooseflesh notwithstanding.

Hook was notoriously foul-tempered before he'd taken his lunch, and as such, Tink tended to spend that time of day far from the decks of the *Jolly Roger*, even when Peter Pan's attentions were otherwise occupied. Such as they were—yet again—that day.

Hence the allure of Mermaid Lagoon. The creatures could be a bit much—frenetic and darting as any gaggle of fairies, which Tink would not have thought possible were she not by then accustomed to it—but in that way, they were also comforting, an unexpected reminder of home.

Tink shook her head. *Don't be silly.* A cascade of pixie dust fell with the chime of bells that the other mermaids by then could understand as her speech (Hook and Tink had fashioned a spell when she first arrived in Never Land allowing others to understand her language).

"Tinker Bell, now. You have a secret," Chelan went on, a smirk pulling at the corners of her lips. Her hair, perennially the color of damp sand no matter wet or dry, bobbed in its ponytail, no less perfectly pert for being waterlogged.

If only you knew, Tink thought.

She didn't have long to dwell on the thought, though. Suddenly, a flurry of cooing erupted, and another series of splashes broke the surface of the water. Tinker Bell and Chelan turned toward the commotion.

"Look!" Penelope pointed at a tiny spec in the sky. She cut through the water and, with a small flip of her tail, gracefully positioned herself at the top of a small cluster of rocks. Immediately, she set to rearranging her starfish crown.

(Tink often thought that mermaids were perhaps the only creatures more vain than she was, and in that, she was not at all mistaken.)

Tinker Bell squinted, and the figure came into sharper relief: spry, well-muscled legs extended gracefully, one arm arced overhead like a dancer, the other swept out to catch the current. A flash of green came into focus, a tunic with a hem that had once been scalloped but was now frayed with wear, and of course the ever-present feather bobbing brightly from a green felt cap.

But most recognizable of all—even from that distance—was the expression on his face: wide-eyed, grinning joy, each individual freckle on his sunburnt cheeks dancing as he surveyed the land, gesturing here and there to point out different landmarks to . . .

A clammy tentacle of dread clutched at Tinker Bell's throat.

Before she could properly react, Arika squealed, "It's *PETER*! He's back!"

And it *was* Peter, of course. Tinker Bell would have recognized his silhouette if her eyes were closed.

The problem was, it wasn't *only* Peter.

There was also a human girl.

She was plain, such that the fairy could scarcely believe this mousy, frail, frightened creature had been the cause of Peter's nighttime flights of fancy. Literally.

She'd wondered what he'd been doing, of course, vanishing into thin air once he thought the coast was clear, not returning until well after the sun began to bleed streaky orange-gold across the horizon. There was a glint to him, too, then—like the essence of London had somehow seeped into him in a fundamental, molecular way.

And finally, when his shadow had gone missing . . .

She almost laughed thinking how he'd tried to play it off, as if he truly thought she wouldn't notice. A person's *shadow*. Just up and gone. He'd left it, or lost it, in London.

And there *she* was, the person—the girl-human on whom Peter had been calling all those nights away. And perhaps Tink had no claim to him (in fact, whatever claims she'd made, they surely involved at least one layer of omission), but that certainly didn't mean she needed to be pleased about this . . . *girl's* arrival. With her . . . strange, lumpy human shape, so graceless as she flew—

Flew.

Tinker Bell's throat tightened. For indeed, the girl,

clumsy though she was, nevertheless *was* gliding alongside Peter. Tink noted that her skin was sallow, like the experience of flight did not agree with her.

Well, of course. It wasn't innate to her. Humans had no pixie dust to illuminate them from within. But that being so, how could this one be flying without pixie dust?

It was simple: she couldn't. Not even the great and all-clever Peter Pan could pull that off on his own. Which meant one thing:

He had found some pixie dust and helped himself to it.

He had taken *hers.*

Tinker Bell swooned briefly before attempting to harness the dark swirl of her emotions. For once she felt the full weight of her inability to hold more than one emotion at a time, and she mourned that shortcoming. Surely there was a nuance, a specificity to the sensation of feeling simultaneously jealous, envious, angry, betrayed, and outraged. But to Tinker Bell just then, those gradations of turmoil swept over her like a brush fire, instant and all-consuming.

He'd stolen a piece of her magic. And given it to this *thing.*

This thing that was flying at them, pale-faced and droopy and unremarkable.

And she had been feeling bad for her deceit as she and Peter grew closer. She'd believed them to be developing a bond. What a fool she'd been.

"What *is* that?" hissed Chelan as Peter and his guest approached. "And is it wearing . . . *nightclothes*?"

Tink nodded. Yes, because Peter had been visiting her at night, in London, which was where he'd misplaced his shadow—though there it was, casting a long tail beneath him as he soared down toward the lagoon. Revolting, the whole of it. Tink cast a baleful look at the shadow, as if *it* were to blame for this disastrous turn of events. The shadow raised a hand and playfully thumbed its nose at her.

She stomped her foot, not feeling at all playful, and turned to the mermaids, who were each craning to get a better look at Peter and his companion. *Peter brings with him a girl-creature. From the city.* She practically spat the words, so distasteful were they.

"Is it wicked?" Arika asked. "It looks wicked."

The wickedest. It would kill and eat a fairy as soon as it would look at one, Tink said. Not necessarily the truth, but no matter. The important thing was that the mermaids recognized this girl as the intruder she was and were prepared to defend themselves and Never Land from her.

As Peter and the girl came in to land, Tink could see that her face had gone a disturbing shade of green. She looked disinclined to eat anything solid, much less a fairy, but Tink wasn't about to change tactics. Not when the mermaids were such a captive audience.

"Peter! You're back!" Penelope exclaimed, swimming up to him with a bright wave. Even her distrust of the newcomer couldn't dampen her enthusiasm. She narrowed an eye at the human. "But who is *this*?"

"Or *what*?" Arika asked. "It looks wicked. And why-ever is it wearing nightclothes, pray tell?"

The human's face flushed. She held out a slender arm as though she meant to shake hands. Tink glared at her and folded her own arms across her chest.

"I'm Wendy. Darling. Of Kensington Gardens, London, England," she added. Like Tinker Bell were some kind of uncultured starling fairy who'd never heard of a far-off land so grand and well known as England!

"And I *am* in my nightgown," this Wendy-thing went on, clearly nervous, though also a bit haughty. "But only because it was the only way to get away, to come visit Never Land, you see. Peter could only take us at night, while our parents were out. John and Michael's and mine. Those are my brothers." She realized she was rambling. "Although," she tilted her head to the sky, "I suppose it's not last night anymore. And so again, I really must apologize for being so indecent."

"You *really* must," Arika agreed.

Wendy blinked. "Well, I—I *do*. I apologize."

For a delightful moment everyone was very, very quiet, and all that could be heard was the ripple of water against sand. It was terribly awkward, and this *Wendy*-girl looked as though she was regretting coming to Never Land.

Good, thought Tink. *Go back to London, and leave Peter to us.*

And my pixie dust to me.

At last, Peter stepped forward. The journey from London seemed only to have made him more robust, unlike poor, wan little Wendy. He was a compact, agile boy who radiated verve even on his worst days, but the gleam in his eyes right then was the afterglow of a long night's adventure. He threw his arms open and laughed. "I think she's waiting for you to accept her apology."

"We know," Arika said, still curt. "I'm thinking about it."

Wendy looked at Peter, mouth open.

He shrugged. "They're . . . thinking about it."

Tink watched as Wendy eyed Peter. "Well, to be honest, I don't think there should be very much to think about," she protested.

"Well, *to be honest*, we don't really care what you think. *We* think you're a guest in our home. And not a very polite one." Chelan rose up to her tallest height from the water. Elegant though she was, it was an intimidating sight.

"This is all getting a little—" Peter started, realizing tensions were elevating.

It's the Wendy bird's fault, Tinker Bell said. She didn't mention the pixie dust. Surely he knew she knew?

"Don't be that way, Tinker Bell," he admonished.

"That—that little fairy? Just spoke to you? What did she say?" Wendy looked astonished and thrilled.

Normally, Tinker Bell adored when others gazed at her with astonishment and thrill. But right then, she was focused on the fact that Wendy couldn't understand her. Unlike all the others in Never Land. *Of course.* Wendy hadn't been in Never Land when she and Hook performed their translation spell. Now she'd never know what Tink was thinking unless Tink wanted her to.

Perfect.

She darted toward Penelope, whispering in her ear, then wove toward Chelan and Arika to fill them in. She glanced at Peter quickly, but he was preoccupied with admiring his shadow in the morning sunlight, contorting his limbs into creative shapes just to watch the patterns play against the sand.

"Peter's right," Penelope cut in. "Everything's getting a bit heated."

"I agree," Wendy said, relieved. "Why don't—"

But whatever she'd planned to say next, the others were never to hear it, as together the mermaids leapt, arcing gracefully out of the water, grabbing Wendy, and pulling her back toward the lagoon.

Startled, Wendy shrieked. "Put me down!" she demanded. "I'm not dressed for swimming!"

"Frankly, you're not dressed for mixed company!" Penelope pointed out, wrapping her hands tighter around Wendy's wrist as she struggled.

It happened so quickly Peter barely had time to react. A splash and another shout from Wendy: *"Peter! Help!"*

Finally, he looked away from his shadow. He jumped

up, twirling in midair and dipping down toward the waves. "Wendy!"

He dove for her, grabbing her elbow. But the mermaids had wrapped themselves around her remaining limbs, enjoying her panic as she thrashed underwater. Bubbles rose as she became more frantic.

Tink dove toward the melee, lighting her path like a bioluminescent reef. By the glow of her otherworldly sparkle, she could just make out Wendy's desperate expression as she wrenched her arms from the mermaids and fought her way back to the surface.

And there, of course, was Peter, cutting sharply through the water and wrapping his arms around the only unclaimed part of Wendy's body, which was her torso. As his hands clasped just over her naval, Tinker Bell's vision went red.

Not now, she told herself. *Stop the Wendy-thing. Peter is altogether too wrapped up in this creature.*

It would not stand, and if the fairy had her way, neither would the human. But it wasn't just Tinker Bell's vision going red—it was Wendy's face as she strained, short of breath. Peter gave a great tug and wrenched her free, sending the mermaids recoiling back, barreling into each other and bouncing off in every direction, churning up great swirls of water all around them.

Tinker Bell took advantage of the chaos and fluttered legs, wings, arms, heart . . . straight up and behind Wendy. She grabbed the girl's ponytail and yanked as hard as she could. She could feel the force of Wendy's teeth as they clattered together. Immediately Tink let go of Wendy's hair and flew toward land, hovering as casually as she could muster as Peter broke the surface with his pet human in tow.

Wendy didn't look very good at all. No longer red or green but a mottled gray, skin puckered, eyes closed, she barely stirred as Peter laid her gently down on the bank. "Wendy," he said, voice hoarse. "Come on, the mermaids were just playing around. They didn't mean anything by it. They get a little . . . well, territorial when someone new comes to visit."

Chelan swam up. "Don't blame us. *She's* the intruder."

"She's my guest!" Peter protested, but he was more concerned with Wendy's complexion, which wasn't improving. He rested his palms flat against her cheeks. "C'mon," he said again. Gently, he tilted her head first to one side, then the other. "Breathe now." When she didn't respond, he propped her up at the waist, rapping lightly between her shoulder blades. "Wendy!"

"I'm *sure* she's just playing," Arika said. "Humans have notoriously bad senses of humor."

"Don't you mean mermaids?" Peter snapped. Just then, Wendy sputtered, sitting up straighter and reaching to brace herself on her own. She shook her head and coughed again, more forcefully, spewing an impressive fountain of water onto the sand.

"Wendy! You're okay!" Peter hugged her.

"I seem to be," she said. "No thanks to *them.*" She shot a look at the mermaids.

"My goodness," Penelope retorted. "You're *fine.*"

"We were only trying to drown her," Arika said with a snort. The other two chuckled, and even Peter's lips twitched for a moment—though only a moment.

Not Tinker Bell, though. She laughed until sparkly pixie dust tears rolled down her face. *She's lucky it wasn't worse.* Wendy glanced at her, knowing she was being spoken ill of but still unable to decipher fairy speak and unwilling to ask for a direct translation.

Good, Tink thought.

"If this is how you're going to welcome my friend, I'll just take her to meet the Lost Boys," Peter said. "Wendy and her brothers will be staying with us for a while."

Tinker Bell's laugh caught in her throat. *A while?* What was "a while"? And since when were droopy new humans allowed in Never Land?

Since when was Tinker Bell's companionship not enough for Peter?

Tink flew toward Peter, assuming she'd follow them to the hideout at Hangman's Tree. But Peter held up a hand. "Just Wendy and me, for now."

Had he spotted her underwater? Had he seen her pull Wendy's hair?

Tink fumed. *Very well.* She watched as the two flew off,

looking for all the world like they'd been doing so forever. *Have it your way.*

It occurred to her that Hook had been waiting for her to give the go-ahead for some time. But for one reason or another, Tinker Bell had been putting off taking the next step in his plot against Peter Pan. Peter was charming, and Tinker Bell, it seemed, had fallen for his considerable charms. And to what end? To be cast aside the moment a shiny new plaything arrived on the scene?

Yes, Peter Pan. Have it your way.

Because soon Captain Hook and I will have it our own.

I'm ready at last.

Are you?

It was midday, the sun high overhead, when Tinker Bell found Captain Hook on the foredeck of the *Jolly Roger*. A table to his left revealed a tray with the discarded remains of a well-enjoyed lunch, including the carcass of a rather unlucky fowl, stripped all but bare, and several mugs crusted with the dregs of an empty carafe of mead.

"Ah! There you are." Hook sat up straighter when he saw her. He gestured to the messy scraps of his meal. "Smee! Why has this not been cleared?"

"I was just getting to that, sir." Smee, who'd been bumbling in the corner, blushed furiously, jumping to his feet and grabbing the plates. But in his nervousness, he sent several of them crashing to the boat's deck. "Oh, dear."

Smee scurried toward the hatch leading belowdecks, slipping briefly then righting himself.

Tink fluttered to the table, hovering delicately within Hook's eyeline while avoiding the less appealing leftovers from lunch. *I have news. About Pan.*

Hook's reaction was completely involuntary, his back going ramrod straight. "Do tell."

She wondered if he'd sensed it, the hesitance she'd been feeling as her bond with Peter had deepened. Emotions were so messy. In many ways, it was far easier to embrace the fury over Peter's betrayal than it was to live in the liminal space where her loyalties shifted with the winds.

He's been to London. And he's returned with guests. (*Using* my *fairy dust,* she added internally. Though of course, Hook had always been adept at reading her. It was a double-edged sword—or a double-pointed hook, as it were.)

Hook wrinkled his forehead. "Humans? From beyond Never Land? But . . . *why*?"

Tinker Bell shook her head. *Well,* I *certainly don't know. I've only met the one, and* she's *nothing special, I assure you. A* girl, Tink added. Tink shook more angrily, showering the captain in a glowing storm of pixie dust that he shooed away easily.

"Ah, but you see—she must be *very* special indeed, in point of fact," Hook countered. Was he . . . *goading* her? "For Peter to have traveled all the way to London for her. And to have brought her back here."

He gave the fairy a deep, knowing look. "He would have needed some pixie dust. And somehow, I rather suspect you didn't give him any." He grinned, an awful expression that made Tink's whole body feel clammy and unclean. "Not willingly, anyway."

He *was* goading her. And of course he had seen straight through her most carefully concealed thoughts.

Tinker Bell stomped at the air. She wasn't sure whom she was angrier at—Peter, for stealing the dust in the first place, or Hook, for sussing out the situation so easily. *She's a lump. In a ratty nightgown.*

"Wonderful!" Hook clapped his one hand—carefully—against his hook in delight, grinning. "Don't you see? She's special to Peter, *and* she's a lump? She'll be all the more vulnerable to our attack."

Tink nodded, but her stomach clenched. Yes, this was what she'd hoped Hook would say. There was no turning back.

Not even if she wanted to.

Of course, did she even know what she wanted anymore? She was a fairy—a minuscule creature with outsized power. Everything about her from the inside out was a contradiction that split her open over and over and over again.

She has brothers, she chimed to Hook. *Two of them. I didn't meet them, but they can't be any more useful than she is.*

"In other words, they'll *all* be easy to defeat. *And* Pan will be distracted, wanting to . . . *protect* them." Hook sneered. "It's always one's passion that ends up one's undoing." He leaned toward her. "Remember that, my tempestuous fairy."

Tinker Bell gestured at his hook. *Really, Captain? Is it* I *who needs to remember?*

Hook threw back his head and laughed deep from his belly. "Touché!" He collected himself, rapping his fingers against his chin. "I'm assuming this means you're finally ready?" Perhaps he had also seen through her various procrastinations, then—insisting on more time to earn Pan's trust, to familiarize herself with his hideout, to whisper in the Lost Boys' ears. . . .

Tinker Bell took a deep breath. The time had come.

She nodded, the sound of her movement echoing daintily around the foredeck. *I am.*

"You'll show me Peter and the Lost Boys' lair and help me infiltrate it?"

Yes.

The forest was still when Tinker Bell returned later that night, Hook and his crew in tow. Though she was still a bit conflicted about delivering Peter to Hook, she knew that if her will faltered, all she needed to do was draw on the image of Wendy soaring over Mermaid Lagoon. Thinking of the wide-eyed gaze Wendy had given Peter made her shudder. *No. No Wendys needed in Never Land, thank you kindly.*

"And so she shall return to London," Hook said, and

Tinker Bell realized she'd spoken that. "That is, if we should let her and her brothers live, after we've captured Pan." This set off a low ripple of laughter among his men.

It's here. Tink paused, wings quivering glitter and gossamer. *His hideout.*

"You'll have to be more specific, my dear." Hook raised his dim lantern. "I see nothing but immutable tree trunks."

Closer. Tink nodded toward the trunk before her, at a hollowed-out knot at its base, just where knotted wood met loamy earth. She cupped a hand over her ear, cocked her head. *Listen.*

It was Smee, unbelievably, whose eyes widened first. "Is that . . . ? Sir—I mean, Captain!" he sputtered, excited and startled. "I hear *snoring*! Down there!" He pointed toward the hollow in the tree.

"*In* the tree?" Hook's gaze swiveled from Tinker Bell to Smee and back again.

Tink bobbed her head. *Indeed. The Lost Boys make their den down there!*

"Sir!" shouted another a few feet away. "There's another opening!"

Each boy has their own, Tink confirmed. *Shall I go distract them, then?*

"Darling," Hook said, his tone somewhat rebuking, "do you really have to ask?"

The scene within the tree was almost disappointing.

The Lost Boys were situated in their usual locations—

one curled on a bearskin beside the hearth and another snoozing gently in a hammock—but Peter was awake.

And he wasn't alone.

He was perched at the edge of his bed with . . . that *Wendy* rapt at his feet. Beside her was a small boy in pink footed pajamas and another boy wearing perfectly round, black-framed spectacles that he adjusted on the bridge of his nose. He, too, wore a nightshirt.

The lumpy brothers themselves. Tink wanted to gnash her teeth. She'd caught them mid-conversation. Peter was boasting about how Wendy had *helped him find his shadow*? And sewn it back on for him?

Tink's mouth filled with a sour taste. Who could possibly care about a silly shadow, anyway? Peter *clearly* didn't need it all that badly, or he would never have lost it in the first place.

"I'm so happy you're going to stay here and be our mother," he said, making Tink's whole body seize like a block of ice.

Wendy looked equally shocked. "Why, Peter," she said, her tone gentle, "John, Michael, and I can't stay here forever."

Peter was indignant. "Why not?" He flew up and around the three siblings and landed in front of them, hands on hips imperiously.

"We're from London, not Never Land," Wendy replied. "And we have a mother—and a father, mind you—of our own."

"Not to mention a Nana," John added, though Tink

didn't know what a Nana was and couldn't see how that was at all helpful.

The little one gazed up at Peter. "But you could come back to London with us."

The one in glasses nodded. He stood on the bed, warming to the idea. "Yeah. Wendy can't be your mother, because she's still got one of her own, and she—*we*—need to go back to her. But you could come, too! Our parents wouldn't mind at all!"

Wendy clapped her hands and jumped up, embracing the boy. "John, what a delightful idea!" She turned to Peter. "He's right. They'd take care of you. They'd take good and proper care of *all* the Lost Boys! I'm certain of it!"

Tinker Bell's skin felt electrified. Her vision narrowed to a tiny pinpoint. All she could hear was the steady rush of her own heartbeat as it sent her pixie blood surging to every channel of her veins. *He isn't saying no,* she realized.

Why *isn't he saying no?*

Forgetting herself in her rage and panic, Tinker Bell darted up to Peter, wings flapping sharply enough to scratch glass. *You can't leave Never Land!*

"Tink! You're back!" He didn't sense her mood, so caught up in Wendy and her fabulous plans was he. The dustup at the lagoon was apparently forgotten, as well. "We had the most splendid day adventur—"

She cut him off. She couldn't bear to hear another second about his grand adventures with Wendy and her splendid brothers and their lovely human family back in

London who not only *wanted* them but would want Peter and *his* "brothers," as well.

And who will want me?

Tinker Bell felt a single tear well in one eye. *You can't go!* she said again, more desperate. Never mind that she'd come with Hook on a mission to destroy Peter. That he would be willing to leave Never Land behind entirely at this human child's fleeting suggestion was the ultimate betrayal. Truly, he cared not a whit for her. Leaving her behind would be as easy for him as casting her off had been for her fairy family.

He held out an arm, as though she were some hysterical creature to be placated. "Tink—"

YOU CANNOT LEAVE NEVER LAND, Tinker Bell exploded. All three of the children and Peter took a step back, giving her a wide and cautious berth.

Finally, Peter Pan had faltered.

Tinker Bell was somewhat surprised at how thrilling it was to see such a thing. The clever and cocksure Peter Pan himself, having a moment of doubt? And because of her!

You don't understand, she said. A cruel smile spread across her lips. *You can't leave,* she went on, feeling the words round and full-bodied inside her, *because of the pixie dust.* Now he would learn. He would know. Her power.

"Whaddya mean?" He shrugged. "It's what we use to fly. So?" His cheeks reddened, and he had the good sense to look mildly sheepish. "Is this because I borrowed some? For the Darlings?"

Buzzing filled Tink's head, hot and furious. Of course

Peter Pan would try to play off his theft as mere boyhood high jinks. *You CANNOT LEAVE,* she said, everything boiling up inside her, *because it is the dust that keeps you young.*

The pixie dust keeps you young . . . and it keeps you here.

"The dust keeps me young?"

John blinked, confused. "I thought you didn't *want* to grow up," he said to Peter. "I thought you *chose* that."

"I did!" Peter insisted.

Ha! Hook *chose that,* Tink corrected before she could stop herself. Then again, there was a great might in watching the realization slowly strip Peter's face of expression. *And* I *made it so.*

The words were out, and there would be no taking them back. Her body felt swollen with power, emotion, force.

At the sound of the captain's name, the Lost Boys awakened like a bell had been rung. The horrid truth was out, could never be put back in. All that could be heard within the space was the crackle of the hearth fire and quiet, even breathing.

Tink and Hook, working together.

Tink and Hook, casting a spell to make Peter Pan young and vulnerable.

"Hook thought if I didn't grow up, I'd be easier to kill." Peter quietly stated the obvious. Tink didn't dispute it.

Wendy gasped, but the others were too stunned to react.

"Well, here I still am," he said darkly. "And where is he?"

A thunderous crash sounded, followed by a shower of loose earth and dust.

When it cleared, there was the captain himself, standing among the group, cutlass unsheathed.

"Fear not, my boy," he said to Peter, gesturing grandly around the space. "I have arrived."

Never After

Instantly the hideout flooded with pirates. The Lost Boys sprang into action, but they were no match for actual swords. John swept up Michael and rushed him toward Wendy. "Take him above!"

"Peter needs us!" Wendy said, looking torn and appalled.

"You're right, he does," the pirate Mullins said gruffly. "Too bad you won't be much help!" He leered at her and lunged, swiping at her with his sword. A thin line of blood quickly beaded up along her forearm.

"You should get out of here," the Lost Boy who was called Tootles warned her. "This is no place for a mother-girl!"

At that, Wendy seemed to regain a sense of composure. "Let's just say I'm a young woman, then. And I *don't* need you telling me my place."

Tinker Bell was overcome with a wave of admiration for the girl . . . the young woman, that was. Until Wendy spun to look at her, eyes flashing. "This is all *your* fault!" she hissed. "You've endangered Peter!" She pointed to where Hook did indeed have Peter cornered, the tip of his sword at Peter's throat. "Was this what you wanted?"

Tink stared at Wendy, incredulous—heart beating as quickly as her wings. How quickly it had all happened.

Of course not.

None of this was ever what she'd wanted. All she'd wanted was to finish her silly mending and while away the day with her friends in the fields. . . .

All she'd wanted was the so-called maturity and independence to use her magic thoughtfully.

So she could spend her afternoons being carefree. Careless.

And look at her.

Her thoughtful and mature application of magic had hurt . . . well, all but Hook, it seemed. Including Tink herself.

Embarrassment flooded her, and she fled.

The journey back to the Hollow was swift. Tinker Bell did not expect to be greeted with any welcome and was surprised when the fairy elders met her at the banks of the river as her lily pad washed ashore. Their faces were smiling, relieved. *We were so worried!*

But . . . you told me to leave, Tink protested.

For a morning, perhaps! For some clarity and fresh air, a bit of distance! You were never meant to vanish so completely.

We shan't let you out of our sight again.

Tink realized, as they embraced, just what it would mean to allow herself to melt back into the fold.

Surely, it would mean Peter's demise.

And yes, of course, her feelings were confusing on the matter of Hook versus Pan (and now, adding to the chaos, versus Wendy and her entire extended family). But hadn't they been conflicted, truly, all along? *Would* she have agreed to Hook's proposal if she hadn't been so raw from clashing with her people?

Perhaps not.

Was she willing to risk Peter Pan's safety—indeed, most likely his *life*—over a *perhaps*?

Perhaps not.

At last, Tink realized, she *did* have a mission. One born of her own passion. It would involve magic—fiery, perhaps more concentrated, more ripened than standard fairy fare. Not dark, as such. But tinted, stained, perhaps. She'd have to find a way to persuade the elders that the moment required such measures.

She found herself more than up to the task.

When the pixies returned to Never Land, they arrived en masse, flying in formation like a flock of migrating birds. Together, they cut a neon streak toward Mermaid Lagoon, the younger creatures marveling at the island that for so long had been cloaked from their awareness.

The mermaids did take a bit of convincing, though.

"Does it mean saving the Wendy-thing, *too*?" Chelan asked.

"And is she still wearing her nightgown?" Arika chimed in.

Ultimately, Tink appealed to their better nature. Her elders, too, cleverly pointed out that should the mermaids and the fairies band together against the pirates, from then on Never Land would not be magically concealed from the fairies; the mermaids would forever have new allies.

Tinker Bell had begun this journey from a desire to be with friends—so much so that she had been willing to overlook the rules and customs of her greater community.

Now she found herself surrounded by community old and new—and commingled, no less!—in a most unexpected turn of events. Was this outcome not worth a bit of self-sacrifice here and there, in whatever form it should take?

Was Peter not worth it?

He did *steal your pixie dust*, she thought.

Perhaps you can take a morning's leave of him, then. For some space and fresh air.

But to do that, you must first save him.

The fairies dimmed their lights as they fluttered single file down the tree trunk passageway to the Lost Boys' hideout. Tink gasped once she got inside. The Lost Boys and the Darlings were all bound hands to ankles and gagged. The space was pure chaos, showing signs of a violent scuffle, with overturned bedclothes, furniture everywhere, and clouds of dust still lingering in the cool underground air.

Peter had been strung up from each limb to various bedposts, also gagged. Unlike the Darlings and the Lost Boys, who were huddled in fear, Peter looked positively defiant even in his vulnerable position.

All at once the fairies burst from their corner, lit brighter than a galaxy. The elders darted straight to the captives. But the younger pixies, led by Tinker Bell, zipped and darted around the pirates, sprinkling enough pixie dust to spark.

Enough pixie dust, that was, to *burn.*

"We're on fire!" Smee shouted. "Run for the water!"

"The boy will escape!" Hook snarled. "You'll all be staying right here!"

The pirate crew wanted to obey their captain, of course—but the fairies were relentless. And their dust rained down like acid. Tink found that the unease that came from always trying to contain her outsized feelings was greatly alleviated with this opportunity to expend some of that wild, raw emotion. It was thrilling. She threw her head back, laughing as the crew retreated.

Then it was just Tink, Hook, and Peter. The Darlings and Lost Boys had been released by the elders. Peter was still strung up, bobbing in his restraints like a kite. Amid the chaos he looked at Tinker Bell with amusement.

"Came back for us, did ya?" His eyes twinkled.

I came back . . . for me.

Hook gaped at the two of them, then allowed himself a low chuckle. "Aye, but that's priceless, love. And here you've been plotting against him since you first arrived, *and* seeing as how he betrayed you."

I haven't forgiven him. But unlike you, Peter Pan never intended to hurt anyone.

"Fair point," Hook conceded. "What do *you* plan to do about it? Since your pixie dust just doesn't seem to have quite the same effect on me as it did on my crew?" He leered.

Tink smiled. She knew something that Captain Hook did not.

At that moment, the mermaids were tunneling an underground channel from Mermaid Lagoon to Hangman's Tree. They'd summoned their own friends from nearby islands. These mermaid pods brought with them the pull of the tides; this was their magic.

Tink knew all this. And she knew they were close.

When they broke through the earth beneath the tree, a surge of water blasted the trunk wide open.

Hook was sent directly into the air, many miles up, before arcing swiftly and returning back down into the pool that had gathered within the Lost Boys' former lair.

He landed . . .

. . . directly in the path of an oncoming crocodile.

Peter looked at Tinker Bell. "Is that . . . ?"

Tink nodded.

It is not an exaggeration to say that Hook's shrieks could be heard all the way to the Hollow that fateful dawn.

Not that any of the fairies were home to confirm it.

Did Peter grow up, and old, then? Once the magic of the pixie dust had been revealed and ostensibly lifted? Did Hook survive his brush with the Crocodile? Did Tinker Bell return to the glade with her pixie family, and if so, what was to become of her friendship with Peter? And what of the Darlings, then? Did they return home to their parents, and did they take in the Lost Boys?

Tink herself would tell you all these things may well have happened. Could have happened, and can still. Rumor tells that when Hangman's Tree erupted, a shower of pixie dust scattered far and wide across the globe. It's there for the taking, up for grabs. Pixie dust!

Tinker Bell would also tell you:

You—yes, you!—can fly. Search! Seek. Find the mission, the magic.
It may be powerful, strong, and frightening.
But it need not be dark.
Indeed, it's out there. For those who believe.

Gonna Take You There

What if Naveen had to get home to Maldonia?

by Farrah Rochon

Gonna Take You There

What if Naveen had to get home to Maldonia?

by Farrah Rochon

The clanging of the call bell summoning Duke's Cafe's sole waitress to the kitchen window could barely be heard above the raucous patrons.

Tiana balanced a stack of flapjacks, two bowls of grits, and five orders of pillowy-soft beignets on a serving tray. She squeezed through the narrow paths between the tables, carefully dodging pointy elbows and protruding feet. The café was packed to the gills with hungry, bleary-eyed customers who'd spent the night either kicking up their heels in the taverns or working the overnight shift in one of the factories in the French Quarter.

"Hey, Tiana, can I get more coffee here?" one customer called.

"Yeah, me too," said another.

"One minute," Tiana said. She quickly made her way to the counter and refilled the carafe with freshly brewed coffee. Several drops splashed onto her fingers, but she didn't have time to wipe off the hot liquid. She was used to such burns.

"Order up," the fry cook, Buford, bellowed from the kitchen window.

"I'll be right there," she called over her shoulder. She darted around the restaurant, refilling empty coffee mugs and picking up dirty dishes. When she returned to the kitchen, she encountered a frowning Buford, his hand propped on his generous hip.

"You want to know why you'll never open your own restaurant?" Buford asked.

"Don't start with me today," Tiana warned.

"It's because you're too dang slow. People want their food hot out the pot."

"Slow!" Tiana motioned to the crowded dining room. "Do you see this place? I can't be everywhere at once, Buford."

He pointed a spatula dripping with egg yolk. "And that's why you'll always be right here, serving folks at Duke's instead of in your own restaurant. You can't handle the heat."

Tiana stepped back in shock. It was bad enough Buford had given away two of her shifts this week, making it that much harder for her to save money for the expenses running her own restaurant would bring. But then he insulted her work ethic?

She'd been on her feet for three hours straight that

morning without a single break. She'd served food, stacked dishes, and cleaned the tables when customers left. She basically did every single thing in the place except the one thing she really wanted to do: cook.

Why was she doing this? Cooking was her passion, yet she spent most of her time watching Buford serve up greasy food prepared without any of the care she would have employed.

Well, not anymore.

"Is that so?" Tiana asked.

"Darn right," Buford replied.

She reached behind herself and untied the apron strings at the small of her back.

"Wrong," Tiana said. "I'm done here."

Buford's mouth fell open. "You . . . you can't quit," he sputtered.

"I just did," she countered. "I'm tired of you picking apart my dream. I'm overworked and underpaid. And I'm not putting up with it anymore!"

Tiana balled up the apron and tossed it on the counter. She grabbed her coat and hat and headed out the back door, ignoring Buford's calls to return. By the time she made it to the end of the alley, her entire body was shaking with a mixture of outrage, fear, and regret.

Had she really quit her job?

The gravity of the situation suddenly hit her. What was she thinking! How could she have made such a rash decision? She couldn't quit. She worked the night shift at Cal's, but the pay there wouldn't cover all her expenses, let alone allow her to continue saving for her dream. And it wasn't like she could afford the luxury of searching for something where she wouldn't have to work her way up to getting the most lucrative shifts. How was she ever going to get her restaurant without Duke's?

She spun on her heel and rushed for the door she'd just walked out of. But with each step she took, the nauseated feeling she got whenever Buford belittled her dream intensified. She needed this job, but should it come at the price of her dignity? If she returned to that kitchen begging for the cook's forgiveness, she would never gain his respect.

Though if she didn't, she might never earn enough money to open her own restaurant.

Maybe her dignity *did* have a price.

Just then, Tiana heard what sounded like bickering coming from the opposite end of the alley. She quietly but quickly walked to the edge of the building and peered around the corner. She spotted two men—one short and portly, the other tall and . . . well . . . rather handsome, if she was being honest—arguing in the street. The shorter gentleman's cheeks were so red it looked as if he'd colored them with rouge. The taller one, who was also younger by many years, grew exceedingly animated, gesturing with his hands as he spoke.

"Will you please just read the telegram for yourself,

Lawrence?" the taller one asked. "According to this message, we must hasten our return."

"I don't care what that telegram says." The other man turned his nose up at the paper the tall one held out to him. "I've decided this will be a new beginning for me. I am done with your family treating me like some peasant, expecting me to change course at a moment's notice. Find yourself another valet to push around."

"Can you not wait until we return to Maldonia to be done with my family?" the handsome one asked.

"No." The one called Lawrence dropped two of the three suitcases he was holding. "Here are your bags, Prince Naveen. You are officially on your own."

Prince Naveen?

Tiana's friend Charlotte and her father, Mr. Eli LaBouff, had been in the restaurant earlier, talking about some prince who was coming into town and attending their Mardi Gras ball. Lottie had hired Tiana to make beignets for the ball.

Dang it! She'd planned to use the kitchen at Duke's to fry up those beignets. How was she supposed to do that when she'd quit her job?

Tiana threw her head back and sighed in frustration. Yet another implication she hadn't considered.

The tableau playing out before her once again grabbed her attention. Tiana watched in fascination as the shorter man stomped off with his bag, leaving the prince standing in the middle of the sidewalk. He looked as lost as an abandoned newborn puppy.

A moment later, the prince's head turned her way and their eyes connected.

Tiana jerked back.

"Ma'am!"

Oh, no!

He approached her, his amber-colored eyes filled with worry.

She swallowed deeply before asking, "Yes?"

"My name is Prince Naveen of Maldonia." He bowed his head slightly, touching the brim of his pageboy cap. "I am in need of assistance. Maybe you can help?"

"What kind of assistance?" Surely he didn't expect her to step in as his valet.

"You see, I just arrived in America today, but a message from my family back home made it here before I did. I need to get back to the port as soon as possible so that I can get on the ship before it leaves for its return voyage. Can you please help me find the best route to the port? I am so bad at directions." He looked around and helplessly raised his hands. "I have no idea where I am."

"What about Mardi Gras?" Tiana asked. "Aren't you supposed to go to Mr. Eli LaBouff's ball tonight as his personal guest? That's a pretty big deal. Are you sure you want to leave?"

He scrunched his forehead. "How do you know I am

supposed to attend the ball tonight? We have never met before, have we?"

Tiana pointed at a discarded newspaper lying in the alley. A photo of him dressed in royal regalia and wearing a charming smile took up a large portion of the front page. "Anyone who can read the paper knows about you."

Prince Naveen stooped down and lifted the paper from the street. "At least the photographer caught my good side, eh?" He shook his head. "That is not important. Neither is the ball. I will apologize to Mr. LaBouff about missing it, but I really must get home." He looked at her with imploring eyes. "Please, help me. I have no one else to turn to."

Pulling her bottom lip between her teeth, Tiana glanced over at the door to Duke's kitchen and then back at the handsome prince. The desperation in his eyes warred with her own desperation to go inside and smooth things over with Buford. She had enough problems of her own without adding the prince's to her load. Besides, he was a grown man, and wealthy to boot! He would figure out a way to manage.

But one look at him told Tiana it wasn't that simple. Prince Naveen needed help. And if there was one thing her parents had taught her, it was the importance of helping those in need.

"Fine, I'll take you to the port," Tiana said.

"Oh, thank you!" Naveen said, his voice saturated with relief and gratitude.

Tiana looked to the door again. Did she have time to go in and apologize to Buford?

"Are we going?" Naveen asked. "Not to rush you, but . . . uh . . . I really need to get there as soon as possible. I need to be on that vessel before it leaves for Maldonia."

"Let's go," Tiana said. She would figure out the Buford situation later.

She gestured for the prince to follow her, and together they headed out of the alley, with the prince's two suitcases in tow.

The port was less than a ten-minute walk from the café, but between navigating the busy city streets and being stopped by curious onlookers who recognized Naveen from his photo in the newspaper, it took them nearly twice that long. As usual, the docks were abuzz with activity. Hundreds of people crowded the pier, angling their way around huge shipping containers bound for the massive cargo ships. Merchants hawked their wares, trying their best to entice potential customers as they walked by.

"Wait a minute," Naveen said. He stood in the middle of the busy pier and scratched his head underneath his cap. "Is this the right dock?"

"The other one is way upriver," Tiana said. "You would have had to take the streetcar or a vehicle to get downtown from there. Is that how you got there?"

"No, Lawrence and I walked," he said.

"Then this is the right dock."

"But the passenger ship I arrived on this morning is not here."

Tiana looked over at the large ships lined up along the long pier. "Are you sure?"

"I am pretty sure," he said. "I was on it for quite a while."

She caught the attention of a dock worker. "Excuse me, sir, but do you know anything about the large passenger ship that was docked here this morning?"

"Yep." The man nodded. "It headed out about twenty minutes ago."

Naveen's eyes widened in dismay as his shoulders slumped in defeat. "No," he said. "Do you know when it will be coming back?"

"About a month's time," the man said.

Naveen shook his head. "That is too long. I cannot wait a month before I get back to my family."

"Well . . ." The man scratched his head. "The ship is making a stop in Mobile Bay to fuel up before it heads across the Atlantic."

"Where is Mobile Bay?"

"Alabama," Tiana and the man said at the same time.

"About a hundred fifty miles east of here," the dock worker added. "That's at least a half day's drive."

Naveen looked to Tiana. She shook her head before he could even think about asking.

"No way," she said. "I offered to bring you to the port,

but that's as far as I can take you. I have too many things to do today."

Like figuring out how she was going to make five hundred beignets for the LaBouffs' Mardi Gras ball without a kitchen to cook them in.

"But how do I get to Mobile Bay?"

"You're a rich prince," Tiana pointed out. "You can hire a driver."

"But what do I do when I get there?"

"You do what anyone would do. You buy a ticket to board the ship and you get on it."

"You make it sound so simple, but it isn't. Who do I see about getting a ticket once I get there? If that port is anything like this one, I will be lost."

Tiana stared at him in amazement. "Don't you know how to do anything for yourself?"

An embarrassed flush colored his face. "Well, not really, actually," he admitted. "I have always had servants or a valet to take care of everything, but Lawrence has abandoned me, and I . . . I do not know what to do."

Tiana had never encountered someone who seemed so utterly defeated. But what could she do? She surely couldn't go gallivanting off to Mobile Bay with him.

"I'm sorry, Prince Naveen, but I just can't—"

"I will pay you."

Tiana's head jerked back in shock. "What?"

"Name your price. I will pay you to take me to Mobile."

Her mouth dropped open in disbelief. "You can't be serious."

"I am. Look, umm . . . what is your name?"

"See, you don't even know my name, and you want me to take you to another state?"

"Please, tell me your name."

"It's Tiana."

"Oh! That is a very pretty name," he said. He shook his head as if trying to clear it. "Look, Tiana. The missive I received was not very forthcoming, but I gather from it that something is very wrong. I need to get home. I want to show my parents that they can count on me. They think I am irresponsible and selfish and a—what is the word? A moocher?"

"Are you?"

"No!" he said. "Well, maybe I have been in the past. But I can change, and this is one way for me to *show* them that I can. Please, help me. Just tell me what would be worth it for you to help me get where I need to go."

Tiana thought about the money stored in coffee cans in her chifforobe. Years of tips she'd collected while waiting tables at Duke's Cafe and working the night shift at Cal's Restaurant. As of now, she had enough for a down payment, but she would need more than that to buy kitchen equipment, tableware, provisions, etc., not to mention start making rent. Tiana did a quick mental calculation of how much she'd need for the first month.

She blurted out the amount to Naveen.

"Deal," he said without hesitation.

"Really?" she asked.

"Yes, yes. I promise to get the money to you as soon as I get to Maldonia."

"I'm supposed to wait until you make it across the Atlantic?" She crossed her arms over her chest and shook her head. "No way."

"Okay, okay, you are right. I would not make a deal like that, either. I will have my family send the money via telegraph."

"I have your word that I'll get the money?" Tiana asked.

He slapped his palm over his heart. "On my honor."

Tiana looked him up and down. If she agreed to this, she would need to find someone to join them. There was no way she could go all the way to Mobile with him without a chaperone of some sort. It would be seen as improper.

But who?

"Do you know how to drive a car?" Naveen asked. "Wait, do you even *have* a car?"

"No," she admitted. "The only car I've ever ridden in belongs to Mr. LaBouff."

Tiana slapped her hand to her forehead.

"Of course," she said. *"Of course!"*

She would get the LaBouffs' driver, John, to take them. She'd known him since she was a little girl and trusted him completely. Not only could John drive, but he would serve as their chaperone, as well.

The LaBouffs were preparing for their ball. They weren't worried about going anywhere. And she should be back in plenty enough time to make the beignets for tonight.

Tiana smiled at Naveen, thinking about how much closer this would bring her to getting her restaurant. "You are in luck," she said. "Because I know exactly how to get you to Mobile."

Twenty minutes later, Tiana and Naveen alighted from the streetcar in front of the LaBouffs' huge mansion on St. Charles Avenue. The grandiose home stood out among the many opulent residences that lined the famous avenue. The flurry of activity at the mansion as a multitude of people readied the house for the night's ball rivaled what Tiana and Naveen had witnessed on the dock.

They were greeted by the butler, who promptly went off to fetch Charlotte.

When her friend appeared at the top of the staircase, her eyes widened at the sight of Tiana and Naveen below. Charlotte hurried down to the first floor.

"Hello," she said, then quickly grabbed Tiana by the elbow and jerked her into the parlor just off the entryway.

"Oh my goodness, oh my goodness, oh my goodness," Lottie mumbled over and over again as she paced. "Tia! Tia, do you know who that is?" She pointed toward the foyer. "That's Prince Naveen of Maldonia!"

"Yes, Lottie, I know. We came here together."

"Why did I leave him standing there? I should have

offered him tea. Or maybe a tour of the gardens. How are things going with the beignets for tonight? I'll bet he'd love to try one." Lottie stopped short. She turned to face Tiana. "Wait a minute. You and Prince Naveen came here together? As in *together* together?"

"No, not *together* together. Just together."

"I'm both confused and intrigued, Tia, and you know conflicting emotions make me dizzy. Now, which one should I be feeling right now?"

Tiana hunched her shoulders. "Probably both. And you may want to add *disappointed* to your list of emotions."

"Would you stop talking in riddles, please? What are you doing with the prince?"

"It's kind of a long story." Tiana took a breath. "Now, I know that you were expecting him to attend your ball tonight, but he won't be able to."

"What? Why not?"

"The prince received word that he is needed back home, and he's trying to get on a boat to Maldonia as soon as possible."

"But he just arrived in N'awlins today. He's going back already?"

"He said he has to. It sounds like something happened with his family."

Lottie's hand flew to her throat. "Something bad?"

"I don't know," Tiana said. "Naveen didn't go into detail, but he's desperate to get back home."

"I guess I understand," Lottie said. "If I got word that Big Daddy needed help while I was away, I would be on the first boat back here to see about him."

"Of course you would. I would do the same if it were Mama," Tiana said. She wasn't sure how to ask her next question, so she just asked it. "Uh, Lottie, do you think John could drive me and Naveen to Mobile?"

"Mobile? As in Alabama?"

Tiana quickly explained the situation, and the need for a driver—and chaperone.

"How about *two* chaperones?" Charlotte asked.

Tiana's eyes widened. "But what about your ball tonight? There's no guarantee that we'll get back in time for it. Matter of fact, it's more than likely that we won't."

"What's the point of attending the ball if the prince won't be there?" Charlotte said with a shrug.

"Do you think Mr. LaBouff will allow it?"

"Don't you worry about Daddy. I'll take care of him."

Tiana bit the inside of her cheek. "I don't know about this, Lottie."

"You want John to take you in one of Big Daddy's cars, right?"

"Yes," she said slowly.

"Well, the car will just have to have me in it."

Tiana folded her arms across her chest and leveled her friend with a knowing grin. "This sounds like blackmail to me."

"No, it would be blackmail if I threatened to tell your mama that you've been sneaking out at night to work extra shifts at Cal's Restaurant." Lottie smirked.

Tiana gasped. "You wouldn't!"

Charlotte searched under her nails for nonexistent dirt.

"Fine," Tiana finally said.

"It's settled." Charlotte let out a squeal. "I'm coming to Mobile."

Despite Tiana's many attempts to talk her out of it, Charlotte remained adamant about joining them on the ride to Alabama. Even worse, when Mr. LaBouff asked where they were going, Charlotte simply told him they were going for a drive out to the country. She claimed it wasn't a total untruth, seeing as the drive between New Orleans and Mobile was mostly country roads.

Tiana knew better than to try anything like that. She had the LaBouffs' driver stop over at the home she shared with her mother, Eudora, in the Ninth Ward. Once there, she explained to her mother exactly where they were going, how long she expected the journey to take, and when she would be returning.

Her mother insisted on meeting Prince Naveen, and it wasn't until she received a promise from John that he would not let Tiana out of his sight that she agreed to allow their road trip. Tiana might have been nineteen years old, but as far as her mother was concerned, she still wasn't old enough to travel through three states without an older adult present.

After receiving her mother's blessing, they set out. Naveen sat in the front seat next to John, while Tiana and Charlotte sat in the back.

About an hour into their drive, Naveen looked back at Tiana and asked, "You are sure we will be there in time?"

"Well, seeing as I don't have a crystal ball, I can't be one hundred percent certain," Tiana said, "but John is going to do the best he can. Right, John?" Tiana called to the driver.

John tipped his hat as he looked at them through the rearview mirror.

"I would love a crystal ball," Naveen said. "Convenient for making plans. And probably a nice conversation starter."

A laugh burst out of Tiana, surprising her as much as anyone else. Naveen grinned at her.

"So," Charlotte said. "What's it like being a prince without a princess, Naveen?"

"Very subtle, Lottie," Tiana muttered under her breath.

"It . . . uh . . . it makes for an uncomplicated life," Naveen said.

"Oh, I know just what you mean," Charlotte said. "I tell Tia all the time how much I hate the thought of being tied down."

Tiana shot her a look of surprise. "You wha—ow!" Lottie pinched her.

"Something wrong?" Naveen asked.

"Oh, she's okay," Charlotte said. "Now, speaking of settling down. I know I will have to do so eventually. I'm sure you have those same pressures?"

"Very much so," Naveen said. "It is something my family tells me all the time."

"Why don't you tell us about your family?" Tiana interjected. Then, realizing that might be a sensitive subject, she changed tack. "Actually, how about telling us what brought you to N'awlins? I'm sure you're disappointed that you're leaving so soon."

"I am," Naveen said. "I have had my heart set on visiting New Orleans for as long as I can remember. I love jazz music, you see. And I have always wanted to visit the place where it was born."

"Oh, I absolutely *adore* jazz music," Charlotte said. "I wish I'd learned how to play." She positioned her fingers as if they were a horn and badly whistled a tune.

"You should learn," Naveen said. "It's never too late."

"I may just do—"

Just then, the vehicle popped up in the air and landed with an ear-splitting crunch.

"What happened?" Charlotte called.

Even before John spoke, Tiana knew the news wouldn't be good. The thick black smoke billowing from underneath the car's hood was her first clue. The pungent aroma of kerosene was the second.

"Uh, that smoke doesn't look good," Naveen said. "Do you think we should get out of the car?"

"Yes. Right now," Tiana said.

They all filed out of the car and backed several feet away from Mr. LaBouff's brand-new Ford Model T Tudor Sedan.

"What happened?" Charlotte asked again.

John pointed to the roadway. "I believe that large rock is to blame," he said. "I'm sorry, you three; I didn't see it."

"This is a disaster," Naveen said. "How far are we from Mobile?"

"It is still several hours' journey, I'm afraid," John said.

A loud whistle rang out, scaring them all. Tiana looked to the left.

Train tracks!

"I have an idea," she said. She motioned for them to follow. After collecting Naveen's bags from the car, they walked through knee-high grass and across a shallow ditch until they came upon the rail cars.

"I knew it," Tiana said. "That's the Southern Railway line. It goes right through Mobile, and directly to the port . . . if I'm not mistaken."

"How can we be sure?" Naveen asked.

"Well, I guess you'll just have to trust me. Unless you have a better idea."

"I think it's safe to say you have all the good ideas," Naveen said.

Tiana smiled despite herself.

"But, Tia, I don't think that's a passenger train," Charlotte said, peering over.

"It isn't," Tiana said. She grabbed the handle with both hands and pulled. The door opened to reveal tightly wound bales of hay. "But at least it'll be a comfortable ride. Who's up for an adventure?"

"Me! Definitely me," Naveen said. Tiana marveled. She had never seen someone so in the moment, despite whatever outside stress he must have been wrestling with. It was kind of refreshing.

Charlotte squealed, clapping her hands together.

"Miss Charlotte, I'm not sure your father would approve," John said.

"Daddy will understand. I'll explain everything to him when we get home," Lottie replied. "Let's go! We'll ride the rails like a group of vagabonds."

Only Charlotte would consider herself a vagabond while wearing a Madeleine Vionnet dress.

"Let's do it," Naveen said. He hefted himself into the train, then held a hand out for Tiana. Charlotte followed her into the train, with John coming up behind, carrying Naveen's bags.

"You're leaving the car?" Tiana asked him.

"Well, I considered which would anger Mr. LaBouff more: leaving the car or letting Miss Charlotte go on without a proper chaperone."

"Good call," Charlotte told him.

"We'll come back for it later," John said.

As they all settled in, Tiana tried to get comfortable, but the hay wasn't as forgiving as she had imagined. It poked and scratched and smelled plain awful.

"Something tells me you're not used to traveling like this," she said to Naveen.

He repositioned himself against the hay bale. "I cannot say I have ever traveled in a railcar full of hay before, but life's an adventure, eh?"

Tiana noticed a little twinkle in his eye. "You never finished telling us why you came to New Orleans. It can't be simply because you wanted to listen to jazz music. You could have done that in the cafés abroad."

He shrugged. "It was more than that. I . . . I am not sure if I should tell you this, but . . ."

"But . . ." Tiana encouraged.

"My parents may or may not have cut me off from the family funds."

"They what?" she cried. "So how will you get me the money you promised me?"

"I will get it," he said. "I know my father. When I tell him why I need the money, he will not hesitate to repay your kindness. You see, they do not have a problem with sharing their wealth, but they have developed a problem with sharing it with their son."

"What did you do?" Tiana said.

"Why am I to blame?"

"Because parents don't just cut their children off without good reason," she said.

He shrugged. "Well, I guess I *was* a bit of a moocher," he admitted. "I have never really had much of a plan, nothing to fill my days. Work is boring to me. I'd rather have fun. Wouldn't you?"

"My work is fun," she said. "At least the work I *want* to do."

"And what kind of work is that?"

A grin traveled across her lips. "I want to open my own restaurant. I've had my eye on this old sugar mill for ages and saved just the amount for the down payment. And now, once your parents send that telegraph, I'll be able to get it all up and running quick. You know what they say—the first month is always the hardest for a new business."

He set his jaw upon his fist and looked at her with keen interest. "What kind of food do you plan to serve?"

"Oh, the usual," she said. "Jambalaya, red beans and rice, crawfish étouffée. But I'm going to put my own spin on all the classics. Except for my daddy's gumbo. I'm not changing a single thing about that recipe. It's perfect just as it is."

"Your eyes light up when you talk about it."

Tiana shrugged as she was hit by a sudden wave of modesty. She'd become so used to folks making fun of her dream that she rarely talked about it with such enthusiasm, especially with a stranger. But Naveen's attentiveness made her forget he *was* a stranger.

"I wish I could find something to do that makes me feel the way you do about your restaurant," he said.

"You know, *your* eyes lit up when you were talking about jazz. You ever thought about playing music for a living?"

His face instantly brightened. But, just as quickly, the

light in his eyes dimmed. "I am afraid my family would never take me seriously if I chose music as a profession."

"But if it's what makes you happy . . . Maybe they just want you to have something like that in your life," Tiana said. "Why don't you have a talk with your parents when you get home? You may be surprised by their response."

Naveen stared at her, a smile slowly building across his own lips. He shrugged and said, "I will think about it. Who knows, maybe you are right."

They rode for some distance in silence, the melodic rocking of the train car almost lulling Tiana to sleep. But her restful state was jarred when the train screeched across the tracks, pulling to a sudden stop.

"What now?" Charlotte asked.

Tiana stood and walked to the door. She pulled it open and peeked outside. "Uh-oh," she said.

"I do not like the sound of that," Naveen said.

"There's a train porter checking the cars," she said. "If they find us here hitching a free ride, we're in a load of trouble."

"I can't get caught. Big Daddy would kill me!" Charlotte insisted.

"And I will miss the ship back to Maldonia," Naveen added.

"What are we gonna do?" Charlotte asked.

"There's only one thing we can do," Tiana said. "Run!"

As they climbed out of the rail car one by one, Tiana was grateful for the cover provided by the weeds that lined the railroad tracks. Their group quickly created distance between themselves and the train, making their way to the dirt road that ran parallel to the tracks.

"What now?" Charlotte asked.

"No use standing around," Tiana said. "Let's get walking. How much farther do you think we have to go, John?"

The driver squinted as he looked out in the distance. "I can't be sure, but I believe we're near the old paper mill, which means the port is another ten miles or so."

"Ten miles?" Charlotte moaned. "I can't walk ten miles in these shoes."

"I have an idea," Naveen said. He knelt on one knee and opened the smaller of his two suitcases. He pulled out a pair of woolen men's stockings—the fancy kind, like the ones Tiana saw in the Sears, Roebuck and Co. catalog.

"These are thick enough to protect your feet." He handed the stockings and garters to Charlotte. "Just try not to step on any sharp rocks."

"Why, Prince Naveen, that is a wonderful idea," Charlotte gushed. "You're so smart and considerate."

"Let's get these on so we can get moving," Tiana said. She helped Charlotte with the stockings as Naveen and John turned their backs for the sake of propriety.

"That *was* a smart idea," Tiana told Naveen. "And generous. These stockings won't be worthy of being used as cleaning rags by the time Lottie is done with them."

"Eh, I have plenty more at home." He frowned at the mention of home. Tucking the smaller bag under his arm, Naveen gripped the handle on the other, and as a group, they started walking east.

Tiana stole several glances at his profile before asking, "You're having trouble with the idea of going back, aren't you?"

"What?"

"Home. You don't want to go home. I can see it on your face."

"My family needs me," he answered.

"Are you sure there isn't anyone in Maldonia who can help . . . your situation?" she asked cautiously.

He turned to look at her. "It seems my father has taken ill. I do not know yet how bad it is." His voice cracked a little.

"Oh, I am so sorry," Tiana said, her heart sinking. She felt foolish for her suggestion. She knew the weight of losing a father. If she'd had a chance to spend more time with him, to help him, or even just time to say goodbye, she would have jumped on it.

"I am his son, and I am next in line for the throne," Naveen continued. "It is my responsibility to be there and help with . . . whatever may come next. Besides, I do not want to disappoint my family. Again."

They marched on for several more minutes before Tiana said, "I know we only met a couple of hours ago, but as far as I can tell, you're a great son, Naveen. Not many people would try so hard to make that long journey back across the Atlantic so soon after arriving in America. Don't be so hard on yourself."

A charming smile spread across his lips. "Thank you for saying that."

She returned his smile. "I could tell you needed to hear it."

"But you are right."

"As much as I love to hear that—about what specifically?" Tiana asked with a smile.

"I would have really liked to stay."

Tiana's heart started to pick up its pace.

"Uh, Tia?" Charlotte called from behind. "Can I see you for a minute?"

Tiana shot an apologetic look to Naveen, though part of her was relieved at Lottie's interruption. What was she doing? The prince was about to get on a ship, and she'd probably never see him again.

"What's wrong, Lottie?" Tiana asked as she backtracked, coming up alongside Charlotte. She could hear John and Naveen talking about the humid weather. "Is it your feet?"

"No, it's you and the prince," Charlotte murmured in a hushed tone, a cagey grin turning up the corners of her lips. "You're not one to notice these things, but he's been making sweet eyes at you since we left N'awlins, and now the two of you are chatting and smiling at each other like a couple of lovebirds. You should go for him."

"Lottie!" Tiana said in a scandalized whisper. "I am not smiling at him—at least I didn't mean to," Tiana corrected when she realized she *had* been smiling at Naveen. "And weren't you determined to marry the man just this morning?"

Charlotte waved her off. "I can find myself another prince. There's bound to be one out there for me. What I see happening between the two of you is true love. Who am I to get in the way of that?"

Tiana rolled her eyes. Lottie believed in silly things such as love at first sight. Tiana didn't have time for any of that.

So why did she feel bereft at the thought of never seeing Naveen again once they reached Mobile Bay? Maybe because she'd had more fun today than she had in ages? And maybe because she could see a big heart beneath all the bravado.

Just a few hours before, all she could think about was getting her job back at Duke's to save her future, but the day had taught her the importance of enjoying the present as well. There was room for both.

"Is that the port?" Charlotte asked.

Tiana looked ahead, and it sure enough looked like the port. "I think it is, Lottie!"

They all picked up the pace, reaching the port within minutes.

"I guess I overestimated how far off we were," John said.

"We made it," Naveen breathed. "Now to find the—there it is!" He pointed to a gargantuan luxury liner parked at the dock.

"Let's find the ticketing agent," Tiana said.

"First, we must find the telegraph desk," he countered. "I'll need money for both the passage home and what I owe you." He took her hands in his and gave them a firm squeeze. "I can never repay you for what you've done."

"Actually, you can," Tiana said with a cheeky grin.

"Well, yes, I can and *will* pay you with money," he said. "But you have given me something more than money can buy. I know what I want to do with my life. And now I will have the confidence to tell my family . . . when the time is right. That is priceless."

"Sire! Sire! Prince Naveen!"

They all whipped around at the sound of someone calling the prince's name.

"Lawrence?" Naveen's forehead furrowed with confusion. "What are you doing here? And how did you get here before I did?"

"I hired a car to drive me," the valet said.

"Let me guess," Charlotte said. "Your car didn't break down on you and leave you to hitch a ride on a railcar?"

Lawrence looked back and forth between Naveen and Charlotte. "What is she talking about?"

"Never mind that," Naveen said. "What are you doing here?"

"Oh, sire, I had to get to you before you left on the boat back to Maldonia. You don't have to go."

"What?"

"Your father is just fine. There was a misunderstanding at the port back in New Orleans. It turns out the telegram you were given was meant for the prince of *Spain*. Not you."

Naveen sucked in a gasp. "My father is well?"

Lawrence nodded. "Yes, he is." He wrung his hands. "I fear I was a bit harsh back in New Orleans," Lawrence continued. "I'm sorry for not reading the telegram when you asked me to. I could have spared you this excursion."

Naveen looked at Tiana and smiled. "It was not so bad. Actually, I had a pretty good time with my new friends."

Charlotte cheered and then announced she and John would search for a quicker way home.

"I'm quite happy you enjoyed yourself, sire," Lawrence said. "But I . . . well, I regret some of the things I said to you. Recent—erm—events have reminded me what an honor it's been to have worked with your family all these years. I do hope you can find it in your heart to forgive me?"

"Yes, of course I forgive you, Lawrence." Naveen clamped a hand on his shoulder. "But you were right. It's time I take care of myself. I have relied on others to do everything for me for far too long. Please, go on—pursue your new interests!"

Naveen turned to Tiana, not seeing his former valet's bewildered expression. For better or worse, it seemed, the valet had gotten the freedom he'd asked for.

"I have been thinking . . ." Naveen said. "Will that restaurant you plan on opening need a house band?"

Tiana thought for a moment. Then she returned his grin. "You give me a few months to open up my restaurant, and you've got yourself a job."

She held out her hand, and he took it—a promise for now and for the future.

At that moment, Charlotte and John approached. "We've found a car for hire. He'll get us back to Big Daddy's car, and then . . ." Charlotte started. Then she saw Tiana's and Naveen's still-clasped hands. She squealed. "On second thought, the car can wait. Let's get back to the party.

"We've got some celebrating to do!"

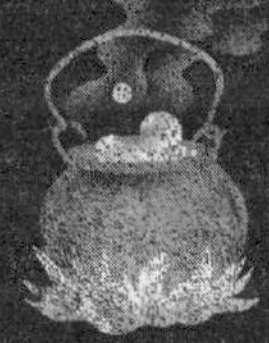

Fates, Three

What if the triplets visited the Witch?

by Jen Calonita

Fates, Three

What if the triplets visited the Witch?

by Jen Calonita

Most mornings, Clan DunBroch awoke to the sound of someone screaming.

Over time, residents of the castle learned not to be alarmed—the disruption was not a sudden invasion. More likely, someone had risen to find:

Frogs swimming in their water basin.

Their undergarments glued to their beds.

Their faces slathered in raspberries that had stained their skin magenta.

The cook's latest dessert missing.

These daily screams were usually followed by a familiar battle cry.

"BOYS!" an exasperated King Fergus would shout.

He didn't need to know what the screaming was about. The early morning ruckus was usually caused by his fifteen-year-old triplets, Hamish, Harris, and Hubert.

Lately, though, the pranking had been orchestrated by one child in particular: the boy whose brain never quieted. The one his mother said had the largest imagination—Hamish.

On one such morning, Hamish heard his father yelling and skidded across a bearskin rug in the triplets' large bedroom. Then he reached behind the dressing partition none of them used (one thing the brothers were not was modest) and retrieved the most beautiful cranachan ever created.

"Time for breakfast, lads!" Hamish crowed, smiling at the massive glass bowl layered with raspberries, toasted oatmeal, crowdie, and honey. It was easy to see why Dad and the cook might be mad. This dessert was a work of art. "Come to Hamish," he said, carrying the dessert over to the table in the center of their room.

At one time that table had held blocks used for creating castles in which the triplets' wood-carved figures fought amazing battles. Later, the table had served as a command center for coming up with pranks. Now the table sat mostly unused—unless Hamish was feeling nostalgic and decided to do some pranking on his own, like today. But if anything was going to get his brothers' attention, it was dessert for breakfast.

"Hubert? Harris?" Hamish called to his brothers, one of whom he knew was already awake. "We've got maybe five minutes before Dad gets here. You don't want to miss this cranachan." He pulled three spoons out of his pocket and dumped them on the table. Neither of his brothers stirred. He tried again. "I don't want to have to eat this evidence alone, but if I have to, I will make the sacrifice."

Across the room, Hubert yawned loudly, the yawn morphing into a burp. He opened his green eyes with a start and sat up fast, his long red locks wild from slumber. (The key to telling the triplets apart was their hair—Hubert's was long, Harris's short, and Hamish's curly bouffant was somewhere in between.) "What time is it? Why didn't you wake me? I should have started training a half hour ago."

Hamish resisted the urge to roll his eyes. Hubert was fixated on proving to their dad he was strong enough to become a full-fledged warrior and train with the clansmen on the coast.

"Forget the training for a minute!" Hamish tried. "Smell the butter and raspberries." He wafted the cranachan scent in Hubert's direction, but Hubert was already standing next to his bed lifting and lowering a carrying pole holding two heavy pails of water balanced on either side. The water sloshed onto the floor as Hubert started counting.

"One, two, three, four, five . . ."

Hamish sighed and looked at his other brother. "Harris? What about you? This might be Grace's best yet. You can taste the crowdie. Heavy cream instead of cheese makes all the difference."

Harris barely looked up from the book he was reading by early morning light. His bed was already made; so tight and smooth, Hamish often wondered how his brother slipped beneath the quilts at night. A stack of additional books sat precariously at the edge of the bed, ready to be devoured. "The what?" Harris asked as he turned a page in his book. "Sorry, I've got to finish this chapter before I meet with my tutor."

Hamish couldn't remember the last time he and his brothers had had a real conversation. Harris devoted all his time and attention to studies, while Hubert was always shadowing the soldiers, trying to become one of them. Hamish missed their company. The only way he could think to get their attention was to do something they'd relate to: pranking their father. King Fergus was their favorite person to trick because he always acted so comically outraged.

Hamish looked from Hubert to Harris to the cranachan again. "You two are going to regret this," Hamish tried again. "This is Dad's favorite dessert for a reason. It's even sweeter than those sweet buns we stole last fall. Remember how Hubert tied a rope to a window and ricocheted through it to grab the tray? No one could figure out how we got out of the kitchen so fast!" Hamish chuckled to himself.

"Sixteen, seventeen, eighteen," counted Hubert, not paying attention to anything other than his water pails.

Harris continued to concentrate on his book, flipping to the next page. Hamish cleared his throat and gave it another shot. "Of course, without Harris, we'd never have gotten that hand-drawn chart showing every hiding spot in the castle."

This time, Harris looked up, a smile playing on his lips at the memory of his genius. "It pays to become friends with your tutor. They never suspect the real reason you want to know the history of your own castle is to learn how to break in and out of it undetected."

Yes! Hamish thought. He was getting through to him. Now he just needed to pull in Hubert. "Without that chart, we never could have pulled off the sea monster myth. There are fishermen in the village who still swear there's a monster in the waters."

Hubert dropped the buckets he was balancing with a loud thud and started to chuckle. "Remember that? The mechanical monster we built was genius!" He held out a hand. "Give me a spoon. I'm starving."

Harris closed his book. "I guess I could take a quick break and have some too before Ham eats the whole thing."

Hamish felt his insides warm as he handed both brothers spoons and they dug in, finishing the dessert together in minutes. This was how every day should start. The three of them enjoying the morning together, the way they always had.

"BOYS!"

At the sound of the king's voice, Hamish hid the spoons while Harris wiped the evidence off the table with a handkerchief he always kept in a pocket. Then Hubert grabbed the bowl and placed it on the window ledge. He was by his brothers' side again when the door to their room flew open and a large man with red hair and a beard sprinkled with gray appeared. (The king might have been getting up there in years, but even with his peg leg, he could move swiftly.)

"Where . . . is . . . my . . . cranachan?" their father thundered.

"How should we know?" Hamish asked. "We just awoke after a restful slumber."

Their father pointed a cane he sometimes used in the morning hours at the three of them. "Oh, you know. Hamish, this betrayal has you written all over it!"

"Me? I helped Grace bake the dessert myself!" Hamish blinked. "Why would I steal it?"

"Hubert and I don't even like cranachan," Harris added smoothly. "Maybe the hounds got to it."

The king's chest rose and fell as he stared at his three boys, waiting for one to crack. Deep down he knew they wouldn't. They never had before. He'd been beaten. Again. "When I find out who did this I will . . . Elinor!" He stomped out of the room and slammed the door behind him.

Harris, Hubert, and Hamish grinned deviously at one another.

"Aaah . . . that was fun," Hubert admitted. "Too bad we'll be too busy for such antics before long."

Hamish's stomach started to swish. He hated talk of the future. When he thought of Hubert and Harris, he already knew what their roles would be in the kingdom: Hubert a warrior at Dad's side on the battlefield and Harris a scholar who could advise them both on the changing world. He just wasn't sure where he fit in the picture. Pranking was the only thing he was good at. And how useful a skill could that be?

"Dad seemed especially worked up over cake, didn't he?" Harris asked as he headed back to his books and bed.

"I heard Mum say he's worried about the MacGuffin clan dinner tonight." Hubert started to put on his gear for the day. "The clans have to decide what to do about that incident with Dingwall. That's why Mum invited everyone to dinner."

Harris groaned. "That's tonight?"

"It's all Mum has talked about all week." Hubert picked up his scabbard and pretended to wield it. "If I have to try on another kilt for it, I'm going to lose my mind."

"Then stop growing out of them so fast," Hamish quipped. Hubert's muscles were getting so large they could have been their own person.

Harris turned as green as an olive. "I'm not sure I can go." He held up a book of Gaelic poetry. "I promised my tutor I'd be done with this by the end of the week. I'll never finish it if I have to sit through a long boring dinner."

Hamish raised his right eyebrow. "Boring? I thought Alastair was coming."

Harris's face reddened. "He is. I don't mean boring. I mean . . . I mean . . ."

Of the three of them, Harris had been the first one to fall in love, a thing none of the brothers knew much about. All they knew was that their painfully shy brother had opened up in a way they had never seen when he'd met Alastair at a clan dinner a few months back. The pair had been writing to each other ever since. Hamish knew his brother looked forward to Alastair's letters, but any time the MacGuffin boy suggested they meet up, Harris made excuses about needing to study.

"You're just nervous because Alastair is going to try to convince Mum you're old enough to attend that snoozy bookfest with him this summer," Hubert said as he swiped at the air with his sword.

Harris's face darkened. "How do you know that? Did you read his letter?"

Hubert momentarily stopped pretend sword fighting and glanced quickly at Hamish for help. "It was fair game. You left it out on your bed. Why haven't you written him back, anyway?"

"That's not your business!" Harris chest-bumped Hubert. "I'm shocked you even knew how to read it!"

"You calling me daft?" Hubert bellowed, pulling Harris into a headlock.

"You just did it for me!" Harris argued, pushing a book into Hubert's stomach.

"Not again," Hamish muttered as he watched his brothers pull each other around the room.

"I am done with this!" Harris snapped. "I can't wait to get away from you this summer!"

"I can't wait to get away from *you*!" Hubert roared, and then turned on Hamish. "And you!"

"Me?" Hamish cried. "What did I do?"

"Nothing! That's the problem. You've got your head in the clouds. All you do is make up stories and plan pranks. It's time to grow up. We aren't kids anymore!"

"Oh, and you're so mature?" Harris countered. "You're dying for an all-out war just so you can show off your strength!" He held up one of his books. "If you stopped and read our history, you'd know fighting isn't always the answer."

"For your sake, I hope it isn't," Hubert spit. "Your books aren't going to make much of a weapon."

"Neither is your pea-sized brain." Harris got in his face. "You're going to get yourself killed on the battlefield, and Mum knows it. She won't let you go train."

"Oh, yeah? Well, she's not going to let you go to another kingdom to read books!" Hubert thundered.

Harris charged Hubert, and he crashed into a decorative suit of armor, sending it to the floor.

"BOYS!" their father bellowed from somewhere below.

All his brothers did was fight! Fight or ignore each other. Meanwhile, Hamish was miserable. Both of his brothers were desperate to leave the castle and see the world, while he was just the boy without a plan. Why couldn't things stay the way they were? Why was everyone so anxious to change? Couldn't his brothers see they worked well together . . . when they weren't trying to kill each other?

He wished Merida were around to talk to about all this—she'd understand. But she was away on some diplomatic mission.

Ah! Diplomatic mission!

That gave him a brilliant idea. Hamish whistled so loudly, the hounds howled somewhere on a floor below. Hubert and Harris stopped arguing and looked at him. "What if I told you there was a way for you both to get what you want this summer?"

Hubert blew a lock of red hair out of his face. "We're listening."

"Hube, you could first let me go," Harris tried, as he was still trapped in a headlock.

"Debating," said Hubert. "Spill it, Ham."

"You both said yourselves—Dad is worried about the MacGuffin dinner, and Mum is worried about you two leaving the castle this summer."

"Go on," said Harris.

Hamish could see the prank laid out in front of him as if it were a live play. "So what if we planned a spectacle so awe-inspiring, the MacGuffin clan is blown away by the brilliance of DunBroch and gives Dad anything he wants? And Mum and Dad are so grateful for the way we handled, er, diplomacy between the clans, they agree to give *us* anything we want?"

"I like it," said Hubert, releasing Harris from his hold. "Ham's plan is going to work."

Harris glared at Hubert. "You haven't even heard it yet."

"It's bound to be good. He has the best imagination out of all of us." Hubert placed his hands on their command center table. "Ham, what did you have in mind?"

Hamish sighed with satisfaction. Once his brothers were reminded about how well they worked together, they'd stop with all this nonsense about leaving DunBroch. This summer it could be the three of them again. Just like old times. Hamish placed his own hands on the table. "Let's talk details."

When the moon was high in the sky and the MacGuffin and DunBroch clans were finally finished greeting one another, showing off their brawn, and bestowing gifts (Queen Elinor was famous for her quilted presents), the groups sat down at long tables to indulge in a meal of quail, haggis, potatoes, and roast carrots. As their father rose to give his customary toast to friendship and goodwill, the boys eyed one another. Well, Hubert and Hamish did. Hubert had to kick Harris to get his eyes off Alastair, who was seated nearby.

"I'm glad the MacGuffins and the DunBrochs could dine together this evening!" King Fergus began at the same moment Hubert pushed a bowl of potatoes off the edge of the table. It smashed to the floor, and his mother gave him a stern look. Hubert motioned that he'd pick it up.

That distraction was all the boys needed to put their plan into action. Hubert crawled under the table, where he'd placed the large crate of the giant copper-and-orange-tip butterflies he'd collected, and prepared to open it. Meanwhile Hamish and Harris put a few more coats of their mashed-banana-and-molasses concoction along the bottoms of chairs to attract the insects. All three boys were back in their seats by the time their father held up his goblet and said, "To the DunBrochs and the MacGuffins!"

The triplets raised their glasses. "To the DunBrochs and the MacGuffins!"

Then they waited. More like they drooled. They could taste victory (and victory tasted better than haggis). Hamish could picture the butterflies leaving the crate and flying up and out from under the table toward the molasses under the chairs and along the walls, creating a spectacular end to their father's speech that would leave Clan MacGuffin breathless. MacGuffins loved special treatment. They were always complaining about Dingwall's lousy dinners. This would put DunBroch on top, and King Fergus would be crowing about it for years.

And then it was happening—the first of the butterflies fluttered up from under the table. Hamish had assumed their father would be just as mesmerized by the insects as the boys were. Instead, their strong, fearless father started to panic.

"Butterflies! Giant butterflies!" he cried out, swatting at

the air. Hamish's stomach dropped as people went running, chairs tumbling, clansfolk barreling to the door.

"Dad, they're just insects!" Harris tried, but it was no use.

People were terrified. Their dad looked like a dancing tattie bogle as he tried to swat at an orange-tip that had become embedded in his hair. He took another swipe with his large hand, and the candelabra in front of him tipped over. The whole table went up like a fireball.

"No!" their mother cried. "Help!"

But before any of them could react, several of the MacGuffin clan threw the table out of the way, jumped on it, and stomped out the flames. The room was silent, full of smoke and people coughing, a few babes crying. Through the haze, Hamish could see his father's chest rising and falling as he stood staring at the crate on the floor and the dripping molasses where the table had been. *And he knew.* He just knew.

King Fergus's eyes locked on his sons. "You three, don't move! Everyone else, *out*!"

The hall emptied very quickly. Their parents looked so angry, even Maudie and the other servants were avoiding coming to clean up the mess.

"Of all the foolhardy things to do." Elinor seethed. "Releasing massive insects, right when we were about to discuss this escalating feud with Dingwall! How could you, boys?"

"Such a ridiculous—so many *wings* . . ." Fergus sputtered.

"And what exactly is on my walls . . . and floors?" Elinor asked, lifting a sticky shoe.

"It was Hamish's idea!" Hubert blurted out. "He thought of the whole thing."

"You liked the idea!" Hamish's forehead started to sweat along with his underarms as he stared at their mother. "We were trying to create a spectacle to impress MacGuffin!"

"Oh, you created a spectacle, all right," Mum said.

"Harris made the molasses-and-banana concoction!" Hubert cried. "I didn't even know that food attracted butterflies!"

"Maybe if you read a book more often, you would!" Harris shouted.

"Why read when I can learn from actually talking to people?" Hubert quipped as he pulled Harris's hair.

Harris growled and knocked Hubert into Hamish. Hamish pushed Hubert off him, and Hubert crashed heads with Harris, who stuck his finger in Hubert's eyes.

"Boys!" their mother said sternly.

But instead of stopping, they turned on Hamish.

"This is all your fault!" Harris seethed. "Look what you've done!"

"Ham was the one who stole your cranachan!" Hubert added. "He hid it in our room!"

"Hubert!" Hamish said, his heart beating fast.

"Silence!" The queen's face turned a nasty shade of violet. (Hamish contemplated running, but his mother had proved to be fast in the past.) "For lads who keep saying how grown-up they are, you continue to act like wee babes!"

"Yes!" King Fergus parroted. "What your mother said!"

"Hubert, this family does not sell each other down the river," Mum said. "And Harris, scholars do not spread molasses on the floor." Harris hung his head. "And Hamish—the mastermind behind the butterflies." She touched his chin, and her voice softened a bit. "Oh, wee one, what are we going to do with you? If only you could put that imagination to good use." She shook her head. "Your father and I had considered letting you three pursue your passions this summer, but this act of recklessness has proven you're not ready."

"But, Mum!" Harris tried, and she shushed him.

"Not ready!" King Fergus echoed. "You lads need some discipline."

"I'm ready for discipline," said Hubert, puffing out his chest.

Their mum scoffed. "You think you're ready for battle, behaving the way you did tonight? You are not ready to train with the clansmen, Hubert."

"Mum!" Hubert cried.

Hamish felt faint. Things were spiraling fast.

King Fergus crossed his arms. "Not ready at all!" he agreed.

"You three need to understand what real work is," their mother went on.

"Yes, yes." Fergus nodded. "Hard work. I agree! Exactly!"

"That's why I think we should send you to Aunt Freya's for the summer break."

"Yes—wait, what?" Fergus's eyes bulged out of his head. "To Great-Aunt Freya's?"

"No!" all three boys cried.

"Mum, no!" Hubert pleaded. "Last time Great-Aunt Freya visited, she expected us up before sunrise, because those were 'the best hours of the day.'"

"'When the moon is still high, and the sun has yet to appear, that's when workers find the most cheer,'" Harris echoed their great-aunt's saying.

"And she makes us help with her embroidery!" Hamish moaned. "Which really means hours of holding her tapestries up and getting stuck by needles while she drones on about the good old days—which are usually just stories about other things she's embroidered!"

"You know none of us can sit still for that long," Hubert pointed out.

"It's true!" King Fergus agreed. "They get their energy from me. I hate when she visits." Elinor cleared her throat and the king backpeddled. "I just mean, Elinor, my love? Don't you think this punishment is a bit harsh?"

"Not at all," Elinor insisted. "Aunt Freya has been

talking about replacing her rushing. I think a few weeks of helping an elderly woman redo the floors of her home, of waking up early and sewing with her, would teach these three a lesson about discipline."

"Not the rushes!" Hamish begged, feeling himself go faint. "Aunt Freya has a dozen dogs! And a cow she keeps *inside*."

"Do you realize how foul her rushes must smell? I can't hold up tapestries in conditions like that," Harris seconded.

Hubert cleared his throat, and it sounded like a gag. The gag kept going, and they all realized King Fergus was retching, too. The queen wasn't swayed.

"It's settled," she said. "We will send word to Aunt Freya that you're coming. Perhaps she can make you grow up, as you so desperately claim to want. Now off to bed, the lot of you!"

The boys said nothing. When their mother was riled up, there was no arguing with her.

Hamish walked slowly behind Harris and Hubert, climbing one of the back staircases to their room, which smelled smoky despite its being several floors above the dining hall. The air felt thick between the ash, the dark sky, and the moon hidden behind clouds that brought the threat of rain. Hamish had heard Harris talk about the astronomical charts he studied and how this summer would be very rainy. Which meant more time stuck indoors with Great-Aunt Freya.

BOOM! A pillow, followed by a book, came flying at him. He ducked, but the flying items continued.

"You've ruined our entire summer!" Harris sounded angrier than Hamish had ever heard him (which was surprising, considering Harris had once threatened to hang Hamish off the roof of the castle for dyeing his hair blue while he slept).

Hubert sent his scabbard flying across the room, and Hamish ducked again to watch it sail over his head and get lodged in their door. "Because of your silly prank, Dad doesn't think I'm ready to ride with the clan!" He pointed a finger at Hamish. "You're doing all the floors yourself! And sitting closest to Aunt Freya's needle!"

"Agreed!" Harris said, and his hands were shaking. "If I can't study with scholars this summer, then I am doing nothing! Good luck getting everything at Aunt Freya's done by yourself."

Hamish closed his eyes for a moment, wondering how he could fix things with his brothers. This was a dire situation. And a potentially smelly one. Forget the floors; Aunt Freya didn't smell like a flower herself. He couldn't imagine spending weeks being used as a human pincushion and listening to the world's most boring tales with no escape in sight. How could he get them out of this mess? And keep Harris and Hubert from hating him for life? He needed a miracle, that's what. He needed magic. He needed—

"The will-o'-the-wisps!" Hamish blurted out.

"The will-o'-what?" Hubert cocked his head to one side.

"He said *the wisps*," Harris snapped. "You do know what wisps are, don't you?"

"Yes," Hubert huffed. "The wisps led Merida to the Witch, who turned Mum and us into bears by giving her—" His eyes widened. "A spell! Hamish, you dog. Just when I want to kill you, you surprise me."

"Oh, no," said Harris, backing away. "We are not going down that path! It could bring danger! And ruin! I hated being a bear! I don't want to do that again."

"Neither do I," Hubert agreed. "A Highland cow wouldn't be so bad, though. They have epic horns."

"No!" Harris cut him off. "No Witch! No animal transformations! No tempting fate! You know what Mum says—the wisps can give you a chance to change your fate, but they can also send you on a path of doom. It's too dangerous."

"You want to go to Great-Aunt Freya's for the entire summer?" Hamish reminded them, and the other two were quiet. He knew that was a no. "Then this is the only way we can fix things. We find the wisps, let them lead us to the Witch, and we make things right with Mum and Dad."

In a bit of irony, the three left predawn—Great-Aunt Freya's favorite part of the day—crossing the foggy, muggy countryside in search of a brownie-like creature that could lead them to a new fate.

"If Merida knew what we were doing, she'd have our hides," Harris said, his eyes sharp as he scanned the tree line for glowing creatures.

"She's not going to find out," Hamish decided. "Maybe the Witch can rewind time, or make Mum and Dad and our clan *and* the MacGuffin clan forget about the table catching on fire."

Harris frowned. "That feels a bit vague, and that's where Merida went wrong. Maybe it's better to be more specific in what we want: for Mum and Dad to let us live our lives."

"Right!" Hubert agreed. "Let us live on the battlefields or listen to boring scholars go on and on about poetry." He yawned.

Hamish frowned. "Your wish isn't specific, either. Live our lives? That could mean live our lives at Great-Aunt Freya's replacing floors and lifting up what has to be the world's heaviest fabric for days." His eyes widened at a sudden thought. "Or live with Great-Aunt Freya permanently, because Mum and Dad have disappeared."

They all retched. Hubert's fake retch was the longest and was why Hamish wasn't sure at first whether he'd actually heard something. A small whisper on the wind, almost like a siren's call. His head swiveled to the right, and through the mist he saw it: a small glowing blue figure—a flaming head and torso with arms that seemed to beckon him forward—bobbing up and down in the air like a firefly.

"Look! A wisp!" Hamish dove for the creature, which went *poof* and disappeared. He groaned. "It's gone."

"No, it's not!" Harris jumped into the air to trap the creature that had reappeared next to him, but *poof!* It was gone again.

He and Harris jumped around, diving and leaping as the wisp continued to play games. It only occurred to him a few minutes later that Hubert hadn't moved.

"Why aren't you helping?" Hamish said, out of breath.

Hubert yawned. "Just waiting for you to let me have a go at the thing."

Harris bowed to his brother. "Be our guest!"

Hubert stepped forward and pulled what looked like a net out of the suede belt around his waist. The wisp appeared in front of him, but Hubert didn't move. He watched as the creature disappeared again. Then Hubert lifted his net, and as the wisp reappeared, *snap!* He dropped the net and pulled the wisp to the ground.

"No more games!" Hubert said in a voice that sounded way older than the one he used with his brothers. "Take us to the Witch, wisp." Slowly he lifted the net off the ground, and Harris and Hamish watched in wonder as the wisp began moving through a clearing of trees. A succession of wisps appeared like a path, lighting the way into the forest. Hubert followed, motioning to his brothers to come along.

Where are we going? Hamish wondered. Merida had told them stories of a small cottage that had appeared to her in the woods that day, but all he saw ahead of them was more forest. They walked for what felt like ages. Hamish could feel his heart beating fast, his mouth going dry. Were they really going to do this? Were they going to attempt to change their fates? Before he could even decide if this plan was still a good idea, the wisps disappeared, and in their place was what looked like a rocky hill covered in moss. Hamish's eyes adjusted to the darkness in this part of the forest, and he realized he was actually looking at a cottage with a roof covered in grass. A small door sat at the center of the structure. Hubert and Harris looked at him. Now what?

"We go in," Hamish said, sounding more confident than he actually felt. His hand reached for the door, which he pushed open to reveal a small, crowded room. Behind him, Hubert gasped.

"Merida wasn't kidding," Hubert said. "This is a woodcarver's shed."

Wood carvings of every size and shape, including small human shapes with feet dangling in the air, covered every inch of the cottage, which smelled earthy, like bark and moss.

"I don't like this," Harris said as he bumped into a rather large carved bear that looked suspiciously like their mother during her brief animal phase. "We shouldn't be here."

"Then go out the way you came," croaked someone in the shadows.

The boys spun around. A tiny woman with large white hair and an even larger nose stood over a table with a small hammer and pick, carving what looked like a miniature table.

"Or stay and look around. Everything is half off," she said.

"You're the Witch!" Hubert blurted out.

The woman looked up and stopped hammering. "I am just a humble wood-carver. See anything you like?" She grabbed a broom and started sweeping.

"No," Hubert repeated. "You're a witch! You helped our sister, Merida, a few years back."

"Helped, hurt, almost destroyed our family, you decide," Harris muttered.

"Now, you see here, lad!" The Witch narrowed her eyes at him and let go of her broom. It kept sweeping. Realizing her mistake, she grabbed it again, but she was too late. "I'm not a witch anymore! Too many unsatisfied customers! Now, if you're not going to buy—"

"Something?" Hamish asked. He'd heard Merida tell this story so many times that he knew exactly what to say to the Witch to appeal to her. "We are willing to buy everything here. And we can pay for it with this." He pulled a bracelet made of agate gems out of his pocket.

The whites of the Witch's eyes flashed. "Oh, my, that's lovely, that is. That could set me up for months." She snapped her fingers, and a cauldron Hamish hadn't noticed came to life, flames lighting underneath it. "One spell, coming up!" She leaned forward. "What will it be?"

"We want to make everyone forget we set fire to the table," Hubert blurted out.

"No!" Harris sounded exasperated. "We have to be specific, or she'll turn us into bears." He glared at her. "We don't want to become bears."

"Maybe Highland cows," Hubert said.

"No Highland cows!" Hamish and Harris cried.

"We need a spell to convince our Mum we should be allowed to live our lives this summer and leave home," Harris said.

"That's not specific enough," Hamish lamented. "We'll wind up knee-deep in needlepoint with Great-Aunt Freya!"

"Boys! Focus! Who is Great-Aunt Freya?" the Witch demanded.

"My spell is good!" Hubert said. "If we just make Mum and Dad forget the table, we'll be fine."

"No!" Hamish panicked. This spell was going to go horribly wrong. He could feel it. "Don't! That's not what we want!"

"What *do* you want?" the Witch tried. "I don't have all day."

"Make Mum and Dad let us live our lives!" Harris insisted. "We want to get away from DunBroch for the summer!"

"I want to battle!" Hubert chimed in.

"Just let us talk this out first," Hamish begged the Witch, but it was hard to hear with all the yelling.

"Dun-wha?" the Witch tugged on her ear. "I don't hear as well as I used to."

"I want to leave DunBroch!" Harris insisted.

"Me too!" Hubert agreed. "Kind of? I want to live on the coast with the clan."

"You're confusing her!" Harris snapped.

Hubert narrowed his eyes. "You calling me daft again?" He lunged for Harris and knocked him into a table full of miniature wooden knights, sending them crashing to the ground.

The Witch gasped. "My babies!" She leaned down to scoop up a wooden knight who had lost his head and trained her eyes on the three of them. "Now you've done it." She snatched the bracelet out of Hamish's hands without even touching him. "I'm picking the spell."

"No!" all three boys shouted.

But the Witch was already stepping outside. The boys had no choice but to follow her. They were outdoors for a mere moment before she snapped her fingers and went back indoors to a fully transformed room, free of wood carvings and darkly lit with candles. "Never cast where you carve," Hamish heard her mutter before she pinched a hair from each of their heads.

"Ow!" Hubert thundered.

But he was no match for the actual thunder and lightning that started as the Witch threw things into her cauldron.

"We're not ready! Wait!" Hamish begged, but the Witch had already begun. Hamish reached for Harris's hand and saw Harris was already holding Hubert's as they waited for what they assumed would be a cake like the one their sister had gotten. But instead the cauldron began to bubble, and a green gas began to seep into the room, making them all cough. The Witch's face was trancelike as she spoke.

"Your fate isn't what needs changing. It's the path you're all on that needs help—divided you fall, together you conquer. Look inside my pot and see for yourself!"

The three stepped closer, staring into the bubbling cauldron. The green light inside it became brighter and brighter till there was a flash that rocked the foundation of the room. Smoke filled the air and swirled faster and faster like a cyclone. In it, Hamish thought he saw his own reflection.

It was actually Hubert with his long hair, riding into battle. He was a fierce warrior, just as he said he'd be; an angry opponent who pushed for war, not diplomacy, and their father appeared to listen to him. On the battlefield, Hubert sliced down all who opposed him. This led to a war on DunBroch's tranquil countryside, to Hubert leading men to their deaths—including their own father.

"No! That's not what I want at all!" Hubert cried out.

The smoke swirled again and a new image appeared. Was this Harris? It had to be, because it was a young man with shortly cropped hair sitting in a massive room among other scholars. He was poring over a stack of books, reading into the wee hours of the night, the candle at his side slowly whittling down to a nub.

"Look, my future is intact! I'm a scholar!" Harris bragged.

"Keep watching!" snapped the Witch.

The Harris in the vision studied and studied, even when his parents came and tried to pull him away from his books. The other scholars ignored him; he was too young to match what they'd already learned, but still Harris tried to keep up. He was too shy to give his opinion, so all he had for company was his books. Even when his brothers came and asked him to join them at a party, he refused. Then Alastair appeared and did the same—begging for Harris to take some time off, to join him for a walk or a dinner, but Harris kept rushing back to his books as if they were the only safe space he knew. The smoke spun faster now, and Alastair appeared—but he wasn't alone. He had another young man with him.

"I waited for you as long as I could," the Alastair in the vision told Harris, "but you never made time for me." He took the hand of his new love, and they walked away.

"No!" Harris shouted at the cauldron. "Wait! I was scared. I didn't know how to talk to you!" He turned to his brothers, the anguish written all over his face.

Hamish grasped his brother's hand harder just as he heard Hubert inhale sharply.

"Your turn, Ham," Hubert said, and the three leaned forward again.

Hamish held his breath and waited, but when the smoke cleared a third time, all he saw was himself in his room, just as he was every day. Things were exactly as they'd always been—him on the same bed he'd always slept in, looking out the window at his two brothers at work and at play. The longer he looked at the vision, the smaller he appeared to himself, like he was a child who'd never grown up. The smoke swirled again and bars appeared on the windows of the room as though it were a dungeon. The him in the vision rushed for the door, but his feet appeared to be stuck in what looked like some sort of mud. The more he struggled, the more he was pulled into the puddle, till he sank out of sight.

"I don't get it," Hubert said. "Your future is you getting eaten alive by our room?"

"It's a metaphor," said Harris. "It means Ham feels left behind." He looked curiously at his brother. "Is that how you feel?"

His brothers looked at him. So did the Witch.

"Go on! Tell them!" she said impatiently, as if she knew what he was thinking.

Hamish's heart hurt as he thought about how he could explain himself without looking ridiculous. His brothers clearly knew what they wanted from life. (Even if these visions showed them screwing things up.) What was he going to say? *Don't leave me?* "No, of course I don't feel stuck. I'm fine. Just fine!"

The Witch sighed loudly. Then she dropped something else into the cauldron. The contents exploded, the whole cottage shaking. The brothers held on to one another to keep from falling. A new vision appeared: all three brothers in one place for a moment, before they were yanked apart by an unseeable force. Then their image fractured down the middle.

Hamish could feel the Witch watching him. Was this what their future was doomed to be? Three brothers divided? Not unlike the story his sister had told them about the prince Mor'du and his own brothers? Shattered bonds, a fractured kingdom, all because he couldn't be truthful with himself or his brothers?

Hamish anxiously looked at the Witch again.

"Are you going to tell them or should I? I don't have all day, you know!" The Witch tapped her foot loudly.

"Fine. I feel stuck!" Hamish felt his cheeks flame. "You two know exactly what you're going to do with your lives, while I have no future! Just like my vision shows."

"Oh, Ham, that's not true," said Harris, putting his hand on Hamish's shoulder. "I feel like you are better off than either of us in that vision."

"I am? I'm stuck in muck."

"You're not stuck. You're our glue," Hubert corrected him. "Literally and figuratively, right?" He looked at Harris, who nodded. "You are the one who brings us together with your stories, your pranks, your ideas. If it weren't for you, life would be boring. Like Harris's books."

Harris nudged him. "Hubert is right. No one can

gather a crowd like you can with one of your stories. You're a better storyteller than even Dad. But don't tell him we said that."

The three laughed, and Harris and Hubert drew Hamish into an embrace.

He felt lighter suddenly as he looked at them. "I've been so afraid of losing you two this summer. I thought if you both left, that would be the end of us."

"We're brothers," Harris reminded him. "You can never get rid of us."

"You're stuck with us, bro, and our smelly room," Hubert said. "Just because we do different things doesn't mean we don't care about each other. Even if I get to go train with the clan, I'll stop pushing Dad to let me go into battle. I'm not ready for war. Being king means stopping wars, not starting them, right?" The others nodded. "It also means taking time for those who love you. Even when I train, I'll be looking forward to the day I come home and get to hear you tell a story."

"Same," said Harris with a grin. "Maybe it's time I share some of your tales with someone like Alastair." He looked at the floor. "That vision is right—if I hide myself away, I may lose Alastair before I even get to know him."

"And maybe I could get out a little more," Hamish admitted, and looked shyly at Harris. "I could come listen to some of your scholars who've written books. I think I might like to write one myself someday, of all our stories."

"Not you and the scholars, too," Hubert groaned jokingly.

Hamish grinned. Maybe not everything they did together had to involve a prank. They could do other things, too—like tell *this* story. He could write it down so they didn't forget all that had happened here. He couldn't wait to tell Merida. "I feel inspiration coming," he told his brothers.

There was a popping sound, and then the cauldron started to bubble again. This time, when they peered into the pot, they saw their joined reflection: three very different boys who would always be united, because they were family.

Hamish had no idea what would happen with Great-Aunt Freya. Maybe their parents would insist they go stay with her for the summer. Maybe they would find a new appreciation for embroidery. Maybe her floors wouldn't smell as bad as they thought. Or maybe on their journey home that afternoon they could come up with a way to talk to Mum and Dad together and convince them they were done with the pranking (for the most part) and could help out around the castle in other ways to make up for what they'd done. They'd fix things with the MacGuffin clan. They'd coach Harris on how to talk to Alastair and help Hubert work on his diplomacy. Hamish would put his storytelling to good use. They'd bond. Hamish smiled, feeling content for once. Then he felt himself bumped from behind.

"Now shoo! All of you!" said the Witch, pushing the boys to the door. "You've already taken up too much of my carving time as it is. Be off now!"

Hubert dug in his heels. "Now hold on a second. We did give you a valuable bauble today."

"That's true." Harris winked at Hamish. "Feels like we should get something in return."

Hamish caught on. "Yes, like maybe you could cast a spell to make Maudie forget I put a bunch of small adders in her bed before we left. They're tiny! Those snakes wouldn't hurt a soul, but . . ."

"Ooh, good one," Hubert said approvingly.

"Nice!" added Harris.

The Witch grabbed her broom. "OUT! All of you! Wee devils! Go home!"

Laughing and linking arms, the triplets ran out of the cottage into the early afternoon sun and a future that felt brighter than ever before.

A Dragon in the Snow

What if Madam Mim and Merlin went to school together?

by Kristina Pérez

A Dragon in the Snow

What if Madam Mim and Merlin went to school together?

by Kristina Pérez

Was there anything better than spreading her wings and taking to the sky?

Mim didn't think so.

She soared and swooped above the Wildwood, purple feathers slicing through the wind. From the corner of her eye, she watched as waves crashed against the rocky shore of the Hidden Isle. Only those touched with magic could even see the island that had been Mim's home for the past five years. Since that fateful day shortly after her thirteenth birthday.

Mim let out a loud caw, reveling in her raven form, pushing away morose thoughts. Up above the din of her fellow students at the Lyceum of Enchantment, she felt her most free, far more comfortable in her own skin—or feathers. The trees didn't judge her. The other birds didn't judge her. Sometimes Mim wished she never had to leave the Wildwood.

She relished the last few blissful moments before her tutor, Taliesin, Chief Mage of the Lyceum, would be expecting her at the Cauldron of Inspiration. Pointing her beak toward the Hidden Isle, she reluctantly began to cross the strait that separated it from the southern coast of Brytannia. Mim was known for her precision, her diligence, and above all, her punctuality.

And yet. And yet . . . when exhilaration fluttered through her luminous wings, when the breeze propelled her higher, higher toward the clouds, she forgot everything else. She forgot herself. A dangerous thing for a young woman tainted by Shadow Magic.

Since her arrival at the Lyceum, Mim had trained harder than anyone else in the ways of Earth Magic, honing her skills to tame the shadows in her heart. Taliesin called them her dragons—dragons whose fire would scorch her heart until it was blackened. He was a kind teacher, almost a second, more understanding father. But Mim suspected part of Taliesin was afraid of her.

Mim promised herself that one day she would demonstrate her worth, prove there was nothing to fear from her, and ascend the ranks to Royal Mage—advisor to kings and queens.

The stone façade of the Lyceum came into view. Mim picked up speed. Sunlight danced off the green and aureate turrets that punctuated the defensive wall surrounding the school.

Mim couldn't imagine ever loving anything but the light. She would never be tempted by the shadows.

She was stronger than that.

As Mim hurried down the steps, deeper and deeper into the caves that lay beneath the Lyceum, she heard singing. A rich male timbre. Taliesin always sang to the Cauldron as if it were a fussy baby.

She tugged at the hastily woven braid that bounced against her spine. Her mane of lilac-colored hair betrayed the source of her magic, and Mim kept it carefully restrained within the walls of the Lyceum. No matter how much time she spent outdoors, her complexion remained pale as moonlight. *Creature of the night,* the villagers would mutter under their breath until Mim's parents had finally sent her away.

Popping and hissing filled her ears as she halted on the threshold of the vast candlelit cavern that contained the source of all mortal magic. Flames licked the enormous iron cauldron from below, cerulean and sapphire.

Taliesin stood proudly beside the Cauldron, stirring the bubbling liquid gently but methodically, soothing its spitting with his voice.

Mim bowed her head to the Cauldron in respect. "May my roots be strong, and my branches reach for the sun," she murmured, repeating the creed to which all practitioners of Earth Magic were bound. At least her eyes were the color of tall grass.

"Good morning, Mim."

Taliesin beckoned her forward with a smile, wrinkles creasing his brown skin, warm like acorns in autumn. His teal silk robes swept the floor of the cave.

Mim returned her teacher's greeting. "Have you been watching over the Cauldron all night?" she asked, coming to stand beside him. She noticed the slightest hints of fatigue beneath his eyes.

"There has been much change in the Summerlands," replied Taliesin. "The Cauldron senses more on the horizon."

Mim nodded. Several years earlier, an ambitious young warrior named Uther Pendragon had conquered the Summerlands, the southern half of the Island of Brytannia. He crowned himself king and established his court at Camelot. He'd made peace with the kingdoms in the north—but it was a fragile peace.

The Cauldron hissed again, as if to confirm Taliesin's words.

"Sing to it, Mim, and see what you hear," he encouraged her.

With trepidation, she opened her mouth. Only the most adept of mages could receive insight directly from the Cauldron in this way. Its magic stemmed from the Other Side, the domain of the immortals who possessed knowledge of the future and the past. Whether the Cauldron had been gifted or stolen was a matter of scholarly debate among the mages, but it had been protected on the Hidden Isle since before human memory.

Mim closed her eyes tight. Her lips pressed together as she concentrated with every fiber of her being. An octave below her reedy alto, she detected a low vibration, a hum that made her skin tingle. Slowly, an image began to form at the back of her mind: iridescent scales swirled behind her eyes, followed by fire. Her throat grew dry.

Footsteps pounded in the distance, rattling Mim's nerves.

The scales and the flames combined into a terrifying gale, spreading outward across the Wildwood, setting the Summerlands alight. Sweat soaked Mim's back.

Was the Cauldron showing her a . . . dragon? What did it mean? Her nerves zinged with warning.

Boom!

Mim was jolted out of the vision, her concentration shattered. When her eyes flew open, she grimaced, gaze training on an unwelcome face.

"Merlin," she bit out.

Another large timber log slipped from his arms and crashed to the ground. He shrugged, stance at once careless and arrogant, brushing the hair from his face. One streak of white stood out amid the midnight-black strands that grazed his shoulders. Not that Mim spent any time thinking about Merlin's hair or the freckles on his slightly crooked nose or the mischievous look in his exceptionally blue eyes.

Surreptitiously, Mim wiped a trickle of sweat from her brow. Taliesin glanced between Mim and Merlin, the side of his mouth quirked in amusement.

"Thank you for joining us, Merlin," said the Chief Mage. "Did you lose track of the time . . . again?"

Collecting the logs into his arms, Merlin said, "Time is all about perception, isn't it?" He grinned cheekily. Mim rolled her eyes.

Taliesin's amusement faded. "No," he said. "The fire beneath the Cauldron must never be allowed to dim. Not for a moment." Gesturing toward the simmering liquid, he commanded, "Add the timber with haste."

Still grinning, not even showing his respects to the Cauldron, Merlin strode forward with the confidence Mim suspected must come from being royalty. Since he'd arrived at the Lyceum six months before, Merlin had charmed all the other students but kept himself apart, coolly aloof.

"And why is it so vital that the fire never goes out?" Taliesin said, voice echoing in the cave. Mim had known the answer since her first days at the Lyceum. Merlin had seen eighteen summers, like Mim, which made her wonder why he'd only just arrived on the Hidden Isle.

As he looked up at the Chief Mage from where he crouched before the Cauldron, Merlin's grin turned wry. "Because if the Cauldron cools, magic will disappear from the mortal realm."

"Just so. And one day—perhaps one day soon—magic will be needed to save our island."

The pronouncement made Mim shiver, but Merlin looked unaffected. Taliesin undoubtedly had more foreknowledge than he would share with his students.

Mim's gaze darted toward a glint of steel near the entrance to the cave. A sword plunged deep into veiny emerald stone. Legend held the sword also came from the Other Side and that only the True Ruler of All Brytannia, one possessing strong Earth Magic, would be able to pull it from the stone. Whether the mages had presented the sword to Uther Pendragon—and whether he had failed the test—was not information to which Mim was privy.

"Join us," Taliesin told Merlin, nodding in his direction. "It is your turn to stir the Cauldron."

Mim's hands had shaken the first time her tutor had extended the gleaming staff in her direction. The rod was hewn from the branch of a silver apple tree that belonged to the Other Side. It was as ancient as the Cauldron and would burn the flesh of those without magic.

Merlin accepted the staff with casual grace, as if it were his due. Taliesin stepped back, allowing Merlin his place beside Mim. She took a short breath, stomach pinching as she detected the scent of the forest—the freshness of moss clinging to an oak. Well, he *had* been carrying timber. Mim shook her head, chiding herself.

Glancing at her sideways, Merlin said, "You're looking lovely this morning, Mim." He held her gaze for a beat and her cheeks flushed. He was teasing her. Of course he was.

"You too," Mim replied, tone implying the opposite. The Cauldron began to boil more violently as Merlin stirred.

"I mean it," he insisted. "Your dress suits you."

Mim's nostrils flared. All final-year students wore a uniform of seaweed green that absolutely did not flatter her pallid face or purple locks or the constellation of moles above her right eye, which she called her Three Sisters. The green suited Merlin's sun-kissed skin. The uniform reminded Mim she would never belong.

Mortification coursing through her, she felt the sting of tears she refused to cry. "You might be a prince, Merlin, but that doesn't give you the right to be cruel," she told him. When she became Royal Mage, he wouldn't dare be cruel to her—nobody would.

Merlin jerked backward as if he'd taken a blow to the chest. "I'm *not* a prince." His eyes flashed with pain. "I'm not *anything*. That's why I'm here."

Mim blinked in surprise. Everyone at the Lyceum knew Merlin's grandfather was the king of Dalriada, one of the three northern kingdoms that had made peace with Uther Pendragon. Merlin circled the silver staff in the bubbling liquid with frustrated, angry yanks. The Cauldron roared.

"Careful!" Mim cried. "You need to be gentle with it."

She darted a look at Taliesin for help, but he retreated farther from his students. Taliesin had been training Mim long enough that she understood he wanted to see how she would handle the situation. A mage must maintain her composure under pressure.

Moderating her voice, Mim suggested to Merlin, "Try breathing in for the count of three with each circle. It stills the mind and heart."

"I know what I'm doing," Merlin protested.

"Do you?" Mim raised an eyebrow. "There are rules for a reason. Not that they seem to bother you."

Merlin narrowed his gaze at her. "Fine, then. Since you know everything—*here*. Show me how it's done."

"With pleasure."

Blowing out a hard breath, Merlin dragged the silver staff through the Cauldron, and a drop of the frothing elixir landed on Mim's hand. A searing pain radiated from the spot, followed by a rush of euphoria. Her heart raced and she felt as if she were back among the clouds. Magic more powerful than she'd ever experienced surged through her.

The beat of her heart grew deafening. The magic hungry, demanding. Shadows swirled behind Mim's eyes. *This is what you've been missing.* The power was delicious. Intoxicating.

Suddenly, someone was shaking her. "Mim?" Merlin's panicked voice pierced her consciousness. "Mim!"

"Let go of me!" she barked.

Merlin dropped his hands from around her shoulders. His face was contorted with worry. "I was just trying to *hel—*"

"You've done quite enough!"

Taliesin drew closer, concern stippling his forehead, as well. "How do you feel?" he asked Mim.

She rubbed her temples. "A bit of a headache."

He nodded. "It could have been much worse," he warned. "Undiluted magic is dangerous. Fatal to most humans."

Mim's bottom lip trembled. "I know."

"You should have been more careful," Taliesin rebuked her.

What? Shame and indignation warred inside her. "It was *Merlin's* fault!"

Taliesin looked from Mim to Merlin and back again. "Merlin is new to the Lyceum. As the more experienced student, you should take him under your wing." Mim felt her face turn scarlet at his words, hands curving into fists at her sides.

"And Merlin," the Chief Mage continued, "let this be a lesson to you that when you do not respect your own power, others are likely to get hurt. Especially those closest to you."

Merlin's head drooped. He stared at the floor of the cave.

"Yes, Taliesin," he said dejectedly.

"You may leave us now."

Merlin glanced up at Mim as he moved to leave. "I'm sorry. I would never want to hurt you." There was an unfamiliar hitch in his voice.

Mim lifted her chin. "I'm not sure I can say the same."

Merlin toyed with his single white strand of hair, saying nothing, and vanished swiftly from sight.

"That was unkind, Mim," said Taliesin when he was gone.

"He deserved it. He swans around the Lyceum like he's better than everyone else and thinks the rules don't apply to him because his grandfather is a king." His entitlement set Mim's teeth on edge. Mim fought every day to be treated like an equal by her peers.

Taliesin pursed his lips. "If you let yourself get to know Merlin, I think you would find you have more in common than it appears."

"I find that hard to believe," Mim said with a pout. He came from royalty, whereas her mother was a humble herb-witch, her father a fisherman.

"Believe what you will," said her tutor. He patted her shoulder. "Why don't you go lie down? You've had a shock."

"If you're sure you don't need any help with the Cauldron?"

"More students will be arriving soon for their lesson."

Mim gave a small nod. "In that case, I think I will."

"And I do mean *rest*, Mim." Taliesin caught her eye. "Not flying." He winked.

As she scurried from the cave, however, Mim knew there was nowhere she would rather be than the Wildwood.

Nowhere better to forget Merlin and this disastrous morning.

Mim perched herself on a high branch of a hazel tree and listened to the sea. The waves were rough in the strait between Brytannia and the Hidden Isle. Her thoughts drifted to her father, wondering if he was on the water that day. She hadn't seen her parents for four years. They didn't visit the Lyceum, and Mim knew she wouldn't be welcomed with open arms in the village of Gurnard. She ruffled her feathers.

Who wanted to live in a place named for a fish? Certainly not Mim.

A melodic trilling rose above the *shh-shh* of the tide, capturing Mim's attention. She cocked her head. The birdcall was doleful, a descant to the moaning of the sea, and it sounded strangely human. In the next moment, a blackbird whizzed past her. Mim glimpsed the telltale shimmer of magic around its wings. Following the blackbird with her eyes, she noticed a streak of dazzling white on its crown.

No. It couldn't be. Was that . . . Merlin? Was he *spying* on her?

Enraged, Mim launched herself into the air. She coasted on the current, keeping the smaller blackbird in her sights. How *dare* he! The bird's call stopped abruptly as it darted between the branches of an enormous maple tree that effervesced with bright red foliage.

Merlin knew Mim was on his trail. If he thought to lose her in the cover of autumn leaves, he was sorely mistaken. Mim had spent years learning every tree in the Wildwood.

She gave chase through tunnels of gnarled hawthorn trees and rowan boughs laden with fiery orange berries. Merlin performed a nosedive through a thicket of towering junipers, their needles tickling Mim as she pursued him. She let out a caw instead of a giggle.

The blackbird's head swiveled to meet her gaze. Mim's and Merlin's eyes locked. Even in his avian form, his eyes were a penetrating blue.

Mim cawed once more, and Merlin flapped his wings harder, zooming far ahead.

Oh, no. She wasn't letting him get away. He was going to explain why he was following her.

Merlin led her toward a clearing between spindly birch trees. He sped out of view for a mere instant. When Mim reached the clearing, the blackbird was gone.

Light streamed through the leaves, dappling Merlin's irritatingly attractive face. He stood in the middle of the clearing, once again wearing his green tunic and leather breeches.

Merlin extended one arm outward as if he were falconer and Mim his pet. Did he seriously think she would deign to come to him? *Conceited prince!*

Mid-flight, Mim transformed into her human form and dropped with ease onto the yarrow covering the clearing. Mastering her shape-shifting to such precision had taken thousands of hours of practice, and it was a skill of which she was immensely proud.

Merlin looked impressed. Then he chuckled. Mim opened her mouth to give him a piece of her mind, but before she could speak, he announced, "Look who we have here, Lady Rulebreaker. So you're not perfect after all."

"What are you talking about?" she retorted.

"If I'm not mistaken, students at the Lyceum aren't allowed to leave the Hidden Isle without permission."

"How do you know I don't have permission?"

Merlin lowered an eyebrow. "Do you?" he said, taunting her with her own earlier words. When Mim said nothing, he snickered. "Exactly," he proclaimed. "You should be more careful. Who knows what lurks in the Wildwood?"

"Other than you?"

He smirked and took a mock bow. Mim snorted. "I'll take my chances with feckless princes."

"I already told you I'm *not* a prince."

Mim tapped her foot on the ground with impatience. "Well, whatever you are, I want to know why you're spying on me."

"Spying?" Merlin spluttered.

"Yes, *spying*. Following me to the Wildwood." She gathered her windblown tresses and almost unconsciously began braiding them together with nimble fingers.

Her foot continued to tap.

Merlin threw his head back in a disbelieving laugh. "You might find this hard to fathom, but not everything is about you. I had no idea you would be in the Wildwood."

"Then why did you run away from me when I spotted you?"

"What I saw was a raven more than twice my size."

Mim scoffed. "Surely you noticed the shimmer—the glow of Earth Magic."

Screwing his lips to one side, Merlin said, "Huh. That's what that was. . . ." He ran a hand through his hair.

"What else would it be?" She crossed her arms in annoyance. "By the Cauldron, what did the mages teach you in the north?"

"Nothing. I never had any training before coming to the Lyceum."

Mim stared at him. "Who taught you to shape-shift?"

He shrugged. "I did."

It was Mim's turn to be impressed. Merlin must be a rare natural mage. Rather than compliment him, she said, "I suppose that explains what happened with the Cauldron this morning."

Scowling, Merlin took two long strides toward her, closing the distance. "I really am sorry about that." He took her right hand in his, rubbing his thumb over the angry welt. Tingles radiated from the spot. Mim bit her lip.

"Does it hurt?" he asked in a soft voice.

"I'm stronger than I look."

"You look incredibly strong, Mim."

Mim found herself caught in Merlin's gaze, a new sensation spreading out from her chest, a warmth that was thrilling and alive. She tugged her hand from his and took a step back.

"You weren't spying on me, then," she said.

"No. I just . . . the Hidden Isle is so cramped. I'm used to roaming the Red Mountains, sleeping outdoors. Sometimes

I feel the walls of the Lyceum pressing in on me. As well as all the rules and protocols, so many things to remember . . ." He forced a teasing smile, but Merlin's words were tinged with sadness, like his blackbird song.

"You grew up at a royal court," insisted Mim. "You must have spent your life adhering to the strictest etiquette, learning to be a nobleman."

Merlin's posture stiffened. "My mother was a princess. *I'm* an embarrassment. My grandfather was happy to leave me to my own devices, let me spend weeks in the wilderness, hunting to survive. The first time I transformed into a bird was to escape the maw of a very hungry wolf."

Mim gasped. "You're kidding."

"I swear—by the Cauldron."

"But, why?" she asked, forehead scrunched.

Narrowing his eyes at her, Merlin said, "You must have heard the rumors."

She had. "Is your father truly from the Other Side? An immortal warrior?"

Merlin's gaze bored into her for so long that Mim wished she hadn't spoken. Finally, he sighed. "The truth is I don't know. My mother wouldn't say anything about him other than he wasn't coming back. My grandfather forbids his name to be spoken. And now my mother is dead, so I'll never know."

Mim touched two fingers to Merlin's elbow. "I didn't realize. I'm so sorry. When did she pass to the Isles of Youth?"

"Last winter. On the Solstice," he replied, tone hollow.

Less than a year ago. "You must miss her," she said.

Merlin nodded swiftly, as if the wound smarted badly indeed. "After an appropriate period of mourning, my uncle decided to banish me to the Lyceum." His jaw clenched. "Because my parents weren't married, my grandfather never granted me the title of prince. Doesn't matter to my uncle. He sees me as a rival for the throne when grandfather dies."

A bitter laugh escaped Merlin's lips. "As if I'd want to rule and protect a people who treated me and my mother like lepers."

Mim gave his elbow a squeeze. "I know something about being an outsider. It's why I escape to the Wildwood . . . without permission."

"*You* feel like an outsider, Lady Rulebreaker?" Genuine shock filled his voice, accompanied by a kinder laugh. "You're the Lyceum's star pupil."

Her cheeks heated at the praise, although she wouldn't deny it. She worked extremely hard to come top in all her subjects.

Mim lifted the tail of her braid. Sunshine glistened on the lavender strands.

"You must have heard the rumors," she told Merlin, offering him a rare coy smile, enjoying turning the tables on him.

Merlin swallowed. "Shadow Magic."

Keeping her tone breezy, Mim said, "Yes, and lavender

really doesn't go well with this shade of green at all." She pointed at her uniform.

"Oh. *Oh* . . ." Merlin banged the heel of his palm against the bridge of his nose. "You thought I was mocking you."

"Weren't you?"

"Teasing, maybe. Making a ham-fisted attempt at flirting? Definitely."

Flirting? Mim's heartbeat accelerated. Mages were discouraged from forming strong attachments with each other because it could interfere with the balance of magic, allow one mage to influence the other. Mim had never envisioned being in danger of such attachment before. It wasn't part of her plan toward becoming the Royal Mage.

Pointedly ignoring Merlin's admission, Mim said, "Life at the Lyceum is easier than in my village. At least the other mages don't stare or point—they just talk behind my back." She inhaled a deep breath. "But someday I'll serve King Uther Pendragon, and all of his subjects will have to respect me, even if they don't like me."

"Take it from me, serving kings isn't all it's cracked up to be," said Merlin. "Kings are still just men." He took a tentative half step forward. "And I already like you, Mim."

Mim laughed a bit too loud. "Half an hour ago, *I* didn't like *you*."

"Ah, but I can tell you're changing your mind."

"Perhaps," she conceded.

The corners of Merlin's playful smile turned downward as he said, "If it's not too personal . . . will you tell me about the Shadow Magic?"

Mim's throat constricted. She'd never talked to anyone about it openly besides Taliesin. She tamped down the instinct to storm off. Merlin had made himself vulnerable with her, and he deserved the same.

"It happened after my thirteenth birthday," she began, a slight stutter to her words. "There were signs before, I suppose." Mim shuddered a breath and forced herself to continue. "One morning I went out with my father in his fishing boat, and as I unhooked one of the mackerels he'd caught, I felt this . . . this *flood* of pity. Suddenly the dead fish came back to life."

Air whistled through her teeth as she paused, not daring to look Merlin in the eye. "My father stared at me with horror," said Mim. "His crew saw, too—called me a cursed child. Unnatural." She flinched at the memory. "I don't know why the Shadows found a home in me."

Her bottom lip trembled. What was so wrong with her? Mim didn't dare ask the question aloud. It must be something terrible.

"All the villagers knew by nightfall. The Lyceum was the only safe place for me to go."

Gently, ever so gently, Merlin wiped away a tear that had leaked from Mim's eye.

"The people in your village are small-minded twits."

Brightening, she told him, "I couldn't agree with you more." She laughed, pushing down the pain. "I'm sorry I judged you for being a not-prince."

He grinned. "Merlin the Not-Prince. I like it."

"Would the Not-Prince be interested in some extra tutoring?" Mim asked, a quaver to her voice. "Taliesin told me to take you under my wing."

"Under your wing, huh?" Merlin's grin deepened.

"I don't like to brag, but I *am* the Lyceum's star pupil."

"You do like to brag, but you've got a deal, Lady Rulebreaker." Merlin extended his hand. "Teach me everything you know."

Shaking on it, "We'll meet here, every day after lessons," Mim decided.

"It'll be our secret." Merlin held her hand a beat longer than was necessary.

For the first time in her life, Mim *liked* having a secret. Especially one she could share with Merlin the Not-Prince.

"Are you nervous about tomorrow?" Merlin asked Mim. Icicles tipped the grass in what she'd come to think of as *their* clearing as autumn gave way to winter.

Mim hugged her fur-lined cloak tighter. The next day was the Winter Solstice, and it had been announced that a competition would take place to find the new Apprentice to the Royal Mage. King Uther Pendragon himself would be journeying to the Hidden Isle to judge it. This was the opportunity of a lifetime, a chance to leave the village of Gurnard far behind.

"No," Mim declared imperiously. In truth, the announcement had taken the entire Lyceum by surprise after the last Apprentice resigned without warning. Mim had expected to have several more years to train for a Mage's Duel.

Merlin canted his head. "Liar," he said. "Your cheeks are pink."

"Because it's freezing! *Brr*," she huffed, and Merlin laughed. Impulsively, Mim reached a hand to his face. "Your cheeks are even pinker than mine," she told him. The soft hairs along his jawline tickled her palm.

Although Mim was determined to prove she was the most talented wielder of Earth Magic among her peers, she couldn't help but be distracted during their training sessions.

Mim was about to remove her hand when Merlin leaned into her touch. Their eyes met and she saw a tenderness in his that she didn't dare believe. "Are you sad about tomorrow?" she asked. "The one-year anniversary?"

"You remembered," he said, words roughened.

"Of course, Merlin."

"I dreamed of my mother last night. You would have liked her, Mim. She was funny and clever, and she had a kind heart—like you."

Mim felt hers thundering in her chest. "I wish I'd met your mother," she said in a quiet voice.

"Me too." Merlin gestured at the hood of her cloak, and Mim lowered it. "You should wear your hair down," he said. "The lavender is radiant. *You're* radiant."

Scowling, Mim replied, "I don't want to remind King Uther that I have Shadow Magic, Merlin. Not if I'm hoping to become the Apprentice to his Royal Mage."

"Who cares what he thinks?" said Merlin with a shake of the head. She dropped her hand from his jaw. He didn't understand. He was still the son of a princess.

"He's a king, Merlin! And *I* do."

"Well, I don't." Merlin shrugged. "I'm only competing tomorrow because Taliesin is adamant I take part."

Mim stared down at the earth, frosted like sea-glass. She took a deep breath, then raised her eyes again. "Merlin, do you promise that whatever the outcome tomorrow, it won't change our . . . friendship?"

The side of his mouth kicked up. "You're asking because you think you're going to win." When Mim's brow creased, he said, "I think you'll win, too. But it won't change how I feel about you—I promise you that."

Merlin framed her face with his hands and lowered his lips toward hers with an excruciating lack of speed. The anticipation was too much. Mim pushed onto the balls of her feet, wrapped her arms around his neck, and drew Merlin closer. When their lips finally met, pure exhilaration surged through her.

Mim's first kiss was just as potent but far sweeter than undiluted magic.

"I've been wanting to do that for a long time," Merlin told her, his cheeks growing rosier, and this time Mim didn't think it was from the cold.

"Will you call me Morrigan? It's my real name," she said. "I couldn't pronounce it when I was little. I called myself Mim and it stuck, but . . ." She looked up into Merlin's gaze. "Will you call me Morrigan when you kiss me?"

"I can definitely do that." Merlin rested his forehead against hers. "Morrigan, I think I'm falling in *lo—*" Mim touched a finger to his lips, stopping him from completing the thought.

"Don't say it." She held Merlin with her gaze. She couldn't love him. She couldn't risk it. "I need my head clear for the competition."

He answered with another kiss.

Snow graced the field that had been designated for the Solstice Competition.

Mim's heart pounded as she watched Merlin duel with another senior student, both currently in the form of bears. Each mage could take on the form of any living creature, and the duel only ended when one mage bowed to the greater power of the other. Merlin's fur was sable with a single white streak, making it easy to identify him—although Mim would know those fierce blue eyes anywhere.

She had won all her duels so far, as had Merlin. Her muscles ached. The students had been paired randomly, progressing through the competition all morning. Mim had bested ten of her fellow mages, qualifying for the Final Duel.

While Merlin might have no interest in becoming Apprentice to the Royal Mage, he wielded his magic with cunning and skill far beyond his years. Mim still couldn't believe he'd started formal training only when he arrived at the Lyceum. She didn't want Merlin to lose, not exactly, yet she also didn't want to be the one to defeat him.

The day before, Mim had refused to let Merlin say the word that would change everything. Could Merlin really love Mim despite her Shadow Magic?

Did he accept her, warts and all?

Mim might have refused to say the word, but she knew the truth in her heart. She couldn't deny to herself that she loved Merlin the Not-Prince.

A roar split her ears as the beige-furred bear knelt in submission.

Merlin had won. Merlin had won, and now the boy she loved was all that stood between Mim and becoming the future Royal Mage.

The king's trumpeter sounded the end of the match. Immediately, Merlin's eyes sought Mim's. She saw apology in them, but also determination.

Taliesin stood on a raised dais, to the left of King Uther's throne. Uther Pendragon looked to be no more than thirty summers, his shoulders broad and muscled, his entire aspect severe. A jagged scar bisected the olive skin of his forehead, leaving little doubt that he had taken his crown by force.

Unease slithered through Mim as she was struck by a sudden knowing that he had failed to pull the sword from the stone. Could it be related to the vision the Cauldron had shown her? Would Mim see the True Ruler of All Brytannia rise in her lifetime? She shook the thoughts away, focusing on the task at hand.

"Merlin of Dalriada, you have won your place in the Final Duel," Taliesin pronounced in a grave voice that carried across the field. Searching the crowd, his gaze landed on Mim. "Morrigan of Gurnard," he said, "step forward to meet Merlin of Dalriada in magical combat."

Mim rubbed her sweaty palms against her thighs. There was no time to exchange a single word with Merlin. She felt the king's glare on her face, imagined his disgust at her shadow-stained hair and complexion. She would show why her magical skill would be a vital asset to Camelot.

As she walked to meet Merlin in the middle of the snow-covered grass, the Royal Mage seated beside the king rose to her feet.

Niniame was a tall, imposing woman of indeterminate age. Her skin was fair but not deathly pale like Mim's, and her face was wreathed with rubicund plaits. Rumor had it her magic was so powerful she could cross to the Other Side at will. More than anything, Mim wanted to be trained by her.

"The rules of the Final Duel remain the same. Each competitor may change his or her shape into any animal known to man with Earth Magic," declared Niniame. "The duel will be considered at an end when one of the competitors admits defeat."

In unison, not daring a glance at each other, Merlin and Mim replied, "May my roots be strong, and my branches reach for the sun." They bowed before King Uther and the Royal Mage, then proceeded to put ten paces between themselves.

Booming to all those assembled, the Royal Mage called out, "By the Cauldron, let the Mage's Duel begin!"

Claps and cheers followed, perforating the air, as a metallic taste filled Mim's mouth. She and Merlin stared at each other for the longest moment of her life. She read the distress on his face. No, this was not the moment to hesitate.

She loved Merlin, but she couldn't let him win.

A glimmering haze silhouetted him where he stood, and then he was replaced by a blackbird taking flight. *A blackbird!* Was Merlin *trying* to lose the duel?

Mim blew out a harsh breath through her nostrils before joining him in her raven guise. Yes, Mim wanted to win, but she wanted to beat him with her magical prowess. Not because Merlin had thrown the competition.

She cawed her frustration. Merlin glanced back at her briefly, twittering ruefully, circling the dais where the king and his retinue watched them intently. This wouldn't do at all. He had to put up some resistance or the Royal Mage would doubt Mim had the requisite skill to be her Apprentice.

Summoning magic from her core as she'd practiced so many times, Mim flapped her plum-colored wings and drove Merlin toward the ground. When the blackbird's beak was nearly touching the snow, Mim siphoned a little more magic, her body growing fever-hot as she transformed from a raven into a fox.

The blackbird warbled in panic. Mim snapped her vulpine jaw, long and sleek. She struck out at Merlin, but he dodged, and the pad of her paw crashed against the snow. A light dusting tickled her purple nose. Mim barked a challenge. She swiped at Merlin again.

Suddenly, the bird was no longer a bird but a menacing lynx. The giant cat had white tips to its pointed obsidian ears. Its eyes flashed like a summer storm.

Yes. This was what Mim wanted. A fair fight.

Exhilaration coursed through her as she ran straight toward Merlin. The lynx might be bigger, but Mim wanted victory more. With an aggressive yowl, she feinted left and ran behind Merlin, leaping on the lynx's back.

Mim nipped at the fur of its neck. The majestic cat roared and threw her off its back. She hit the frozen earth with a thud. *Ow.* Her shoulder throbbed.

The lynx prowled closer. Merlin let out a feline whimper. He was sorry, Mim knew, but she didn't want him to stop fighting. She remained prone, luring him closer, using his concern for her against him. The instant Merlin's muzzle hovered above her, Mim released a ripple of magic and changed shape once more, becoming a wolf—the lynx's natural predator.

Mim remembered how Merlin had shape-shifted for the first time when confronted with a wolf, and she wanted to frighten him into action. The lynx went stock-still.

Baying at the midwinter sky, Mim scrambled onto her hind legs, shaking out her violet coat, and leapt for Merlin's jugular.

This time she didn't hold back. Howling, she grazed the cat's neck with her fangs.

Merlin tried to shake her off. Mim held on tighter. Her body vibrated with a low, demanding growl. The lynx rolled onto its back, trying to use the momentum to dislodge the wolf's teeth.

Admit defeat, Mim beseeched with her growl.

His blue eyes widened, and all at once, a shudder ripped through Mim. In her mind's eye, she saw them kissing in the clearing. A pink sheen surrounded them. Intensity of feeling overwhelmed her. Love. Love so strong it pained her.

Mim's heart seized. The world spun around her, tunneling as if she were falling to the bottom of a very deep well. *No, oh, no . . .* Was this what she'd been warned about?

Her yowl transformed into a scream. A very high-pitched, human scream.

Still staring into the lynx's eyes, Mim frantically ran her hands over her face—her mortal face—with desperate panic.

The king's trumpeter signaled the end of the match.

Merlin stared at Mim, stunned. The big cat's whiskers twitched.

"Merlin of Dalriada, you are the champion of the Solstice Competition!" proclaimed the Royal Mage. "You may regain your human form."

"No!" The word escaped Mim, plaintive and mangled. She took a stride toward the dais. "No, I do not admit defeat!"

Niniame regarded her with a mixture of scorn and pity. "You may not admit defeat, but your magic does. You lost control. You could not maintain your animal form."

"That's not true! It wasn't *me* who lost control," Mim protested. Gasps erupted among the audience when she dared to contradict the Royal Mage. She glanced in the direction of the lynx and her gaze snagged on Merlin, a boy once more, expression bleak.

"Tell them, Merlin," she insisted.

"I . . ." He hesitated. "Royal Mage Niniame, I don't know what happened."

Mim clenched her jaw. "You broke my magic, Merlin. You *cheated*!" she said, her fury boiling over.

Niniame surveyed them dispassionately. "Morrigan of Gurnard, your tutor, Taliesin, has extolled your talents to me. Therefore, you must be aware that to break the magic of a fellow mage, you must share an incredibly close bond."

Tears of humiliation threatened as Mim swallowed hard. Merlin reached for her hand, and she pushed him away. His consolation was the last thing she wanted.

"But the rules of the duel state that a mage should change his or her own shape—not that of their opponent!" Mim shot back, using all her willpower not to let her voice quaver.

"She's right," said Merlin. "I acted on instinct. I didn't know what I was doing, but it was against the rules."

The Royal Mage exchanged a weighted look with Uther Pendragon. The king gave an almost imperceptible shake of the head.

"You were betrayed by your own emotions, Morrigan of Gurnard. Not by your fellow mage. Merlin of Dalriada exploited a weakness in your magical defenses," Niniame went on. "A Royal Mage must prize protection of the realm above all—including her own heart. I am sorry, Morrigan, but you are not yet up to the task. Merlin of Dalriada will be my new Apprentice."

Mim's eyes burned. She could no longer hold back the tears. She ran from the field of combat as the spectators cheered, "Merlin! Merlin! Merlin!"

Taliesin grabbed the sleeve of her dress as she passed the dais.

"Mim, don't leave. You performed well today. I'm proud of you."

She laughed caustically. "I followed the Lyceum's rules, and it wasn't enough. *I'll* never be enough. I'm done trying."

"You're upset," Taliesin said patiently, as if he were pacifying the Cauldron. "Take a few moments to calm down, and then come congratulate Merlin."

"I won't congratulate a cheater—not even if he's your favorite."

Her tutor frowned. "You're letting your Shadow Self control you."

"Maybe it's about time. It's who I am, after all," she said, and Taliesin winced at her words.

"Magic or no, we all have shadows inside us," he chided. "It's what we do with them that matters."

But Mim was sick of the Chief Mage's advice. "I always knew you were afraid of me."

"I'm afraid *for* you, Mim. There's a world of difference."

"Either way, I'm not your responsibility any longer. I quit. I'm leaving the Lyceum."

Mim stormed away from her former teacher and took to the sky.

Snow flurries fell above the Wildwood in an unhurried fashion. Mim lugged two large leather satchels behind her. She shivered beneath her cloak, stopping to catch her breath in a birch tree clearing. The sun had set, and the gloaming tinted the snow a pale pink. Mim would need to find shelter for the night.

A desolate song echoed through the wood.

Mim groaned as the blackbird caught up with her. "Go away!" she shouted.

Merlin stood before her in the next moment, flushed—with victory she presumed. He took a step closer, and she drew back. "Where are you going, Mim?"

"I don't know. But as long as you aren't there, I don't care."

He flinched. Running a hand through his hair, Merlin said, "Then I'll go with you."

Of all the nerve. "You're not invited. Besides, shouldn't you be packing for Camelot?"

"Mim, this—this isn't how I thought today would end," he told her. "I never wanted to hurt you."

"You keep saying that, Merlin. And yet you keep hurting me."

"That's not fair."

"Nothing is fair. You proved that today. Apprentice Rulebreaker. Or should I say, *Prince* Rulebreaker?"

Merlin drew in a sharp breath. "You know the best ways to hurt me, Mim."

Her entire body panged, but she refused to show it. Her love for him had been her downfall. If he hadn't made her care for him, she would be the new Apprentice.

Daring another step toward her, "I love you, Morrigan," Merlin declared.

"You don't get to say that," she replied, voice breaking. "You don't get to love me after you betrayed me. If you really loved me, you wouldn't have used my own heart against me."

Merlin's face crumpled. "I didn't betray you, Mim! I had no idea I could do what I did," he pleaded.

"I taught you to hone your natural talent, and this is how you've repaid me?" Mim balled her hands into fists. "I risked my heart, and you stole my future!"

"I'm sorry. You have no idea how sorry I am, Morrigan. It's the worst thing I've ever done." He got down on one knee. "By the Cauldron, I swear I'll never cheat or bend the rules again. I hate myself for hurting you."

She swiped angrily at her fresh tears. "If that's true, then tell the Royal Mage you decline her offer. Tell her that I should be her new Apprentice."

Merlin pushed to standing. He worried his jaw from side to side. Before he spoke, Mim knew what he would say.

His decision was etched into every line of his face.

Inhaling deeply, he said, "I've been speaking with King Uther, and he thinks that having a mage from the Red Mountains will help him keep peace with my grandfather and the other northern kings."

"Your grandfather sees you as an embarrassment."

A hiss escaped Merlin as he sucked his lips together. "Even so. For once I can see how my mixed parentage can help me do good in the world."

"So much for serving kings not being what it's cracked up to be," Mim retorted.

"It's not about the kings, Morrigan." Merlin closed the remaining space between them. "I felt my mother with me today, during the competition," he said, dropping a hand on Mim's shoulder. "My grandfather didn't want to make peace with Uther, but my mother convinced him. This is my chance to continue my mother's legacy, do you see?"

Mim did see. With perfect clarity, she understood why Taliesin had insisted that Merlin take part in the competition.

She let out a soft, shrill laugh.

"I'll always be the better magic-wielder, Merlin," she told him. "But it doesn't matter because my mother wasn't a princess. We were never in the same competition. We were always being judged by different rules."

Merlin's lips parted. "I don't understand."

"No, you can't understand. As much as you claim otherwise, you're still royalty. The choice today was political. It was never about talent." Pointing at herself, jabbing an angry finger at her own chest, Mim said, "*I* will always be an outsider, Merlin. The Lyceum let me believe that if I suppressed my Shadow Magic, if I embraced all of their rules, I could succeed—that I had as much chance as anyone of becoming Royal Mage."

Her laughter grew hysterical. "It was all lies. I rejected so many parts of myself trying to be like everyone else."

Mim shrugged off Merlin's touch. She unpicked her carefully plaited braid, letting the purple tresses blow freely in the snow-laced wind.

"When the rules are unfair, the only smart thing to do is to break them and create your own," she declared.

"The Lyceum should fear me. Camelot should fear me. All Brytannia!"

"You're acting mad, Mim," said Merlin in a low voice. Glancing at the darkening sky, he said, "Let's get back to the Hidden Isle. You'll feel differently tomorrow."

"I'm not going anywhere."

"You can't stay in the Wildwood. It's not safe."

Mim scoffed. "*I'm* the most dangerous thing in these woods."

"Fine." Merlin planted his feet. "Then I'll stay, too."

"How many times do I have to tell you that you're not invited?" she said, raising her voice. "Go back to your rules and your king. I don't want anything to do with them—or with you."

His face contorted as if she'd slapped him. "You don't mean that, Morrigan. You can't just turn your back on what's between us."

"You can't be with me and serve the king. You have to choose."

Silence followed her ultimatum. The whole Wildwood went quiet. Only the sound of falling snow echoed in Mim's ears. Behind her eyes, the snow turned to flickering flames.

The vision she'd had from the Cauldron made sense to her now. It wasn't Uther Pendragon she'd seen. Not quite. His rule was unjust. Brytannia would never be safe for those with Shadow Magic while he was king. Uther and Camelot were her enemies.

Merlin pressed his arms to his sides. Sadness filled his winter-blue eyes.

"I must choose peace. It's what my mother would do," he said, resolved.

"Then we are enemies. From this day forward, there will be nothing but enmity between us."

"Not on my part, Morrigan. I will keep hoping that you'll find it in your heart to forgive me."

She bit her lips together, fury surging, breathing harshly, chest rising and falling.

"You are no longer in my heart, Merlin."

"*Please*, Morrigan," he said, tone ragged. "Please don't say that."

"I will never love anyone or anything again. You showed me that love is weakness. But I should thank you because I've torn the tenderness from my heart and cauterized the wound."

Merlin shook his head. "I don't believe you."

"Then watch this—and just try to break my magic!"

The shadows encroached from every corner of the Wildwood. Mim beckoned them, invited them, as if they were kittens and her rage a saucer of milk. She lifted her arms toward the night sky. The darkness sheathed her. She drew it into herself: a cold that burned, raw and intense. Bitterness fueled her, a limitless source of energy.

A lifetime's worth of tears could be combustible.

This was what Mim had been missing. The icy shadows

that swarmed her heart belonged there. They made her powerful. They were home. She was home.

She was the dragon.

Mim felt the violent flame at her core, and then her mortal form fell away. Snow fell on her iridescent scales as she grew and grew. Wings towering above the trees, she was incandescent, her underbelly exposed yet tough. A royal-purple dragon. A beautiful monster.

"Morrigan!" gasped Merlin. The horror was plain on his face.

She answered with a roar of fire.

He bent his knees and squared his shoulders, closing his eyes. Mim watched the intense concentration on Merlin's face. She felt petty assaults against her magic. They bounced off her like pebbles against a coat of armor.

Sweat dripped from Merlin's temples. He gritted his teeth so hard, it looked like they might break.

Merlin was no match for her. She had traded love for shadows, and now she was invincible.

Finally, he opened his eyes. Surprise lit them, then despair, as she pounded the snow with her dragon tail. For the first time, Mim realized she was seeing her true self.

"You've proved your point," said Merlin, breathless. "You don't love me." His shoulders curled forward, and she took delight in his exhaustion. "Hate me all you want, Mim, but come back to the Lyceum. You don't have to be alone."

Except Mim *was* alone, and she always had been. She seared the clearing with her breath.

"I'll come back tomorrow," said Merlin. "And the day after that. And the day after that."

But Mim wouldn't be there.

The snow shimmered around Merlin as he transformed. He circled Mim's head as a blackbird. She yawned, releasing a burst of flame that singed Merlin's wings.

He raced back toward the Hidden Isle, a lament suffusing the air.

Mim remained alone with the shadows, where she belonged, where she was meant to be. At long last, Mim was free to be herself.

Mim was free.

And she would bring Camelot to its knees.

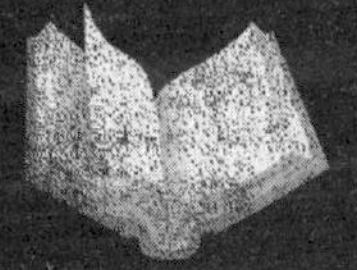

The Journey Home

What if Belle had to take her father's place at the fair?

by Farrah Rochon

The Journey Home

What if Belle had to take her father's place at the fair?

by Farrah Rochon

Inharmonious squawks pierced the peaceful morning as a brood of hens flocked to Belle's feet.

"Calm down. There's enough for all of you," Belle said, laughing. Using her father's latest invention, she sent chicken feed arcing through the air with a flourish. She sprinkled the last of the feed near the chicken coop before entering the house she and her father shared.

The minute she cleared the threshold, a loud crash boomed from her father's workshop. It was quite normal to hear strange sounds coming from the workshop, but this one sounded especially worrisome. When Belle heard a small strangled cry, alarm swept through her.

"Papa?" Belle yelled. She raced to the workshop and pushed open the heavy wooden door. The sight before her stole her breath. "Papa!"

She rushed to the mountain of logs that had tumbled to

the floor and began chucking them aside, searching for her father.

"Oh, Papa," Belle said upon finding him. His face was streaked with dirt and grime. She dropped to her knees and brushed bits of tree bark from his mustache.

"I'm . . . I'm okay," Maurice said.

"Maybe I should get the doctor, just to be safe."

"No, Belle!" He held out a hand to her. "Just help me up. I'll be fine."

Belle caught his wrinkled hand, the papery feel of his skin reminding her that her beloved papa was growing older with each passing day. How long would he be able to keep up this pace before she was forced to intervene?

"See? Good as new," Maurice said. He took one step and immediately crumpled to the floor.

"Papa!" Belle wrapped her arms around his torso and led him out of the workshop and to his bed. "I will fetch the doctor. You stay right there."

"Belle, I have to show my invention at the fair in two days' time. This is too important to miss."

"You can barely walk," she pointed out. "Please, promise me you won't move until I return with the doctor, at least."

She grabbed her cloak and raced into town. Belle wasn't entirely confident in her ability to summon the local doctor. The man was just as small-minded as the others in town. They'd all labeled both Belle and her father odd and treated them as outcasts. All because her father spent his time coming up with brilliant—albeit sometimes strange—inventions, and because she would rather read a book than participate in town gossip.

Her father needed the doctor's expertise, small-minded or not.

After much haranguing, Belle convinced the doctor to follow her back home. Her stomach tied itself into knots as she observed the physician's spindly fingers pressing into her father's leg, which was already turning a pale rose from bruising.

"How is he?" Belle asked cautiously.

"I don't think anything is broken, but he should stay off his leg for the next week at least."

"No, no." Maurice shook his head. "I can't."

"I will make sure he does," Belle told the doctor. She guided him to the door. Once there, she shook his hand, placing his fee in his palm. "Thank you for coming."

The man tipped his hat to her, but before he crossed the threshold, he said, "Maurice could further injure himself if he does not give his leg time to rest."

Belle acknowledged his warning with a nod. She closed the door behind him and rested her head against it, her eyes falling shut as she prepared herself for the argument she knew would commence the moment she walked into her father's room.

But when she returned to his room, the bed was empty.

"Papa?"

That stubborn man!

Belle took off for his workshop. She found him hobbling toward his log-splitting machine: the invention he hoped to show at the fair. "Papa, you heard the doctor! You cannot leave this house!"

"I must, Belle. I've worked too hard for this." His eyes grew misty as he lowered his voice and said, "This is my best work."

Belle's heart broke; she knew how much it meant to her father to share his inventions with the world, to have them mean something, to improve the day-to-day lives of those who could use them.

"Fine." She sucked in a deep breath, then said, "I'll go."

Maurice whipped his head around, his eyes wide with apprehension. "No." He shook his head. "You can't—"

"I can, Papa," Belle said. She ran to him and took his hands in hers. "I can do this. I've been at your side the entire time you've been working on this invention. I know how it works. Let me go to the fair in your stead."

"But . . . but you're a young woman."

Belle's mouth fell open. She was so taken aback she could scarcely think of what to say. "Is that a hindrance in your eyes, Papa?"

"Of course not, Belle. *I* know you are capable of doing anything you set your mind to, but there's many people in this world who would disagree."

"And I, for one, am tired of allowing those people to dictate what I can and cannot do. Why should anyone else have a say in whether or not I present your invention at the fair?"

"It's not just that, Belle. The fair is in Annecy. It's a full day's journey. You've never been that far from home before, and certainly not on your own."

"I know," Belle said, a thrilling sensation fluttering in her stomach. After years of yearning to see beyond the borders of her provincial little town, the thought of journeying someplace new, even if it was only to show her father's invention at a neighboring village's fair, made her heart race.

Maybe she would encounter a merry theater troupe on their way to perform the latest play. Or maybe merchants traveling with their wares to trade on the Silk Road. Oh, wouldn't it be wonderful to meet a newly married couple heading to Paris or Verona to celebrate their honeymoon? Who knew what types of adventures awaited her!

"I know exactly how to demonstrate the machine, Papa," Belle said. She walked over to the log-cutting machine and opened the small door on its side. "The coal goes here." She quickly ran to the other side. "Then I just pull this lever." She gave the lever a hard tug, and the contraption sputtered to life. Steam bellowed from the top, and within moments the sharp axe at its helm splintered a log in two.

"Well, look at that," Maurice said. He scratched his head. "But, Belle, I don't know about this. Venturing out on your own—it could be dangerous."

"Not if I'm careful," she said. "And I won't be alone; I'll have Philippe with me." She captured her father's shoulders and planted a kiss on his cheek. "You've done so much to take care of me all these years. Let me do this for you, Papa."

Belle observed the apprehension playing across his face. She was just about to make a stronger plea when he said, "Maybe it won't be so bad, as long as you stick to the path."

Yes!

"It's decided," Belle said. "I'll leave first thing in the morning."

Belle sat on the edge of her bed, her eyes trained on a fence post outside her window. Her heart pounded wildly against her chest as she waited for the first sliver of sun to break through the stillness of early morning darkness. She had awoken more than an hour earlier, her excitement making sleep almost impossible. Hesitant to light a candle and wake her father, she'd dressed by the faint light of the moon and quietly packed a bag of provisions for her journey to the village where the fair would take place.

Her most difficult choice had been which book to bring. She couldn't decide between something she'd never read before and one of her favorites.

So, of course, she'd packed two: a pirate adventure story she'd borrowed from the bookseller just the day before and the beloved book of short stories her mother used to read to her when she was a child.

A warm smile stretched across Belle's lips at the thought of her mother and the love of reading she'd instilled in her only daughter. She'd also nurtured Belle's sense of adventure.

"I'm finally going on one of my own, Mama," Belle whispered. "A true adventure."

The moment the sun crested the horizon, she hopped off the bed. According to her father, if she left at the first light of dawn, she should arrive in the town of Annecy before nightfall.

"It's time," Belle said excitedly. Goose bumps popped up along her arms as she thought of what awaited her.

She went into the kitchen and grabbed the tray she'd assembled for her father. It included almost everything he would need for the next three days. She didn't want him venturing out too much and tripping over things around the house.

Belle knocked at his bedroom door and let herself in. "Good morning, Papa," she greeted. "How is your leg?"

"Better," he said.

Her heart dropped.

"But I hate to admit that the doctor seems right," Maurice continued. "My leg is still not strong enough to go to the fair."

Belle knew she should feel guilty at the relief that rushed through her. It was not that she wanted Papa to be in pain. But now that this grand adventure lay before her, the thought of not going was more than she could bear.

She arranged his tray on the bedside table, then fluffed a pillow. She placed his leg on it and covered him with the worn blanket her mother had made for him years before.

"Now, Papa, you are certain you have everything you need here?"

"Yes, yes. And you remember the plan for your lodging? You will find a small inn just on the outskirts of Annecy. Tell the innkeeper you are Maurice's daughter, and he will give you the best room available." Her father sighed. "Oh, Belle, I'm still unsure about this."

"I'll be fine, Papa." She crouched down and wrapped her arms around him. "You raised me to be brave, and to make smart choices. I'll make you proud. You'll see."

"I am always proud of you." He squeezed her tight, then released her. He handed her a rolled piece of parchment. "Now, remember. Don't veer off the path."

Belle tucked his rudimentary map into her bag. "Well, I guess this is it. Philippe and I will be back before you know it." She gave her father another kiss before leaving his room.

She grabbed the bag she'd packed and then left the house, a mixture of anticipation and the tiniest bit of apprehension traveling along her spine as she made her way to the stable and saddled Philippe. The Belgian draft horse was her most trusted companion. She didn't have anything to worry about with Philippe at her side.

You can do this.

She'd spent too many years of her life in this tiny village, confined to a certain role because of the small minds of the people who lived here. Belle could only imagine what they would say about Maurice if they discovered he was allowing her to travel alone to Annecy. To show off one of his inventions, no less. They already considered him a loon; then they would call him an irresponsible father.

But Belle believed in her father's abilities as a parent just as much as she believed in his amazing inventions. She was going to show the people of this town just how wrong they had all been—about both of them.

Especially that loathsome cad Gaston.

Belle was convinced the arrogant huntsman was the driving force behind how the town viewed her family. He had the townspeople wrapped around his sausage-sized little finger, and if Gaston decided someone should be shunned, most obediently followed his lead. His cruelty toward Belle and her father had escalated after she turned down his advances, but she would endure the censure of every person in town before she gave in to Gaston.

Belle gathered the reins and gave Philippe a firm pat with her booted foot. "Let's go, Philippe. We have a long journey ahead of us."

They started out with a slow but steady canter, her horse's hooves kicking up tiny plumes of dust on the country road as they clomped along the path. Belle switched the reins to her left hand so she could use the other to tighten the cloak at her neck. The wind was brisk, but at least it wasn't wet.

A cold, featherlight snowflake landed on her nose.

"Wonderful," Belle said with a sigh. "I guess I should have expected this, huh, Philippe?"

She would not allow the snow to put a damper on her journey. She'd waited too long to taste the freedom of the open road, to see the world she'd only read about in her beloved books.

Not that there was much to see here. So far, her father's map had led to one long, boring road with nothing but trees on either side. She could hear a gurgling creek in the distance. Would it hurt to venture out just a little? To find a shortcut, perhaps?

"No," Belle said. Her father had warned her that she should remain on the path he'd drawn out for her.

But soon she was given no choice. For lying in the middle of the roadway was a massive tree. It had fallen over and blocked the path.

"Maybe we can go around it," she said to her horse.

She tried directing Philippe one way, then the other. But no matter how they maneuvered, her father's log-chopping machine was too big to fit through the narrow space between the uprooted tree trunk and the trees that remained standing along the road. The snow started falling with more fervor, and the chill in the air had become biting.

Belle lifted the hood of her cloak and looked around. She spotted a small trail winding its way through the thicket, blanketed by leaves and bits of snow that was starting to stick.

"Yes," she said. "Look, there's another path through the woods, Philippe."

When she tried to steer him toward it, the horse brayed and stubbornly stuck his nose in the air.

"Come on, Philippe."

She tugged his reins until he finally relented. They entered the forest, and the little light that had managed to break through the heavy clouds quickly became shaded by the trees overhead. Belle kept her eyes straight ahead and tried not to look at their spindly branches, which reached out and grazed her like the gnarled fingers of an old witch.

A brisk wind whipped up the snow that had accumulated on the ground. Combined with the fat flakes that had begun to fall in earnest from the sky, it made her travels that much more disorienting.

The deeper they ventured into the forest, the more Belle began to question the wisdom of her detour.

She pulled on Philippe's reins, halting his steps.

"Whoa there, boy. Let's go back. We'll try another route," Belle said. But when they turned, she found herself more than just disoriented; she was completely turned around. The path she'd set out on was indistinguishable from the rest of the forest floor.

A lump of terror lodged in her throat, but Belle managed to swallow it down. She inhaled deep stinging breaths in the frostbitten air—an effort to get her rapidly beating heart under control.

The horse took a tentative step. Belle leaned forward and ran a hand along his mane.

"Careful, Philippe," she whispered.

One wrong move and the horse could trip over a hidden tree stump or fall into a snow-covered divot. There were so many hazards lurking all around, dangers she hadn't taken very seriously when she'd volunteered for this journey.

Belle straightened her spine and held up her chin. She would not allow fear to grab hold of her. The characters she'd read about in books over the years always faced some type of hardship, didn't they? And they always managed to find a way out. She would do the same.

She slowly guided Philippe across the terrain. On more than one occasion, she jumped down from the horse and walked ahead of him, testing the ground before allowing him to drag her father's invention across it.

Belle tried not to think about how much time had passed, but she knew this had set her back at least a half hour so far. She dreaded traveling these roads past nightfall and could only hope she would be able to make up some time once she and Philippe were back on the right path.

Belle looked ahead and gasped.

"Look, Philippe!"

There was an opening through the trees. Just to the right of it, she could make out the tree that had fallen on the roadway. Somehow she'd managed to find her way back, and on the right side of the tree no less.

Relief buoying her, she climbed onto the saddle and pressed her booted feet gently into the horse's flanks, urging him forward.

But just as they cleared the tree line, Belle heard a loud clomp and was jerked back.

No. *No!*

Belle jumped down from the saddle and raced to the wagon that carried her father's machine. The front wheel was firmly lodged in a muddy, snowy rut.

"No, no, no," Belle cried aloud in vain. She grabbed hold of one of the spokes and tugged at it, knowing it was a wasted effort. Between the log-chopping machine and the wagon, she wouldn't be surprised if this load weighed a thousand pounds. She could have muscles the size of boulders and she wouldn't be able to get that wheel moving without some help.

She kicked the wheel in frustration, gaining a scuffed boot for her effort.

Maybe there was a way to dig the wheel out.

She spun in a slow circle, searching for something to use as a shovel. The snow had begun to fall in earnest, making it hard to see more than a few yards in any direction. Belle walked over to a barren tree and pulled at the bark, but the largest piece she could break off was no bigger than her palm.

Unable to think of a better solution, she returned to the wagon and began scooping snow out from around the wheel. But she couldn't keep up with the rate of the snowfall. She needed something bigger.

Belle looked around, then peered up at the shiny axe at the helm of the machine.

Maybe . . .

She shook her head. She knew a bad idea when it scurried across her mind. Even if she were able to free the axe from the myriad knots binding it to the machine, she wouldn't risk detaching it without being certain she could put it back in place. Besides, with the way her luck was going that day, the sharp axe would slip out of her hands and chop right through the wheel.

Belle turned and rested her back against the wagon, her shoulders slumping in utter defeat. This was not going as planned. She could deal with one mishap, but the blocked roadway, worsening snowstorm, *and* sunken wheel were overwhelming.

She considered her options, each less appealing than the last. Leave the wagon and her father's most prized possession? Find a way home to get tools and help (from whom, Belle did not know) and somehow manage to retrace her steps to this spot? Or wait for help in the middle of the woods in increasingly dangerous conditions, putting both her and Philippe's lives at risk?

Onward, Belle.

She heard the words spoken in her mother's soft, encouraging voice—words she would say whenever young

Belle felt stuck. Belle stood up straight and wiped away the wayward tear that had escaped. Her chest swelled with confidence she wouldn't have considered possible just a few minutes earlier.

"Come on, boy," Belle said, rounding Philippe's side. She grabbed hold of the bridle strapped to his chin and tugged. The horse lunged forward, but the wagon didn't move an inch.

"Again," Belle said. "Give it another try."

He extended his elegant neck, the muscles in his chest standing out in stark relief as he tried to pull the heavy load.

The wagon groaned.

"Wait! Stop!" Belle yanked on Philippe's bridle.

She stooped low and confirmed what she'd already suspected. Instead of pulling free, the wheel had only lodged deeper in the rut.

Could this day get any worse?

Just then, Belle heard a faint sound somewhere in the distance. She crouched lower, her eyes darting from left to right. She did her best to calm her frantic breaths and to hear over the chaotic thumping of the blood rushing through her veins.

Holding herself very still, Belle listened intently.

There it was again.

The sound was muffled, barely discernible over the wind rustling through the trees, but she had definitely heard it. She looked all around, searching the area the sound had come from. She saw the tree branches shake and then heard it again. It sounded like a horn of some type. And . . . laughter?

More shaking branches. More laughter.

She looked just west of her, toward snow-laden trees. What emerged made Belle's skin crawl and her stomach wrench.

Gaston.

Great. Just what she needed.

Moments later, his sidekick, LeFou, scampered up behind him, clutching a quiver of arrows in his hands. The bow's thick leather strap was stretched tightly across Gaston's massive chest.

Belle knew better than to hope they wouldn't see her, not with the way her father's colorful contraption stuck out in this white landscape. Still, she tried to make herself as small and invisible as possible. Maybe they would think someone had abandoned the wagon.

"Well, well. What do we have here, LeFou?" Belle's eyes slid shut at the sound of Gaston's voice. "This looks like the inventor Maurice's fine steed, doesn't it? This horse is wasted on that loony old man if you ask me."

"Yeah, Maurice doesn't deserve a horse like this," LeFou said.

Philippe neighed, and Belle had to curb the urge to lash out at that towering buffoon and his little minion. And then she realized their voices were getting closer. It was only a matter of time before they spotted her.

Instead of allowing Gaston to find her crouching like a frightened church mouse, she stood.

"Belle?" Gaston called. There was genuine surprise in his voice. No doubt he was expecting to find her father. "What are *you* doing out here?"

"Having a cup of tea," Belle replied, the words dripping with sarcasm.

LeFou started muttering about wanting a nice warm drink before Gaston shot him a look.

"Well?" Gaston turned to Belle, bracing his feet apart and crossing his gargantuan arms over his equally gargantuan chest.

"If you must know, I am on the way to the fair in Annecy," Belle said. "But as you can see, I've found myself in a bit of a rut. Quite literally."

Gaston rounded the wagon. He rubbed his chin with his big meaty hand. "It's no wonder, a girl taking out a wagon alone."

Belle cringed. She would never understand why the women in town fawned over this Neanderthal. He had the grace of a water buffalo and the temperament to match.

Huh . . . Belle suddenly had a thought. If the tales he so often told all about town were true, he also had the strength of *ten* buffaloes. While she rarely put stock in anything Gaston said, his physical prowess was undeniable.

And that mighty strength of his was exactly what she needed.

If she, Gaston, and LeFou tried, it was possible they could lift the wagon out of the trough.

But to ask a favor of Gaston? There was nothing Belle could think of that she would rather do less.

Well, that wasn't entirely true. There were several things she could think of that were worse when it came to Gaston. The man wasn't one to do favors for anyone. Anything she asked of him would come at a price, and just the thought of what that price might be made Belle want to hurl herself into the first icy river she came upon.

She opened her mouth to tell him to get on his merry way, but then she looked at her father's invention gathering snow, at Philippe's trusting gaze.

What choice did she have? She could not get out of this quagmire she found herself in. And she hadn't seen another soul on the path all morning. Only fools would venture out as the snowfall increased. She needed muscle, and unfortunately, the only muscle here belonged to the bane of her existence.

She sucked in a deep breath before she began.

"Gaston," Belle started in her most conciliatory voice. It galled her to have to use this approach, but a man like Gaston thrived on such things. She would have to be her most pliant and amiable self if she wanted his help. "I know we've had our disagreements in the past."

"Disagreements?" He arched a thick, bushy eyebrow. "You've been downright disrespectful to me, Belle. When

I have offered you more than a girl like yourself could ever hope for."

Maybe she could just live in this forest forever. That would be better than being beholden to this leech.

Belle forced a smile. "I will admit that I have been less than pleasant at times, but that's all water under the bridge."

"Is it, now?" Gaston murmured.

"Yes. In fact, I consider you somewhat of a—well, a *neighbor*," Belle continued, struggling to find the right word. "And as a neighbor, I was hoping for your assistance in a certain matter."

"What is it you want?"

She stared at him. Wasn't it obvious? "I need help dislodging my wagon. If I don't get moving soon, it will be dark before I can reach Annecy."

"So you need my help?" Gaston said. He looked over at his sidekick. "Did you hear that, LeFou? Little Belle here, who has turned that pert nose up at me whenever I've come near her, actually *needs* me."

She shook her head, immediately regretting her decision. She should have unstrapped Philippe and walked home with him. It would have been better to admit to her father that she'd made a mistake in coming here than to rely on Gaston for anything.

"Maybe I would be willing to help," Gaston said. "If you would be willing to do something for me in return."

And there was the other shoe.

She had known this despicable barbarian would exact a price.

"What do you want?" Belle asked.

"Dinner," Gaston said. He rubbed his hands together. "If I free your little wagon from this rut, you will agree to have dinner with me at the tavern this coming Saturday night."

Suffer through an entire meal with Gaston? At the tavern? On a Saturday night? That would be all but a declaration that they were courting.

"Why don't you let me pay you instead?" Belle asked.

He laughed. "I don't want or need your money, Belle."

"What about if I baked you something? Maybe some cakes you could sell at the tavern."

Gaston rubbed his chin. "If I didn't know better, I would think you were ashamed to be seen in public with me, Belle."

Ding. Ding. Ding.

The thought of being seen in public with him made her queasy.

"It's not that. . . . It's just . . ." She hesitated.

"Belle . . ." Gaston looked down his nose at her. "You have my price. What is your answer? You must admit that dinner with me is better than anything else you have planned for this Saturday."

"Yeah, it's way better than having your nose stuck in one of those books," LeFou said.

A book? A book!

"That's it," Belle whispered.

She scrambled up the side of the log-chopping machine and grabbed her bag from where she'd tucked it behind the seat. She searched around inside until she found the book she'd gotten from the bookseller. She hated the thought of ruining it, but there was no way she would use the collection of short stories from her mother. She would apologize and pay the bookseller when she returned. Hopefully with some of the winnings from the fair.

"What are you gonna do with that?" LeFou asked.

"Just you wait," Belle said.

She climbed down, taking care not to slip on the snow-covered step of the wagon. Then she knelt next to the wheel and started digging up the snow surrounding it.

"Belle, have you gone mad?" Gaston asked.

"No. I'm getting out of this mess," she said as she wedged the book between the wheel and the ground. "On my own."

LeFou pointed to the book and laughed. "What in the world is she doing, Gaston?"

"I'm making a ramp for the wheel," Belle answered for herself. She ran over to Philippe and climbed into the saddle. She pressed her legs into the horse's flanks. "Let's go."

With a heave, her horse surged forward. The wagon inched ahead.

"That's it, Philippe," Belle said. "Again."

The horse pressed on with a loud neigh, and the wagon rolled out of the rut.

"Way to go, Philippe."

"Look there, Gaston!" LeFou said, clapping his hands. "Can you believe it?"

Gaston growled at his sidekick.

Belle looked down at the two of them. "Well, gentlemen, it looks as if I won't need your assistance, after all. Gaston, I'm sure you can find some willing woman in the village to join you for dinner Saturday night, but it won't be me. And now I have some important things to do, like demonstrating my father's invention at the fair."

She straightened and gave Philippe the cue to start moving.

"You may want to get out of this snow. It looks as if it will only get uglier," she threw over her shoulder.

A trail of sweat pebbled at Belle's hairline, despite the chill that remained in the air.

This was the most important aspect of her trip. If she didn't have a good showing at the fair, everything she had gone through on her harrowing journey the day before would be for naught.

"It takes only a small amount of coal to fire it up," she explained to the judges as she shoveled coal into the pit. She closed the door, then mentally crossed her fingers. "Here we go," Belle announced in a cheerful voice to hide her nerves. She pulled on the lever, and the machine came to life.

As the judges observed her father's invention, she studied their faces, trying to gauge their reactions.

When the axe landed on the first log, there was an audible gasp from the crowd. And when it split the log perfectly down the center, everyone burst into applause.

Relief sluiced down Belle's spine. And several minutes later, her entire being was on the verge of erupting in glee as she stood on the stage and accepted a blue ribbon from the head judge.

"Thank you. Thank you so much," Belle said. "My father has worked on this invention for years, because he knows how much a device like this can help busy families in the winter."

"I'd take one of those," the head judge said.

Another person said, "Here, here!"

"Me too!" said another.

Belle's chest felt as if it would burst with pride.

This was vindication, for both her and her father—against all the naysayers in town who called her father a loon for his inventions, and all those who thought a woman could not travel alone, or do anything as well as a man, for that matter. This blue ribbon proved them all wrong.

Belle spent another night at the inn on the outskirts of Annecy. She treated herself to a celebratory dinner of mutton stew and cobbler and enjoyed the singing and dancing of others in the tavern. Then she read her mother's fairy tales by the fire in her room before going to bed. She didn't need to be accompanied by Gaston to have a good time in a pub. She was perfectly capable of entertaining herself.

At the first light of dawn, she set off for home, arriving well before nightfall.

"Papa!" Belle called. She went into his room and found him sitting up in bed, sipping on a cup of tea.

"Belle, you're back!"

"Yes. And guess what?" She produced the blue ribbon from behind her back. "Your invention won first place! Oh, Papa, everyone loved it."

His face lit up. "First place? I . . . I don't know what to say." But then he sobered. "Actually, I do know one thing I should say. I'm sorry, Belle."

"Sorry? For what?"

"For ever doubting you," her father said.

"Papa, it's okay." She laughed. "Goodness knows there were moments during the trip when I doubted myself."

"Oh, Belle, I am sorry," Maurice said again. Then he looked at her, and she could see his inventor's mind churning. "What helped?"

She wrapped her arms around her father's shoulders. "What always does: your innovation, Mother's confidence, and of course"—she smiled—"a book."

Three years later . . .

Just as Belle alighted from the rolling ladder that glided

along the wall of bookshelves, the bell above the shop door chimed with the arrival of another customer.

"Bonjour, monsieur," Belle greeted the cheesemonger. "Back for another?"

"Yes," he said. He held up the book he'd carried in with him. "You were right about this one. The swashbuckling pirate was my favorite character." He pantomimed a sword fight. "Who knew one could find such fun in a book!"

Belle tipped her head to the side. "Hmm . . . who knew?" she said with a chuckle. "Lucky for you, I just received a new shipment." She lifted a leather-bound tome from the shelf and handed it to him. "If you thought the pirate was a great character, just wait until you meet this sailor marooned on a desert island!"

The cheesemonger's eyes lit up. "I can't wait to read it!"

She walked him to the door, delighting in his joy as he left with his new purchase. She'd witnessed that same look of excited anticipation on the faces of many of the villagers in the year since she'd taken over the bookshop. The same people who'd mocked her for her love of reading, and gossiped about her father, now cozied up with a good book while enjoying a fire fueled by wood cut with her father's wood-chopping machine. Many minds had been changed those past few years.

Particularly when word of her father's prize-winning invention had spread and Monsieur René le Prince, an entrepreneur (a new profession, funnily enough, born out of the word *adventurer*), proposed a partnership. With Monsieur le Prince's resources, Maurice's knack for machinery, and Belle's cleverness, they had formed a formidable team. They traveled to other fairs and looked for new innovations to support, Belle often finding successes in the inventors no one else would take a chance on. After a while, the trio had made a name for themselves.

More than once, Belle had suggested she and Maurice move to Paris or Nice or at least a different village—start a new life for themselves anywhere else. And yet, he could not bear to leave the little cottage, the last place he had seen his beloved wife. So they always returned to the small town.

And then, when the local bookseller let Belle know he was intent on retiring, Belle had bought the business and taken it on as a passion project, stocking the shelves with titles she acquired on her travels and ordering new ones. Most of the villagers had come to visit the shop out of curiosity, having learned how famous and beloved Belle and her father were throughout the country. They made conversation, sheepishly at first and then more earnestly as Belle got to know them and their tastes and could make book recommendations that lifted their spirits in ways they had not known they'd needed.

Slowly, friendships had been forged, and Belle and Maurice had become pillars of the village. And when Gaston ended up moving away to marry a widowed baroness (one who, if the rumors were true, made him wait on her hand and foot—something he had *not* anticipated when first presented with the opportunity), what was left of the old tensions eased.

Belle no longer sought to move away. She enjoyed the trips to Annecy, Doussard, and the other places she and her father and Monsieur le Prince visited, attending fairs around France and abroad. But after so many years of longing to break free from this town, Belle had learned to love the idea of having a small special corner of the world to return to, of having relationships to maintain.

Through her parents, her books, and her neighbors, she had found her path onward, the most rewarding journey of all—the journey home.

Call It a Hunch

What if Hercules's first day as a god didn't go as planned?

by Jen Calonita

Call It a Hunch

What if Hercules's first day as a god didn't go as planned?

by Jen Calonita

"Well?" Hercules leaned in closer. "What do you think?"

Meg looked over her shoulder at the azure sky that surrounded the cushiony cloud they were seated on. As if for effect, an eagle swooped past them, whistling a high-pitched call miles above land. She gave Wonder Boy a look. "I'll tell you one thing—no one has ever taken me on a date like this."

Hercules's whole face lit up. A silver tray floated past him, and he plucked a grape off it and fed it to her. "That's a good thing, right? Aphrodite—I mean, *I* thought this would be a romantic way to celebrate our new jobs."

"You're the one with a job," Meg reminded him as she took another piece of the best cheese she'd ever had in her life. "Mine is more like a hobby. A *new* hobby."

"Don't sell yourself short," Hercules insisted. "This is going to turn into something big for you. I can feel it! No one is better suited for solving crimes."

Meg cocked her head to one side, her fiery-red ponytail swaying in the light breeze. "If you consider the scheming I did for Hades crime work, then maybe. But let's not get ahead of ourselves. This is one small gig." A gig that would barely pay the rent, but she couldn't be choosy. There wasn't a large market for women who'd recently been freed from the Underworld, and she needed to make money. She was still surprised Darius, the wealthy businessman who owned several shops in the agora, had agreed to her fee for tracking down his missing Athena statue. It had disappeared from a fountain in front of the marketplace on the east side of town two days before, and business had plummeted. No one, not even the authorities, liked to touch crimes that involved the gods—too risky, too unpredictable. But Meg had always liked a challenge.

Hercules's blue eyes sparkled. "All you need is one gig to get started."

Meg shook her head. "That's what I love about you, Wonder Boy. You're the eternal optimist." She touched his chiseled chin. "It's why you will make the perfect god of heroes."

Hercules blushed. "It still feels funny hearing you use my new honor."

"Well, get used to it. There's no one better to advise someone on their hero's journey. Your father picked a good role for you—you're going to make a heck of a god."

"You think so?" His blue eyes were pensive. "I really

want to make my parents proud. I don't want them to think they made a mistake giving me such a big title."

When Hercules had renounced his godliness to stay on Earth to be with her, she was sure Zeus would rain thunderbolts down from the heavens. Instead, Zeus had taken the news quite well. (Turned out the god was a romantic.) He insisted Hercules remain a god ("You earned it!" he'd boomed). After Zeus talked to his wife, Hera, the two agreed their son could have dual residency on Mount Olympus and on Earth so he could be with Meg. Wonder Boy had been beside himself, and it was his first day of training, which was why Meg had brought him a good-luck present.

"And if you need reminding that this is the role you were born for, just look at this." Meg reached into the satchel she'd brought with her when Pegasus picked her up that morning at an unearthly hour. (Did gods sleep? Probably not much. She'd have to get used to dating one.) Out came the small parcel she'd carefully wrapped for him.

Hercules's eyes lit up. "You got me a present?" He unwrapped it with one tear from his gargantuan hands. A coin was nestled inside the paper. He held it up in the early morning light that Helios provided. "Hey . . . is there a tiny bow and arrow etched on this coin?"

Meg smiled. "Yes. It's to remind you that your aim is true and to always trust your instincts," she said softly. "They've never steered you wrong before." Including about her. Even when she'd been conflicted, he'd seen the trueness of her heart. She'd saved him, then he'd saved her, and now they were ready to start something new together.

Hercules leaned in and kissed her softly. "I love it. It's the perfect present." He tucked it into a slot in his leather belt. "I have a gift for your first day, too." He snapped his fingers, and a small gold pin appeared in the palm of her hand.

Meg stared at a tiny crown of olive leaves. "It's beautiful," she murmured. She couldn't remember the last time she'd received a gift, let alone one from someone she loved. It certainly hadn't happened in the Underworld. "Thanks, Wonder Boy." She pinned the delicate crown to her purple gown, right above her breastbone.

"It's for luck," he said. "Not that you need it."

"I don't know about that." Meg didn't want to admit she was nervous, but this was the first "real" work she'd had since she'd left Hades, and she wanted it to go well. Not only did she want it to lead to more folks hiring her to solve god problems no one else would, but she wanted to be able to afford dinner that night. She couldn't have every meal catered to her on a cloud. "I don't have a clue what I'm doing."

"Yes, you do," Hercules insisted. "Just do like you told me—trust your instincts. They won't let you down." He skimmed her nose with his own. "They led you to me, didn't they?"

"Yes, they did." She leaned in for another kiss.

They didn't come up for air till she heard the tinkling of bells.

"Hello there, lovebirds!" Hermes said, the little blue god's winged helmet helping him flutter in front of their cloud. "Hercules, your father wants you to report for god training at once. The early bird gets the worm, so to speak. And Zeus has a long list of worms—uh, birds, for you already."

Hercules and Meg stared at each other, their noses still touching even though their lips had parted.

"Your father is right about the worm thing," Meg murmured. "I should go, too. I want to talk to Darius before the marketplace opens for the day."

"Pegasus will give you a lift down," Hercules said, "and then he can bring you back here afterward and we can have dinner. Talk about our day."

"A man who wants to see me twice in one day? Who are you?" she joked, and he kissed her again.

"Good luck, Meg. Knock them dead! Just not literally," Herc said before he faded away in front of her eyes.

Hermes, however, was still there, watching her through his spectacles, which had fogged up in the early morning dew.

There was something about the little blue devil's mischievous smile that gave her pause.

"Yes?" she asked.

"Nothing!" His winged helmet fluttered faster. "Just wanted to wish you a great first day at your new job!"

Meg stared. These gods knew everything. But before she could reply, Hermes was gone, and Pegasus was already flying into her line of vision, ready to whisk her back down to the city of Thebes far below.

Up on Mount Olympus, Hercules's excitement was already waning. What had he gotten himself into?

"It's easy!" Zeus said in a jovial tone. (He was clearly a morning person.) "Once you get the hang of catching the cries for help, you'll be able to hear them in your sleep. Literally. Just last night, I woke up twice to the sounds of mortals calling my name. The key is concentrating."

Hercules scrunched up his face, trying hard to sense if someone needed his help. He didn't hear anything. Did the people below even know he held a place among the gods on Mount Olympus? Last he'd seen them, he was still a mortal, and yes, he'd been on a roll, defeating monster after monster, but was anyone going to call on him for god stuff? He couldn't hear anything but the sound of his own nervous breathing, which was rapid and shallow.

"Concentrate . . . concentrate . . ." he told himself, closing his eyes and listening. But the only sounds that came were those of a nearby waterfall. "Father, I don't hear anything."

"Sometimes it takes a bit of time. When someone is

calling me, I get a tingling in my fingers. Do you feel any tingling, Son?"

Tingling . . . did he feel tingling? He didn't think so. Hercules shook his head.

"Really steady your breath, then you should feel the humans. Or perhaps you can actually see them!" Zeus touched the cloud he was standing on and parted it, staring down at the tiny world below. "Ah! There's Georgios standing over his farmland, asking me to bless it so that he has a fruitful harvest. See him, Son? Right there?"

Hercules looked down, squinting to visualize something so far away. He saw the tops of trees, a few mountains, but nothing smaller. He looked harder, and maybe, just maybe, he thought he saw the outline of a donkey and a man in a hat. The image was gone in a flash. "I think I did for a second."

"That's good!" Zeus clapped him on the back, the larger god's strength knocking Hercules onto a different cloud. "And, oh, look! That fellow over there is calling for you!"

"Me?" Hercules, excited, attempted to part his own cloud. The cloud wouldn't separate. "Where? Who? What does he want?"

Zeus laughed. "Let's see if you can figure it out on your own. Start again from the top. Take a deep breath and—"

POOF! Hermes appeared. "My lord? Hades has been spotted topside again."

"He *what*?" Zeus's whole body turned red, and storm

clouds rolled in behind him. A clap of thunder made the ground shake. "I'll be right back. Work with your mother, Son. She'll tell you what to do."

"But . . ." Hercules's father disappeared before he could finish his thought.

Hera, with her sparkling pink gown glittering in the morning light, appeared in Zeus's place. "How is it going, my dear?"

Immediately, Hercules felt calmer. "Good. I think. I mean, I might have seen a human calling for me for a split second. I can't be sure, but Father said he was, so I'm trying hard to part this cloud and see for myself."

Hera touched the cloud with her pointer finger, and a hole appeared. "Ah, yes, young Perseus. I believe he's fighting one of the Gorgons today." She smiled at Hercules. "He could use a hero's blessing."

"Blessing? But I can't even see him, let alone bless him," Hercules lamented, trying again to catch a glimpse of what was happening on Earth.

Hera reached out to touch her son's arm. "Here's my advice: Picture yourself in a young hero's shoes—what do they need? How can you guide them? A single blessing can work for more than one hero on a journey." She peered back down, pausing for a moment. "And from the sound of things down there, you've actually got at least a dozen people in Thebes who could use your help today."

"A dozen?" Hercules cried, starting to get anxious. His breathing grew rapid again. "I can't see any of them."

"Perhaps you're worrying too much." His mother's voice was gentle. "I want you to take a deep breath. Close your eyes. Forget about me and everything around you. Now breathe in and out. In and out," Hera repeated.

That's what his father had said, too, so Hercules tried again, taking deep inhales and exhales while imagining Perseus and the heroes calling on him.

Oh, god of heroes, hear my plea. . . .

Hercules, I could use your help. . . .

Can you hear me, Hercules? If you can . . .

"I hear something!" Hercules exclaimed. "I can hear them!"

"I knew you could do it," Hera said proudly.

He couldn't believe it. He was doing it! An abundance of voices rushed over him, talking all at once . . . over one another . . . making it hard to understand the requests or who was asking for what. Wait. This was a lot of voices. "But there's so many. How do I know how to focus on just one voice at a time?"

"For that, you need to—oh!" Hera looked at the sun as Helios and his chariot zoomed past. "I have to go, Son, but you are doing great."

"Wait! You're leaving, too?" Hercules cried.

Hera looked at Thebes below. "I have business on Earth that I need to attend to right away, but if you really need help, I'm sure . . . Athena! Athena? Can you help Hercules decipher the calls of the mortals praying for his help?"

The god of wisdom and war, her trademark owl perched on her shoulder, glided across a series of clouds to appear at his side. Her expression was unreadable, the glow of her skin bright blue. "I am pretty busy today. Another one of my statues has gone missing in Thebes."

Hera paused. "That's the second one in two days. How could a mortal move such a thing?"

Athena narrowed her eyes. "I don't know, but when I find out, they'll regret it."

Hera nodded. "I'm sure they will. We won't keep you. I was just hoping you could advise Hercules for a moment before you go. Thank you!" And then his mother, too, disappeared.

"What do you need?" Athena asked plainly.

Hercules swallowed hard. Athena was an intimidating presence, even when she wasn't in a rush. "I was hoping you could explain how to know which voice goes with which mortal?"

"You separate the voices, like this." Athena pushed a nearby cloud aside and divided it into a dozen smaller clouds. "See? Concentrate."

Hercules peered over at the clouds, and this time they slowly became more translucent, like mist. Not only could he see small figures below, but he could hear them. The closer he got to one cloud, the better he could hear which voice belonged to which.

"Yes!" he said excitedly. "I think I see what you mean.

But once I know who is who, how do I decide who to help first? Do I help them all? Or—"

"Hold on." Athena listened intently to something in the distance. Her small owl hooted. "I have to go." She disappeared before Hercules could stop her.

The new god hung his head. This wasn't going very well. Every god on Mount Olympus was too busy with their own charges to help him learn how to care for his. He needed guidance, and fast. But from whom? *Phil?* Then Hercules quickly remembered: the satyr had told him he was putting off his retirement a tad longer to run a special "So You Wanna Be a Hero?" camp on his island. ("Hundreds of kids signed up!" Phil had told him. "Got to strike while the iron is hot! And Phil is hotter than the Underworld at the moment!") He couldn't interrupt Phil in the middle of training a bunch of newbies.

He'd have to figure things out on his own.

Meg was also trying to figure things out, which was proving difficult. The Athena statue didn't appear to be anywhere near the center of Darius's fountain, where he swore it had been before the theft, and for the life of her she couldn't figure out how anyone could have made off with such a large monument.

"It's massive!" Darius described, echoing her thoughts. "As tall as half a dozen men. Or at least Alcyoneus. And strangely enough, in its place were piles of olive pits." He narrowed his eyes. "I wouldn't put this past Kostos. He's always been jealous of my agora. He may have better olives at his marketplace, but my cheese is the freshest in the city! I'd start with him."

She was not going to tell Darius this, but anyone who was anyone shopped at the agora on the west side of town. Kostos's olive stand was truly second to none. "Who wouldn't choose fresh cheese over olives?" Meg said instead. She stared at the gurgling fountain from all angles and wondered where the Athena statue could have gone. And who would have left olive pits floating in the water as a clue?

Suddenly her hair seemed to stand on end. Was someone watching her? She always sensed when Hades was lurking in the shadows, but this felt different. A shadow fell over her, and she looked up. The early morning sun had given way to thickening clouds. It made her curious how things were going for Wonder Boy upstairs.

"Look, can you find the statue or not?" Darius pressed. "After the Titan attack, people are afraid to go shopping. And no shopping means no money. That's why I need Athena's presence back here as soon as possible. She is the protector of this agora." He sighed, looking around at the nearly empty market. "And she won't be pleased when she gets word about what happened. I need the statue back today."

"Today?" Meg sputtered. "That's impossible."

Darius shook his head. "I guess this is what I get for agreeing to give a woman a job like this."

Meg placed her hands on her hips. "Oh, I'm sorry. I didn't realize that as a man, you were making such good headway on your own without me."

Darius glared at her.

She paused, gathering herself. "Give me the day to get some leads, and I'll report back with what I've learned. We'll go from there. Deal?"

"I guess I don't have a choice." Darius glanced at the sky himself. "The last thing we want to do is make the gods angry."

Darius hurried back inside, which was fine by Meg. She didn't need the businessman looking over her shoulder as she canvassed the marketplace. If anyone had seen the statue stolen, it would be the people who lived and worked right where she stood. Meg turned to the first person she saw, a woman selling pomegranates from a basket on her arm at the entrance to the agora.

"Excuse me, were you working here two days ago?" Meg asked.

"Yes," said the woman warily.

Good start, Meg thought. "Did you see the Athena statue here in this fountain?"

"Yes," the woman said again.

"And when did you notice it missing?" Meg asked.

The woman thought for a moment. "The statue was here till I sold my last piece of fruit in the late afternoon. I left before it was taken." A clap of thunder made them both look up. "The gods are unhappy, as you can see."

It's just rain, Meg thought, but she wasn't about to argue. "Who is the last person out of the market after closing?"

"Usually Darius. Although the night before it went missing, I did see Kostos, the owner of the other market, shopping at our spice stand."

"Kostos, you say?" Between that and the olive pits, Meg supposed it was time to pay the competing agora a visit.

It took a while to get across town. After the Titans' battle, people were still cleaning up crumbling buildings and destruction all over Thebes. Several roadways were blocked, while construction had started in other areas. By the time she'd reached the other marketplace, the sky had turned menacingly dark. Most of the marketplace vendors were moving indoors, but there was a commotion at the entrance that kept several people outside.

"She will not be happy when she sees this."

"Of course, not! It's disrespectful."

"Who would do this?"

"What's going on?" Meg asked two women holding babies.

"The Athena statue at the entrance to the marketplace is missing," said one.

Meg paled. If another statue was missing, this was a deliberate attack. But by whom? "When did you notice it was gone?"

"When we arrived to work this morning," said the first woman.

A rumbling of thunder in the distance made everyone look up.

"We've angered the gods, and now we will be punished," moaned the second woman.

"The gods will find fault with all of us," said a man pushing a cart. "Athena's statues are missing all over the city."

Meg whipped her head around. "Did you say all over the city?"

"Yes," the man insisted as more people gathered around. "They're missing at both marketplaces, plus the one at the temple is gone, as are the one near the sea and the one at the southern entrance to the city! All gone as of this morning! Who knows how many others?"

That was a lot of missing statues. Meg had to wonder who would risk angering Athena. Even Hades himself wouldn't be such a fool. He didn't fear many, but he always got anxious when Athena's name came up in the Underworld.

"No wonder the skies are so dark," said the man. "Athena knows we have removed our statues, and she is furious. She will strike us down for such a crime."

Meg squared her shoulders. "She's not going to strike anyone down if I can help it. Tell me the last time you saw your statue—was it last night?" They both nodded. "And who is always the last person in this market?"

"Kostos's son, Otis," said the first woman. "He was

closing up, and he said one minute the statue was here, and the next it was like, poof! Gone!"

Raindrops began to fall, and the two women hurried inside. Meg didn't mind getting wet. She walked over to the site of the missing statue and knelt in the damp earth. She picked up a handful of small rough pellets. More olive pits.

"Megara."

Meg's name was spoken so loud it sounded like thunder. She quickly stood and turned around. Before her was the subject of the investigation herself: Athena, and she did not look happy. Meg inhaled sharply. It was one thing to see the god's likeness in stone and to hear tales about her greatness, even to see flashes of her when visiting Wonder Boy up on Mount Olympus. It was quite another to see the god of war and wisdom looming before her.

"Where are my statues?" Athena demanded.

"That's what I'm trying to find out," Meg told her.

"Work faster," Athena said. "The people are concerned, and I find this thief's lack of respect infuriating." Lightning crackled in the sky above her. "I want them returned today."

Great. Another person with an impossible deadline, Meg thought. "I understand. I'm working on it. I just need more time."

"Time is not something on your side, Megara," Athena told her. "I suggest you move faster before I inform Zeus what is happening and who is *not* doing what they can to make things right." Lightning flashed again, and Meg shielded her eyes. When she opened them, Athena was gone.

If Athena told Zeus she wasn't getting the job done, who knew how Wonder Boy's father would react? This was now about more than earning a living or getting a recommendation for another job. It was about upsetting the gods above and her boyfriend's family in one fell swoop.

Think, Meg. Where could Athena's statues be? She needed to talk to the olive vendor's son. She ran over to a man covering his shop with tarps. "Do you know where I can find Otis?"

"He went to see Darius at the other agora," he said as thunder rumbled again ominously. "You just missed him."

Meg covered her face with her hands. *Wonder Boy, I hope you're having a better day than I am.*

Hercules was getting very good at controlling his breathing. He was pretty proud of that fact and wanted to share the news with someone, but there wasn't a god to be found that morning on Mount Olympus. Hermes popped in and out, giggling to himself, but Hercules could only assume that was how Hermes always acted. In his short time on Olympus, he could tell no one made Zeus laugh like Hermes did.

But breathing right and figuring out whose voice belonged to whom wasn't enough. Now Hercules had to figure out how to actually *help* the prospective heroes.

Take Despina, for example. Harpies had stolen her food.

To get it back, she'd need to climb Mount Aigaleo. But she'd never ventured that far before or faced Harpies. She was understandably frightened. She was asking for the courage to take her journey. Could he grant someone courage?

Then there was Calisto, a young girl trying to defend her friend against a group of ruffians who kept tormenting her. And Tobias, a goatherd whose entire herd was stuck on an embankment while he was on the other side of the flooded river. How was he going to get them across?

Then, of course, there was Perseus. He had amassed a number of weapons to fight a Gorgon but knew his first move was his most important. He was asking Hercules to guide him in figuring out what it was.

Hercules wasn't sure what he was supposed to do. He could grant all their requests or swoop down and take care of their problems. But if he did, where were their hero's journeys exactly? If he gave them ships to get across seas, swords to slay monsters, and strength to fight men, was he taking something away from them? Then again, what was the right call when so many lives hung in the balance?

Lightning flashed above Thebes, and Hercules frowned. He wished his own inspiration would strike.

Meg watched the lightning hit a nearby olive tree and sighed. She had gone from one end of the city to the other and back again to Darius's agora after hitching a ride on a wagon, convincing the driver, Tassos, it was in his best interest to take her. There would be no one to hire him if Thebes got smote. The wind was whipping up, sending things flying. What she wouldn't give to hang up her sandals and head home herself. Her dress was soaked, and she was no closer to figuring out where Darius's Athena statue was, let alone a whole city of them. On the ride over, Tassos had mentioned three other missing statues—two in front of theaters and one in front of another temple. Once Darius heard this, he'd fire Meg—if Athena didn't turn up again and unleash her wrath first.

Meg looked up, once again getting the feeling she was being watched. No one was there. If it was the god of war and wisdom, she would have made herself known. Athena was anything but subtle.

Meg absently waved to Tassos as he drove the carriage away, just as Darius stormed out of his market.

"Well? Anything?" he demanded.

"The good news is Athena isn't only angry with you—she's mad at half the city," Meg said, pushing her wet hair out of her eyes. "There are Athena statues missing all over the place."

"And that news helps me how? I hired you to find *our* statue, Megara, not learn what's going on elsewhere." He shook his head. "I should have called on Hercules. They say he's a god now. He would have found it."

Meg's cheeks burned, but she held her tongue. *Find the statue; collect your pay.*

But Darius wasn't finished. "Some investigator you are. I told Otis you wouldn't be able to help us."

"Otis?" Meg stopped glowering and narrowed her eyes at him. "Why are you talking to your competitor's son?"

Darius reddened. "It's none of your business."

Huh. Darius had specifically asked Meg to look into Kostos, not his son. Why would Darius get chummy with the competition?

Meg pushed the thought aside. "I was actually looking for Otis myself. He might have been around when one of the other statues was stolen. Do you know where he is?"

Darius paused, then pointed in the direction of the first stall, where a young man with short brown hair was talking to a vendor.

"Otis!" Meg called to him, running over. "I was just at your agora. I'm told you were the last person to see the Athena statue at your market."

"I didn't take it, if that's what you're getting at," he said gruffly. "It would take ten men to lift that thing."

"I know that," Meg said, though she thought he seemed quick to defend himself. "What I wanted to know was when you last remember looking at the statue—before it was gone. When did you last pray to it?"

Otis paused for a moment. "Right before I told everyone to go home for the night. I said my nightly thanks to Athena for protecting us and our city, and then I turned to the stalls to tell them to pack up. As I did, I heard a loud pop. Almost like a clap of thunder, but not quite as booming as this," he said, motioning to the stormy weather. "Then the statue disappeared. It seemed like a trick."

A pop and a trick.

Meg's mind was racing. She ran through all the facts. Multiple, immovable protection statues had magically disappeared in the past two days. Olive pits had been left in their place—at least in the spots she had visited—which was more than a little strange. And while the two agora owners Darius and Kostos were not on great terms, they'd *both* had statues stolen. It didn't seem likely they'd steal from each other. Though, oddly enough, Darius and Kostos's son, Otis, were friendly with each other.

Meg shook her head to clear it. Something wasn't sitting right about the timing. It seemed kind of ironic that a bunch of Athena statues went missing on Wonder Boy's first day on the job—a day when many gods would be helping him.

And then she had it—a hunch.

The more she thought about it, the more a certain someone came to mind—someone with the means and the motive to get the job done.

Of course, an accusation of this magnitude would be risky. She'd have one chance to get it right. If she was wrong, Athena would not look on her fondly, and her reputation for this line of work would most likely be tarnished. She had to be sure. And the only way to do that was to talk to the suspect directly.

But how?

Wonder Boy. The thought of him at her side calmed her. He'd believe her reasoning without concrete proof, maybe even talk out her theory with her. Meg sighed. Calling on Hercules was the easy way out. She couldn't always rely on her god of a boyfriend to help solve her problems. And besides, it was his first day on the job. By the looks of this weather, he probably had his hands full with any heroes caught in the storm. She would have to handle this on her own. *Wonder Boy,* she thought, touching the pin on her chest. *What would you do?*

Another crack of thunder sounded. A toddler in a nearby stall began to cry.

"Mama!" he called out, racing into a nearby woman's arms.

That's when Meg had an idea. And it involved her boyfriend's mother.

High above, Hercules sat on a cloud, feeling like a fraud. He'd give anything to talk to Hera, but she was long gone. So was his father. Maybe it was for the best. Did he really want to go crying to his parents about not knowing how to do his job? No. He didn't want Zeus regretting his decision to let him be a god.

Pegasus swooped down and landed next to him, nuzzling Hercules's chest. The horse was so large, he accidentally knocked Hercules over.

Hercules laughed. "Whoa, boy." He sat back up, and

something fell from his belt. Nestled in the mist was the coin Meg had given him that morning. He picked it up. *To remind you that your aim is true and to always trust your instincts,* she'd said.

Trust my instincts, Hercules thought. He looked down at the separated clouds again, each one representing a different hero in need. When Phil had trained him, he hadn't stepped in and taken over. He'd talked to him—taught him techniques, told him about heroes from the past, given his best advice—then let him make up his own mind. That was what a coach was for. Hercules knew what a lot of these heroes were going through. He'd walked in their sandals himself. He'd taken his own journey—he'd beaten many a monster and fought a god of the Underworld. He knew what it was like to be afraid of the problem, but he also knew what it was like to take aim and hit your mark.

Hercules stood up and looked down at the heroes in training in his city. He knew what he needed to do. *Talk to them. Tell them you're rooting them on. Tell them they know what to do because they can trust their own instincts.*

Hercules focused on his breath and on each voice. They came in loud and clear. This time, they didn't feel so overwhelming. "Hello? Despina?" he started. "I hear you."

One by one, he reached out to them. He told Despina to climb the mountain and not fear the Harpies. He advised Perseus on what blade to use to fight the Gorgon. He encouraged Calisto to defend her friend. He commiserated with

Tobias the herder, then reminded him to use his strength to knock down a log that his goats could walk across. Then he sat back on the cloud (the newly parted cloud!) and watched as his charges took charge of their own destinies, fought their own monsters, forged their own paths, and made their way in the city.

"Wahoo!" Hercules crowed, jumping up and high-fiving Pegasus as he watched one hero after another complete their quests. "We did it, Pegasus! We had our first day as a god of heroes, and we actually helped a few people *become* heroes. On our own! I can't wait to tell Meg!" He ruffled the horse's mane. "Want to head down and get her, boy? She's probably finishing up herself."

Meg's day was not done. Not by a long shot. Not if she couldn't find those Athena statues. She was almost positive she knew who had them, and she was about to do something very risky—especially coming from a mortal. If things went south, she might not be invited back up to Mount Olympus. She sighed and thumbed the pin Hercules had given her. *Okay, Wonder Boy. It's time to be bold and take a risk. That's what you'd tell me to do,* Meg thought. She cleared her throat. It was now or never.

As the rain started to fall harder, Meg walked out into the open square and stood in front of the fountain with the missing Athena statue. "I know you're there," Meg said, raising her voice. "You've been watching me all day." The rain fell harder, splashing into the fountain and causing waves. Meg rubbed her shoulders to keep warm. "I'm not one to ask for favors, but if it's you, Hera, I could really use your help about now."

A glow as bright as the sun appeared in the center of the square, pink and vibrant. And then the god herself appeared with a crown on her head, her long flowing locks billowing out behind her in the wind much like her Grecian gown. Her blue eyes narrowed.

"Are you accusing a god of spying on you, Megara?" Hera asked.

"Accusing? No," Meg said. "Guessing? Yes. It's what I would be doing if I had a son who almost renounced his heritage to date a mortal. I'd want to know if she was worth all the fuss." Meg shrugged. "Call it a woman's hunch."

The god appeared to relax slightly. Meg might have even detected a small smirk.

"I'm not helping you with your quest, Megara," Hera said. "You must find the statues on your own."

"And I think I have," Meg said. "But to get to the bottom of all of this, I need your help in summoning another god."

Hera raised an eyebrow. "Bold move. If you're wrong—"

Meg cut her off. "I know. I'm as good as back in the Underworld." Thunder boomed. "But I'm sure."

"All right, then," said Hera, clasping her hands together. "Once I make this call, you are on your own. Understood?" Meg nodded. "Who do you want me to summon?"

Meg took a deep breath. "Hermes."

She saw Hera almost smile before she yelled for the god. "Hermes!"

POOF! The tiny god appeared at once, not making eye contact. "You called, my lady?"

Hera stepped aside, motioning to Meg. "This mortal has something to ask you." But the god didn't leave. It looked like they would have an audience.

Hermes looked from Hera to Meg, and she saw his face flicker. "What's up, buttercup?"

Meg straightened her shoulders. Might as well go for it. "Athena's statues are missing all over the city." She leaned forward. "And I think you took them."

"Me?" Hermes squeaked, his wings slowing down slightly. "What proof do you have?" He side-eyed Hera, but the god looked at them neutrally.

Meg tried to sound firm. "Every person I interviewed said the statues were there one minute and gone the next—as if by magic. In their place were olive pits. To me, this sounds like a practical joke, something I know Zeus is quite fond of. And I know you love an audience with the big guy." Hermes said nothing. "I know you'd never deliberately be disrespectful to Athena. But she's furious."

"Furious?" Hermes repeated. "Over a statue guarding an olive stand?"

"Oh, yes," Meg said, nodding vigorously and cutting a quick glance at Hera. "Really angry. I got the impression if they're not returned, heads will roll, cities will burn, wars will start, all that sort of thing. But I'm sure if the statues reappeared, all would be forgotten. She never even has to know it was you. I, for one, wouldn't tell her."

"Aww, geez . . . I didn't think she'd get *that* mad. Everyone is so touchy these days after the Titans. . . ." He sighed. "Fine." Hermes snapped his fingers, and a three-story-tall Athena statue appeared behind them in the fountain. "They're all back, exactly the way they were." He glared at Meg. "You really messed with my joke about statues being the pits."

"Ah, I'd wondered about that part," Meg said. "Well, thank you. Today has been a real slice."

He shook his head and poofed himself gone. The rain stopped suddenly and the clouds instantly started to clear.

Hera looked up. "Athena is pleased, it seems, and I suspect your client will be, too." She smiled. "See you upstairs for dinner, Megara. Good job today."

Meg dropped into a bow. "Thank you, Hera."

As the god faded away, Meg saw Darius running from the marketplace.

"You did it!" he cried. "But when? And how? How did you get Athena back in the fountain?"

Meg stood up straighter and pushed her ponytail off her shoulder. "I can't reveal all my secrets, Darius."

He dropped a bag of jingling coins in her outstretched hand.

"I just have one question," she said. "Why did you send me to Kostos when you were talking to his son?"

Darius looked down sheepishly. "Otis has been

wanting his dad and me to put our differences aside and work together as the two largest agoras in the city. After the statues got stolen, I realized he might have a point. Better for us to be a united front and find ways to encourage shoppers to come to both agoras with our best wares—his olives, my feta—no matter what's happening above."

"Ah, I see," Meg replied.

He smiled at her. "Anyway, I should thank you, Megara. I'll be sure to recommend you to my brother, Letha, who can't remember where he buried his fortune. He thinks the god Tyche might have something to do with it."

Meg clutched the coins in her hands and started to sashay away. She could already see Pegasus flying toward her in the distance. "You know where to find me."

Minutes later she was climbing atop Pegasus and flying into the heavens, straight for a buoyant cloud where Hercules had amassed a huge feast with trays of every delicacy Meg could imagine.

"We're celebrating," he said as she dismounted and ran into his arms. He spun her around. "Thanks to your coin, I helped a bunch of potential heroes today."

"And thanks to your advice, I found not just one Athena statue—I found half a dozen of them."

Hercules's blue eyes widened. "Half a dozen? Who took them?"

That part's not important," she said. "All you need to know is I found the trickster, and I don't think they'll be messing with me or Thebes again anytime soon."

"I can't imagine anyone messing with you, Meg." Hercules caressed her cheek. "You're the strongest person I know."

"I think that's you," Meg murmured, running her fingers through his hair. "Literally."

Hercules grinned. "Tied for first place, then?"

Meg agreed with a long, lingering kiss. "So what's next for *your* journey?"

"Hmmm . . . I'd say taking things one step at a time. Listening as much as possible. More of this?" He hugged her, and Meg smiled. "And for you?"

"A lot of the same, I suppose. Also carving a name for myself as someone who can get to the truth of things. And maybe knowing when to ask for help." Out of the corner of her eye, she saw Hera and Zeus sitting at a long table filled with more godly delicacies. Hermes filled Zeus's goblet with a pout on his face. "Hey, would you mind if we joined your parents for dinner tonight?"

Hercules lit up. "Great idea!" They gathered their trays of food to share, then made their way to the large glistening table.

"Hello, you two," Zeus boomed.

"Come find your seat," Hera said. They looked down. There were two extra place settings with cards beside them—one that read *Hercules* and another labeled *Megara.*

Hercules's eyes widened. He turned to Meg. "How did you know they'd be expecting us?"

Hera and Meg shared a smile. "Call it a hunch," Meg said.

The Reluctant Prince

What if Bambi didn't want to be the next Great Prince of the Forest?

by Liz Braswell

The Reluctant Prince

What if Bambi didn't want to be the next Great Prince of the Forest?

by Liz Braswell

The snow had finally disappeared: only small white pockets of it still remained in the deepest, shadiest gorges. Forest streams rushed and burbled and overran everywhere with meltwater as cold as icy frost.

This made the beavers joyful and busy, of course; all dawn and dusk they paddled back and forth across the ponds to attend to their dams, then swam up the river to build new ones. Their ceaseless activity provided no end of delight to the otters, who had been recently deprived of their snowbank slides and runs. Cold mud wasn't *quite* as fun to slip down and slink over, and sometimes you had to clean your coat extra carefully after. But also sometimes you ran across a frog groggily emerging from her buried winter den, pale and slow from a season asleep. Yum!

Birds sang without break—sometimes right through the middle of the day—joyful at the arrival of spring. Robins, back from wherever they went for the colder seasons, trilled and warbled until snoring old Friend Owl hunkered down in annoyance. A sibling pack of blue jays tore through the canopy and meadows, screeching and playing tag, their feathers a striking blue in the sun, dollops of white on their backs like the snow that had so recently melted. Chickadees called out to declare which tree was theirs, when there was trouble to avoid, and where there was food. Mourning doves cooed hauntingly . . . although *they* had been singing since late January, the first ones to sense better days ahead. They strutted about, smug in their predictions.

The troutberry trees had already bloomed and gone; on the forest floor, delicate white petals of starflowers and gold-thread and Carolina springbeauty sparkled when a stray beam of sunshine caught them. Wild onions were the only plant that had fully leafed out, brilliant bright green under maple and elm and birch and oak whose own leaves were still pregnant thoughts.

All of nature was just waking up, fulling, becoming large and new.

In one protected thicket, not so different from the one Bambi himself had been born in, Faline the doe was resting her own growing body. Occasionally she stretched her long neck out to curl around her belly, feeling its warmth against her cheek. Dreaming of the days to come.

Bambi watched and felt a lightning bolt of joy shoot through him like he was a fawn again. He couldn't entirely restrain himself but didn't entirely give in to the overwhelming urge to bellow and leap as high as he could. He pranced excitedly in place instead, front legs bending and shifting, his rear legs shuffling to accommodate the weight.

Then, in a graceful dip and turn, he moved away from the thicket, unwilling to disturb Faline but unable to stand still.

Bambi was going to be a father—of *twins*, it looked like! How magical and lucky was that? He needed to distract himself, to tell the world the good news, to find a friend to expend some excess energy with. Get into *high jinks* with, like in the old days.

Of course that meant Thumper or Flower.

Flower had been out of his winter torpor for a while now. Although he and his family didn't go to sleep for the whole season the same way bears did, they tended to hunker down and doze through the coldest nights. Thumper and his kin stayed awake and out the entire season. Both would be ready for some fun, a last jaunt before the babies came. . . .

Suddenly everything around him fell silent. There was a thick pause in the life of the forest. He flicked his ears, trying to locate the disturbance.

"Your doe is beautiful, Son."

The Great Prince of the Forest stepped out of invisibility, dipping his full, branching rack of antlers in respect.

"Her name is Faline," Bambi said politely but firmly.

His father turned his head a little, keeping his son focused in his big black eyes.

And completely ignored what he had just said.

"You have lived through the winter . . . through fire and wound, through cold and loss. You, too, are healthy and strong—and are starting your own family now."

Bambi felt his front legs twitching again, begging to run, and not out of joy. His ears flicked; there was something ominous about these words. But he was not a fawn anymore, and frankly, "ominous" and "pompous" were quite similar in nuance. He willed himself to stillness.

His father continued.

"Fawns will be born . . . but some animals did not make it through the winter. Some will not last through to summer. The forest is renewed with bud and grass, with the sun and the bodies of those who passed. Spring is the time of greatest change.

"It is time for a new Great Prince of the Forest."

The old buck bowed his neck low, low, and lower still—until he curled one leg back and was nearly touching the cool, packed leaf duff with his velvety nose.

"Oh," Bambi said, eyes widening. "But . . . why? *You're* the prince."

The buck's own eyes gleamed in the closest he ever came to a true smile. "I *am* strong. And fast. And the forest knows me. But for how many more seasons? The sun won't warm my back forever, Bambi. The forest needs a strong leader, one they know will help protect them in the years to come."

There was silence, and his father gazing at him wisely . . . or maybe just silently.

"And . . . that's *it*?"

Even as his hooves shifted nervously in the dirt, Bambi felt a strange warmth of emotion flow up his throat and bloom into his head, settling at the base of his (much smaller) antlers. Surprise, maybe. Or perhaps something more heated. "You were prince, and now you're done, and now it's my turn? Just because I'm your son?"

"That is how it has always been."

"I've lived through *one winter*," Bambi said. "I got *hunted* before the sun had even begun to set earlier. I don't know anything about leading—any more, I suppose, than I know anything about being a father. And surely you have other children—older ones more experienced in the ways of the forest?"

"There have been other bucks," the old prince said neutrally. "And there are does. There is no one like you, Bambi."

"There's nothing special about me," Bambi snorted. "And until the fire, I barely ever saw *you*, Father. You appeared, led us to safety, and disappeared again. You found me when I was hurt and lost and brought me to the herd. *And then disappeared* again. Is this the sort of prince I'll be? Majestic and mysterious, unapproachable except in emergencies?"

The old buck's eyes gleamed in amusement. "Are you challenging me?"

"No, Father," Bambi said shortly. "I'm not."

He turned his back on the prince—for the first time ever—and wandered away slowly but pointedly, not even listening for whether or not the buck left as well.

The original promise of spring seemed to suddenly dim. Somewhere above the tall white pines a caul of clouds clung stickily to the sun. Without its friendly golden beams illuminating new growth, the forest floor became dismal and wintry again. Bambi bent down distractedly and nibbled something that looked green and inviting, but he didn't really taste it. He didn't pay attention to where his long legs took him, either: up a gradual slope, along a narrow path hard packed through much use by the forest folk, and finally across the chattering stream in one halfhearted, desultory leap.

He didn't know exactly what about the exchange with his father bothered him. Shouldn't he have been thrilled to be told he was going to be the next prince? Shouldn't he be proud and excited?

The view from Chestnut Ledge was wide open with the underbrush not grown in yet. Bambi stepped out onto its stony outcrop, his hooves making little *clonk* noises against the bare rock. A pebble he kicked tumbled over the side and down into the tops of trees nearly twenty feet below.

From here he could see the wide swath of the land that hugged the forest: the low meadows, the beaver swamp, the great river. Its grassy banks were still covered with the brown-and-golden stalks of reeds dead from the year before. To the north was a great pasture that eased into a valley where Man came from, the place of hunters and dogs. They rested in the field with their fires and tents before following the deer with their guns.

All of this belonged to the herd; all of it would be Bambi's domain if he became prince of the forest.

With a start he suddenly realized that this ledge was the place his father had appeared the year before, gazing out over the herd, eyes resting briefly on his young son. This was where he called to the herd in times of trouble.

Standing there, Bambi felt childish. Not regal and huge, not determined and thoughtful and wise. He was fast and uncertain, like a twig racing down a stream, ignorant of its path but adamant, giving itself to the current with wholehearted conviction, rumbling one end over the other as it bounced off rocks.

Before he could stop himself, Bambi had sprung down, bouncing back and forth on the steep and narrow rocky ledges. He dove to the shadier side, careening through the trees as thoughts and seasons buffeted his mind.

Where *was* his father—the Great Prince of the Forest—when there wasn't an emergency? Where did he spend his time?

If the prince just stayed with the herd, couldn't he protect everyone better? *Have* protected?

What good was a prince who was only a prince in times of disaster?

Who would ever want to be prince, anyway?

As these thoughts whirled around in his mind, a light began to break through the chaos.

Faline would know what to do. Faline was great at thinking through things like this; she could help him answer some of these questions! He turned, started to head toward the thicket where she rested.

But . . .

She was busy answering her own questions. Pregnant and sometimes exhausted, sometimes struck with strange whims that made sense to only her own certain self. How silly and annoying it would be for Bambi to interrupt her rest with quizzes and egotistical pondering about what it meant to be a prince.

He changed directions. Instead of diving into the shadows of the forest, he was a tawny lightning bolt striking the edge of a clearing that would eventually be filled with bright purple blossoms. Violets first, then lupines that would make little crowns across the sweet-smelling milkweed, the summer ending with mounds of aster.

"Oh, hullo, Bambi."

Flower was right where Bambi had known he would be: at the base of the tree where his wife had a den. His striped coat fairly sparkled in the sun—but in the shadows, when he sat still, he blended in with everything, becoming a shadow himself.

"Flower," Bambi said, "I've just had some strange news. I'm going to be the Great Prince of the Forest."

The skunk shrugged and smiled. "Well, your father was prince. Isn't that how it works?"

"I don't *want* to be prince." Bambi stamped impatiently. "I want to roam the forest with you and Thumper. I want to run in the fields. I want to spend more time with Faline— I want to see my children. And spend actual time with them! We only have a year before they're grown. . . . I don't want to miss that. I don't want to miss the wind in my ears."

Flower frowned a little at the last bit, confused. He thought hard for a moment.

And despite what anyone might have said about the skunk, he *did* have good thoughts—it just took a little longer for them to occur to him than it did other animals.

"But *someone* has to be prince," he finally said.

"Well, obviously. But does it have to be me?"

"I think so, but . . . I don't know. I'm not royalty, or wise. Why don't we ask Friend Owl? He'll know for certain."

"Of course!" Bambi cried. "That's a brilliant idea. Let's get Thumper. We can all go together."

Flower nodded happily and trundled behind his friend. Bambi had to remember to walk slowly; the skunk had nimble fingers and clever teeth but walked as unhurriedly as a porcupine.

On the other side of the clearing the ground became grassier; it was flat from the heavy snows of the winter but would soon tuft up all over the hill, making it look like its furry residents. There were thick tangles of old dead growth, hummocks, and ditches, where dozens and dozens of Thumper's kin lived and raced and bounced and danced in the twilight and dawn.

"Hey," Bambi said loudly, stomping his feet. "Thump! Come out!"

Springing like—well, like nothing else Bambi could really think of; even frogs didn't do this—springing like a *Thumper*, the rabbit shot straight out of a tuffet behind the two friends. He barely landed before springing up again and again, laughing in the warm sun that had come back out. *Maybe like a springtail,* Bambi thought, the tiny black insects that appeared in the purple shadow of snowy ditches, then jumped and disappeared like magic.

"Hey, you two—isn't it a glorious day?" Thumper crowed. "I'm going to have six children, I think. Maybe seven. Do you want to go down and see what the beavers are doing? Sometimes it's fun to throw old crabapples at them. They work too hard. My wife is beautiful! Have you seen her ears?"

"Thumper's twitterpated *hard*," Flower said with a low whistle. "Just like Friend Owl warned us. He's so madly in love with her!"

Bambi laughed. "Actually, Thump, we're going to go see the old owl right now."

"Bambi doesn't want to be prince," Flower whispered poorly, behind his paw.

"Prince? Omigosh, that's right! Like father, like son! *Prince!*" Thumper's eyes brightened even more, and his ears stood at attention. "I know a prince! I have a prince for a friend! Wait—you don't want to be prince?"

"I don't know the first thing about it, and there are other things to do," Bambi said a little primly.

"Huh." Thumper looked at him for a moment—*really* looked at him, going completely still in the way that rabbits did, all the way down even to his thumping foot. "I'd want to be prince if it was offered. No one asks rabbits, though."

"They're too small," Flower pointed out reasonably.

The three friends strolled side by side deep into the woods, and for those few moments all was perfect. A warm breeze blew that somehow smelled of the sun. Stone flies, the first real insects of the year, delicately hovered and sparkled in drifts of sunlight like magic. Everything seemed right and true in the world. Peaceful.

When they came to the giant beech tree where Friend Owl slept, Thumper marched right up to it and turned around, choosing to *thump* on the wood soundly with his right hind leg instead of politely knocking.

Unhappy screech owl noises soon came from high up in the tree. A single brown feather floated down, rocking slowly back and forth. It was accompanied by murmurs, groans, and irritated-sounding whistles.

Bambi smiled—and then wondered. The owl could be silent when he wished, when he hunted. He didn't *need* to make these noises. Were they only for his visitors' benefit? They certainly made a rabbit feel comfortable enough to wake him: *Look, it's just Friend Owl, grumpy and chatty and complainy.*

Bambi frowned. What a strange and new thought.

On feathers as noiseless as the still air on a hot summer day, the owl reluctantly descended to a lower branch, muttering to himself.

"It's the middle of the *day*. What nefarious business are you three up to?"

He closed one eye and squinted, peering down at the three mammals below as if he were nearsighted. But he wasn't, really.

"Bambi's got some questions about being prince," Thumper called up.

"He doesn't want to be," Flower added shyly. "Prince, I mean."

"Doesn't want to be *prince*?" the owl demanded, jumping and flapping his feathers. "But but but your father is the prince! And his father before him! And his father before him!"

"And someone else can be now," Bambi said easily. "Why is it just because I'm his son, that makes me prince?"

"Some would question your sanity, son," the owl muttered. "Who doesn't want to be prince?"

"Me."

"What does being prince even mean?" Flower asked dreamily.

"You got a crown," Thumper pointed out, twitching his ears at Bambi's rack.

"Every buck has a crown," his friend retorted.

"You should see Ronno's," Flower said without thinking. "It's a beaut."

Thumper thumped him. Flower tumbled prettily over, gloriously furry tail arcing overhead. He giggled.

"Without a prince, who is going to protect the herd?" the owl demanded. "Ever thought about that, laddie? Who will scent Man when he comes with his guns and the fire, when the acorns fall and the leaves of the swamp maple turn red—"

"Wait," Bambi interrupted. "When the acorns fall? Like—*every* time the acorns fall?"

"Well, yes, Bambi."

"So the hunters come every year, at the same time?"

"Is there something wrong with your hearing?" the owl asked grumpily. "*Yes*, boy. Every year. Every fall. Like a plague."

"Did my mother know this?"

"I don't know if your mother knew it. Maybe she did. Your father does. He's the prince." The owl shrugged, as if this explained everything.

"*I* didn't know it," Flower said.

"My folks always run and hide whenever *anything's* weird, or there's Man around," Thumper said. "Every season. Any season."

"Flower—nobody hunts skunks, you daft thing," the

owl said impatiently. "And, Thumper, you're fair game year-round. Running and hiding is *always* a good idea for your folk."

"Wait, wait," Bambi said, tossing his head, feeling the weight of his rack as its tips clawed the air. "How do you know all this? That no one eats skunks, and when the hunters hunt, and who they hunt?"

"He's Friend Owl," Thumper said with surprise.

"He knows everything," Flower added, nodding.

"I am a venerable gentleman, yearling." The owl puffed up his chest. "Son, I *knew* your father's father, and his father before him. My own great-grandowl was alive when the Great Prince was a unicorn, not a deer. When you see enough seasons—and listen to enough chatter from you twittering ground-dwellers—you see patterns and remember things. And then when the prince asks you questions, you have answers."

This answer felt good to Bambi. Satisfying. But it also scraped up other things, like when he pawed the ground for mushrooms but instead found acorns a lazy squirrel hadn't buried deep enough. Bumpy things that didn't fit back in the soil. It was one thing to think of the owl as someone wise and old, endless and always there . . . it was another thing to think of him actually having friendly chats with Bambi's father. And his grandfather. Princes standing under the branches of this tree for generations.

"I can think of a better question to ask," the owl said,

preening a little in between his words. "Why are you asking these questions to begin with? Question your questions, my lad! Quoo-who!"

Bambi sighed. Maybe they had used up all of the owl's wisdom for the day. It had been easier to put up with some of the bird's more . . . nonsensical verbiage when Bambi was a fawn and could listen to the old bird prattle on for hours. But it was like he had just been led to the cusp of something great, and the owl was back to being his usual chatty, silly self again.

"Come on, let's leave him to his nap," Bambi said, jerking his head to get his friends to follow.

As they left, Friend Owl could be heard still mumbling to himself about princes and boys and fawns and how twitterpation was making it hard for anyone to think right these days.

The three wandered without any formal discussion down to the beaver flats. An icy little breeze that must have come from someplace higher up, somewhere north, slapped their feet and tousled Flower's glossy tail. Thumper rose up on his hind legs, scenting the air. For a moment his eyes grew distant.

"Ever wonder what's beyond the forest?" he asked. "What's beyond the meadows?"

"What's a prince, what's beyond the forest," Flower said in a singsong. "'Why are you asking these questions'?"

"I guess a prince has to stay with his forest," Bambi said moodily. "No exploring the world for him."

"Everything I love is right here," Flower declared. Then he shrugged. "Although someone was telling me about these boxes where humans leave food—*garbage cans*, I think they're called. I'd love to see one someday. They're supposed to be amazing."

"Garbage cans," Thumper said. "Huh. Probably the only thing that smells worse than you, *Flower*."

"Uh-oh," Flower said, ignoring him and pointing. "Here comes trouble."

Picking his way regally through the thinning trees at the edge of the woods was Ronno. His rack was broader and pointier than Bambi's, his coat a lusher shade of brown. He walked like he owned the forest. Like a real prince.

He saw the three of them and smirked. "Aw, are the little playfriends hanging out again? It's *spring*, Bambi. Shouldn't your thoughts be on other things? Like Faline and her coming children?"

Bambi felt itchy and had an overwhelming urge to lower his head and snort. Handsome and imposing the other buck's rack might be, but Bambi had already bested him once. That time it was to win Faline. Here he would be winning nothing beyond dominance over the other deer.

Which would make it look like he was being a prince, he supposed, if anyone was watching.

"My thoughts are on *many* things. The forest is large," he said instead, turning to go.

"Hunh," Ronno said with a sneer. "If they're not on

your children and your doe, or your herd, maybe someone *else* should be thinking about them." He pawed the ground and snuffed.

Bambi sighed. This was a waste of energy and time. Nothing good would come from an extended fight between the two biggest yearling bucks in the area. Just blood and wounds and scars—which Bambi already had some of, *thank you very much, Man-with-gun.*

Without the usual ritual snort that normally marked the beginning of such a thing, without posturing or stamping or any of the usual beautiful movements that were inked deep into Bambi's instincts, he swung his rack around silently—like an owl—and charged the other deer.

Unprepared, Ronno couldn't lower his head in time to deflect the blow. Bambi caught him in the side of his neck, the meaty part where it met his shoulder. Hard enough to bludgeon and bruise, but not enough to really wound.

The other deer made a noise Bambi would never forget: a gulp of breath that was forcibly punched out of him, an inverse-snort of surprise. It ended with a squeak.

If this had been a normal fight, at some point they would have both called out and flattened their ears and glared at each other until one of them turned away, admitting defeat. Civilized. Or it would have become a long, epic tangle of antlers, the slow, beautiful struggle between two equals with the clicks and slides of shining rack on rack.

But it was not that kind of fight. Ronno was not that

kind of opponent. He was a bully who needed to be put in his place, not a worthy nemesis.

So Bambi did not attack again; he just glared icily down his muzzle at the other buck, daring him to say or do something.

Ronno lowered his head sullenly and turned to go.

Bambi started to sigh in relief, to turn to his friends—

When Ronno lowered his rack and lunged.

Bambi reared up on his hind legs and twisted. He seemed to dance, nimbly moving himself out of the way.

With his target suddenly gone, the other buck fell forward. He crashed hard, headfirst, into a jumble of old blackberry canes. And poison ivy.

"Wow," Thumper said, jaw dropping. "Dang."

"Let's head out," Bambi suggested casually, as if nothing at all had happened. "It's feeling a little close in here, under the trees."

Ronno shook his head free of the vines and chuffed, his black eyes full of anger.

"Just because you're in line to be prince," he spit, "doesn't mean you deserve it."

"This has nothing to do with who or what I am," Bambi said. "This has to do with who and what *you* are, which is a thorn in my side. Don't bother me again, Ronno. Stay away from me and Faline. Tend to your own doe and family." He didn't add *if you have one*. That would have been cruel and unnecessary. And he really didn't want the other buck to be sad and alone; happy and having found his own place in the herd would mean far less trouble for Bambi in the future.

"You won't always be strong," Ronno snorted.

"No, none of us will," Bambi agreed.

Although at that minute he felt invincible and eternal: it was always spring, and he was always a yearling who had just defeated his enemy. But he knew that this feeling, while pleasant, was a lie. The breeze always told the truth. Underneath the warmest, greenest scent of spring was always a little bit of decay from old leaves rotting all winter under the snow, from the bodies of bear and deer and others who didn't make it. Nothing was eternal except for the forest and the cycle of seasons.

Ronno snorted again and trotted away as if he didn't care, which for a deer meant keeping your eyes anywhere except on whatever it was that drove you off.

"That. Was. *Amazing!*" Flower said in awe. "You showed him!"

"I didn't want to," Bambi said a little crossly. "This was supposed to be a fun spring day—spending time with Faline, and you two . . . then my father comes and makes these silly pronouncements about me being a prince, and Ronno appears. What's next? A thunderstorm? Hunters? Blackflies?"

"He wanted to fight you because you're the next prince," Flower said slowly, trying to work it out. "But you didn't want to fight him. And you don't want to be prince. You didn't want to prove you were a prince . . . or anything."

"Yes, what's the point there, Flower?"

"Maybe he means that the people who don't *want* to be princes are the ones that should become princes," Thumper interrupted impatiently.

Flower's eyes widened in surprise. "No, that's not what I was thinking. But I do like it!"

"Hunh." Bambi tossed his head. "That doesn't even make any sense."

But it went round and round in his head, refusing to go away. An itching mosquito of a thought.

"Hey, Bambi, why don't you talk to Faline?" Thumper suggested brightly. "She always makes you feel better about things. I mean, as long as you're not still acting all twitterpated around her. You could talk to her like, like you do *us*. Not like to a doe, I mean."

For some reason Flower found that hysterically funny, and almost fell over himself giggling.

"I was going to . . . but I don't know. I don't want to disturb her," Bambi admitted.

"Naw, I think Faline would love to help you," Thumper said, shaking his head. "And she probably won't love you *not* talking to her about this important stuff. You being prince affects her, too, you know."

"I hadn't thought of that. You're absolutely right, Thump. I'm so jumbled up and just thinking of myself today. I'm a mess."

"We'll walk you to the edge of the thicket," Flower offered, recovered from his giggles and grooming the twigs out of his fur. "We can always visit the beavers tomorrow."

"It's a deal," Bambi said with a smile. "Thanks, guys. You're the best friends."

"Aww," Flower said, holding his tail and blushing a little.

The sun was soft and warm and there was a slow peacefulness to the afternoon, like a rest before the furious growing of spring began again. Thumper paused to nibble a blossom. Flower admired a slow-buzzing, fuzzy bee for a moment before casually popping it into his mouth. Bambi didn't really feel like grazing, but he bit at some old, bright red bearberries still there from the previous fall and enjoyed the sour taste in his mouth.

Faline was easy to scent; she was with a small group of does, two of whom were playing like fawns, bounding back and forth over a low stone wall just for the fun of it. Faline took a turn herself, gracefully jumping higher than the other two in a spring of pure joy.

"Hey, be careful," Bambi said, eyes widening. "Aren't you—"

"A pregnant doe from a long line of pregnant does, all of whom ran, galloped, leapt, played, and fought until the moment they were giving birth? Why, yes, Bambi, I am," she retorted with a laugh. Then her smile faded as she saw the strain around Bambi's eyes. "Bambi, what's wrong?"

"My father wants to make me the next Great Prince of the Forest. He told me today."

Faline's eyes widened. "Why, Bambi, that's wonderful. And it makes sense. . . ."

"I don't know if I want to be prince," he said quickly, feeling a little foolish.

Faline grew thoughtful. She flicked her ears; the other two does wandered off as if they suddenly had something else to do.

"Seems like if anyone should be the prince of the forest, it should be you," Bambi said wryly. "You already have your own herd."

"As do you," she said, nodding at Flower and Thumper, who were also disappearing into the shadows.

"They're not deer."

"Yes, most of the residents of the forest aren't," Faline noted blithely. "What's wrong with you, Bambi? You're grumpy about a marvelous thing. And how could you be in a bad mood at all on such a beautiful day? Just look around!"

In the space of a breath she was leaping again, bounding away through the woods. She tossed her head back at Bambi and laughed.

He sprang after her.

The two deer ran for the sheer joy of running, flashes of sunlight gleaming on their flanks and their white tails, the otherwise invisible and dark shapes moving at unbelievable speed through the forest. Smaller animals dashed and dipped out of their way. A still-sleepy bear, the only creature in the forest close to them in size, watched them go and wondered at the calories they were expending for no reason. Small foraging flocks of birds exploded up out of trees as they passed, chickadees and nuthatches and titmice exclaiming in irritation and amusement.

By the time they reached the meadows, Bambi had easily caught up—but he let her stop first, slowing himself as if she had won. She didn't even notice.

"I'm so happy," Faline said, panting. "But do *you* feel any better?"

"I do," Bambi admitted. "I always do when I'm with you. It doesn't change things, though. I just . . . I just don't want to be prince. Not now, anyway. Maybe not ever. Who knows?"

Faline looked thoughtful. "But what *does* 'prince' mean?"

"Oh, now you sound like Flower."

"What a clever little skunk, then. But listen, Bambi: you can't say you don't want to be something until you know exactly what you think that something *is*. So what is it that you think 'Great Prince of the Forest' means?"

"It means acting all high and mighty," Bambi said in exasperation. "It means only showing up in the most dire times, and yes, helping—but never being around for anything else. Like just swooping in and being the savior. It means walking around all slow and snooty and dispensing wisdom without being asked and holding your rack up and only getting involved when it's really necessary."

"Is that what a *prince* is," Faline asked pointedly, "or is that what your *father* is? To you?"

"But he *is* the prince! They're the same!"

"No, he's *a* prince. There was one before him, and there will be one after him. I don't know what your grandfather was like. Maybe you should ask someone. If Ronno beat you and drove you out of the forest, I know what kind of a prince he would be."

"But . . ."

But nothing. She was right. He had never thought of it that way before. *Prince* and *father* were all tangled up together in his head. But there were other things, too. . . . "He's all alone."

He didn't specify whether he meant his father or the prince.

"Maybe he *likes* being alone," Faline said gently. "Maybe what you're thinking of as *aloof* is just that: him wanting to be alone. Or maybe he *is* a snob. Who knows? But *you're* not like that. You have friends, ones who aren't even deer. I have a phoebe friend, you know—he'll sit on a branch above me and twitter and talk the day through, or just perch quietly, catching bugs and *being* with me. I wouldn't stop being friends with him if I became a prince, or anything else. So if you were a prince . . . by definition, you would be a prince with friends. Just like being a deer with friends.

"And isn't that better, anyway? If you're prince of the

whole forest, doesn't that mean looking after *everyone*? Not just deer?"

Bambi was silent, and Faline, too, fell silent, seeing that he was thinking about what she had said.

"Faline," Bambi said after a long moment, "*you* should be prince. You're wiser than I am, and more patient, too. You're right—I can be a different kind of leader.

"But only if you can be a mother *and* a friend. A doe *and* an advisor. A deer and a companion and someone who listens to phoebes, who will tell me when I am being grumpy, or wrong, or angry, or aloof."

"Of course I can, Bambi," Faline said with the quiet confidence in herself that Bambi so admired—and envied a little. "Whatever you decide, I'll be here, racing you and making you take a harder look at yourself."

Bambi let his breath out in something that wasn't quite a sigh. He still didn't know exactly what to think about his father, but Faline was right again: he didn't actually know all that much about him. That was a question he could work on answering over the next season. Maybe he could even get his father to open up and talk to him a little.

As for being prince—true, it wasn't necessarily the future he had imagined. But maybe with Faline, Thumper, and Flower by his side it wouldn't be so bad.

And Friend Owl, of course. Even if he wasn't *quite* as wise as he thought.

Gazing at Faline, Bambi realized the truth: the funny old bird didn't really understand what true *twitterpation* was.

The Rose and the Thorns

What if Aurora knew the truth about her curse?

by Elizabeth Lim

The Rose and the Thorns

What if Aurora knew the truth about her curse?

by Elizabeth Lim

The only thing that Princess Aurora hated more than being cursed—was *knowing* that she was cursed.

Every day and everywhere she went, *someone* would remind her that she'd been doomed since birth. That the great and evil fairy Maleficent had condemned her to prick her finger on the spindle of a spinning wheel before the sun set on her sixteenth birthday—and die.

Aurora really wished everyone would stop being so dire. After all, the good fairy Merryweather had watered down the curse significantly so that Aurora would only sleep, not die. Did she really need to be protected by bodyguards everywhere she went and be caged up in a drafty old castle? Sixteen years was such a long time to wait for something inevitably terrible to happen.

Sometimes, secretly, she wished that her parents had sent her far away. She could have grown up as a peasant, away from Maleficent's prying eyes. She could have been free.

But she knew that was a selfish thought. The King and Queen would have missed her too much, and she loved her parents. She couldn't imagine a life without their daily lunches and dinners, without her mother teaching her the harp or how to dance. She couldn't imagine trying not to laugh at Father as he tried to hide his burps during the royal dinners.

What she resented, though, was how everyone treated her as if she were made of glass. She resented having to spend every afternoon learning how to protect herself from some all-powerful, likely inevitable curse. Almost every day, Aurora suffered through magical protection lessons with the three fairies Flora, Fauna, and Merryweather, who now lived in the castle and used their magic to place wards around the royal grounds.

Her very first word had been "careful," instead of a normal "Mama" or "Dada," because it was the word she had heard most often.

"*Careful*, Your Highness! Don't prick your finger on that fountain pen!"

"Oh, no, that hook is sharp! *Careful!* You might hurt yourself!"

Ironic that when Aurora turned thirteen, Merryweather had decided she should take fencing lessons. "A form of defense," the youngest fairy had said to convince the King and Queen. The swords were wooden and dull, of course, but Aurora could have kissed Merryweather on the first day of her lessons. Three years later, she was far from an accomplished swordswoman, but she relished the time spent hacking at straw dummies and letting out her frustrations. Plus, it was the only of her lessons that was outdoors, and it let her view the world beyond the castle walls.

And spend some time with Phillip.

"Be careful with that quill," her tutor warned, breaking her daydream. "The nib is sharp. You might—"

Don't say it.

"—prick yourself."

Aurora sighed. "It's a writing quill, not a needle."

"Even still, Your Highness. The future of our very kingdom rests on your shoulders. Only one month to go."

Yes, Aurora was aware of how much time there was before her sixteenth birthday. She was reminded of it every day; every single subject in her parents' kingdom had been counting down the years, months, weeks, and days until their princess would be safe from Maleficent's horrible curse.

Thirty days, twenty hours, fifteen minutes to go.

Well, no one was more tired of it than Aurora herself. When she was sure that her tutor wasn't looking, she let out a loud gasp and dropped her quill with a dramatic thud. As inelegantly as she could, she crumbled off the chair and onto the ground.

The tutor sighed. "Your Highness, this isn't funny. Twice in a month is too much, even for you."

A beat passed. Then another. "Aurora!"

Her tutor knelt and shook her by the shoulders. Aurora didn't move. "Your Highness? Oh, dear." Footsteps thudded against the rug as her tutor ran out of the room. "Help! The curse! Her Royal Highness pricked—"

Aurora didn't bother listening to the rest. Once her tutor was gone, she sprang up and crept out the door. Looking out the window, she could see that the drawbridge was down. Just a few more corridors, then the garden. She'd grab the disguise she stashed under the rosebushes, then skirt past the guards to the portcullis. . . .

She got as far as the north wing, two halls before the garden entrance, before a familiar voice rang out from behind: "Just where do you think you're going?"

The princess halted in her step.

Merryweather.

The fairy flew to Aurora's side. She was in her smaller form, which made her only slightly larger than a blue butterfly. Even still, Aurora could make out her crossed arms and furrowed brow.

"Why, Merryweather." Aurora put on her brightest smile. "I was just . . . going out for some air."

"In the middle of your writing lesson?"

"What better time for a walk is there?" Aurora said.

"I thought I saw the royal guards running up toward

the lesson hall. Did you by any chance pretend to fall to your curse again?"

There was no use lying. "Oh, Merryweather, I'm going out, just for an hour. I'm almost sixteen. What harm would it do to have an hour to myself? I'm in lessons all day."

Merryweather didn't look moved. If anything, she crossed her arms tighter. "You *are* almost sixteen—that's the entire point. This is the time to strengthen our defenses. For you to lie low, keep hidden, and not draw attention. In one month, the curse will be broken."

"I've been keeping hidden for sixteen years," Aurora countered. "I might as well be a rabbit in a cage. Maleficent knows exactly where I am. At least let me go out into the village. It's my fault everyone in this kingdom has to suffer through Maleficent's curse. I'll wear a disguise, watch out for ravens." Aurora made a pleading look. "Please? Everyone in the kingdom must hate me."

"They know it isn't your fault."

"Can't I at least go up to the ramparts and see them?" Aurora paused. "I heard my father say some of the villagers are unhappy that they can't make their own clothing. That they're living in rags. I could send someone to give them some of my clothes. I could give a speech from the balcony. I want to do my part."

"You'll do your part by staying put in this castle."

"You sound like Flora and Fauna," said Aurora.

"No, I don't."

"Do too!"

Just like that, Merryweather smiled. Just a little.

Of the three fairies that had helped raise Aurora, Merryweather was the easiest to talk to. She didn't coddle Aurora as though she were a glass slipper that might shatter, nor did she snitch on Aurora whenever she ran off from her tutors. But she still could be stern, and she was as fiercely protective as the others.

"Very well," relented Merryweather. "I suppose your tutor's already left. You can go on a walk around the ballroom."

"But . . ."

"That's my offer."

Aurora sighed. "All right."

"Good. I'll give you an hour before I tell Flora where you are."

Aurora knew it was the best she'd get, and she hugged the fairy. "Thank you!"

"Not so fast," said Merryweather. "I'm coming with you."

"Oh."

Merryweather waved her wand and instantly changed to her normal size. "Oh? You don't want to walk with your favorite fairy anymore?"

"It's just that . . ." Aurora's mind reeled. "Don't you have a meeting with Mother and Father? I thought you were strengthening the castle's defenses. . . . It is only a month until my birthday, after all."

"You never remember my schedule, Princess. What are you—" Merryweather's expression turned coy. "Are you meeting Phillip?"

Aurora blushed.

The fairy leaned forward and said in a low voice, "Has he kissed you yet?"

"Merryweather! He's just a friend."

The fairy shrugged, but her eyes twinkled. She had a soft spot for Prince Phillip. "Remember how your curse gets broken? True Love's Kiss."

True Love's Kiss. Those three words had haunted her ever since she was old enough to understand what they meant.

How would she even know what true love was?

A question she'd tried asking the fairies multiple times, but they'd blustered half-formed responses. Aurora knew better than to ask again. Deep down, she worried she didn't *have* a true love. After all, she wasn't even sixteen years old yet.

But if she didn't have a true love and she fell to the curse, she'd stay asleep—forever. When put that way, was Merryweather's adjustment all that much better than the original curse?

Why a kiss? Aurora wanted to ask Merryweather, but the words that came out instead were:

"Why did you even bother telling me? Why not whisk me away so I could hide? Another kingdom? Or even the middle of the forest? At least I'd have animal friends to talk to."

"The King and Queen couldn't bear the idea of giving you up," explained Merryweather, for the umpteenth time. "We told you the truth as soon as you could understand. That way, you'd have a better chance of defending yourself against Maleficent."

Aurora sighed. For the past sixteen years, she had studied every magical defense spell in the fairies' book, in addition to taking the fencing lessons. She'd even secretly learned some archery from Merryweather. She could spot a raven a mile away. But Maleficent had never come. Sometimes Aurora even wondered if the curse was real.

"Where are you meeting Phillip, anyway?" said Merryweather, suddenly suspicious. "I didn't see Samson in the stables this morning."

Aurora swallowed. "In the garden," she fibbed. "He's probably been waiting for me. We were supposed to meet on the hour."

"In the garden," Merryweather repeated.

"Can I please go?" said Aurora. "I've practiced my spells, and Phillip's got his sword. I'll look out for ravens, I promise. And we won't talk to anyone, not even the guards. Please let me go."

"I don't know. . . ."

"Please, Merryweather? It's not like I'm going out into town."

"Phillip will be with you the entire time?"

"Yes, but you know I can take care of myself, too—thanks to your training. And Flora's and Fauna's."

Merryweather chuckled at the flattery. "All right. Only for an hour. . . . If it weren't for this meeting, I'd come, too. But be careful."

Aurora nodded, her heart leaping with joy. "I will."

The garden was Aurora's favorite part of the castle. It was the only place where she felt a semblance of freedom, and where there weren't guards lurking at every corner making sure she wasn't in danger. Of course, every rose and bramble bush had been carefully pruned, and there were archers on the lookout for ravens and flying spindles, but she could at least pretend she was alone.

Here was also the place where she and Phillip had met—outside of formal ceremonies and meals—for the first time. It was years before, but Aurora still remembered everything. It was after a magical defense class with Flora, and instead of going straight to her dreaded luncheon with Father, she had transformed her dress into a shirt and trousers and sneaked out onto the lawn surrounded by topiaries. Who knew that Phillip had dreaded the lunch as much as she had and pretended to be sick? He'd borrowed a page's outfit and had instead gone exploring in the castle.

Aurora had thought him an actual page sent to find her and had immediately ducked into a rosebush. Of course, Phillip had seen her.

"Hiding from someone, Ms. Rose?" he'd said, peering at her.

"Shh." Aurora hushed him. "Go away, or they'll see me."

"Who?"

"The guards." Aurora smiled. "They never think to look past the thorns."

"Really?" Phillip said, stepping into the rosebush himself. The guards passed, not seeing either of them. Once they were out of sight, he said, "You're right! Why didn't I ever think to hide here?"

"You?" Aurora said. She frowned. "Aren't you a page?"

"No, I'm Phillip."

"Phillip?" Aurora's eyes widened. She stepped back, almost forgetting that she was inside a bramble bush. "The prince?" She burst into a fit of giggles.

"What's so funny?"

"I'm . . . I'm Aurora," she said between laughs. "I think . . . I think we're engaged. Funny, I've never seen you without that ugly blue hat—with the red feather. You look much better without it."

Phillip started laughing, too. "Father makes me wear it. It's either that or a crown. Crowns are surprisingly—"

"Heavy?"

"Exactly."

"Not very good for hiding in bramble bushes." She tilted her head, still smiling. It was different seeing Phillip face to face, without the pomp and rigmarole of an official ceremony, or in the presence of their parents. "I think your hat would look better in red."

"I'll remember that for next time." Phillip grinned. "I'll

bring you one, too, if you want. All the seamstresses in my kingdom do is talk about what you wear. They're the ones making all your clothes."

"What do they say?" Aurora asked, genuinely curious.

"They lament that they never get to see their dresses on you because you're locked up in your room."

Aurora made a face. "Only half the day, when I'm not at my lessons."

"They say you're not allowed to go anywhere."

"Well, that's true. I'm not allowed to leave the castle. Thankfully, it's large. I'm not to touch anything sharp. Mother and Father don't even let me have a knife at dinner, as if I'll cut myself." She rolled her eyes.

"But the curse was only for a spindle of a spinning wheel, I thought."

"They won't take any chances. Which doesn't make any sense, because Merryweather insisted I learn fencing, and she's secretly been teaching me archery."

Phillip raised an eyebrow.

"To defend myself," she explained. "In case Maleficent comes after me one day. But my tutors always let me win, and they're too afraid to ever even hurt me."

"How about I be your practice partner, then?" Phillip gestured at the archery range on the other side of the garden. "If I beat you, you have to figure out what to tell our parents when we're late to lunch, and if you beat me, same goes for me."

"It's a bet," said Aurora, sharing her first smile with Phillip.

From then on, they'd become fast friends, and their parents couldn't have been more delighted. Aurora counted down the days until Phillip visited again, and when he did, they spent every moment they could together. Often they sneaked off to the garden, hiding from the guards, chasing the rabbits that roamed the castle grounds, or competing in archery and sword fighting. Then, as they grew older, they schemed a way to get Aurora out into the nearby townships. Never once did they mention that one day, in the near future, they would marry.

Her cheeks flushed just thinking about it. Phillip had been her future husband ever since they were children, but lately when they saw each other, her stomach did somersaults and she became tongue-tied and sometimes she forgot what she meant to say. She was sure he'd notice, and that made her nervous to see him.

She pushed her nervousness aside as she approached one of the rosebushes in the garden. After a quick glance to make sure no one saw her, she crouched, grabbed the set of peasant clothes under the roses, and threw them over her dress.

All her life, she'd tried to find ways to sneak out of the castle. Ironically, only last year, she'd discovered the best way to sneak out was to actually pay attention to her lessons. Her magic lessons, that was.

"Rays of sunshine," she whispered, "align!"

As soon as she spoke the words, a powerful ray of light shone upon Aurora, concealing her from the guards' views. It wouldn't last long, so she hastily clambered over the castle wall.

"Sorry, Merryweather," she said softly as she landed. But ever since she'd finally seen the world beyond the castle walls, and had seen the toll that her curse had taken on the kingdom, she couldn't stay still and do nothing.

She whistled for Phillip's horse, Samson. Reliable as ever, the stallion was waiting to take her into the village—where Phillip was waiting.

Phillip was sitting on a tree stump beside Mrs. Vall's cottage, where Aurora often stopped to help with the laundry while Phillip cut wood. He was wearing his usual disguise for outside the castle: a simple red cap and matching cape over his gray tunic. Just the sight of him made Aurora smile, and she inhaled sharply, hoping her pounding heart wouldn't give her away.

"You're late," he greeted, a teasing smile on his face.

Aurora made a face. "Blue caught me."

"But she still let you skip your lesson? She must be getting soft, since you've only got a month left to go."

"A month still feels like forever," said Aurora. She glanced at the cottage and dropped the satchel of clothing she had brought for the children. "Where's Mrs. Vall?"

"She took the children to buy thread."

Thread was expensive. One spool was the price of three meals. Aurora gritted her teeth as she touched the fraying threads on her own sleeve. Mrs. Vall had been a weaver before the curse, and these days, instead of creating tapestries at her loom, she'd recycle old clothing into strips and weave them into new garments. Aurora brought what scraps she could from the castle and distributed the freshly made clothes to the rest of the village.

Because of her, spinning wheels had been banned for sixteen years. All needles were prohibited, even if for knitting. This meant that children wore ill-fitting dresses and trousers that were far too big or far too small, and nearly everyone had worn their clothes thin, until they'd become rags. Peasant or lord, it didn't matter. Everyone was affected by the King's ban on spinning wheels, and the people felt it most keenly during the winter, when there were barely enough blankets and coats and socks to keep the kingdom warm.

During Aurora's visits to the village, she brought as many of her own clothes as she could. Though she was a princess, her wardrobe was meager—she had no more than a handful of dresses—yet she still had far more than most. She shared what she could, but she knew it wasn't enough.

Seeing her people suffer made her angrier with Maleficent. With this stupid curse that she couldn't do anything about—except wait it out.

The only good thing that had come of her curse, it seemed, was that her country now traded more heavily with the neighboring kingdom for essentials, and that had brought the two countries closer together. Moreover, the trade accord meant the neighboring king visited often—and he brought Phillip.

Thanks to her curse, Aurora and Phillip had grown up together. She couldn't imagine a world in which he wasn't her best friend, her confidant. Her favorite person in the world.

"What's the matter, Aurora?" said Phillip, noticing how she was staring ahead.

"A month until the curse ends, but Maleficent will still be out there. What if she decides to curse me again? With something worse this time. What if it's not clothing, but food?" Aurora looked up at him. "I understand why my father banned spinning wheels—I know it's to protect me. But should we be living in fear like this?"

"Your father can't exactly send an army into Maleficent's lair. The moment he lets down his guard around the castle, she'll send one of her ravens after you. Or worse yet, one of those enchanted spindles she's supposed to have. They'll come flying after you, and . . ."

He didn't need to finish; Aurora knew what would happen. She sighed. "I don't even know why she cursed me in the first place."

"Well, I've got some news for you," Phillip said. He

paused, making her curiosity grow. "Father slipped . . . finally."

Aurora's eyes widened. "About the curse? What did he say?"

Phillip lowered his voice. "That Maleficent was upset she wasn't invited to your christening ceremony, so she cursed you."

Aurora's eyes widened. "That's all?"

"That's all?" Phillip laughed. "What did you imagine was the reason?"

Aurora shrugged. "Oh, I don't know. Maybe she was in love with my father, and he spurned her." She flushed at the ridiculousness of the theory. "Or maybe when I was a baby, I accidentally scratched her or bit her. Who knows? I've had a lot of time to think about it, and I still have no idea."

She linked arms with him and started dragging him back home.

"Where are we going?"

"Back to the castle." Aurora was never in a rush to go home, but this was an exception. "We need to talk to Flora, Fauna, and Merryweather. They'll know more."

"Who did you hear this from?" Flora demanded, frowning as Aurora posed her question to the three fairies.

Phillip made a sheepish smile. "From me."

The three fairies exchanged glances. Aurora had known the three long enough to read their expressions. Flora was in favor of keeping the answer secret, Merryweather was turning as blue as her dress and ready to tell everything that she knew, and Fauna, in the middle, had her lips pursed. Aurora appealed to Fauna with her eyes. It was always up to Fauna.

Fauna sighed. "Well, it doesn't hurt for her to know the reason, I suppose. She knows everything else."

"So it's true," Aurora exclaimed. "This entire curse was over a party invitation." She crossed her arms, unable to believe it. "Has anyone tried looking for Maleficent? Or tried apologizing?"

Flora glowered. "No, no, that isn't how you deal with Maleficent. It isn't just about your christening, Princess. It goes far deeper than that."

"How?" queried Aurora.

"Well . . ."

"Maleficent doesn't need a reason to do something vile," Merryweather said with a huff. "She was born evil."

"She was born different," said Fauna, bringing a kinder light to Maleficent's story. "Whereas fairies like Flora, Merryweather, and I have the talent for nurturing beauty and happiness in the world, Maleficent's powers—"

"Bring misery," said Flora staunchly.

"It's balance," Fauna said.

Flora and Merryweather made faces, but they couldn't disagree.

"You see, Maleficent's been different ever since she was a girl. We tried to treat her like a sister, but—"

"She frightened us," Merryweather interrupted. "She made all our flowers wilt, she made the animals sick, she made the rain turn into poison."

"She didn't mean to, at first, but she couldn't help it. It was her own choice to go away, to seclude herself from the rest of the fairies. But I guess her loneliness twisted her heart."

A pang touched Aurora's heart. "That's sad."

"Well," Flora huffed, "don't you go around feeling sorry for Maleficent. She revels in the misery she brings everywhere."

"Well, I don't," Aurora said. "Every day of this curse, the kingdom suffers. Has anyone tried . . . talking to her?"

"The last person who tried talking to her turned into stone," replied Flora. "Don't you get any ideas."

"No ideas," Aurora assured them. "I only wish you'd told me earlier."

"We were trying to protect you, child," said Flora.

There it was again, the speech Aurora heard every day of her life. She twisted away from Flora before the eldest fairy could pat her on the arm.

"Thank you," she said. "I'm glad you told me." She towed Phillip out of the room by the arm. "I think we're late for dinner with our fathers."

Of course, the last thing on Aurora's mind was dinner with her father—or Phillip's.

Once she was out of the fairies' earshot, she crossed her arms. "I should've known that they were hiding something from me."

"Don't be too hard on them. It's their job to keep you safe."

"You try to keep me safe," she retorted. "But you don't coddle me and hide terrible secrets."

"I'm also not a fairy," Phillip replied. "Though if it's that curse we're still talking about, I could simply kiss you," he teased. "Maybe that would break the spell."

Aurora's face went hot. More than once, she'd imagined that Phillip might be her true love. She couldn't imagine anyone other than him waking her with a kiss. But they were friends. Best friends, at that.

He probably thought of her as a sister. Someone he was obligated to marry because their fathers were best friends. She bet he even felt sorry for her.

"You'd have to be my true love to do that," she blurted. She instantly regretted it, but it was too late to take the words back.

"You're right," Phillip said, after the briefest pause. He raked his hand through his hair and chuckled as if he'd made a joke. "What a silly thing for me to say. Come on, Rose."

Rose had been his nickname for her since they were six years old, and it never failed to make her smile when she heard it.

"Where are we going?"

"To the garden, of course." He grinned at her, but his smile didn't reach his eyes. "We haven't had an archery contest in a while. I want to see if you beating me last time was a fluke!"

Aurora smiled, but her heart tightened as she followed Phillip to the archery range. She couldn't stop thinking about what the fairies had told her about Maleficent. About the innocuous origins of a curse that had uprooted her entire life and that of her kingdom. If Maleficent had been biding her time all these years, gathering her powers and her forces, what good was it for Aurora to sit in the castle like an archery target? Surely there was something she could do.

"Everything all right, Rose?" Phillip asked.

She could find her true love, she thought immediately at the sound of his voice.

You'd have to be my true love to do that. The words still rang in her ears, and how she regretted them. "I'm fine," she said, mustering a smile. "Archery always clears my mind."

"I know."

She drew her bowstring, its tension singing against her cheek. She'd loved Phillip for years now, and so many times she'd wondered whether he felt anything for her.

"Ready?" Phillip said. "On the count of three. One. Two—"

Her arrow hit the target. Perfectly.

She set down her bow. "You know," she said slowly, "I've spent my whole life trying to avoid the curse. Staying put in the castle, being shuttled away from anything sharp, even pen nibs. Maleficent knows exactly where I am and exactly how to find me. I'm tired of waiting for Maleficent to lure me into a trap or find a spindle wheel in some dark corner. You know what she wouldn't expect?"

"What?"

"*Me* to break my curse. *Before* my birthday."

Phillip hid his reaction well, for his face remained calm. "How will you do that?"

"I'm going to seek her out and ask her to lift the curse."

"She's the mistress of all evil," Phillip pointed out. "I don't think reasoning with her is going to get her to lift the curse."

"Then we'll bring extra quivers of arrows, and I'll start asking the fairies to teach me some more advanced spells. I'll actually go to my lessons with Flora, too." Aurora nodded, more determined with every breath. "Will you come with me to find her?"

"Go with you to find the lair of the most dangerous person in the world?" Phillip chuckled. "What are best friends for?"

Aurora grinned back at him, ignoring that skip in her heart. "Let's get planning."

Aurora had spent all her life learning to hide, to defend and protect herself. Now she needed to learn to go on the offensive. For the next month, she and Phillip worked together, spending every spare moment they could plotting out their soon-to-be encounter with Maleficent and training to sneak into her lair and past her guards.

Far too soon came the morning of her sixteenth birthday.

The castle came alive in a way Aurora had never seen before. Every maid, steward, and cook was in a frenzy preparing for the celebration, a spectacular party that would begin at sundown, once the curse was officially broken.

There were cookies in the shapes of spinning wheels, and noodles that were cut to look like spindles. No expense was spared to celebrate the end of their dear princess's curse! Even the fairies were partaking in the preparations. Flora was sewing a dress for Aurora, Fauna was overseeing the royal birthday cake, and Merryweather was helping with decorations in the Grand Hall.

No one noticed that Aurora wasn't in her bed, sleeping peacefully.

Quite the opposite. At dawn, Aurora and Phillip were already on horseback, traveling for the blot of darkness that touched upon the King and Queen's kingdom. A forbidden part of the realm that no one dared enter—that was where Maleficent lived.

Maleficent had a castle guarded by hundreds of monsters, each clad in iron armor and armed with an axe or spear.

Aurora gulped when she saw the army. "Maybe this wasn't such a good idea after all."

A raven cawed, loudly.

"They're here," rumbled the soldiers. "She's here!"

At once, Maleficent's army surrounded the princess and the prince, many of them jumping with glee when they recognized who had walked into their mistress's lair.

In a blast of bright green fire, Maleficent emerged. Black horns shot out from her temples, and her eyes were chillingly yellow.

"You've come of your own accord," said Maleficent. "I'm impressed. You've made it easy for me, coming to my home. Saved me the trouble of going to yours."

Aurora shivered as she clenched her bow. "I'm not here to fight you," she said. "I want to talk."

The raven at Maleficent's side warbled something, and the fairy inclined her head. "Ah, how rude of me to forget." A pause. "Happy birthday, Aurora."

Fire spurted from Maleficent's staff, knocking both princess and prince off Samson.

The flames took on the shape of a spinning wheel, and Maleficent spoke. "You've come because you wished to spare your family the anguish of witnessing your fall. Sixteen years I've waited for this. It was wise of you to realize that no number of wards or protections your fairies cast will keep you from me."

"You won't hurt her!" Phillip said, stepping in front of Aurora.

"How quaint. The princess brings her knight in shining armor." Maleficent laughed. "But you see, I, too, am prepared."

Maleficent raised her staff, and Aurora's breath left her

as its fiery light illuminated thousands of spindles floating above her.

"Each spindle has been enchanted to bring eternal sleep to anyone it pricks," said Maleficent as the spindles glimmered green. "Shall I send them over to your kingdom now? Perhaps we can start with the good king and queen. Or right here with your dear prince."

"No!" Aurora cried.

The mistress of evil gave a chilling smile. "As I thought. Will you come forward?"

Aurora glanced at Phillip, who mouthed a hard *no*.

But they were surrounded—by both soldiers and enchanted spindles. What could Aurora do?

She stepped forward. "Why curse me over a party invitation?" she demanded. "At least tell me that."

The light from Maleficent's staff shook as she laughed. "Do you think it was over a party? Do you know what your name means, child?"

Of course she did. "The rising sun."

"Yes, gold of sunshine in your hair," Maleficent said, twisting a lock of Aurora's hair with the end of her staff. "Lips that shame the red, red rose. You are a bearer of light. And all light is a threat to the kingdom of darkness I was born to rule. That is why you must die."

A shiver twisted down Aurora's spine. "You don't have to do this. The fairies told me that your magic is unique, but you don't have to hurt anyone, Maleficent. Least of all yourself."

Laughing wickedly, Maleficent raised her staff. "What makes you think I don't enjoy this?"

Suddenly, she began to transform. Her black gown stretched and wings grew from her sleeves. The ground trembled, and the dark skies rioted with a coming storm.

Aurora and Phillip backed away fearfully, and Samson dipped his head, urging the two to mount him so they could get away from there. But it was too late.

Maleficent's laugh transformed into the roar—of a dragon!

The princess, prince, and stallion raced across Maleficent's kingdom, and Samson reared as the drawbridge crumbled under the weight of Maleficent's falling tail. At the last moment, he leapt across the gap—his hind legs barely landing the jump.

A feat that did not please the dragon.

Spiked vines burst from the ground, blocking their path. "We can't get any farther," Aurora cried, leaping off Samson and drawing her sword. Nothing had trained them for this.

Together, the prince and princess began slicing at the vines, but as they cleared a path for themselves toward Maleficent, sharp points began to protrude from the branches.

"Rose!" Phillip cried. "There's thorns!"

Oh, Aurora saw. And they weren't just any thorns. They were the spindles that Maleficent had enchanted. All of them, attached to the vines.

Fear churned in her gut. If one of them touched her . . .

"That's right," Maleficent hissed. "One touch, and you'll be mine."

Phillip dismounted their horse and charged at Maleficent, throwing his sword into her belly. But a new vine burst from the side and pricked him in the back.

"Phillip!" Aurora cried as the prince fell forward.

She rushed to him. He was asleep, as she would be.

"Did you think your prince would be able to kiss you awake?" Maleficent laughed. "Each thorn is cursed with the sleeping spell. With your true love asleep, no one will be able to wake you now. There will be no true love's kiss."

Aurora clenched her jaw. "Come on, Samson. It's you and me now."

Fire spewed from Maleficent's jaws, and Aurora used the magic she'd learned to enchant Phillip's shield, holding it up at the last minute before the flames burned her into ashes.

The vines moved like arms, swinging relentlessly at Aurora. She leapt out of the way, at every turn casting defensive magic she had learned from the three fairies. Changing blasts of fire into flowers, changing the spikes that flew at her into bubbles. She was growing tired. There was no chance she'd ever make it to Maleficent. No chance she could get a clear shot at the fairy.

A familiar voice cried out. "Hurry!"

Flora—and Fauna and Merryweather! They had come!

"This was very rash of you, Aurora," greeted Flora with a frown. "We'll talk about this later. Right now, do you remember your spells?"

Yes, Aurora did. She'd been casting them to deal with the bursts of fire and to evade the thorned vines that swung at her back every other second.

She leapt to avoid another vine. But this time, Merryweather turned the vine into a silk ribbon. With a whirl of her wand, Fauna confronted a blast of fire and turned it into a jet of rainbows. The fairies' interference enraged Maleficent.

While the fairies distracted Maleficent with their magic and protected Aurora from the vines, Aurora reached behind her back for her arrows. She had only three left.

"Arrows of Virtue," Aurora cast upon her bow. "Fly true!"

Aurora aimed at Maleficent's heart, then released her arrow. True indeed it flew, straight for the dragon's chest. But no sooner did the arrow fly to Maleficent's heart than the dragon caught it and waved it aside.

Aurora readied another arrow. The same thing happened; Maleficent evaded the attack. This wasn't working.

Only one arrow left. Aurora bit down on her cheek.

"Is that all you have?" Maleficent screeched, laughing as she blew more fire into Aurora's path.

The heat was almost unbearable, and Aurora staggered back behind Phillip's shield. Then she had an idea. She reached for her last arrow and aimed for one of the spindles behind Maleficent. The dragon was so used to flicking away Aurora's attacks that she didn't bother looking.

And that was her error.

Maleficent's wing brushed against the enchanted spindle, and she let out a screech as she realized what she'd done.

In one last attempt, her tail came swinging at Aurora. The princess leapt out of the way, diving into the arms of her protector fairies as Maleficent collapsed, falling into the canyon beneath her castle as an eternal sleep claimed her.

The three fairies surrounded Aurora and the unconscious Phillip, pointing their wands at the sky to protect one another from the falling boulders and rubble. Then, when the earth went still, the fairies dared step apart.

"It's done," Flora breathed. "Maleficent is no more. The curse is lifted."

So it was. The spindles on the vines no longer glowed green with Maleficent's magic, and the ghoulish soldiers of her army transformed into men, groaning awake—as if they'd been long under a terrible spell.

"Look!" cried Fauna. "The darkness."

The night that cloaked the lands surrounding Maleficent's domain receded. For the first time in what might have been centuries, sunlight burst from behind the clouds, banishing the shadows that wreathed the mistress of evil's castle.

Aurora knelt beside Phillip. The ground was still warm from the fire, but the vines were gone. Vanished, as if they'd never existed.

She swept Phillip's bangs from his brow, hoping beyond hope that she was his true love. Because she couldn't bear the thought of him staying asleep forever—of losing him. And she knew with clarity he was hers.

"Wake up, Phillip," she whispered in his ear. "Who's going to fence with me and tell silly jokes every time I take down your guard? Who's going to dance with me in the garden when the roses bloom or sneak into town with me to play with Mrs. Vall's children? Who's going to talk to me when I'm lonely and make me believe that true love is real?"

She swallowed hard. Here it was, the moment she'd dreaded for sixteen years. But instead of being cursed herself into an eternal sleep—it was Phillip! Phillip, her best friend. Her confidant. Her favorite person in the world.

She knew the way to break his curse, but what if it wasn't her? What if she kissed him and nothing happened?

"Only one way to find out, Aurora," she told herself.

Slowly, she pressed her hand against his chest and leaned forward. She thought she ought to close her eyes, but she couldn't. She was too nervous. Then she thought about all the times she'd waited to see him, and how he'd made life at the castle so much more bearable. She thought about how much she loved him. With a smile, she pressed her lips against his.

They'd held hands plenty of times, even hugged. But this was their first kiss.

His lips were cold at first. Then warmth sprang to them, and he was breathing.

Tears pricked the edges of Aurora's eyes, and she cried out in joy. "Phillip!" she said, hugging him. "You're awake."

He tried to jump to his feet, but Aurora didn't let go of him. "Maleficent's gone."

Phillip smiled back. "Funny, in my dreams, it was always me kissing you."

"I thought you meant it as a joke."

"Never." Phillip touched her cheek. "I was only worried you'd be disappointed."

"Never," Aurora echoed. "I wanted it to be you."

Phillip glanced behind him, hearing the thundering gallops of what sounded like hundreds of horses. "Sounds like your parents sent the entire army out to look for you."

So they had.

As soon as Aurora helped Phillip to his feet, an entire legion of royal soldiers appeared behind them. "Your Highnesses!" they cried.

"Maleficent is sleeping," Aurora announced, gesturing at the dragon slumbering below the broken drawbridge. Maleficent had fallen deep into the canyon below, but the dragon's belly rose with breath. She was still alive. "Only True Love's Kiss shall awaken her."

The princess, prince, and fairies looked upon the

dragon solemnly, knowing that whatever love Maleficent might once have had in her heart had been twisted by the path she'd chosen, full of resentment and rage.

The three fairies flew over the sleeping Maleficent. Flowers and trees grew over the dragon, covering her sleeping form so she was forgotten. And the last of the darkness that had cloaked Maleficent's castle turned to light.

Day had returned to this part of the land, and Aurora remembered Maleficent's words. Light had won against the darkness.

And Phillip . . . Phillip had been her true love all along, just as she'd known he was.

Phillip gazed at her tenderly, as if he could read her mind.

She took his hand. "I hear there's a party at the castle, and the guest of honor's late. Shall we sneak inside and steal some cake?"

He grinned at her. "That's the best idea I've heard all day. Race you."

Together they ran after Samson, back for the castle, to begin their happily ever after.